THE GILDED ONES

ARE WE GIRLS OR ARE WE DEMONS?

ARE WE GOING TO DIE OR ARE WE GOING TO SURVIVE?

Deka lives in fear of the blood ceremony that will determine whether she can become a member of her village. If she bleeds red, she will belong. But on the day of the ceremony, her blood runs gold – the colour of impurity, of a demon.

The consequences force Deka to leave her village with a mysterious woman, destined to join an army of girls like her – the alaki, girls who are near-immortals with rare gifts, and the only ones able to stop the empire's greatest threat.

But as she journeys to the capital to train for the battle of her life, Deka discovers the great walled city holds many surprises. Nothing and no one are quite what they seem – not even Deka herself…

To my father, who taught me how to dream.

To my mother, who taught me how to do.

And to my sister, who supported me all the way.

First published in the UK in 2021 by Usborne Publishing Ltd., Usborne House, 83-85 Saffron Hill, London EC1N 8RT, England, usborne.com.

A CIP catalogue record for this book is available from the British Library.

Trade paperback ISBN 9781474959575
Waterstones exclusive paperback ISBN 9781801310277

05233/1   FMAMJJASOND/21

Printed and bound in Great Britain by CPI Group (UK) Ltd, Croydon, CR0 4YY.

THE GILDED ONES

NAMINA FORNA

THE GILDED ONES *includes scenes of violence, including some graphic violence, which some readers may find distressing.*

Harukana

Eastern
Provinces

Zhang-Do

Sembugard

Ebungard

Gar Suma

Gar Nasim

Gar Sinkarie

Gar Shekou

Gar Satu

N

W   E

S

Gar Fatu

Unknown Lands

ONE

Today is the Ritual of Purity.

The nervous thought circles in my head as I hurry towards the barn, gathering my cloak to ward off the cold. It's early morning, and the sun hasn't yet begun its climb above the snow-dusted trees encircling our small farmhouse. Shadows gather in the darkness, crowding the weak pool of light cast by my lamp. An ominous tingling builds under my skin. It's almost as if there's something there, at the edge of my vision…

It's just nerves, I tell myself. I've felt the tingling many times before and never once seen anything strange.

The barn door is open when I arrive, a lantern hung at the post. Father is already inside, spreading hay. He's a frail figure in the darkness, his tall body sunken into itself. Just three months ago, he was hearty and robust, his blond hair untouched by grey. Then the red pox came, sickening him and Mother. Now he's stooped and faded with the rheumy eyes and wispy hair of someone decades older.

"You're already awake," he says softly, grey eyes flitting over me.

"I couldn't sleep any longer," I reply, grabbing a milk pail and heading towards Norla, our largest cow.

I'm supposed to be resting in isolation, like all the other girls preparing for the Ritual, but there's too much work to do around the farm and not enough hands. There hasn't been since Mother died three months ago. The thought brings tears to my eyes, and I blink them away.

Father forks more hay into the stalls. "'Blessings to he who waketh to witness the glory of the Infinite Father'," he grunts, quoting from the Infinite Wisdoms. "So, are you prepared for today?"

I nod. "Yes, I am."

Later this afternoon, Elder Durkas will test me and all the other sixteen-year-old girls during the Ritual of Purity. Once we're proven pure, we'll officially belong here in the village. I'll finally be a woman – eligible to marry, have a family of my own.

The thought sends another wave of anxiety across my mind.

I glance at Father from the corner of my eye. His body is tense; his movements are laboured. He's worried too. "I had a thought, Father," I begin. "What if…what if…" I stop there, the unfinished question lingering heavily in the air. An unspeakable dread, unfurling in the gloom of the barn.

Father gives me what he thinks is a reassuring smile, but the edges of his mouth are tight. "What if what?" he asks. "You can tell me, Deka."

"What if my blood doesn't run pure?" I whisper, the horrible words rushing out of me. "What if I'm taken away by the priests – banished?"

I have nightmares about it, terrors that merge with my other dreams; the ones where I'm in a dark ocean, Mother's voice calling out to me.

"Is that what you're worried about?"

I nod.

Even though it's rare, everyone knows of someone's sister or relative who was found to be impure. The last time it happened in Irfut was decades ago – to one of Father's cousins. The villagers still whisper about the day she was dragged away by the priests, never to be seen again. Father's family has been shadowed by it ever since.

That's why they're always acting so holy – always the first in temple, my aunts masked so absolutely, even their mouths are hidden from view. The Infinite Wisdoms cautions, "Only the impure, blaspheming, and unchaste woman remains revealed under the eyes of Oyomo," but this warning refers to the top half of the face: forehead to the tip of the nose. My aunts, however, even have little squares of sheer cloth covering their eyes.

When Father returned from his army post with Mother at his side, the entire family disowned him immediately. It was too risky, accepting a woman of unknown purity, and a foreigner at that, into the family.

Then I came along – a child dark enough to be a full Southerner but with Father's grey eyes, cleft chin, and softly curled hair to say otherwise.

I've been in Irfut my entire life, born and raised, and I'm still treated like a stranger – still stared and pointed at, still excluded. I wouldn't even be allowed in the temple if some of Father's relatives had their way. My face may be the spitting image of his, but that's not enough. I need to be proven for the village to accept me, for Father's family to accept us. Once my blood runs pure, I'll finally belong.

Father walks over, smiles reassuringly at me. "Do you know what being pure means, Deka?" he asks.

I reply with a passage from the Infinite Wisdoms. "'Blessed are the meek and subservient, the humble and true daughters of man, for they are unsullied in the face of the Infinite Father'."

Every girl knows it by heart. We recite it whenever we enter a temple – a constant reminder that women were created to be helpmeets to men, subservient to their desires and commands.

"Are you humble and all the other things, Deka?" Father asks.

I nod. "I think so," I say.

Uncertainty flickers in his eyes, but he smiles and kisses my forehead. "Then all will be well."

He returns to his hay. I take my seat before Norla, that worry still niggling at me. After all, there are other ways I resemble Mother that Father does not know about – ways that would make the villagers despise me even more if they ever found out.

I have to make sure I keep them secret. The villagers must never find out.

Never.

It's still early morning when I reach the village square. There's a slight chill in the air, and the roofs of nearby houses drip with icicles. Even then, the sun is unseasonably bright, its rays glinting off the high, arching columns of the Temple of Oyomo. Those columns are meant to be a prayer, a meditation on the progress of Oyomo's sun across the sky every day. High priests use them to choose which two days of the year to conduct the spring and winter Rituals. The very sight of them sends another surge of anxiety through me.

"Deka! Deka!" A familiar gawkish figure waves excitedly at me from across the road.

Elfriede hurries over, her cloak pulled so tightly around her, all I can see are her bright green eyes. She and I both always try to cover our faces when we come into the village square – me because of my colouring and Elfriede because of the dull red birthmark covering the left side of her face. Girls are allowed to remain revealed until they go through the Ritual, but there's no point attracting attention, especially on a day like this.

This morning, Irfut's tiny cobblestone square is thronged with hundreds of visitors, more arriving by the cartful every minute.

They're from all across Otera: haughty Southerners with dark brown skin and tightly curled hair; easygoing Westerners, long black hair in topknots, tattoos all over golden skin; brash Northerners, pink skinned, blond hair gleaming in the cold; and quiet Easterners in every shade from deep brown to eggshell, silky straight black hair flowing in glistening rivers down their backs.

Even though Irfut is remote, it's known for its pretty girls, and men come from far distances to look at the eligible ones before they take the mask. Lots of girls will find husbands today – if they haven't already.

"Isn't it exciting, Deka?" Elfriede giggles.

She gestures at the square, which is now festively decorated for the occasion. The doors of all the houses with eligible girls have been painted gleaming red, banners and flags fly cheerfully from windows, and brightly coloured lanterns adorn every entrance. There are even masked stilt dancers and fire breathers, and they thread through the crowd, competing against the merchants selling bags of roasted nuts, smoked chicken legs, and candied apples.

Excitement courses through me at the sight. "It is," I reply with a grin, but Elfriede is already dragging me along.

"Hurry, hurry!" she urges, barrelling past the crowds of visitors, many of whom stop to scowl disapprovingly at our lack of male guardians.

In most villages, women can't leave their homes without a man to escort them. Irfut, however, is small, and men are in scarce supply. Most of the eligible ones have joined the army, as Father did when he was younger. A few have even survived the training to become jatu, the emperor's elite guard. I spot a contingent of them lingering at the edges of the square, watchful in their gleaming red armour.

There are at least twelve today, far more than the usual two or three the emperor sends for the winter Ritual. Perhaps it's true what people have been whispering: that more deathshrieks have been breaking through the border this year.

The monsters have been laying siege to Otera's southern border for centuries, but in the past few years, they've gotten much more aggressive. They usually attack near Ritual day, destroying villages and trying to steal away impure girls.

Rumour is, impurity makes girls much more delicious…

Thankfully, Irfut is in one of the most remote areas of the North, surrounded by snow-capped mountains and impenetrable forests. Deathshrieks will never find their way here.

Elfriede doesn't notice my introspection, she's too busy grinning at the jatu. "Aren't they just so handsome in their reds? I heard they're new recruits, doing a tour of the provinces. How wonderful of the emperor to send them here for the Ritual!"

"I suppose…" I murmur.

Elfriede's stomach grumbles. "Hurry, Deka," she urges, dragging me along. "The line at the bakery will be unmanageable soon."

She pulls me so strongly, I stumble, smacking into a large, solid form. "My apologies," I gasp, glancing up.

One of the visiting men is staring down at me, a thin, wolfish smirk on his lips. "What's this, another sweet morsel?" He grins, stepping closer.

I hurriedly step back. How could I be so stupid? Men from outside villages aren't used to seeing unaccompanied women and can make awful assumptions. "I'm sorry, I must go," I whisper, but he grabs me before I can retreat, his fingers greedily reaching for the button fastening the top of my cloak.

"Don't be that way, little morsel. Be a nice girl, take off the cloak so we can see what we've come—" Large hands wrench him away before he can finish his words.

When I turn, Ionas, the oldest son of Elder Olam, the village head, is glaring down at the man, no trace of his usual easy smile on his face. "If you want a brothel, there's one down the road, in your town," he warns, blue eyes flashing. "Perhaps you should return there."

The difference in their size is enough to make the man hesitate. Though Ionas is one of the handsomest boys in the village – all blond hair and dimples – he's also one of the largest, massive as a bull and just as intimidating.

The man spits at the ground, annoyed. "Don't be so pissy, boy. I was only having a bit of fun. That one isn't even a Northerner, for Oyomo's sake."

Every muscle in my body strings taut at this unwelcome reminder. No matter how quiet I am, how inoffensive I remain, my brown skin will always mark me as a Southerner, a member of the hated tribes that long ago conquered the North and forced it to join the One Kingdom, now known as Otera. Only the Ritual of Purity can ensure my place.

Please let me be pure, please let me be pure. I send a quick prayer to Oyomo.

I pull my cloak tighter, wishing I could disappear into the ground, but Ionas steps even closer to the man, a belligerent look in his eyes. "Deka was born and raised here, same as the rest of us," he growls. "You'll not touch her again."

I gape at Ionas, shocked by this unexpected defence. The man huffs. "Like I said, I was only having a bit of fun." He turns to his friends. "C'mon, then, let's go get a drink."

The group retreats, grumbling under their breath.

Once they're gone, Ionas turns to me and Elfriede. "You all right?" he asks, a worried expression on his face.

"Fine. A bit startled is all," I manage to say.

"But not hurt." His eyes are on me now, and it's all I can do not to squirm under their sincerity.

"No." I shake my head.

He nods. "My apologies for what just happened. Men can be animals, especially around girls as pretty as you."

Girls as pretty as you…

The words are so heady, it takes me a few moments to realize he's speaking again. "Where are you off to?" he asks.

"The baker," Elfriede replies, since I'm still tongue-tied. She nods at the small, cosy building just across the street from us.

"I'll watch you from here," he says. "Make sure you're safe."

Again his eyes remain on me.

My cheeks grow hotter.

"My thanks," I say, hurrying over to the bakery as Elfriede giggles.

True to his words, Ionas continues staring at me the entire way.

The bakery is already packed, just as Elfriede said it would be. Women crowd every corner of the tiny store, their masks gleaming in the low light as they buy delicate pink purity cakes and sun-shaped infinity loaves to celebrate the occasion. Usually, masks are plain things, made out of the thinnest bits of wood or parchment and painted with prayer symbols for good luck. On feast days like this, however, women wear their most extravagant ones, the ones modelled after the sun, moon, and stars and adorned with geometric precision in gold or silver. Oyomo is not only the god of the sun but also the god of mathematics. Most women's masks feature the divine symmetry to please His eye.

After today, I'll begin wearing a mask as well, a sturdy white half mask made out of heavy parchment and thin slivers of wood that will cover my face from forehead to nose. It's not much, but it's the best Father could afford. Perhaps Ionas will ask to court me once I wear it.

I immediately dismiss the ridiculous thought.

No matter what I wear, I'll never be as pretty as the other girls in the village, with their willowy figures, silken blonde hair, and pink cheeks. My own frame is much more sturdy, my skin a deep brown, and the only thing I have to my advantage is my soft black hair, which curls in clouds around my face.

Mother once told me that girls who look like me are considered pretty in the Southern provinces, but she's the only one who's ever thought that. All everyone else ever sees is how different I look from them. I'll be lucky if I get a husband from one of the nearby villages, but I have to try. If anything should ever happen to Father, his relatives would find any reason they could to abandon me.

A cold sweat washes over me as I think of what would happen then: a life of enforced piety and backbreaking labour as a temple maiden or, worse, being forced into the pleasure houses of the Southern provinces.

Elfriede turns to me. "Did you see the way Ionas looked at you?" she whispers. "I thought he was going to whisk you away. So romantic."

I pat my cheeks to cool them as a small smile tugs at my lips. "Don't be silly, Elfriede. He was just being polite."

"The way he was looking at you, it was—"

"What? What was it, Elfriede?" a mincing sweet voice interrupts, titters following in its wake.

My entire body goes cold. *Please, not today...*

I turn to find Agda standing behind us, a group of village girls accompanying her. I know immediately she must have seen me talking to Ionas, because her posture is brittle with rage. Agda may be the prettiest girl in the village, with her pale skin and white-blonde hair, but those delicate features hide a venomous heart and a spiteful nature.

"You think that just because you might be proven today, boys will suddenly start thinking you're pretty?" she sniffs. "No matter how hard you wish otherwise, Deka, a mask will never be able to hide that ugly Southern skin of yours. I wonder what you'll do when no man wants you in his house and you're an ugly, desperate spinster without a husband or family."

I clench my fists so hard, my fingernails dig into my flesh.

Don't reply, don't reply, don't reply...

Agda flicks her eyes dismissively towards Elfriede. "That one, at least, can cover her face, but even if you cover your entire body, everyone knows what's under—"

"Mind your tongue now, Agda," a prim voice calls from the front of the store, cutting her off.

It belongs to Mistress Norlim, her mother. She walks over, the numerous gems on her golden mask glittering sharply enough to blind. Mistress Norlim is the wife of Elder Norlim, the richest man in the village. Unlike the other women, who can afford only gold half masks or full silvers, she wears a formal gold mask that covers her entire face, a sunburst pattern replicated around pale blue eyes. Her hands are also decorated, swirls of gold and semi-precious stones pasted onto the skin.

"'The words of a woman should be as sweet as fruit and honey'," she reminds Agda. "So sayeth the Infinite Wisdoms."

Agda bows her head, sheepish. "Yes, Mother," she replies.

"Besides," her mother adds, the pity in her eyes at odds with her cheerfully grinning mask, "Deka can't help that her skin is as dirty as her mother's was, any more than Elfriede can hide her birthmark. That's the way they were born, poor things."

My gratitude curdles to anger, the blood boiling in my veins. Dirty? Poor things? She should just call me impure and be done with it. It's all I can do to keep my face docile as I walk towards the door, but I somehow manage. "Thank you for your kind words, Mistress Norlim," I force myself to grit out before I exit.

It takes every last bit of my strength not to slam the door.

Then I'm outside, and I'm inhaling and exhaling rapidly, trying to regain my composure, trying to push back the tears of rage pricking at my eyes. I barely notice Elfriede following behind me.

"Deka?" she asks. "You all right?"

"I'm fine," I whisper, hugging my cloak closer so she won't see my tears.

My fury.

It doesn't matter what Mistress Norlim and the others say, I tell myself silently. I will be pure. Doubts surge, reminding me that I have the same uncanny differences Mother did. I push them away. Mother managed to hide hers until the day she died, and I'll do the same. All I have to do is make it through the next few hours and I'll be proven pure.

Then I'll finally be safe.

TWO

I spend the remainder of the morning preparing for the Ritual of Purity: pressing clothes for Father and me and polishing our shoes. I've even made a garland of dried flowers for my hair; their bright red colour will contrast nicely against the ceremonial blue of my dress. I'll be going to the village feast immediately following the Ritual, and I must look my best. This is the first time I've ever been invited to a feast, or any other village celebration, for that matter.

To calm my nerves, I concentrate on the gooseberry tarts I'm taking to the feast. I try to make each one as perfect as possible – edges neatly folded, dollops of whipped cream just so – but it's difficult to do so without a knife. Girls aren't allowed to be near sharp things from the moment they turn fifteen until the day after they're proven by the Ritual of Purity. The Infinite Wisdoms forbids it, ensuring that we do not bleed a drop before the Ritual. Girls who injure themselves during their fifteenth year are taken to the temples for cleansing, their families ostracized and shunned, their marriage prospects destroyed. All they can hope is that they heal properly and that they're proven by the Ritual. Even if it weren't for that, most men won't marry girls who have scars, especially ones with scars from their fifteenth year. It's considered taboo.

"Despised are the marked or scarred, the wounded and the bleeding girls, for they have polluted the temple of the Infinite Father." These words have been drummed into my head from birth.

If Father had more money, he would have sent me to a House of Purity, to spend the entire year before the Ritual protected from sharp things in its soft, pillowed halls. But only rich girls like Agda can afford Houses of Purity. The rest of us have to make do by avoiding knives.

I'm so deep in thought, I don't notice Father's footsteps approaching. "Deka?" he calls. I turn to find him shifting nervously behind me, a box clutched in his hands. He opens it with a hesitant smile. "This is for you," he says, offering me the embroidered dress inside.

I gasp, tears blurring my eyes. The dress is dyed the deep blue of the Ritual and has tiny golden suns embroidered on the hem, but that's not the most exciting thing. Peeking out underneath it is a delicate blue half mask with white silk ribbons to tie it on with. It's finer than anything I've ever seen, the craftsmanship light and elegant despite its wooden base.

"How?" I breathe, gathering it to my chest. We don't have money to spare for new clothes, much less masks. I altered one of Mother's old dresses for the Ritual.

"Your mother made them for you in secret last year," he answers, pulling something else from the box.

"Mother's favourite necklace…" I whisper, a happy sob

bursting from my throat when I take in the thin, finely crafted gold chain and the delicate gold sphere hanging from it, that old, familiar symbol emblazoned across it. It almost looks like the kuru, the sacred symbol of the sun, but there's more to it, another marking so worn I've never been able to make it out, not even after all these years. Mother used to wear the necklace every day without fail.

To think that she had all this ready for me so long ago.

My chest feels tight now, and I rub it, trying to soothe away my tears. I miss her so much, miss her voice, her smell, the way she always used to smile whenever she saw me.

I wipe my eyes as I turn to Father.

"She made sure I kept it for you," Father says. Then he clears his throat, colour rising in his cheeks as he pulls one last thing from the box: a garland of fresh flowers, their bright red shimmering in the light. "The flowers, however, are from me. The merchant told me they were long-lasting."

"They're beautiful," I cry, feeling overwhelmed as I look at him. This is the first time I've received so many gifts. "Everything is beautiful. My deepest thanks, Father."

Father awkwardly pats my back. "Ready yourself, quickly now. Today, you'll show them you belong."

"Yes, Father."

I hurry to do as he says, determination firming inside me. I will show them. I'll wear my new dress and flowers, and then, once the Ritual has ended, I'll wear my new mask to match. I'll wear it so proudly, even Agda won't be able to deny me.

I grin at the thought.

* * *

It's late afternoon when we reach the temple. The village square is packed by then – well-wishers and curious onlookers jostling for space; girls in their ceremonial blues lined up before the temple steps, their parents on either side of them. Father takes his place beside me just as the drums sound, and we watch as the jatu march solemnly towards the steps in preparation for Elder Durkas's arrival, their red armour a gleaming counterpoint to the sea of deep-blue dresses, their gnarled war masks glowering in the dull afternoon light. Each mask resembles a terrifying demon face, and can be attached and removed from the helmet with ease.

Since the doors haven't yet opened, I take in the temple's stark white walls, its red roof. Red is the colour of sanctity. It's the colour pure girls will bleed when Elder Durkas tests them today.

Please let mine be red, please let mine be red, I pray.

I spot Elfriede at the front, her entire body rigid. She must be thinking the same thing. Like all the other girls, she stands with her face revealed one last time, although she hunches slightly to hide her birthmark.

The temple doors creak open, and the crowd hushes. Elder Durkas appears at the top of the stairs, his usual pinched, disapproving look on his face. As with most priests of Oyomo, his mission is to root out impurity and abomination. That's why his body is so thin and his eyes are so intense. Religious fervour leaves little room for eating or anything else. A golden tattoo of the kuru – the symbol of the sun – gleams in the middle of his clean-shaven head.

He extends his hands over the crowd. "The Infinite Father blesses you," he intones.

"The Infinite Father blesses us all." The crowd's reply reverberates through the square.

Elder Durkas raises the ceremonial blade towards the sky. It's carved from ivory and sharper than the most finely honed sword. "'And upon the fourth day,'" he recites in the deep, booming voice he likes to use for these occasions, "'he created woman – a helpmeet to lift man to his sacred potential, his divine glory. Woman is the Infinite Father's greatest gift to mankind. Solace for his darkest hour. Comfort in…'"

Elder Durkas's words fade to a low droning as my skin begins to tingle, the blood rushing underneath. It's coupled by sudden awareness: the stillness of the wind, the crackle of melting icicles, and, somewhere in the distance…the crunch of heavy footsteps on fallen leaves.

Something is coming… The thought flitters through my mind.

I force it away. Why is this happening now?

Father must have noticed my distracted expression, because he sighs ruefully, eyes squinting against the sun. "Ever has your mind been inclined to wander, Deka," he whispers, voice low so the others won't notice we're talking. "You're so very much like your mother."

When his lips turn down in sadness, I frown at him. "You'll develop lines," I say.

Now he smiles, suddenly looking like the hearty man he used to be, before the red pox and Mother's death conspired to shrink him to a shadow of himself. "A bit like the river condemning the stream for rushing too fast, don't you think?" he jokes as the line begins to move.

I nod, return my attention to the temple steps. Elder Durkas has finished his recitation. The Ritual of Purity will now begin.

Agda is the first girl to walk into the temple, and her face is pale with nervousness. Will Oyomo favour her or judge that she has succumbed to impurity? The crowd leans forward, tense. The chattering, the whispered conversations – all fade to a hush, until soon the only things you can hear are the disgruntled yips of the dogs and the huffed breaths of the horses tethered to the nearby stables.

Moments later, a startled cry erupts from inside the temple. Agda emerges soon after, her blue scarf clutched across her chest, where Elder Durkas cut her with the ceremonial blade. Once she arrives at the top of the stairs, she pulls off the scarf and holds it above her head to display the red blood it's saturated with. A relieved cheer swells through the crowd. She's pure. Her parents rush to embrace her, and her father proudly fixes her first mask onto her face, a delicate gold half mask in the shape of the budding moon to declare her newfound womanhood. She casts a victorious glance around the crowd, her lips curling into a smirk when she glimpses me.

Once she walks back down the stairs, the next girl enters, and the Ritual of Purity begins again.

I train my eyes on the door. The sight of it – large, red, and imposing – frays my nerves, causing my stomach to clench and my palms to moisten. The tingling strengthens – a low hum now, fine hairs lifting, awareness rising.

Something is coming. The thought filters through my mind again.

It means nothing, I remind myself firmly. I've felt such things many times before and never once seen anything strange—

Terror slams through me so suddenly and heavily, my knees buckle. I grasp Father's hand to remain standing. He frowns at me.

"Deka, are you all right?"

I don't reply. Fear has frozen my lips, and all I can do is watch in horror as a sinister tendril of mist snakes around Father's feet. More of it is slithering into the square, chilling the air. Above us, the sun flees, chased away by the clouds now rolling across the sky.

Father frowns up at it. "The sun is gone."

But I'm no longer looking at the sky. My eyes are on the edge of the village, where the winter-stripped trees crackle under the weight of snow and ice. The mist is coming from there, heavy with a sharp, cold smell and something else: a distant, high-pitched sound that jitters my nerves.

When the sound shatters into an ear-piercing shriek, the entire crowd stills, petrified statues in the snow. One word whispers across the square: "Deathshrieks…"

Just like that, the lull is broken.

"Deathshrieks!" the jatu commander calls, unsheathing his sword. "Arm yourselves!"

The crowd scatters, the men racing towards the stables for their weapons, women herding their daughters and sons back to their homes. The jatu plough past the crowd, heading towards the forest, where colossal grey forms are appearing, inhuman shrieks heralding their approach.

The largest deathshriek is the first to step foot over the

leafy border marking the edge of the forest. A hulking beast of a creature, it's rawboned to the point of gauntness, its clawed hands dragging almost to its knees, spikes erupting all the way down its bony spine. It seems almost human, black eyes blinking, slitted nostrils flaring as it surveys the village. It turns to the village square, where I'm still standing, terror-struck, and my breath shallows – short, fast spurts of air now.

It opens its mouth, inhales...

A shriek blasts through my skull, white-hot agony slicing into my body. My teeth grind together; my muscles lock in place. Beside me, Father collapses to the ground as blood begins to pour from his ears and nostrils. More villagers are already writhing there, faces contorted into grimaces of terror and anguish.

Other than me, only the jatu remain standing in the square, their helmets specially soundproofed against deathshriek screams. Even so, their eyes flash white behind their war masks and their hands tremble on their swords. The jatu here are mostly recruits, newly initiated into the ranks, just as Elfriede said. They haven't yet fought in the borders of the South, where the deathshrieks lay constant siege – haven't ever even seen a deathshriek before, probably. It'll be a miracle if any of them survive this.

It'll be a miracle if any of us survive this.

The thought jolts me from my paralysis, and I whirl to Father. "We must flee!" I shout, pulling him so hard, he nearly jerks off the ground. Fear has powered my muscles, made them unnaturally strong. "We must go!" I glance at the lead deathshriek again, its hair writhing and lashing fitfully around it.

As if it senses me watching, it turns, and its eyes connect to mine from across the distance. There's a look in them…an intelligence. The breath rips from my lungs. Every muscle in my body suddenly feels weak, frozen under that predatory black gaze. By the time I find the sense to cower, it's already stalking onwards, as are the others. The many, many others. They're emerging from the mists, leathery grey forms bristling with menace. Some lope to the ground from the trees, claws scoring the snow as they run on all fours.

"Defend the village!" the jatu commander roars, lifting his sword. "For the Infinite Father!"

"For the Infinite Father!" the jatu repeat, running towards the beasts.

A horrified gasp bursts from my chest as Father staggers up and echoes the call along with the other village men, who are all now hurriedly wrapping kerchiefs or belts around their ears. "Run to the temple, Deka!" he shouts at me.

Before him, the jatu commander is bearing down on the lead deathshriek, but the creature doesn't retreat. Instead, it stills, cocking its head. For a moment, amusement seems to glitter in its eyes. Deadly amusement. Then it moves, violently backhanding the jatu across the square. His body cracks on impact, blood spewing everywhere.

A signal for the other deathshrieks to attack.

They race into the village, smashing through the jatu's shields, disembowelling them with fatally sharp claws. Screams echo, blood sprays, the odour of urine rises. The jatu try to fight back, but there are too few of them, and they're too inexperienced against the deathshrieks' monstrosity.

I watch, horror choking me, as limbs and bodies are severed

with inhuman abandon, heads ripped off with ferocious glee. Within minutes, the entire jatu force is overwhelmed, and then it's on to the village men.

"Don't let them get past!" Elder Olam roars, but it's already too late.

The deathshrieks are ploughing through the villagers, some leaping onto their victims, others slicing into them with claws and teeth. The more the village men scream, the more frenzied the deathshrieks become. Blood splatters the ground, startling crimson across the white of the snow; corpses lie in a tangle of viscera and dried leaves.

It's a massacre.

Terror knifing my heart, I turn to Father. He and two other villagers are engaged in combat with a deathshriek, pushing the creature back with swords and pitchforks. He doesn't see the other deathshriek racing towards him, bloodlust in its eyes. He doesn't see its claws unsheathing, reaching for him.

"NOOOO!" The desperate cry erupts from my chest before I can quiet it, so powerful it seems as if it's layered with something else. Something deeper. "STOP, PLEASE! Leave my father alone! Please, just leave us alone!"

The deathshrieks whirl towards me, eyes deep black with rage. Time seems suspended as their leader moves forwards. Closer, then closer still, until—

"STOP!" I shout, my voice even more powerful than before.

The deathshriek abruptly stiffens, life draining from its eyes. For a moment, it almost seems a husk – an empty vessel, rather than a living being. The other deathshrieks are the same: frozen statues in the late afternoon light.

Silence descends upon the village. My heart pounds in my ears. Louder. Louder. Then…

Movement.

The lead deathshriek turns and staggers towards the forest, the others following behind it. The mist swiftly withdraws behind them, almost seeming to trail in their footsteps. In less than a minute, they're gone.

I'm drunk with relief, floating, as if I'm only barely connected to my skin. A hazy feeling is taking over now, making my entire body feel as light as thistledown.

I glide towards Father, a glazed smile on my face. He's still standing where he was, but he doesn't seem to feel as relieved as I do. His face is pale, his body slick with sweat. He almost looks…terrified.

"Father?" I ask, reaching for him.

To my surprise, he recoils. "Foul demon!" he shouts. "What have you done with my daughter?"

"Father?" I repeat. I take another step towards him, confused when he once more recoils.

"Don't you dare call me that, beast!" he hisses.

The other men have gathered around him now. The women have begun to spill out of the houses, Elfriede among them. There's an expression on her face, one I've never seen there before. Fear.

"Your eyes, Deka. What's happened to your eyes?" she whispers, horrified.

Her words melt a bit of the haze surrounding me. My eyes? I turn to Father, about to ask what the men are saying, but he nods to someone behind me. When I look, there's Ionas, a sword gleaming in his hand. I frown at him, confused. Has he come to protect me, as he did earlier today?

"Ionas?" I ask.

He thrusts the sword into my stomach. The pain is so sharp, so exquisite, I barely notice the blood spilling into my hands.

It's red…so very red at first, but then the colour begins to change, to glimmer. Within moments, the red has turned to gold – the very same gold now racing across my skin.

Shadows cloud my vision as the blood in my veins slows to a trickle. The only thing that remains moving is that gold, pouring into my hands like a river, slowly gliding over my skin.

"As I always suspected," a faraway voice says. When I look up, Elder Durkas is looming over me. His expression is dark with satisfaction. "She's impure," he declares.

That's the last thing I hear before I die.

THREE

It's dark when I wake and strangely quiet. The noise and crowds of the village square have disappeared, replaced by shadows, cold, and silence. Where am I? I glance around, my breath coming in short, laboured spurts, and discover I'm in what looks like a cellar, with neatly stacked casks of oil lined against dark stone walls. I try to rise, but something stops me: rough-hewn iron shackles, one set for my feet and a matching pair for my wrists. I tug and twist, breaths heavier and heavier now, but the shackles still don't move. They've been hammered into the wall behind me. A scream builds in my throat.

"You're awake." Ionas's voice slices through my panic. He's standing in the darkness, examining me with the cold intensity he usually reserves for beggars and lepers. The expression is so harsh, I jerk back, frightened.

"Ionas," I say, tugging at the manacles. "What's happening? Why am I here?"

Ionas's mouth turns down with disgust. "You see me?" he asks. Then he adds, as if to himself, "Of course you can."

"I don't understand," I say, sitting up. "Why am I here? Why am I chained?"

Ionas lights a torch. The brightness is so overwhelming, I have to shield my eyes. "You can see me in complete darkness, and you dare to ask why you're here?"

"I don't understand," I repeat. "My head, everything is all confused."

"How can you not remem—"

"Don't speak to it," a cold voice commands.

Father rises from the corner, a harsh expression on his face. A pillar concealed him before, but there he is now, clear as day, despite the shadows cloaking his corner. Why can I see him so clearly? Ionas only lit one torch. A fearful twinge shoots through my stomach as I remember Ionas's words: *You can see me in complete darkness...*

Father nods curtly to Ionas. "Summon the others."

Ionas hurries up the stairs, leaving Father, a wraithlike figure in the darkness. His eyes burn with a strange emotion as he approaches. Anger? Disgust?

"Father?" I whisper, but he doesn't reply as he crouches before me, his eyes flicking over my body until they land on my stomach. There's a jagged hole in my dress, revealing a stretch of unmarked skin. I cover it self-consciously, something niggling at me.

What am I forgetting?

"Not even a scar," Father observes in a strange, removed sort of way. He has something clutched in his hand: Mother's necklace.

He must have taken it from my neck as I slept.

33

A tear slides down my cheek.

"Father?" I say. "Father, what is this? Why am I here?"

I reach out to him, then stop. There's a harsh, forbidding expression on his face. A simmering disgust. Why won't he answer me? Why won't he look at me? I would give anything for him to embrace me and tell me how foolish I am for being so frightened, his sweet, silly girl.

He does none of these things, only looks into my eyes with that awful, removed disgust. "It would have been better if you had just died," he spits.

And then I remember.

I remember the Ritual of Purity, the deathshriek leader's approach – how cold those black eyes were as they met mine. Then the jatu and the village men's counterattack. Blood on snow. Father in danger. And then that voice emerging from me...that awful, inhuman voice...followed by the look in Father's eyes as he commanded Ionas to cut me down. The look that I understood only when I saw the golden blood dripping down my belly.

"No..." I whisper, sobs wracking my body. I can almost feel the jagged edge of the sword again, feel the darkness descending upon me.

I rock back and forth, so deep in my horror, I barely notice the footsteps echoing down the stairs, barely see the figures approaching. Only after they've been standing before me for some minutes do I look up, discover Elder Durkas reading fervently from the Infinite Wisdoms, a bandaged Elder Olam and the village elders standing silently beside him. There are only five of them now. I wonder about the others, and the image of two elders' spines shattering under the sweep of deathshriek claws blisters through my mind and my stomach lurches.

I double over, vomit pungent on my tongue. Elder Durkas steps forwards, his eyes filled with disgust. "To think, we sheltered such a creature in our midst."

His words freeze the vomit in my throat. I surge to my knees, holding my hands out to him. "Elder Durkas," I plead, "please, this is a mistake! I'm not impure! I am not!"

Guilt surges inside me, a horrific reminder: my skin tingled when the deathshrieks came, and when they left, it was only because I told them to.

Because I commanded them.

Elder Durkas ignores me and turns to the other men. "Who will purify this demon and rid our village of her abomination?"

His words terrify me. I begin begging again. "Please, Elder Durkas, please!"

But the elder says nothing, only turns to Father, who glances at me. There's an expression in his eyes, an uncertainty.

"Remember, that is not your daughter," Elder Durkas reminds him. "She may look human now, but that is the demon that has possessed her – the demon that called deathshrieks to our door and killed our families."

Called the deathshrieks? The words splinter, choking me with horror. "I didn't!" I protest. "I didn't call the deathshrieks."

You made them leave, however… The reminder slithers in my mind and I force it away.

Elder Durkas ignores me, continues talking to Father. "You brought her impurity into this village. It is your duty to cleanse her."

To my horror, Father nods grimly, then steps forwards and holds out his hand. Ionas places a sword inside it.

When it gleams, its blade reflecting the dim light, my fear explodes. I scramble against the wall. "Father, no! Please, no!"

But Father ignores my pleas and approaches until he's standing just before me, the tip of the sword resting on my neck. It's cold, so icy cold... I look up at Father, trying to see any hint of the man who once carried me on his shoulders and saved the creamiest portions of milk because he knew I liked them best.

"Father, please, don't do this," I beg, tears pouring down my cheeks. "I'm your daughter. I'm Deka, your Deka, remember?"

For a moment, something seems to spark inside his eyes. Regret...

"Cleanse her or the jatu will come for you and the rest of your family," Elder Durkas hisses.

Father's eyes shutter. His lips thin into a tight, grim line. "I cleanse you in the name of Oyomo," he declares, raising the sword.

"Father, no—"

The blade slices through my neck.

I'm a demon.

I know it the moment I open my eyes. I'm still chained in the cellar, but my body is whole again. Not a single scar or blemish marks my skin – not even the portion of my neck where Father beheaded me. I touch it, a whimper wrenching from deep inside me when I feel the skin there, once more silky smooth under my fingers. It's as if I've been completely reborn. Even my childhood scars are gone.

I hurriedly kneel, bowing my head in prayer. *Please don't abandon me, Infinite Father,* I beg. *Please purify me of whatever evil has taken hold. Please, please, please…*

"Your prayers won't reach him," Elder Olam says from the corner. It's his turn to watch me, it seems. Unlike the others, he does so with fascination rather than disgust. "He's already rejected you from His Afterlands twice."

His words are like an arrow piercing my heart. "Because I'm a demon," I whisper, horror and disgust an acrid bitterness in my mouth.

"Indeed." Elder Olam doesn't bother to prettify his answer.

He doesn't have to. What kind of cursed creature doesn't die from a beheading? Even deathshrieks topple when their heads are cleaved from their bodies. I close my eyes against the memory, try to breathe out my rising panic.

"Where's Father?" I ask.

The Elder shrugs. "He took to his bed."

Something about his tone makes me stiffen. "When?"

"Five days ago, when the fibres of your neck stretched their way back to your body and reattached."

Vomit rises to my throat again, and I retch loudly, emptying my stomach. There isn't much left in it now but water and bile. Once I'm finished, I wipe my lips, mentally push back frenzied thoughts and acid guilt.

All those years, Father endured being sneered at and excluded – for me. For the promise that I would one day be proven and show everyone I belonged in the village. But I am exactly what they said I was, only worse – so, so much worse. And now look what I've done.

Elder Olam continues watching me. "Your friend Elfriede is pure, in the event you were wondering," he says. "We are watching her, nevertheless. She spent a great deal of time with you. You never know how such associations can taint a person."

The words jolt through me. "She is innocent," I whisper, horrified. I'm the one who heard the deathshrieks. Who commanded them… "Elfriede has nothing to do with this."

Elder Olam shrugs. "Perhaps. Time will tell, I suppose…"

The callousness of his answer is terrifying, but I can't dwell on that now.

"Father," I remind him. "What is his condition?"

Elder Olam shrugs again, unconcerned. "He won't survive for long. Not if you remain undying," he adds pointedly.

I flinch, shame and guilt roiling in my belly. Now I understand why Elder Olam is here – why the others made sure he took Father's place. He's good at making people see his way. Before he became head of the village, he was a very successful trader. He had a way of making his patrons believe that they wanted what he wanted.

He doesn't have to do so with me. I look down at my veins, stomach lurching as they shimmer, the gold glittering inside them, demonic essence forever marking me impure. I want to rip them out, want to dig so deeply I empty them.

Suddenly, I think of the villagers, huddled in their homes, and Father, on his sickbed. And even Elfriede. Distinctly now, I remember the fear in her eyes when she looked at me.

The disgust. What happens when the demon in me rises again? What happens if it decides to lash out? To attack the village? To call more deathshrieks?

All those dead villagers scattered in the snow...

My breath shallows, and I try to breathe, surrender myself to Oyomo's grace. Elder Durkas told us it was always around us, there if we only reached for it – if only we submitted ourselves to His will.

I will submit. I will do anything to cleanse myself of my impurity, of my sins.

I look up at Elder Olam. "Kill me," I whisper, the tears sliding down my cheeks. "I know you must know how. I am an abomination in the eyes of Oyomo. I am an abomination."

A grim smile slices Elder Olam's lips. Victory. "They say fire is cleansing for the spirit," he murmurs, taking a torch from the wall and staring meaningfully at the flames.

Another scream rises, but I swallow it down. It'll be all right, I tell myself. All I have to do is submit, subject myself to the flames, and perhaps then Oyomo will forgive me for my impurity.

Even as I think this, I know it's a lie. Fire won't kill me. Perhaps nothing ever will. Even then I have to try – have to submit and bear the pain until Oyomo gives me His grace again. Or until He grants me the mercy of death.

Click. Click. Click.

A sharp, insistent tapping penetrates my ears.

When I blearily open my eyes, there's a woman sitting before me. She's small and delicate, and dark robes cover her from head to toe. Even stranger, her hands are covered by white, bonelike armoured gloves – gauntlets. They have sharpened claws at the end, and they glow dimly in the darkness of the cellar. It almost looks as if she has ghostly white hands. White Hands... Perhaps that's what I'll call her.

When she notices me watching her, White Hands stops drumming her fingers. Her wooden half mask gleams under her hood, a gnarled, frightening demon caught mid-roar. I blink. For just a moment, I thought it was a war mask, but only men wear those. Is she really a nightmare? A fever dream? Please let her be a dream. Please, no more pain – no more blood.

Golden rivers, coiling down the floor—

Tiny daggers bite into my chin and neck. "No, no, you will not ignore me, alaki," White Hands says in a lilting, heavily accented voice.

I jerk away from her gauntlets, gasping. This isn't a dream; she's really here! The scent of ice and fir trees wafts from her cloak, chasing away the ever-present stench of burning flesh, melting fat, charred bone. As I inhale deeply, savouring the smell, White Hands abruptly crouches, her eyes boring into mine. Fear shivers over me.

They're dark – so very, very dark – those eyes. The last time I saw eyes so dark was on a deathshriek, but they didn't have whites surrounding their pupils.

White Hands is human. Terrifyingly so.

"You are awake. Good," she murmurs. "Are you lucid?"

I blink back at her.

White Hands slaps me so sharply, my head jerks back from the blow. I touch my cheek, shocked, until she grips my chin with those claws again. "Are. You. Lucid. Alaki?"

There it is, that word again. *A-la-key*. I pronounce it silently in my mind, focusing on its strange, forbidding edges as I sit up. "Yes," I rasp, licking my lips. My voice is a raw nerve, my tongue drier than our lake bed in midsummer. I haven't spoken in days...or has it been weeks? Months? How long have I been here? My memories blend in an orgy of blood and terror – of gold, shimmering on the cobblestone floor as the sword slices down, tearing past reattaching muscles, reconnecting tendons...

The elders bring out buckets, gold-lust in their eyes. They're going to dismember me again, going to rip me apart to harvest the gold that flows in my veins. A scream pours out, shrill, unhinged. It mixes with my prayers. *Please forgive me. I didn't mean to sin. I didn't know about the impurity in my blood. Please forgive me.*

Then the icy sweetness of the knife, slicing through my tongue—

White Hands snaps her claws. "No, do not drift off again." She rummages in her cloak and unearths a small glass vial, which she wafts under my nose.

An acrid smell sears my nostrils, and I jerk upright, blinking wildly as the memories flee back to their hidden corners. White Hands moves forwards with the vial again, but I quickly turn my head away.

"I'm awake, I'm awake," I rasp.

"Good," she says. "I dislike being ignored by alaki."

"Alaki?" I repeat.

"It means worthless, unwanted. That is what they call your kind." White Hands peers at me. I can almost feel her frowning under her hood. "You do not know what you are?"

I struggle to understand what she's saying. "I'm impure," I reply. Rivers of golden blood flow past my eyes.

Amusement glimmers in hers. "Undoubtedly, but that does not fully explain what you are."

Something stirs inside me, a dull echo almost resembling curiosity. "What am I?" I ask. "And what do you mean by my kind?" Does she mean the other impure girls, the ones who died here?

More memories surface – impatient whispers in the darkness.

Why won't she die?

They always die by the second or third death. Beheading, burning, drowning. It's always one of the three.

She's unnatural, this one.

Unnatural…

"If you make the correct choice, I will tell you."

The sound of White Hands's voice returns me abruptly to the present.

"Choice?" My head throbs and I want to go back to sleep.

I begin to close my eyes again, but she pulls something from her pocket. It's a seal made of solid gold, with a circle of obsidian stones in the middle of one side and an old Oteran symbol on the other: an eclipsed sun whose rays have been turned into wickedly sharp blades. This is the first time I've ever seen one so close before. Only officials carry seals, and it's rare they come to Irfut. There's something strange about the circle on the first side. I squint, forcing it to take shape.

Stars. The stones are shaped like stars.

"The ansetha." White Hands's voice answers my unspoken question as she points to the symbol on the seal. "It is an invitation."

Confusion lines my face, and I frown at her. "An invitation for what?"

"For you, Impure One. Emperor Gezo has decided to create an army of your kind. He invites you to join it and protect our beloved Otera from those that would oppose her will."

White Hands begins untying her mask, and I recoil, unnerved. Is this a trick? Some kind of bizarre test? Women never remove their masks in front of strangers, only family or their dearest friends. I shut my eyes, frightened of what I'll see, but White Hands's amused laugh filters into my ears.

"Look at me."

I squeeze my eyes tighter.

"Look at me." There's iron behind the command now.

I look.

White Hands is the most beautiful woman I've ever seen. My jaw drops nearly to my chest when I take full stock of her. Small of stature, she has short, tightly curled hair and glowing skin that gleams a smooth bluish-black, like the night sky at midsummer. Her most striking feature, however, is her eyes, deep black and fathomless, as if she's seen the worst of humanity and survived to laugh at it all.

I thought I'd endured tortures, but something tells me White Hands has not only endured but thrived, become stronger for her pain.

She's monstrous... The realization shudders through me, along with another. This is why the Infinite Wisdoms cautions against talking to unmasked women, against even looking at them.

They may be demons in disguise.

White Hands moves closer. "Now, then, tell me – what have you decided? You have only two choices, after all: remain here, where the elders can bleed you while pretending to enforce the Death Mandate, or come with me to the capital and make something of yourself – something even those greedy bastards upstairs cannot sneer at."

"I'm impure," I say slowly, pushing back the futile hope that surges at her words. There's no reprieve for me, no freedom. Nothing will change that.

Oyomo, give me grace. Oyomo, forgive me my sins. Oyomo, please absolve me.

I turn my head away, but White Hands's gauntlets immediately return, digging into my skin. She forces my eyes to meet hers. "You can decide your fate, alaki, an option that was not given to your predecessors." Her tone is pleasant enough, but there's pure steel behind it. "However, if you do wish to have the Death Mandate enforced—"

"Death Mandate?" This is the second time she's mentioned it.

"'Never allow an alaki to live, nor anyone who aids her,'" White Hands recites, as if reading from a scroll. "Those are the exact words of the Death Mandate for your kind – the words that ensure that every girl in Otera undergoes the Ritual of Purity so that all your kind are found and executed without delay."

The ground falls out from under me. So that all your kind are found and executed... The elders suspected all along what

I was, were just waiting for the Ritual to confirm it so they could finally end my life—

"Listen well, alaki," White Hands says, moving so suddenly, I feel the sting on my chest only after she's sliced it open with her gauntleted claws. Unease shudders through me when I look down and see she's made a cut in the same place Elder Durkas would have, had I gone through the Ritual of Purity.

Gold is already welling up, staining my skin with its evil. I jerk away, cover the wound, but White Hands lifts a droplet and rubs it between her fingers.

"This is the cursed gold." She extends gold-stained fingers towards me. I watch them, mesmerized.

Cursed gold?

Such awful words....

"It's what marks you as inhuman, demonic."

Tears prickle my eyes, a mixture of horror and futile humiliation. White Hands doesn't have to remind me of what I am. I know I'm a demon, foul and unclean, despised by Oyomo. No matter how much I beg, no matter how absolutely I submit, He never listens, never even hears me.

Why won't you hear me?

I'll try harder, I won't scream, I won't cry, not even if they dismember me again, knives slicing through fat, cutting past bone and—

White Hands grasps my chin, claws digging in deep, and my thoughts still once more. "It also marks you as a precious commodity." She rises to her feet. "The deathshrieks have begun migrating, and the southern borders are nearly overwhelmed. The jatu there will not be able to withstand the attacks much

45

longer. Every day, those…creatures come closer and closer to the empire. It is only a matter of time before we are overrun, defeated by them."

I shudder from the memory, remembering the predatory look in the deathshriek leader's eyes as they met mine. "What does that have to do with me?"

White Hands shrugs elegantly. "Who better to fight a monster than another monster?"

Shame wells up again, and the tears burn hotter in my eyes. I can't even watch White Hands any more as she continues: "You have died, what, seven, eight—"

"Nine," I tiredly correct, the methods flowing through my head. Beheading, burning, drowning, hanging, poisoning, stoning, disembowelling, bloodletting, dismemberment…

Several dismemberments, only one of which actually killed me.

The elders bring out buckets, that gold-lust surfacing in their eyes.

"We'll sell it in Norgorad. I know a merchant there who pays a fair price."

"Nine times." White Hands's voice wrenches me from my turbulent memories. "You have died nine times and revived each time. That means you have already been proven. You are perfect for what the emperor wants."

"He wants demons?" I ask.

"No, he wants warriors. An entire army of impure ones, fighting for the glory of the One Kingdom."

My eyes widen. There are enough other girls like me to create an army? Of course there are. All those sisters and distant cousins taken over the years…

White Hands looks down at me. "Once every hundred years, deathshrieks migrate to the primal nesting ground, the place from which they all originate. This year begins a new migration, and Emperor Gezo has decided it is the perfect time to strike.

"In eight months precisely, when all the deathshrieks have fully gathered at the nesting ground, his armies will march on them and destroy them and their accursed home. We will obliterate them from the face of Otera." Her eyes pin me in place. "Your kind will lead the charge."

My kind... Foreboding shivers through me, mixing with a twinge of disappointment. For a moment, I hoped White Hands was an alaki too. I force myself to return her stare. "Even if that's true, why should I agree?" I rasp. "What would I gain from it, other than an eternity of painful deaths on the battlefield?"

"Freedom from this farce." She gestures around the cellar. "While you cower here in misery, those elders sell your gold to the highest bidder so nobles can make pretty trinkets from it. They enrich themselves off your suffering – parasites, quite literally draining the blood from you."

Nausea swells my mouth and I struggle to swallow. I've known what the elders were doing, known that they were dismembering me for the gold. But I have to submit, have to pay the price for my impurity.

Oyomo, forgive me; Oyomo, grant me—

"Absolution."

My heart nearly stops when White Hands utters this word.

"That's the other thing you would gain."

Everything is so quiet now, I barely hear her continue.

47

"Fight on behalf of Otera for a period of twenty years, and you will be absolved, your demonic nature cleansed. You will be pure again."

"Pure?" I repeat, all other thoughts disappearing, chased away by those incredible words: pure. Absolved. Human again, just like everyone else...

No more tingling, ever again.

I look up at the ceiling, tears stinging my eyes.

You were listening. This whole time, you were listening. You heard me after all.

I barely notice White Hands as she nods in affirmation. "The emperor's priests can ensure it, yes," she replies.

By now, so many thoughts are whirling through my head, so many feelings – relief, joy – it's all I can do to keep from jumping up in agreement.

Then I remember. "What about the elders? My father?" I ask.

White Hands shrugs. "What of them? I am an emissary of Emperor Gezo himself. A living embodiment of his will. To go against me is to go against Otera."

Relief surges again, determination swift on its heels. I can be pure. I can find a place that accepts me, and even belong for the first time in my life. I can have a future – a normal life, a normal death...

He will finally allow me into His Afterlands.

"A word of warning, alaki." White Hands's voice interrupts my thoughts. "The training will be ten times more brutal than that of the regular soldiers."

When I cower back in alarm, she shrugs. "You are an accursed demon, a despised abomination in the eyes of Oyomo, and they will treat you as such." As I look down, ashamed, she adds a few more words. "However, given what you have endured here, I doubt there is anything you would encounter during training that will ever come close."

She leans nearer, that seal dangles from her hands. An invitation. A warning. "Well, have you decided?"

Decided? Is it even a question? All these days, I have been praying, submitting, in the hopes of belonging somewhere, and here I have it – the answer, the one I have been seeking. I look at her, my eyes certain now.

I accept the seal.

"Yes," I say, "I have. I agree – on one condition."

An amused smile curls across her lips. "Oh?"

"You will make them tell my father that I am dead."

FOUR

In the end, Elder Durkas doesn't even argue with White Hands about my fate. All it takes is a pointed arch of her eyebrow, and I'm unchained and dressed with such extraordinary speed, it's as if the hounds of the Afterlands themselves have risen to nip at the elders' heels. The elders may hate to lose the wealth I've brought them, but they dare not go against an emissary of the emperor.

It's night outside when they lead me to the steps of the temple, and so dark the moon only barely sparkles on the snow-covered ground. A blast of icy-cold wind hits my face, sending tears to my eyes. It wouldn't sting so much if I had a mask to cover my face, but I'm an impure woman. I'll never be able to wear a mask now.

I've been freed from the cellar. I never thought I would be. I never thought I'd feel the wind again, never thought I'd glimpse the sky again. This almost feels like a dream – the blissful ones I have whenever I die and my skin takes on the same golden sheen as my—

"Take these," Elder Durkas snarls, shoving something coarse and heavy into my hands. "They're an offering for the emissary's mounts."

I look down, surprised to find a burlap sack filled with plump red winter apples. A sob chokes me. Winter apples are harvested only at the height of the cold season. If these are as fresh as they seem, I've been locked in that cellar for two full months, perhaps more.

More sobs come, each one more wracking than the last.

Elder Durkas's lips curl into a sneer at the sound. "Wait here," he growls, walking towards White Hands's wagon: a small, rickety wooden affair with tiny windows on each side and a single door at the back. Two large creatures are attached to it. They look almost like horses, but there's something funny about them.

As I blink, trying to make them out through my tears, Elder Durkas calls out to White Hands: "I've brought the demon, as you commanded."

Demon. I should already be used to the word, but shame curves my shoulders, and I huddle into my coat. That is, until White Hands guides the wagon nearer, and I see the creatures clearly for the first time.

The breath rushes out of me. Those creatures aren't horses at all; they're equus: horse lords. They have human chests sprouting from their horselike lower bodies and talons where hooves should be. Mother used to tell me about them – how they ran through the desert on their talons, herding horses and camels. Similar creatures roam the more remote mountains of the North, but they're larger and much more heavily furred. Strangely, these equus are wearing heavy coats over their glossy white bodies, and they even have furred boots over their talons. It must be too cold in the Northern provinces for their kind.

The larger one sees me staring and nudges the other as they near the steps where I remain, huddled into myself. "Look, look, Masaima, a little human to eat," he says. He has a stripe of black hair in his otherwise pristine white mane, and his nose is so flat, it's almost a muzzle.

The smaller one is pure white from head to tail, and his eyes are a large, gentle brown. "Looks tasty, Braima. Shall we share her between us?" he says with a smile.

I shrink back, alarmed, but White Hands turns to me with an amused smile. "Do not worry, alaki, Braima and Masaima are vegetarians. They only eat grass…and apples," she adds pointedly.

I blink, then hurriedly remove two apples from the sack. "Oh, here, these are for you," I say, walking over. I slowly offer them up, mindful of how much the equus loom over me.

Greedy, long-fingered hands snatch the apples out of mine.

"Mmm, winter apples!" Braima, the black-striped equus exclaims, crunching into his. Suddenly, he doesn't seem dangerous at all – more like an overgrown puppy playing at being fierce.

He's obviously the elder of the twins. I realize that's what they are now, because other than his larger size and the black stripe in his hair, he and his brother are identical, both beautiful in that ethereal, otherworldly way despite their powerful physiques.

White Hands shakes her head fondly. "You should be nicer, Braima," she chides. "Deka is our travelling companion." As I frown at this strange description of our circumstances, she turns to the elders. "What are you waiting for, then? Hurry it up."

The elders quickly do as they're told. Warm clothes and a few packs of food are bundled into White Hands's covered wagon, as are several flasks of water.

The entire process takes only a few minutes, and then White Hands helps me up into the back of the wagon and shuts the door.

To my surprise, someone else is sitting among the furs packed there – a girl my age with a plump figure and the blue eyes and blonde hair so typical of the Northern provinces. She smiles at me cheerfully, her face half covered by an ocean of furs, and a tingle rushes under my skin, one distinctly different from what I felt when I first sensed the deathshrieks. This tingle feels almost like…recognition… Could she be one of my kind? An alaki too?

"Hullo," the girl says and gives a pleasant little wave.

She reminds me of Elfriede, the way she seems so shy and eager at the same time. Only the accent is different, hers flowing in the rhythmic up-and-down of the remotest Northern villages, the ones so high in the mountains it takes weeks to reach them.

I'm so taken aback to find someone else sitting here, I barely notice the clinking until I glance up to see Elder Durkas approaching the front of the wagon, a pair of manacles in hand. White Hands is already seated at the reins, and she watches impassively as he nods at me, disgusted.

"That one is unnatural, even for an alaki," he sneers. "Refuses to die no matter how many times you kill her. Best to keep her chained away from the other one, before her bad blood spreads its influence."

I flinch at the words, shame growing, but White Hands's expression freezes colder than the wind now whipping through the air. "I neither fear little girls nor need shackles to compel them," she says, ice dripping from her words. "Now if you will excuse me."

She clicks the wagon's reins.

Just like that, I'm riding out of the only home I've ever known.

Elder Durkas watches me, a chilling hatred in his eyes. Who will he bleed for gold now that I'm gone?

As we pass the last houses on Irfut's outskirts, White Hands gestures towards the girl. "Deka, this is your travelling companion, Britta. She is going to the capital as well."

"Hullo," Britta says again. Surprisingly, she doesn't seem scared of me at all, even after what Elder Durkas said. But then, she's an alaki like me.

I manage a small, shy nod. "Evening greetings," I mumble.

"Britta will explain to you more about your kind," White Hands says. "She should know. She's the same as you. Well, almost."

I cautiously examine Britta from the corner of my eye. She catches my look and grins again. Other than my parents and Elfriede, no one's ever smiled at me so much. I fight the urge to duck my head in embarrassment.

"So yer new to this alaki business too," she whispers conspiratorially.

"I just heard the word for the first time today," I reply, glancing down.

Britta nods eagerly. "I didna know about it meself until I

started bleeding the cursed gold durin' me menses. Me da nearly keeled over when me ma showed him mine. But they did me right, called herself." She nods at White Hands. "She came an' took me two weeks ago. Apparently, I'm one of the lucky ones."

When I glance up at her, confused, she explains: "Afore, most girls got executed in the temples the moment they were discovered, an' their families were punished so they'd never speak of it. Now everybody gets sent to the capital. They've even started takin' the younger girls, the ones who haven't been proven by the Ritual of Purity. The minute they suspect ye, they cut ye an' that's that."

Despised are the marked or scarred, the wounded and the bleeding girls... The quote from the Infinite Wisdoms rushes through my mind, and I nearly laugh at the irony, the wickedness of it all. Now I understand why they don't want girls to get cut or wounded before the Ritual of Purity. It's so the impure ones like me don't discover what we are, don't ask any questions before it's too late. It's also likely the reason they don't kill impure girls before the Ritual. Kill an impure girl any other time and her family will protest, the other villagers will ask questions, voice their objections... It's the Ritual that gives legitimacy to the murder.

An impure girl is despised by Oyomo, her very existence an offence to Him. Her murder is sanctioned by the Infinite Wisdoms, and who can argue with the holy books? Who would dare even try? All the families can see from then on is the demon that somehow invaded their bloodline. The sheer wickedness of it stings.

Britta looks at me, pity rising in her eyes. "Must've been

55

horrible, wha those bastards did to ye back there. I'm so sorry for wha happened to ye."

More memories, all so sudden and powerful, my body trembles from the force of them. The cellar…the gold… Blood rushes to my head, and light becomes pinpricks. I close my eyes against it, faint.

"Ye all right?" Britta asks, concerned.

I slowly nod. "I am," I say. Then I clear my throat, try to change the subject. "So what did White Hands tell you about our kind?"

Britta's eyebrows rise. "White Hands? That's herself's name?"

Her surprise is so unexpected, so genuine, I smile and shake my head. "I don't know what her real name is. I gave it to her because of the gauntlets."

Britta nods, quickly understanding. It's bad luck to ask the emperor's emissaries directly for their names. Never invite trouble into your house, as the saying goes.

I prompt her again. "So what exactly am I? What are we? White Hands never explained fully."

"Demons," Britta says, the word a shard of ice through my heart. "Well, their descendants, leastways." She leans closer, eyes wide as she whispers, "She says we're the descendants of the Gilded Ones."

"The Gilded Ones?" I repeat, alarm rushing over me.

I know the Gilded Ones – everyone in Otera does. Four ancient demons, they preyed upon humanity for centuries, destroying kingdom after kingdom until everyone finally banded together for protection, forming Otera, the One Kingdom. It took several battles before the first emperor was finally able to destroy them, and he only did so using the might of Otera's combined armies.

Every winter, villages enact plays chronicling the Gilded Ones' defeat. Elderly aunts wear masks carved in their images to frighten naughty children, and men burn straw figures in their likeness to scare away evil.

And I'm being compared to them. Being called one of them. Heart drumming a sudden and panicked beat, I rummage in my pack and unearth the golden seal White Hands gave me, quickly counting the stars embedded in the ansetha. When I see what's there, tears sear my eyes. Four. Four stars in the symbol. Four Gilded Ones.

Why didn't I suspect this? I should have known, should have at least suspected, the moment my blood ran gold. The Gilded Ones were female, after all, and they were always depicted with gold veins running over their bodies. No wonder Oyomo took so long to hear me, no wonder I had to submit to the executions, the bleedings, for so long. I am an insult to the natural order itself.

Britta doesn't seem to notice my despair as she smiles at me. "Oh, ye got one of those too," she says excitedly, holding a golden seal identical to mine. "White Hands gave it to me when me ma an' da handed me over. Most saddened they were to see me go, but it was—"

"You were telling me about the Gilded Ones?" I quickly remind her, trying to stop her from saying anything more about her parents, about her life before now.

She's not even horrified. Not even the slightest bit disgusted by what she is. But how could she be when her parents protected her, kept her from harm – from dismemberment – while mine… Tears prick at my eyes when I remember Father's words: *It would have been better if you had just died.*

Did he even cry when he heard of my death, or was he just relieved – grateful to be free of his unnatural burden? Does he even think about me any more?

I dig my nails into my palms to stop the thoughts from circling and try to focus on Britta as she answers my question. "Oh yes – the Gilded Ones," she says brightly. "By the time Emperor Emeka destroyed them, they'd already intermixed an' had all sorts of children with humans. We're the result – their grandchildren thousands of times removed, I suppose."

"So we are demons," I conclude, a dull, heavy feeling settling over me.

"Half," Britta corrects. "Less than a quarter, probably. White Hands says we change only when we near maturity, which is sixteen for our kind. Once we begin our menses, our blood gradually turns gold, an' that makes our muscles an' bones stronger. That's why we heal so fast an' are quicker an' stronger than regular folk. It's 'cause we're like predatory beasts now, like wolves an' such."

Predatory beasts. Bitterness jolts me at the words.

I remember the surge of strength I experienced when the deathshrieks came, remember how I could see in that dark cellar even when there weren't any torches. Now I understand why. It's because I'm no better than an animal – a fiend skulking at the edges of humanity. Perhaps that's even why I could sense the deathshrieks, why Mother could sense them as well.

But that doesn't make sense. Mother wasn't alaki. If she was, she would have bled the cursed gold when the red pox turned her insides to sludge, and then she would have fallen into the gilded sleep, her body taking on a golden hue and repairing itself while she slept. Then she would have come back.

She would have come back...

"By the time herself came, I could almost lift a cow." Britta grins. "Very helpful when yer milking an' they begin to get all unruly. I heard yer a farm girl too."

I nod slowly, but my mind is far away. I have a lot to think about. A lot to grieve.

FIVE

The next week passes swiftly, a blur of howling snowstorms, freezing roads, and frightful nightmares. Even though I'm no longer in the cellar, I sometimes have dreams that the walls are closing in on me again, that the elders are approaching, knives and buckets in hand, gold-lust in their eyes. I wake up in the wagon crying, chest heaving with great sobs, while Britta edges ever nearer, concern in her eyes. I know she would hold me if I let her, but I'm not ready to be touched by another person's hands.

Most days, I just feel like screaming until my throat collapses.

Sometimes, when I wake, the furs covering me are in tatters. I've ripped them apart in my sleep, shredded the tough leather underpinnings as if they were parchment. Even the strongest men in the village couldn't manage such a feat. More confirmation I'm unnatural, the spawn of reviled demons rather than a child of humanity.

It's almost a relief when I look up after eight days of travelling to find we're in Gar Melanis, the port city where we'll board the ship to the capital, Hemaira. The entire city is smothered in darkness when we arrive – the ramshackle, soot-covered buildings huddled against each other, dim oil lamps lighting murky interiors. Our ship, the *Salt Whistle*, creaks at the dock, an aged, squat passenger vessel with greying sails and chipped blue paint on its sides. Wiry sailors dart across the snow-slick deck, settling passengers, hauling baggage and supplies. Families huddle together against the cold, mothers in their plain brown travel masks, fathers with miniature copies of the Infinite Wisdoms on their belts to ensure travelling mercies.

The moment we board, I find a quiet corner and look up at the night sky. Bright green and purple lights are rippling across it: the Northern Lights, heralding the return of Oyomo's chariot to its Southern home. It's a sign: after all those weeks in the cellar, Oyomo has finally answered my prayers. I'm on my way to Hemaira, to my new life as a soldier in the emperor's army – a life that will bring me absolution.

Thank you, thank you… The prayer of gratitude circles my mind.

"Enjoying the view?"

White Hands is approaching, Britta and the equus at her side. As usual, there's that look in her eyes, that amused smirk that's always visible under the shadow of her half mask. It makes the skin on my arms prickle, an uneasiness I do my best to stifle. What if White Hands is lying? What if all of this is a trick – an underhanded plot to corral all our kind into the same place? I wouldn't put it past her. I've never met anyone so secretive in my life, not even the priests. Britta and I have spent over a week in her company, and she still hasn't told us her real name. We now call her White Hands outright, since she's made no objections.

I school my features and turn to her. "It's beautiful," I reply.

"Isn't it?" Britta is in such a hurry to join the conversation now that I'm talking, she doesn't even pay attention to her surroundings as she walks over. "Almost reminds me of the sky in – ARGHH!" she yelps, tripping over a mound of netting, but she's up in seconds, dusting herself off and smiling ruefully, not a hint of embarrassment to her. "Almost broke me neck. Lucky our kind is hard to kill, ain't that right, White Hands?" she quips.

The older woman shrugs. "Most alaki die very easily, actually," she murmurs.

Britta's forehead wrinkles. "But wha about the gilded sleep?" she asks.

"That happens only if it's an almost-death."

It's my turn to frown now. "An almost-death?" I ask, walking closer. I've never heard of such a thing.

"For alaki, there are two types of death," White Hands explains. "Almost-deaths and final ones. Almost-deaths are fleeting, impermanent things. They result in the week-long gilded sleep, which heals the body of all wounds and scars – except, of course, those acquired before the blood turns."

A chill shudders through me. I no longer have any scars – not even the ones from childhood. They all disappeared the moment I had my first almost-death.

I'm so uneasy now, I barely notice Britta frowning down at a tiny scar on her hand. "Guess I'll never get rid of this, then," she says and sighs.

White Hands ignores her and continues. "An alaki can have several almost-deaths, but she has only one final death – one method by which she can truly be killed. For the vast majority of alaki, it's either burning, drowning, or beheading. If an alaki doesn't die from one of these, she's practically immortal."

I suddenly feel light-headed. Practically immortal? I don't want to remain undying for ever, to live despised and reviled as I am. I don't want to remain like this one moment longer than I have to.

I have to win absolution. I have to!

Beside me, Britta has an awed look on her face. "Immortal…" she breathes. Then she gasps. "Does that mean we can live for ever?"

"I said 'practically'," White Hands corrects her. "Nothing is undying except the gods. Your kind does, however, age very slowly – hundreds of years to each human one. Add to that the swift healing, the ability to see in the dark, and no wonder people are so frightened of your kind – especially the ones that are hard to kill, like Deka."

Britta's eyes flit to me again, and I tense, waiting for that look to come into them – that disgust I saw so often reflected in the elders' eyes.

But she's not even looking at me. Her entire face is screwed in thought as she stares at White Hands.

"White Hands?" she asks. When the older woman turns to her, she continues. "We're not going to start eating people, are we? I mean, the Gilded Ones did, an' we're their descendants with all these abilities an'—"

"Have you started developing sharp teeth?" White Hands asks, cutting her off.

"What?" Britta frowns, taken aback. "I mean, no, but—"

"Does the thought of eating human flesh appeal to you?"

Disgust mottles Britta's face. "No, of course not!"

"Then don't ask me any more stupid questions. Eating people indeed." White Hands humphs, shaking her head. She motions for us to leave. "Run along and secure your beds. It's a long journey to Hemaira."

As Britta and I walk towards the stairs leading down into the hold, Britta grumbles to herself. "I don't think it was a silly question," she mutters. "All that talk of predators an' seein' in the dark an' such – it was a logical conclusion."

Britta sounds so offended, a laugh bubbles inside me, momentarily pushing aside my dread. I try to hold on to the feeling as we walk through the door and enter the hold.

"Here we are." Britta's cheerful voice is like a balm to my thoughts, which have been steadily darkening since I entered the hold.

I try not to notice the shadows, the walls curving inwards. Try not to notice the black edging my vision, the sweat dripping down my back. *This isn't the cellar… This isn't the cellar…* I whisper to myself.

The cellar was dark, still. It smelled of blood and pain, not sour wine and seawater. There were no torches flickering in the shadows, no passengers unpacking their belongings and settling into their spaces.

I force my attention back to Britta, who's pointing at the corner we've been given, where there's just enough space to spread out two pallets and string a curtain for privacy. "Once we put our pallets down, it'll almost feel like home," she says.

There's a strange note in her voice, but she avoids my eyes when I glance at her, and hurriedly bustles about, chattering ever more cheerfully.

"Course, it could use a few touches... Mebbe a bright cloth or somethin'. But it really is nice, really it is." Her voice sounds even more strained now, and when I look down, I see that her hands have clenched her skirts so tight, her fingers have turned the colour of bone.

Finally, I understand.

Just like me, Britta has been branded impure, wrenched from everything she ever knew, and forced into a terrifying new life. Family, friends – even the village she grew up in is lost to her. For the first time in her life, she's completely alone in the world. And she's afraid.

That's why she tried to get closer all this week, comforting me when I cried from my nightmares, pretending not to notice whenever I screamed for no reason... She's not like me – used to being alone, being hated. She needs to be accepted, to be part of a community. Except I'm the only community she has now – she and I connected by our demon ancestors and the golden blood that binds us. That's why she was always there, waiting if ever I wanted to reach out and talk to her.

But I've been so focused on my own misery, I never did.

I try to breathe back the crowding darkness as I turn to her. "It must have been difficult, leaving behind your family, your village," I whisper. A tentative opening to conversation.

Britta's eyes flick to mine, and her chin trembles slightly. "It was…but they'll be waiting for me when I return." Her lips firm into a bright, determined smile. A mask that does its utmost to hide the pain, the uncertainty shining in her eyes. "Once I'm pure," she declares, "I'm going back home to me village. An' then I'll see me ma and da an' all me friends."

I nod quietly, not knowing what to say. "That's good. It's good to have friends."

"We should be friends."

Britta leans closer, her mask of a smile desperately brittle at the edges. "I know we just met," she says, "an' I know after wha happened, ye find it difficult to trust anyone, but Hemaira's a long way away, an' I don't want to do this alone. Yer the only one who understands wha it feels like. Who understands…"

She extends her hand. "Friends?" she asks, hope and fear shining in her face.

I look down, considering her extended hand. Friends… What if she betrays me like everyone else did? Like Father, Ionas, the elders… But no, Britta isn't one of the people who cast me out and tortured me, she's an alaki – the first and only one I've ever met.

And she needs me just as much as I need her.

"Friends," I agree, taking her hand.

Britta beams, eagerly moving closer. "I've been so afraid of going to Hemaira, of becoming a soldier," she confesses, a river of words rushing out of her. It's as if she's been saving them up this entire week – a dam just waiting to burst. "Now that we have each other, mebbe it won't be that bad. Mebbe ye can even

66

come with me back to me village when it's all over! I know yers wasn't the best…

"An' anyway, everyone's friendly in Golma, an' we have lots of handsome boys too. 'Course they won't be the same ones I left behind, but there'll be all sorts of lovely ones to pick from." She peers at me speculatively. "Ye ever kissed a boy, Deka?"

"What – me? No, never!" Where did the question even come from? I've never spoken to anyone about such a thing before, but Britta, it seems, has no such reservations now that the gates have opened.

"I did once, during one of the village festivals. It was bad, very bad. His mouth tasted like sour milk." She wrinkles her nose, turns to me. "So why didn't ye – kiss a boy, I mean?"

I look down, that awful feeling rising inside me again. "No one ever wanted me," I whisper. Besides, Elder Durkas always told us kissing led to impurity, and I tried so desperately to be pure, for all the good it did me.

Britta frowns. "Why? Yer so pretty." She actually sounds perplexed.

"I'm not." I shake my head, awful memories of Ionas, smile on his face, sword in his hand, flashing across my mind. *Girls as pretty as you…* What awful lies he told.

Britta's snort cuts through the awful memory. "Ye are pretty, Deka," she says. "Yer hair curls around yer face all pretty-like, and yer skin is nice an' brown even in this deep winter." Then she adds, as if it's an afterthought, "An' yer shapely. Men like shapely women. And plump ones." She grins. "They've always liked me."

67

"But they don't like Southerners – at least, not in Irfut."

"Then maybe it's a good thing we're headed south," Britta says, patting my arm as the ship creaks into motion.

I nod, sending a silent prayer up to Oyomo that this proves true.

SIX

"**D**eka, Deka, wake up. Please wake up! We're here, we're here!"

Britta's voice comes as if from far away when I wake, the heat around me so overwhelming it feels like a boulder pressing down on my chest. The remnant of a dream teases at my thoughts, heavy and insistent. I try to grab onto it, but it disappears when a large, warm weight insistently shakes my shoulder.

"I'm getting up," I say, blinking open my eyes.

To my surprise, the light around me has changed. It's not the cool blue of winter but the warm yellow of deep summer. Even stranger, the smells of the sea now are mixed with a new, exotic fragrance. Flowers. But I've never smelled flowers like these. These are subtle and elegantly scented, their fragrance shimmering around me on delicate waves.

Where's the smell of ice and snow? Where's the cold?

I turn to Britta, whose eyes are wide with relief. "Why is it so warm?" I rasp, confused. My tongue is as dry as our haystacks in midsummer, and sweat slicks my hair and clothes so they stick to my skin.

Britta hugs me tightly. "I thought ye would never wake! It's been four weeks! White Hands told me ye would, but four whole weeks—"

"Four weeks?" I frown, pulling away from her. When my muscles protest this simple movement, I wince, startled. Why do they feel so tight? "What do you mean, four weeks?"

"You've been asleep for almost a month." This explanation comes from White Hands, who's watching me calmly from against the wall.

Sunlight filters bright and warm through the door at the top of the stairs behind her. It shimmers over Braima and Masaima, whose heavy fur coats and boots are long gone. They're bare-chested in the heat, talons flexing against the wooden floor. Flies buzz around them, and they whip them away with their tails.

"A month?" I echo, flabbergasted.

"Naughty alaki, to make her friends worry." Masaima tsks, shaking his head.

"But the quiet one needed her rest, Masaima," Braima says, tossing his black-striped hair. "You would too if you knew you'd be travelling for weeks in a nasty, nasty ship's hold after being trapped by priests in a nasty, nasty temple cellar."

"But I'd at least tell you I was sleeping a long time, Braima," Masaima sniffs.

White Hands gets annoyed by their back-and-forth. She points to the stairs, where the other passengers are now filing out towards the door. "Upstairs with you both," she commands. "Prepare the wagon."

"Yes, my lady," they chime, their talons clacking up the wooden steps.

"I'm so sorry, I don't know why – how – I slept so long," I say, still in shock. I turn to White Hands. "Is that something that happens to alaki? Is it normal?"

"No," she replies. "But you needed your rest. Experiences such as the one you had can take their toll. Even humans, when faced with your circumstances, sleep away their pain. Better now than when you reach the Warthu Bera."

I frown. "The Warthu Bera?" I've never heard those words before.

"The training ground where me an' ye are assigned," Britta says excitedly, tapping the old Hemairan symbol on the back of her seal. "That's wha this symbol means. It's the most elite one."

My forehead scrunches in confusion. Why would we be sent to the most elite ground when we haven't even done any training yet?

I can't comprehend it. I can't comprehend anything right now. That dream resurfaces, a vague memory edging at my thoughts. It flitters away when White Hands passes us each small sticks of what looks like charcoal. I recognize them immediately: tozali. My mother used to line her eyes with it every day to protect them from the sun.

"Rub this on your eyes. You'll need it. We depart upon the hour."

"Yes, White Hands," we say as she leaves.

Once she's gone, Britta and I apply the tozali using a small jug of water as a mirror. My hands tremble as I rub the stick against my eyelids. My muscles have become so weak now, every tiny movement has them howling in protest. It's even

71

worse when I begin packing up what remains of my things. When did I eat last?

And how could I have slept so long? My limbs feel rubbery – new – the way they felt every time I woke up after the gilded sleep. Even worse, there's a strange feeling somewhere deep inside me, as if something is changing...growing... I can't help but feel that I've become different somehow, in a way I don't yet understand.

Britta watches me the entire time, a perplexed look in her eyes.

"What is it?" I ask, my mind still racing.

"Why is it that ye survive even when ye do not eat?" she whispers. When I glance at her, startled, she explains: "Ye didn't have a bite of food or even a drop of water. I had to eat all your meals so the other passengers wouldn't notice you were asleep for the entire journey. I told them ye were sick – that's why ye weren't movin' or talking. But they would've wondered about ye if ye never ate. So I ate for ye. I mean, I knew ye were strange, but this..." Her voice lowers to a whisper. "This is unnatural, Deka."

Unnatural... There it is, that word again.

I know Britta didn't mean to hurt me, but the word still stings. Even worse, it's true. I don't feel any hunger any more. It's disappeared, vanished to a place where I cannot find it. I shrug sadly, trying to push back all the horrible feelings rising inside me, the fears at this new, worrying sign of my impurity.

"I don't know. It's never happened before. It must be like White Hands says, I was sleeping away everything that happened in that cel—"

"Are ye hungry now?" she asks quickly.

I know she's interrupting so I don't have to finish the devastating words. I nod gratefully. "I suppose I could eat."

She quickly hooks my elbow with hers, offering me a bright smile. "Then let's feed ye before yer stomach starts dancin' the Northern jig," she says, pulling me up the stairs.

We emerge to sunlight so blinding, I have to shade my eyes against the glare. Crowds upon crowds of people mill across the docks, their voices a formidable wave of sound emerging from every ship, street, and stall. There are too many people, too many sounds... I have to fight the urge to block my ears.

"Oyomo preserve us!" Britta exclaims. "Have ye ever seen so many people in yer life?"

As I shake my head, speechless, Britta waves goodbye to the sailors and other passengers. To my surprise, they wave cheerfully back. "Travel blessings, Britta," a grizzled old sailor calls.

Britta beams in return. "And the same on yer next journey, Kelma!"

When she sees me looking, she shrugs. "We became friends," she explains. Then she leans closer, whispering: "They told me all sorts o' things over the journey. Deathshrieks have been attacking Hemaira! Every night, a few of them slip in, an' no one knows how."

My eyes widen. Deathshrieks in the capital? How is that even possible? It's said the walls of Hemaira are impenetrable, that the city itself has been made into a walled garden impervious to siege. That those creatures could already be here, so close – my mind shudders at the thought.

"And what do they say about us – the alaki?" I ask.

She shrugs. "People don't know about us yet. Only the priests and elders know. But then, they've always known."

I nod bitterly, until a motion catches my attention: White Hands, beckoning to us from the docks, where Braima and Masaima are already saddling themselves to her wagon.

"Hurry, hurry, Quiet One," Braima calls. "The day is passing faster and faster."

I hasten my pace, aware that people are giving Britta and me curious stares. We're two unmasked girls of Ritual age, no male guardian present to oversee us. It won't be long now before we're stopped. Just as I think this, a plump, pious-looking man, embossed Infinite Wisdoms scroll under his arm, separates from the crowd and begins walking towards us, a severe look on his face. Before he can reach us, however, White Hands smoothly cuts in front of him, waving us onward.

"Come along now, girls," she says loudly. "Hemaira awaits, as does your service to our great empire." The emperor's seal swings officiously from her belt.

The man's eyes flicker to it, and then to us. He hisses under his breath about ungodly women as he walks away, disgusted.

"I hate pompous, puffed-up meddlers, don't you?" White Hands humphs. Not waiting for us to answer, she points upward. "Look. The gates of Hemaira."

As my eyes follow her hand, my jaw drops when I see the colossal walls rising above the docks, twin warrior statues guarding each of its gates. So these are the walls of Hemaira Father always told me about.

Father…

I stifle the thought by concentrating on the walls. There are only three. Three walls with three gates. Why? I turn to White Hands to ask, but she's gesturing towards the nearest and largest entrance.

"We're headed for Gate Emeka," she says, nodding at the twin statues of the same stern warrior with a crown upon his head.

Emperor Emeka, the first emperor of Otera – I recognize him immediately. Tall and dark, hair closely cropped, except for the beard. His image is engraved in every temple and every hall. Those stern eyes, flaring nostrils, mouth tight and severe, are unmistakable, and so are the statues now soaring above us, their swords casting massive shadows on the crowds gathering below.

I look up at them, fear and unease rushing through me. "Well, here we are," I whisper, bracing myself with a deep breath.

"Here we are," Britta agrees, doing the same. Her face is even paler than usual, no trace of a smile on her lips.

Her hand nudges mine, and I squeeze it, nod tightly. She doesn't have to say what she's thinking; I already know. She and I will survive this – together.

White Hands leads us directly to Gate Emeka, where a river of people and animals is already streaming into the city. Westerners, Easterners, Southerners, Northerners – they all vie for space with horses, camels, and other, more exotic animals I recognize only from Father's scrolls. Orrillions – hulking silver-furred apes with strangely humanlike faces – pull nearby chariots, their sharp horns blunted by curved golden sheaths. Mammuts plod at the front of caravans, multiple tusks protruding underneath their long, flexible trunks, ivory spikes all along their gigantic, leathery grey backs, and yet more spikes at the rounded ends of their tails. Caravan masters sit inside little tents atop them, blowing horns to herald their approach.

I wish Mother was here. She was always telling me about the Southern provinces. Even though she never regretted leaving to marry Father, she always missed the lands of her birth. All she ever wanted was for me to see them someday. To see the other side of my bloodline.

She would never have imagined me coming here as a newly recruited soldier.

Britta points to the emperor's guards manning the gates. "Would ye look at all those jatu, Deka," she says, gaping. Unlike the ones we saw up North, these jatu are wearing not armour and war masks, but splendid red robes, as they direct the lines of travellers and carefully inspect their documents. They all have the jatu insignia, the golden lion against the rising sun, pinned to their shoulders.

"They look very officious," I reply, a twinge of unease running through me.

I'm distracted from them by a flash of blue. A carriage rattles past us, led by two large lizardlike creatures with wings. They make strange squawking noises deep in their throats.

"Zerizards!" I gasp, excited.

Another type of creature Mother told me about. They're found only in the South, where the sun is warm and the forests are endless. I squint, trying to take in their feathery blue tails, the bright red plumage crowning their heads.

"My mother loved riding them when she was young," I say.

"They're beautiful," Britta replies, in awe.

Braima sniffs, tossing his black-striped hair. "They're not as impressive as us, are they, Masaima?"

"Certainly not," Masaima agrees.

"You're both very beautiful too," I soothe.

The equus twins stomp their annoyance as they lead the wagon away from the main gate towards a small side entrance, where a line of ominous-looking wagons gathers. The drivers are wearing black robes similar to White Hands's, their faces hidden by heavy cloth hoods. At the sight of all those iron-barred doors and windows, my blood races faster and faster. These must be the wagons carrying the other alaki. Each one looks big enough to hold at least six.

Britta shifts uncomfortably in her seat. "It's the others, isn't it?"

"Most likely," I reply. I can almost feel the despair rising from the wagons.

Britta reaches out her hand, and I take it. We remain silent while White Hands leads the wagon to the front of the line, where two jatu are playing owareh, a Southern board game Mother loved. The moment they glimpse her, they jerk to attention.

"My lady." They salute, rushing to open the narrow gate.

To my surprise, they're both speaking Oteran instead of Hemairan. But then, Hemairan is the language of the nobles and the aristocracy, the language used in the Infinite Wisdoms.

The only reason I even know how to understand it is because Father's father forced everyone in the family to memorize the Infinite Wisdoms as penance for our long-ago impurity.

I don't know why I expected common jatu to use it.

The gate comes open with a small squeak, and I return my attention to the road before me. My eyes widen nearly past their sockets.

There, just beyond the gate, is a massive lake, which shimmers into the horizon. The city rises from its centre, a series of lush green hills connected by high, arching wooden bridges. Rivers and waterfalls cut through like streets, with cheerfully painted boats gliding across them, their embroidered umbrellas protecting passengers from the sun.

"Oyomo preserve us," Britta breathes, staring at all the sights. "Have ye ever seen anything like this in yer life?"

As I shake my head, unable to voice an answer, something else seizes my attention: the majestic building thrusting up from the peak of Hemaira's highest hill like a jagged crown. I've seen it numerous times before, printed on every Oteran coin. Oyomo's Eye, the ancient palace of the Hemairan emperors. The kuru, Oyomo's sacred sun symbol, decorates its multiple spires, and groups of smaller buildings, the Halls of Administration, cluster among the hills below it. I recognize them immediately from every description of the capital I've ever heard.

It's all so splendid, so…much…I can barely comprehend it. So this is Hemaira, the City of Emperors.

"Be careful to close your mouths before flies invade them," says White Hands, laughing at my astonishment as the equus canter happily into the bustling thoroughfares.

"It's good to be home, Brother," Masaima says, grinning.

"No more the itchy furs and the cold, Brother," Braima agrees.

The deeper we go into the city, the more crowded it becomes. Zerizard- and equus-pulled carriages battle for space on tightly packed streets. Along the pavements stroll pedestrians, most of them male, all of them luxuriously robed and groomed, with precious jewels threading red-clay-starched beards, tozali swirling in elaborate patterns around masculine eyes.

The few women about are even more elaborately masked here than they are in the North, gold and silver gleaming on every face instead of wood and parchment. There are several variations: round sun masks to glorify Oyomo; silver fertility masks, cheeks exaggerated like the pregnant moon; oval good luck masks, beaded symbols to invite blessings on the forehead and chin; black formal masks, horns curving from smooth obsidian foreheads.

Even some of the little girls here wear half masks, visible representations of their family's wealth moulded in gold and silver. A pang of sadness passes over me whenever I see them. I'll never wear a mask now, never be able to adorn myself in the sacred coverings of purity.

The thought flitters away as we head deeper into the city. Something else has attracted my attention: a dull, almost indistinguishable humming that becomes louder the closer we get to the central bridges. By the time we reach the massive bridge that leads towards the central hill upon which the palace and other administrative buildings stand, it's a roar reverberating in my bones.

"Do you hear that?" I ask Britta.

She nods, brows furrowed in confusion. "What do ye suppose it is?"

"Emeka's Tears," White Hands replies, turning to us.

I frown at her. "Emeka's Tears?"

White Hands points, and I follow her finger towards a gap in the city's walls, where a single statue rises, this one female. "Keep watching," she instructs, leading the equus towards the topmost portion of the bridge.

The moment we reach its peak, the breath rushes out of me. There, at the very edge of the city, a massive waterfall cascades into the Endless Sea below. Now I understand why Hemaira has only three walls. The capital is a city on a cliff, the waterfall at its edge an unscalable barrier against any force that would seek to attack from the sea. The statue I saw thrusts from the edge of the waterfall, a woman with tightly curled hair and a slender but sinewy build. She gazes out into the water, her arm outstretched towards the horizon in warning.

"Fatu the Relentless, mother of the first emperor and keeper of the waters around Hemaira," White Hands explains, her words piercing through my awe. There's a tone in her voice, an emotion I don't understand. Sadness? Regret? "A fitting sight to end your journey. Now it's on to Jor Hall." She gestures towards the administrative buildings rising just below the palace. "Prepare yourselves."

I silently nod, anxiety knotting in my chest as the equus continue onwards, talons clacking over the main bridge. Oyomo's Eye looms above us, a silent condemnation. Our journey will soon be over. Our new lives are about to begin.

* * *

By the time we reach the streets bordering the administrative buildings, dread has coiled like a hooded snake in my stomach. I barely notice how orderly the streets are here, barely notice the lush gardens clinging to grand, towering buildings almost as old as Otera itself. All I can think about is my impending change in circumstances. What will Hemaira hold for me? Will it be as White Hands promised? Will any of her promises hold true? There's still that lingering doubt, that prickle of unease I get whenever I'm in her presence.

Please let them be true, I pray silently as we make our way down the street. We're approaching an enormous red building, the jatu insignia prominently displayed on its banners. Jor Hall, the hall of administration for the jatu. Father spoke so often of it from his time in the military, I recognize it by sight. Lines of girls are wrapped around its side, an acrid, unpleasantly familiar smell wafting from them: the stench of unwashed bodies.

I know then, even without asking, that those girls are alaki. The same shivery feeling I felt with Britta trickles through me.

Nausea churns my gut the nearer we pull to them.

The other alaki are all painfully thin, their clothes torn and dirty, their feet bare and scabbed over. Not a single mask covers their faces – no cloaks or cowls protect their modesty from the burly, black-robed guards who leer as they check the symbols on the back of their seals before directing them into different lines. A few are wounded, blood dripping from their robes, scars criss-crossing exposed arms and shoulders. They haven't died, at least not recently. Their wounds and scars would have already been completely repaired by the gilded sleep if they had.

But then, physical death isn't the worst thing an alaki can suffer. I can tell from the haunted expressions in the other girls' eyes, from the way they don't resist when they're roughly unloaded, seven, eight at a time, from the backs of wagons, that they've all suffered greatly. Even when the guards prod them towards Jor Hall, its banners flapping sullenly in the breeze, most of them don't make a sound. What methods did the other transporters use to keep the girls in line? A chill shivers through me just thinking about it.

Thank Oyomo for White Hands. A surprising thought, but nonetheless true. Despite all my doubts about her, the most she ever did during our journey was lock the wagon's doors at night so we wouldn't run away. She never hit or abused us, never belittled us with foul words, though I suspect all these things and more happened to the other girls.

I wait, anxiety growing, as she stops the wagon before the hall, then walks over to open the back for us.

"This is where we part ways, alaki," she says, beckoning for us to dismount.

I do so tentatively, arms folded tightly over myself. The guards are watching us now, scowls burning into my shoulders. I suddenly wish I had my old cloak, the one I left in Irfut. It was tattered and shabby, but it always protected me from view, always made me feel safe. Here, I have no such shielding – not even the half mask I'd imagined I'd be wearing by now.

As I shuffle to the front of the wagon, stomach lurching, palms sweating, the equus twins turn towards me with mournful expressions. "We must say goodbye now, alaki," Braima says with a pout.

"We liked all the winter apples you gave us, Quiet One," Masaima adds, glancing at me. "They were very delicious."

"Next time we see each other, I will give you more apples," I say softly, petting him and his brother.

They nod, and I turn to White Hands. The side of her mouth is quirked, as usual, but her eyes are shuttered behind her half mask. She seems almost...regretful as she glances at me, although I don't understand why.

"White Hands, I—"

"I must leave you now," she says, stopping me with a gesture. She glances from me to Britta. "Do not be stupid, and you won't die too many times."

We both nod quietly. She reaches over and squeezes our hands. It's the most affection she's ever shown us in the month we've travelled together, and the very gesture heightens the fear rising inside me. I try to stifle it as White Hands continues her farewell.

"Remember, this will be tough, but you will overcome it. May fortune guide you," she whispers.

"I wish the same for you," I reply, but she's already walking to her wagon. She rides on, Braima and Masaima waving goodbye.

As she disappears, that fear coils tighter inside me, accelerating my heartbeat.

Please, please, please let me be able to endure what's next.

SEVEN

"**T**hey were hurt, weren't they, the other girls?" Britta asks some minutes later.

I don't answer, my muscles too tight with tension to even speak as we walk down the dark, cavernous hallways in Jor Hall. Each leads to a chamber for one of the different alaki training grounds. Judging from the number of lines, there are ten.

As Britta and I keep pace with the line headed towards the chamber for the Warthu Bera, the training ground White Hands told us about, the other girls cower against one another, some of them sobbing under their breath, others trembling with every step. They're scared of the jatu patrolling the corridors, the ones with the ansetha, the star symbol, gleaming on their shoulders. White Hands warned Britta and I about these jatu – told us to treat them with caution. They've been specially trained to subdue both alaki and deathshrieks and, as such, are much more brutal than their compatriots. They're the reason the odour of sweat and fear has been rising steadily ever since we entered the hall.

Well, one of the reasons.

The other is the girls with torn robes and hooded eyes that shuffle beside us, their movements slow and stiff as if their souls have been snatched right out of their bodies.

I recognize that look, that posture.

It's the same one Elder Durkas's temple maidens sometimes have. The one that tells everyone they're not maidens any more. Once again, I'm grateful for White Hands. What would have happened to us had we had other transporters – male ones? I shudder to think of it, the price some of the girls here have already paid to earn their absolution.

"Deka?" Britta prompts, her eyes flicking back to the empty-eyed girls.

"They were hurt in more ways than we can imagine," I finally answer, my expression grim.

She glances at me, fearful tears glazing her eyes. "We were lucky, weren't we?"

I squeeze her hand. "We still are," I whisper firmly. "We have each other." And I mean it, mean every word. I'm lucky to have Britta at my side, to have someone else to endure this with.

She nods as we reach the double doors at the end of the hall.

The room we enter is so immense, it's hard to see the other side of it. Ornate golden carvings decorate glossy black stone walls, and the floor is much the same. I struggle to keep my mouth closed, I'm in such awe. The only black stone I've ever seen was in Irfut's temple, and there was only enough of it to decorate the altar. The amount in this room could keep every family in Irfut fed for a thousand years or more.

Even more daunting is the line of boys waiting for us, all of them wearing armour and war masks.

I nearly stumble at the sight.

There are about one hundred boys in total, roughly the same number as we alaki, and they're standing at attention, backs straight, hands over their hearts. They range in age from sixteen to about twenty, and they all seem stern and forbidding, their eyes filled with disgust behind their war masks.

My heartbeat doubles into a frantic, fearful beat. I have to physically resist the urge to clasp my arms over myself.

"Wha's happening? Why are they here?" Britta asks, moving nervously closer to me.

I shake my head. "I don't know."

I'm so unnerved by the sight of all those boys, it's some moments before I notice the platforms. Ten in number, they thrust, solid and imposing, high into the air above us, stairs trailing up either side. Officials sit in eight of them, yellow robes spread out, scrolls and ink pots at their fingertips. The centre two, however, are occupied by jatu commanders, both tall and dark and wearing war masks. My eyes are immediately drawn to the commander on the left. It's not just his hair, which is braided in an intricate style and daubed with bright red clay, but his stature, which is smaller than the other's and more graceful despite its muscularity.

He seems almost...female, but that can't be possible. Women are not allowed to be jatu commanders.

"Straighten the line!" the guard beside us calls, startling me out of my gawking.

As he pushes the girl in front of me forward, an angry shout suddenly echoes through the hall. "Get your filthy hands off me!"

It comes from the end of the hall, where a tall, thin girl is struggling against a group of transporters, at least four of them. She pushes so fiercely, a few go flying into the wall. I rub my eyes, blinking again and again to make sure I'm seeing what I'm seeing. She shook the transporters away like they were fleas. I've never seen that done before, not even by a man. Is this the alaki strength White Hands told us about, the one that sometimes allowed me to rip apart the fur blankets as I slept?

When she grabs a sword from one of the transporters and brandishes it threateningly, a few of the jatu run over, spears raised. Within moments, they're circling, sharpened spear tips inches from the girl's throat.

"Let her go!"

Everyone turns, as do I, towards this sudden and powerful command. It comes from the tall, well-muscled boy now emerging from the line, each of his steps slow, deliberate as he walks towards the proud girl. "She is a soldier in the war against the deathshrieks," he declares in the clipped and clearly articulated manner of someone more used to speaking Hemairan than Oteran. "And soldiers have rights."

Rights? The word circles in my mind, shimmering and unbelievable. Rights are the domain of men and boys – not women, and certainly not alaki. Even so, the word blossoms, like a distant hope I'm afraid to even touch.

"Is that not so, Captain Kelechi?" The boy glances at the taller commander.

To my surprise, the commander nods. "Indeed, Recruit Keita," he replies. "Everyone here has rights, although there are some that would stretch them to the bounds of common decency." He turns a disapproving eye towards the proud girl, who spits on the floor in disgust.

Making an irritated sound in his throat, the commander motions the boy – Keita – forward. "Inform her of her rights as a new member of the emperor's army, Recruit Keita."

"Yes, sir."

Keita walks towards the proud girl, removing his helmet and war mask as he goes. I'm startled to discover he's dark like me – well, darker – although his hair is so closely cropped as to make him look bald, and his eyes are golden and sharp as a hawk's. He's about sixteen or so, but there's a hardness to his eyes, an experience that speaks of a deeper maturity.

Who is Keita, that he knows the commander so well?

His armour seems different from that of the other jatu, more ornate. Father once told me that each jatu's armour is inscribed with Hemairan symbols celebrating battles long ago fought, victories won. Keita's has several more symbols than any jatu armour I've ever seen, and an emblem of a snarling orrillion adorns each shoulder.

Perhaps it is an heirloom passed down to him by a father or uncle. The aristocracy have several such items. Either way, it marks him as something more than the jatu surrounding him. Richer, undoubtedly. He must be one of the Hemairan nobles I've always heard so much about. It would explain his relationship with the commander, as well as why he feels so comfortable speaking out of turn.

Mistrust lines the girl's proud, refined features as he approaches.

"Come no closer!" she snarls, her dusky-brown skin flushed

with anger. "I will listen to no more of your lies! Soldiers in the emperor's army? Absolution? Lies – all lies! You just want our blood on this floor, so you can sell it, you worthless bastards!" She jabs her sword towards him.

Keita lifts his hands in an appeasing gesture. "It is the truth. You are free to do as you like," he says. He glances to the rest of us. "You are all free to do as you like. If you wish to leave now, you may do so."

Whispers rise into the air, uncertain but hopeful. Beside me, Britta shifts. "Do ye think it's real, wha he says?"

For one brief, glittering moment, I allow myself to believe in Keita, allow myself to believe in his words. Then I remember Ionas, remember how he thrust that sword into my belly only hours after telling me how I pretty I was.

Tension clenches my body again.

Keita will be no different when the time comes. No matter what he does now, he will show his true colours soon enough. They all do.

"No," I say, shaking my head.

I watch with jaded eyes as the other jatu turn to the commanders in protest. "But, Captain Kelechi—" one jatu gasps.

"Surely you will not let this stand!" another pleads.

The taller commander lifts his hand for silence. "Recruit Keita is correct," he booms. "Either the alaki want to be here or they don't. An unwilling soldier is a useless one. You're all free to leave if you desire, but remember that you are impure, and the world outside will only ever see that. Not to mention deathshrieks will come hunting for you wherever you hide."

He nods and the jatu reluctantly open the door, following his command.

I watch all this, tense, as does Britta.

Around us, the girls murmur among themselves, wondering what to do.

Keita steps forward once more. "We can guarantee your safety to the border of Hemaira," he says. "After that, it's up to you." He glances pointedly at the proud girl, and whatever hope I had crumples like ashes in my mouth.

There it is, the condition. Yes, we can flee here, but once we leave Hemaira's gates, we return to our old lives – to the Death Mandate, the constant threat of deathshricks... Keita is just like all the rest, giving us impossibilities and calling them choices.

The proud girl seems to know this, because she looks from the open door back to him. "We have your word?" she asks distrustfully, glancing from him to the commander, who nods.

"I swear upon Oyomo's kuru," Keita replies, referring to the sacred sun symbol. "I will, however, say this: you can make something of yourself at the training grounds. You can be fighters, and once you're done, you will be given absolution. Or you can spend your lives as outcasts, always fearing the Death Mandate. The truth of the matter is simple: you're either with us or against us. The choice is up to you."

Giving her a quick, short bow, he returns to his position in line. I'm thankful he's gone – angry at myself that I almost believed their words. Why did I think, even for a moment, that he would be different from Ionas and all the others?

My attention returns to the girl now standing in the middle of the hall, her eyes shadowed and dark. She looks towards the door again, and then back at the line. Her gaze flickers between the two – door, line, line, door. I can see her mind racing, making the same calculations mine has. Finally, she makes her choice. She straightens her back and walks over to her line, as regal as a queen. She's staying.

I can almost feel Keita's pleased smile as, slowly but surely, the other girls follow her lead.

EIGHT

Once all the girls are back in line and everything is as it was, the taller commander walks to the edge of his platform and removes his war mask. His face is both haughty and commanding at once: so dark it's almost the colour of the midnight sky, and so severe, his severe, dark-brown eyes pierce us from above cheekbones sharp as knives.

"I am Captain Kelechi, commander of the jatu assigned to the Warthu Bera, your honoured training ground," he declares, his voice ringing through the hall. "Before you stand the newest recruits to the Warthu Bera." He gestures to the line of boys, who quickly remove their helmets and war masks. "They are here to serve as your uruni, your brothers in arms. After your first three weeks of initial training are completed, they will join you and provide aid for the coming months of combat. It is our hope that you will form lasting and deep partnerships with them, which will extend well past the time you leave these walls."

"Brothers?" Britta whispers under her breath, her dismayed expression echoing my own. I can't imagine any of those haughty-looking boys as our new brothers.

Beside us, a girl with long braids scoffs under her breath: "More like spies, ensuring that we remain firmly in our places."

The captain continues, ignoring the rising whispers: "As you all no doubt know, deathshrieks have begun massing in their primal nesting ground near the N'Oyo Mountains, hundreds of thousands of them."

"Hundreds of thousands..." Britta whispers, an echo of my panicked thoughts. I knew there were a lot of deathshrieks, but I could have never imagined the true scope of their numbers.

"What you may not know is that Hemaira lies on their path. That is why Emperor Gezo has decided that all alaki – even the neophytes – must go on monthly raids, both thinning out their forces and preparing yourselves for the campaign. You must know everything about your enemy, every strength, every weakness, before you face them on the battlefield, and the recruits will aid you in this task."

Whispers explode. Monthly raids? Does he mean we'll actually have to face deathshrieks out in the wild?

As my breath catches in horror, Captain Kelechi continues: "In the coming months, you will face the most fearsome monsters in all of Otera, but you will not face them alone. Your new uruni will be with you every step of the way. Even when you're completing your initial training, they'll be just on the other side of the wall, waiting to join you, your brothers in arms."

He motions to the recruits, and they march to form a single line behind him, their bodies at attention. The smaller commander, who has remained silent all this while, motions for us to do the same. It takes us a little more time, the jatu shoving at us, but after some moments, we are standing in an opposite line, so that the two commanders face each other.

Once we're in place, the captain and his silent companion motion again, and the recruits take one step to the side, then slowly begin to file past our line.

Now I understand. This is how we receive our partners: by matching with whichever jatu stops next to us when Captain Kelechi calls for a halt.

My heart rises to my throat with each step the recruits take. *Please don't match me with a cruel boy, or one who hates alaki,* I silently beg Oyomo. Ionas's face flashes in my memory, and I push it away, praying even harder. *Please, please, please...*

The procession continues, seeming to stretch on for ever as the recruit line continues slowly and deliberately towards the end of ours. Boys walk past – tall, short, plump, thin; Southerners, Easterners, Westerners, Northerners; all with similar forbidding looks on their faces, many with barely hidden sneers. I'm so nervous now, my hands are sweating and my stomach is in knots. I'm suddenly keenly aware of my shabby appearance – tattered hair and robes, unmasked face.

I lower my eyes and then keep them studiously fixed on the floor, unable to look any more. There's no way my prayers will be answered. The boys seem as reluctant to be here as we are – some of them even angry, unwilling to look at our faces. I can only imagine what they think, knowing that they will have to work with impure girls. Descendants of demons who are strong enough to toss them away like the proud girl did.

I keep sweating, my eyes firmly lowered, until I finally hear the command: "Stop."

For a moment, I can't look up. What will I find if I do – disgust? Fear? I swallow deeply, steeling myself for disappointment. Then I raise my head. To my surprise, standing before me is a short Western boy, hair black, three tattooed lines from chin to lip. When he smiles at me, brown eyes kind and gentle, I feel a tremor of relief. He's not one of the larger boys, the threatening ones. In fact, if I squint, he looks almost girlish, with his long lashes and shy smile. I smile back, the knots in my stomach loosening.

Then Captain Kelechi calls out, "Recruits – take one more step and face your partner."

Take one more step?

Horror douses me as the Western boy shrugs ruefully in apology and then obeys the command, going to stand before a girl with flaming red hair. I look up and despair washes over me. Stern golden eyes are peering down into mine. Recruit Keita's. He's my new partner.

I barely hear Captain Kelechi when he speaks again, barely hear anything past the panicked beating of my heart. "Make your introductions!" he commands.

Keita looks down at me, his face expressionless. "I am Keita," he says. "Keita of Gar Fatu."

It takes everything I've got to force myself to continue looking at him instead of ducking my head in shame. Finally, I manage a reply. "Deka of Irfut," I mumble.

He nods.

By now, Captain Kelechi and his partner have turned to face each other. "Hold out your hands," the captain instructs us, extending his hand to the silent commander, who is still masked, unlike all the other men.

Now, more than ever, I'm certain she's female.

She clasps his forearm, and he does the same, an obscene imitation of the marriage ritual. "Extend them to each other in the spirit of fellowship."

Keita and I face each other and do the same.

I shiver when his hand touches mine. It's warm, calloused… He has capable hands – a swordsman's hands. The type of hands Ionas used to thrust that sword through my belly. The memory shakes me, and I have to force myself not to jerk my hand away. I look up into his eyes, trying to push past my fear.

But his eyes slide away, a cold expression shuttering his face. His grasp on my arm loosens.

I'm almost thankful when Captain Kelechi speaks. "From now until the moment of your deaths, you are bonded," he says. "Brothers and sisters in arms. Uruni."

The words send a shiver through my spine. It feels almost like…foreboding… When I look up again, Keita's expression is darker and more severe than ever. I can barely breathe, barely remain standing so close to this boy who will now be my connection to the normal world. A world I'm not certain I want any more part of. A world that certainly wants no part of me.

"Well met, Keita," I say, forcing myself to push my discomfort away.

He nods brusquely back. "Well met, Deka of Irfut," he replies.

Then he lets go of my hand.

* * *

96

With that, the ceremony is at an end. The boys file out from the other end of the hall, the commanders following behind them, and the transporters file back in. It all happens so fast, I barely notice two yellow-robed officials take their places on the empty platforms, barely notice as we line up once more – this time before the platforms. Now the actual intake begins. Girls walk up to the officials, who examine them and inscribe their details into scrolls with the help of the brown-robed assistants now scurrying to and fro like ants. The girl at the front of my line – a frail, sickly-looking Southerner – sobs quietly while the assistants poke and prod her, loudly calling out her details.

"Height – five hands, three knots. Severely malnourished. Primary indications of scurvy."

A frown knots itself into my brow. Malnourished? How is it that this girl is malnourished and I'm not after all those weeks asleep in the ship? *Unnatural…* The word whispers in my head again, banishing all thoughts of Keita and the cold way he stared down at me. I ignore my whispering fears, try to think of other reasons why there are differences between me and the girl. Perhaps some alaki are sicklier than others and some, like me, are just naturally healthier. There are so many potential explanations.

The girl's transporter, a stocky bearded man, raises loud objections when he's given only half a bag of gold as payment. "I was promised sixty otas a girl! Sixty!" he splutters.

The assistant's reply is loud and implacable. "That one is sickly and ill-fed. You were warned not to maltreat the emperor's property."

The emperor's property. Disgust sweeps over me at the words.

I thought we were supposed to be soldiers.

By now, all the transporters have made their way to the middle of the chamber except for White Hands, not that I'm surprised she isn't here. I don't think she really needs the gold they're doling out for the transporters' services. Our journey seemed more of an amusement for her than anything. Not for the first time, I wonder who exactly she is and why she would embark on such a journey for what seemed like the sport of it.

As I turn the question over in my mind, a horrible burnt smell wafts past my nostrils, desperate screams following just behind it. I whirl towards the sound, muscles strung tight. There's an assistant dipping a red-haired girl's hands into an urn of what looks like liquid gold.

The cursed gold, our own blood.

My mouth sours, vomit surging up, but I swallow it down, glance at the girl, who's now weeping uncontrollably as she stares at her hands. They've been gilded – golden now from fingertip to elbow. It's almost like she's already dead – halfway into a gilded sleep. The thought forces little rivulets of sweat down my back as the line advances again.

The gilding won't hurt, I tell myself encouragingly. It'll only sting a little. Just a tiny bit. But I know that's not true. That burnt smell is intensifying now, fresher and more visceral than the smell that sometimes plagues my memories. There's something about the cursed gold in that urn, something about the way it's been prepared, that causes it to stick to alaki skin.

More screams rise, and darkness edges my vision. I feel like I'm jumping out of my skin, like my entire body is on edge.

"Deka, breathe. Deka!" Britta's voice comes as if from far away.

Soft arms encircle me. Safety. Warmth. "I'm here, Deka," her voice whispers. "You're safe with me. Safe."

Safe…

It takes some moments, but finally, I take a ragged breath and manage to nod. "I'm fine," I croak.

I swallow back my nausea and straighten just in time to glimpse the assistant gild the girl in front of me. When she removes her hands, the gold now gleams on her skin. My hands tremble. It's my turn next.

The Eastern official sitting above me is pale and intimidating in the dim light. "Step forward, child," he beckons, adjusting his spectacles in an imperious manner.

Once I do so, he turns to his assistant. "Name?" he asks the assistant.

"Deka of Irfut," the assistant dutifully reads out.

"Are you here of your own free will?" the official asks.

"Yes," I whisper. Across the chamber, another girl screams as both her hands are dipped in the urn. The smell of burning flesh rises, and with it, my fear.

"Louder."

"Yes, I am," I say. I try not to look at the urn again.

"Do you seek absolution?"

"Yes, I do."

The official nods, satisfied.

I stiffen as one of the assistants begins to examine me, rough hands tugging at my body. "Weight – moderate, height – five hands, five knots, hair – black, eyes – grey, no distinguishing marks, excellent health."

Once this assessment is done, the assistant directs my

attention back to the accountant, who continues his questions. I crane my head up towards him.

"Do you swear fealty to Emperor Gezo and his armies?"

This was a question I had not anticipated, so it takes me a moment to answer. "Yes," I finally reply. More screams sound, cold sweat drenches my back.

"You were brought here by the Lady of the Equus."

"The Lady of the—" It takes me some moments to understand he is talking about White Hands. Of course they would nickname her that, because of Braima and Masaima. She treats them more like companions than steeds, after all. "Yes," I answer, forcing the words out past my panic.

The official nods again. "She did not physically harm you nor attempt to sell your virtue to others?"

I blink, taken aback by the question. Now I understand what happened to the empty-eyed girls. The transporters weren't supposed to harm them, but one thing I've learned in the past few months is that people often do things they aren't supposed to. A vision of the elders flashes behind my eyes, their knives and buckets looming as they prepare for yet another bleeding. I inhale, exhale out the memory.

"No," I finally answer.

"Well, that's a relief," the official says under his breath. "No additional scrolls to fill with this one."

My teeth grit. Girls had their virtue forced from them, their lives devastated, and all he cares about is doing more work. He's like the jatu that just left with their false promises of rights and freedoms. I have to exhale again to keep the rage from showing on my face.

He turns to his assistant. "The gold," he commands.

As the assistant moves to bring over the urn, the official directs his eyes to me. "This gold has been formulated specially to mark you as the emperor's property. It will fade with every year that passes and disappear once you reach your twentieth year of service. A gilded sleep will not fade it, so don't try killing yourself to lessen your time."

Don't try...killing yourself...

I'm in such a state now, my thoughts are barely more than half-formed things. By the time I finally piece together what he's saying, the assistant is already pulling my sleeves up, then he's dipping my hands into that urn. A whimper escapes my lips, even though all I feel is a brief, icy stinging before the gold covers my skin. I try not to react to the smell of my burning flesh, but my body trembles again and the sourness in my mouth intensifies as that horrible odour wafts past my nostrils.

"She is gilded," the assistant says.

"She is duly accounted for," the official concludes. Now he looks down his spectacles at me. "Bring pride to Otera in the coming years, alaki – both you and your uruni."

I vomit the moment I'm led out of the hall.

NINE

There's nothing in my stomach. Nothing but bile and dust. And that's the only thing that saves me from the wrath of the two jatu overseeing my group when I retch violently outside the hall. My hands are still raw and stinging from the gilding, but I can already feel them healing, new skin forming under the thin sheen of gold, which, strangely, is just as supple as the skin underneath it. There really is something uncanny about the gold they used.

The shorter jatu sneers, disgusted. "Get a hold of yourself, creature." He shoves me towards the line of hulking, prisonlike wagons waiting in the back of the hall.

There are twenty wagons in total, each a different colour designating the different training grounds scattered on the hills at the very outer edges of Hemaira. Britta and I are headed for the forbidding red wagons waiting at the very end of the line. They're the ones destined for the Warthu Bera. At least one hundred girls will be taken there before this night is ended. The jatu recruits are no doubt already on their way, ready to do their own initial training.

The scent of fear grows stronger the closer we get to the wagons, girls clutching each other desperately and whispering to each other – rumours, suppositions, anything they've heard over the course of their journey. But Britta's mind is still on our new uruni.

"Wonder why they don't want us to start training with them now…" she murmurs. There's a strange note in her voice.

I glance over to find she's tentatively pressing the gold on her hands. She hisses softly, tears flooding her eyes, and I move closer to her. "The skin under it will heal soon," I whisper. "Everything'll be all right, you'll see."

Britta inhales shakily, nods.

"Did you hear?" the red-haired girl I saw gilded whispers, drawing our attention to her. "The training grounds are going to be overseen by Shadows, the emperor's personal spies."

"I heard that they were all female," another replies, this one short and dark.

The memory of the smaller commander immediately flits through my mind.

"Female?" says another girl. "That can't be possible. Whoever heard of female teachers?"

I certainly never have.

The Infinite Wisdoms forbids women from working outside the house except in service to their husbands and families. And yet there might be female teachers at the Warthu Bera – female spies.

I've heard of the emperor's Shadows – everyone has. They're the ones sent whenever the emperor needs something swiftly and silently done. It's said that they have powers above those of normal people, that they can blend into the shadows that are their namesakes and strike down enemies from enormous distances. They might be our teachers? I can't even fathom it.

Beside me, the red-haired girl shakes her head. "I heard they had no choice but to use women. Too many incidents happened with the male transporters. You saw some of the girls—"

"Britta, Asha, Adwapa, Belcalis, Deka," the short jatu barks, reading our names from a scroll. "Move yer arses!"

I hurry along, struggling to ignore the subtle tremors still wracking my body as I rush towards the wagons. The gilding wasn't that painful, but that smell, that awful burning smell, still lingers in my nostrils, wafting up memories I would prefer stay firmly buried. As the jatu and his partner open the door to deposit us inside, I glance at Britta. She seems a little better now, some of the colour returned to her face.

"Any better?" I ask.

She nods as the short jatu locks the door securely behind us. "Loaded!" the tall one shouts, banging the roof.

"Proceed!" the short one shouts.

"Proceed!" the tall one echoes, banging again.

The wagon lurches into action, rattling onto the street. As we head away from Jor Hall, I glance around the wagon's interior. There are three other girls here with us. Two of them are twins – both so midnight dark I know immediately that they must be Nibari, a fiercely independent tribe that lives in the mountains of the remotest Southern provinces. It must be a very unfortunate series of events that brought them here. The Nibari are fiercely loyal to each other, and Mother once told me that they don't really worship Oyomo, only some secret god they have kept from the time before the many tribes became the One Kingdom.

Even more alarming is our last passenger, the proud girl. She huddles as far away from the rest of us as she possibly can, black hair wild around her face as she fixes that determined gaze upon the grated door separating us from the outside world. Perhaps she's already regretting her decision to stay.

There's no escape, I want to tell her. Even if metal grating wasn't barring the door, there would also be the jatu to deal with. There's a contingent of them assigned to each caravan of wagons, and all of them are the ones specially trained to deal with alaki. I wouldn't even be surprised if there were some recruits among their number, riding along to accompany their new "sisters". I have to swallow back the bitterness that rises at the thought.

The wagon rattles on, its wheels loud against the cobblestones. Despite this, the silence is deafening – as is the tension that swirls around us, as smothering as smoke. Britta squirms beside me. She's one of those people who hate awkward silences – or any silence, for that matter.

"Well, here we are," she says, summoning her most cheerful smile. When everyone's eyes turn to her, she shifts uncomfortably but gamely soldiers on. "Anyone have any idea wha's waitin' for us when we get there? Other than the recruits, that is." She laughs nervously at this painful attempt at a joke.

"Do you think this is a game?" the proud girl snaps, aquiline features whipping, hawklike, towards Britta. "Do you think that we're off to court, to learn how to be proper maidens and do needlework?" The girl leans closer, a sneer on her face.

"We're monsters, and they're going to treat us like monsters. They're going to use us, bleed us, and when they're done, they're going to find whatever our final deaths are and execute us one by one."

She leans back against her seat, scoffing. "Uruni – can you believe the lies? More like spies, here to ensure we don't step one foot out of line or run off during the raids." She turns hardened eyes to Britta. "The sooner you understand that, the better off you are."

Britta reddens, tears springing to her eyes, and anger abruptly swells inside me. Who is this girl to speak so harshly to Britta? And today of all days, after everything we've just endured, after all the humiliations. Why add to the pain, the suffering? Why attack the one person trying to make things better?

I turn to the proud girl. "You don't have to do that – you don't have to scare her," I say.

Eyes the colour of midnight glance at me. "I don't? You may be under illusions of what this is, being partnered with Recruit Keita and all," she sneers mockingly, "but I'm not, and I would prefer to prepare myself in silence."

Heat blazes over me before I even notice it. "Who I'm partnered with has nothing to do with my feelings," I snap. "And, to be clear, you chose this, same as us. You had a choice, and you decided to remain here."

"No," the proud girl says. "I chose to escape the Death Mandate, if only for a few more days. I chose to survive, rather than being executed the moment I walked out that door. Don't mistake my decision for anything more."

"Oh, please, we all chose to escape the Death Mandate," an annoyed voice interrupts.

When we turn, two pairs of eyes are watching us, irritation plain in them. The taller twin's bald head gleams in the darkness of the wagon as she drawls, "That's the path we all chose. Whether we were forced or not doesn't matter. We're here now. We make the best of it or we die, simple as that."

I'm surprised she spoke on my behalf. Northerners and Southerners never fare well together, and my accent very clearly marks me as a Northerner, despite my appearance. Perhaps she doesn't care about the grudge between the Northern and Southern provinces.

I can only hope everyone else here feels the same.

She and her sister seem older than us – perhaps eighteen or so – although she's much fiercer-looking than her shorter, smaller sister, whose black hair is braided in tiny rows down her back. When she shrugs, moonlight dances across the intricate scars on her cheeks and shoulders. My heart tightens in recognition. Those are tribal scars, probably carved well before her blood turned and the cursed gold began healing all wounds. The Southern tribes use them to mark their members. Mother had two on each cheek.

"Then let's make the best of it by becoming friends," Britta says. The others turn to her, and she shrinks inward for a moment. Then she stiffens her shoulders. "Or allies, l-leastways," she stammers. "True ones, I mean, not like our new partnerships."

I can't help but admire her for her bravery. "Britta's right," I say. "We are all going to a place we don't know to face horrors we cannot imagine. We could bear it alone." A dark cellar. Golden blood on stones. "Or we could band together, help each other. Britta's helped me before. I slept through our entire journey across the sea, and she ate my food so others would not start asking questions about me – about how I could survive without eating."

"Must have been such a sacrifice for you." The proud girl's eyes examine Britta's plump form dismissively. "A few days of feasting to your heart's content."

Her sarcasm prickles me. "It was four weeks," I say coldly. "Almost a month."

Now her eyes widen. "A month?" she gasps.

The Nibari are shocked as well. "A month?" the taller one muses. "You look healthy for not having eaten for a month."

The smaller one nods in agreement but still does not speak. I'm starting to wonder if she can.

"I don't think our kind dies of starvation," I reply.

"We don't." The grim expression in the proud girl's eyes says she knows this from experience. "We do, however, show its ill effects. Our ability to heal goes only so far, and we need food to fuel it." She looks me up and down. "Your hair is full, and your body isn't thin. Your skin's unwrinkled, and you don't have sores around your mouth. How long ago were you starved?"

As I try to remember, Britta leans forward. "She still hasn't eaten yet."

I blink, startled to realize she's right. When last did I eat – or even have a drink? I try to pin down the day, but my memories shift away, the same way they've been doing since my time in the cellar.

The proud girl's lips curl into a sneer. "You're unnatural," she says, disgusted.

As I wince at the word, the shorter Nibari rustles beside me and turns to the proud girl. "We all are – you as well," she sniffs. Like her sister, she has shrewd eyes and a defiant expression. Ritual scars also cover her cheeks and shoulders. "How else do you think you tossed away all those guards in Jor Hall? What human woman do you know who possesses such strength?"

The girl stiffens. "Of course I know—"

"Can't sneer at someone else for being unnatural when you're considered exactly the same by other people," the shorter Nibari interrupts.

"All the more reason we should band together," Britta announces, extending her hand out to the twins. "I'm Britta," she says.

The twins look at her hand, then at each other. The taller, bald one takes it first. "I'm Adwapa, first daughter of Tabelo, high chief of the Nibari."

"And I'm Asha, second daughter of Tabelo, high chief of the Nibari," the shorter one says, braids swinging as she nods.

When both turn to me, I extend my hand as well. "Deka of Irfut," I say, clasping each of their hands in turn.

"Well met," they intone together.

We all turn to the proud girl. At first she just looks at us, disgusted. Finally, she sighs and rolls her eyes. "Very well, I am Belcalis of Hualpa," she says, naming a far Western city near the border to the Unknown Lands.

"Well met," we all say.

"This does not make us friends," she snarls.

Britta's broad smile exposes the dimple in her left cheek. "But it does make us allies."

I nod. "Let us watch each other's backs and aid each other as much as possible."

This stipulation seems to calm Belcalis. "As much as possible," she says, then adds, "but understand this: I will flee this hellhole as soon as possible."

Britta's brows gather. "Don't ye want to be pure, then? 'Blessed are the meek and subservient, the humble an' true daughters of man, for they are unsullied in the face of the Infinite Father.' That's wha the Infinite Wisdoms says."

Belcalis rolls her eyes. "You actually believe that dreck? Purity is an illusion. So is absolution and anything you read in that cursed book. You'd think you fools would understand that by now."

My jaw nearly drops. I've never heard anyone talk about the Infinite Wisdoms that way before, much less about purity. I quickly glance upward, sending a quick prayer for forgiveness from the Infinite Father. *Please, please, please don't punish us for this,* I beg.

I turn to the others. "Perhaps we should pray," I suggest.

"If you're so moved," Adwapa says with a shrug. It's clear she has no intention of doing so. Neither do her sister or Belcalis. Is there something about the Southern provinces that makes people defy the Infinite Father so?

I don't want any part of it. I don't want any part of anything that could lead back to that cellar – back to all that blood, that pain...

I'm relieved when Britta squeezes closer. "I'll pray with ye,

Deka," she says, reaching out her hand.

"Thank you," I whisper as I take it.

We silently pray together as we begin making our way towards the edges of the capital.

Our destination, as it turns out, is a series of isolated hills at the very outskirts of the city, just next to the wall. Night has fallen, so an oppressive gloom engulfs the caravan of alaki wagons threading towards the hill. Despite the darkness, I see everything perfectly: the large building at the top of the largest hill, its windows as small as pinpricks, its walls slick and red. There's an imposing, almost ominous feeling about it, but that's the way it's designed. Those walls, those tiny windows – they're as much to keep the inhabitants inside as they are to keep others out. This must be the Warthu Bera, our new training ground.

My mouth slackens at the sheer size of it. Those rolling hills, the lake in the middle – the Warthu Bera is large enough to house a village. In fact, it's very much like a village, all those smaller buildings surrounding the big one at the very top. The only difference is, everything here is built for war. If I squint, I can see what looks like a sandpit in the distance and sharpened spikes jutting from the depths of the surrounding moat. I don't have to ask to know they're there for any alaki who thinks of escaping using that route. Lookout towers thrust from the walls, all of them swarming with armoured jatu. Our new captors. Keita and the others may claim that we're soldiers with choices, but I know better. Even regular soldiers are punished for desertion, and we're as far from regular as can be.

It's an unpleasant thought, so I try to push it away as the gate opens and we cross the bridge to begin our ascent. Finally, we reach the courtyard of the largest building, where orange-robed middle-aged women are lined up beside a statue of Emperor Gezo. Shock jolts me when I realize they're all unmasked, their heads uncovered, with what look like short wooden walking sticks sheathed at their sides. I turn my eyes away, overwhelmed by the sight.

Are these the women who are going to train us?

My tension builds, the blood prickling under my skin, as the wagons roll to a stop. "Dismount!" The cry echoes from jatu to jatu. "Release the alaki!"

When keys click in the wagon's lock, Britta and I look at each other one last time.

"Be strong," she whispers to me, her face pale in the darkness.

"You too," I whisper back.

It's still warm outside when we exit the carriage, joining the mass of girls gathered in the courtyard. Temperatures don't plunge here the way they do in the North, it seems. The air is moist and tinged with a sharp, metallic odour. I don't have to inhale deeply to know that it's blood – cursed gold. After my months in the cellar, I can recognize the scent with barely a whiff.

My tension rises when a robust matron with a formidable chest separates herself from the group. She almost resembles a bull, all jutting brows and tiny, beady little eyes. I look down, unnerved by the sight of her unmasked face, and that's when I notice the small, sunlike tattoo on the back of her hand, its bright red colour immediately distinguishable. A gasp wrenches itself from my throat. The ylm-kuru, the emblem of the red sun. The emblem of the temple maidens, those unmarried women unfortunate enough to be bound into service to temples and other places of worship.

Now I understand why all these women are revealed, their faces unmasked even in the presence of the jatu. They aren't our new teachers, they're the women serving them.

"Follow me, neophytes!" the matron barks, walking into the building.

I've never heard the word neophytes before today, but I know she must be talking about us. I fall into line behind the other girls from the wagons, following her through the massive archway. There's that eclipsed sun symbol on the largest stone above the entrance, although it is beaten and weathered. A frown furrows my brows. Something about the weathering has changed the symbol, made it seem more familiar, like I've seen it somewhere other than on the Warthu Bera's seal before.

But where?

"Hurry it along!" the matron bellows, rushing us down the steps into the bowels of the building, to an underground bathing chamber consisting of a series of tiled baths.

Assistants in yellow robes stand beside each bath, thin towels and sharpened razors at their sides. My heartbeat doubles at the sight of them.

"Disrobe!" the bull-like matron barks.

As we all turn, startled by the command, she fingers the hilt of the stick strapped to her side. We take off our clothes, all of us doing so swiftly to ensure we aren't seen. My cheeks heat, my eyes dart to the floor, the ceiling – anywhere but to the other girls' bodies. Even then, I catch glimpses: bodies of all sizes and shapes, some covered in hair, others smooth except for the hair on their heads – a few like the Nibari, with tribal scars or tattoos from the time before their blood changed into cursed gold.

I'm stunned by how different the other girls' bodies are. Mother and I were never welcomed in the women's baths in Irfut, so she's the only woman I've ever seen fully naked before, her body dark and shapely like mine. Soon, only one girl remains clothed.

Belcalis.

She wraps her arms around her body, a defiant gesture despite the uncertainty, the shame, now flickering in her eyes.

The matron walks over to her and lifts her chin with the butt of her whip. "I heard it said there was a troublemaker among you," she says in a heavily accented voice, *rs* and *ls* rolling like waves across her tongue. "It must be you. Tell me, alaki, why do you refuse to heed my order?"

"I don't wish to disrobe," Belcalis grits out.

"A modest one, are you?" the matron sneers.

"If it pleases you."

"It pleases me for you to disrobe!"

I hear the stick before I see it, a low whooping sound through the air, just as its weighted hilt cracks into Belcalis's back. She lets out a hollow, gasping sound as she falls to the floor, golden blood spurting down her back. Air catches in my throat. That walking stick isn't a stick, it's a rungu – a club soldiers throw at opponents. I've seen one in action before, witnessed Father practising with it and the many other weapons he kept from his time in the army. His, however, didn't have barbs on the weighted end for ripping into flesh and bone the way the matron's does.

So this is how they will keep us in line.

The matron walks over, puts her foot on Belcalis's back, pressing her deeper into the floor. Belcalis grunts, pained, but the matron doesn't move her foot. She just smirks down at her, a chilling look in her eyes.

"Insolent beast," she sneers, ripping the rungu out.

I clap my hands over my mouth, stomach lurching as more golden blood goes spurting into the air. The sight of all that blood is sickening, but even worse is what's underneath: a mass of scars, each one layered so thickly across Belcalis's back, even the rungu's barbs couldn't penetrate completely. Now I understand why she seems so defiant, why she doesn't retreat when threatened by authority. She's used to being beaten, bled – even starved. Her exposed ribs, gaunt spine, and flat, removed expression all tell a story, one of unspeakable horror.

Is that the way I looked in the cellar – that detachment, that resignation?

The matron grows impatient. She strokes the rungu again. "You will not listen, alaki?" she sneers. "You will not follow the path? Then I suppose I will just have to beat you across it." She raises the stick again, and Belcalis flinches.

It's a broken, ugly movement.

"No!" I gasp before I can stop myself. "Please don't hurt her."

The matron turns to me, a chilling expression of amusement

115

on her face. "What's this? The troublemaker has a friend." Abandoning Belcalis, she walks over to me. Now I see her face close up, jaw squat and severe, nose blade-thin. Her brows furrow, those tiny eyes gleaming under them. "You have a familiar look about you," she murmurs. "Have we met before?"

I shake my head.

"Part your lips and speak up, alaki."

Terror dries my throat, but I somehow find the strength to swallow. "No. We've never met," I rasp.

She humphs. "Very well, then," she says. "Now, you had something to say about your friend. What was it again?"

My eyes flicker to the golden blood snaking across the stones. I remember that blood, remember how it pooled around me in the cellar… "Don't hurt her…please," I whisper.

I swallow to push back the darkness as the matron steps closer, strokes my neck with the weighted end of her rungu. Her tiny eyes gleam when she notices me wince from the barbs. "I didn't mean to offend," I croak, "only to say that Belcalis is very…devout. She's not used to being bared near others."

"Devout?" The matron guffaws at my lie. "As if Oyomo would give His attention to any of you infernal beasts." As I wince at this insult, she turns to Belcalis, a thin smirk slicing her lips. "And you – so your name is Belcalis. That's good to know."

Across the room, Belcalis shoots me a baleful glare, and alarm ripples over me. I didn't mean it, I try to explain with my eyes.

The matron approaches her again, but this time, one of the assistants steps in front of her and respectfully bows her head.

"Matron Nasra, the hour approaches. The karmokos await you."

Matron Nasra huffs. "Very well. Ensure that the girls are all clean, especially her" – she points at Belcalis – "and give them all the closest of shaves. There will be no lice in the Warthu Bera," she barks as she walks out.

Once she leaves, the assistant who spoke turns to the girls. "Wash yourselves, hurry now. Time grows short." She directs another assistant towards Belcalis. "Take her to a private chamber. I'll not have cursed gold in the water."

The assistant bows, escorting Belcalis out. "Yes, ma'am," she says.

When they pass me, Belcalis catches my eye. "Next time you have the urge to aid me – don't," she hisses.

Then she's gone, and the rest of the girls, including me, enter the water. One of the assistants approaches with a blade and scrapes it over my head. I try not to see the curly strands of black hair falling into the water, try not to give in to the tears pricking at my eyes. I don't even know what to think any more. Exhaustion, emotion, the gilding…they all overwhelm me now, making me teary-eyed with confusion.

But I will survive it all, I remind myself sternly. I will survive this and whatever else happens next.

Oyomo, help me endure it.

TEN

In less than an hour, I'm clean and clothed in scratchy green robes and leather sandals. I'm also as bald as all the other girls subjected to the assistants' razors. If I ever had any doubts about my new status, they were erased the moment my hair was tossed into the furnace like it was nothing. The Infinite Wisdoms states that a woman's hair is her greatest pride, the source of her gracefulness and beauty.

Now none of the girls here have any.

As of this moment, I'm truly nothing more than a demon, my last claim to femininity stripped away. The realization roils inside me, a nausea that builds as the matrons and their assistants usher us down the building's warrenlike halls into a massive central hall. A line of girls is waiting there, each one clothed in leather armour and bearing wooden swords. Like ours, their hair was shaved clean, but it's regrown to nape-length for most. I suppose that means they've been here a few months at least.

These must be the girls who were sent here before us, the older alaki.

At the very front stand a trio of unmasked women, the red and gold banner of the Warthu Bera rising proudly behind them. My eyes are immediately drawn to the woman in the middle. She has dark-brown skin, powerfully muscled arms, and a stern, unflinching gaze. Most striking of all is the bright red clay that daubs the intricate braids coiled around her head. It's immediately familiar, as is the woman's silhouette.

The silent commander from Jor Hall!

It's her – only now she's unmasked and wearing dark green robes, a large golden pin at her shoulder. On it is the eclipse symbol from the archway. Where have I seen it before? The question niggles at me.

I have to force myself not to look down when she steps forward and raises her hand in salute. Around me, other girls do the same, pained expressions in their eyes. This is probably the first time they're seeing so many unmasked women too.

"Hail, our honoured alaki neophytes," the stern woman calls out.

"Hail!" the armoured girls echo her, their voices a single, powerful entity.

Chills rush through me at the sound.

The stern woman continues talking, her booming voice echoing through the hall: "On behalf of his Imperial Majesty, Emperor Gezo the Fifth, honoured sovereign and ruler of the One Kingdom, our beloved Otera, I bid you welcome to the Warthu Bera."

"Welcome!" the armoured girls repeat.

"I am Karmoko Thandiwe," the woman says, "head instructor at the Warthu Bera, the glorious training house in which you stand. Refer to me with any other title, or mispronounce my name, and I will cut out your tongue for your insolence and put it in a jar to keep me company."

At her words, the atmosphere chills and girls look at each other, frightened. I silently try to sear her name's pronunciation into my memory: Than-DEE-way, Than-DEE-way.

Karmoko Thandiwe continues her speech. "To my left is Karmoko Calderis."

She motions, and a brunette of almost bearlike proportions lumbers forward and examines us with the single bright blue eye not covered by a leather eye patch. The eclipse pin gleams at her shoulder as well.

"She will serve as your weapons master in the coming months." Karmoko Thandiwe motions again, and Karmoko Calderis steps back with a curt nod.

"To my right is Karmoko Huon," Karmoko Thandiwe says.

A small, kind-looking woman with pale skin and dark eyes steps forward. Her black hair cascades like a river down her back, tiny jewelled flowers adorning it. She doesn't seem like a warrior at all, and her gentle smile as she nods at us only reinforces this impression. She also wears the eclipse pin, and when she absently strokes a finger over it, my heart beats faster, though I don't know why.

"She will serve as your combat master," Karmoko Thandiwe says.

The kind-looking woman steps back, her dark eyes glancing almost tentatively over us. Again, I silently wonder how this woman was chosen to become our combat master. She's like a butterfly, so delicate and beautiful, you could crush her if you weren't careful.

Karmoko Thandiwe continues: "From now until such time as you leave the Warthu Bera, we, your karmokos, your teachers, will serve as your guides. Each of us standing before you has served as his Imperial Majesty's Shadows, the deadliest of all his assassins. We have all earned notable places in the Heraldry of Shadows, the book that lists the exploits of our kind – the book that sits here, in the famed Warthu Bera, the House of Women.

"We are proud to have been trained within these very walls, and are even prouder to give you the same honour. From now until you leave this training ground, you will work harder and feel more pain than you have ever felt in your life, until we mould you from the weak, useless girls that you are into warriors – defenders of Otera. Conquer or Die, this is our motto here."

My eyebrows gather. Warriors? Defenders? Are the karmokos certain they're talking about us? I peer at Karmoko Huon again, trying to imagine her as a deadly assassin. If she of all people can be a warrior, perhaps the same is possible for—

Something is coming...

The unwelcome premonition tingles under my skin, and I stiffen. "Britta," I rasp, my breathing shallow as I turn to my friend. Does she feel it too – heightened awareness, panic crawling up her spine?

Do the other girls? They all seem as calm as ever, but they have no idea what's about to happen. I remember all too keenly what happened at the village the last time I felt this way. The blood, the fear, the bodies littering the snow...

"Wha is it?" Britta whispers back.

"Deathshrieks," I whisper. "They're here."

"Wha do ye mean, here?"

As Britta glances around, panicked, Karmoko Thandiwe walks towards us, her eyes stern. "You have all heard of deathshrieks, yes?"

Around me, the girls nod their heads.

"Have any of you encountered them before?" When the girls nod timidly again, Karmoko Thandiwe bellows, "Open your mouths and use your tongues! The correct response is 'Yes, Karmoko!'"

I nearly jump out of my skin, her voice is so powerful. I've never heard a woman speak like that, never heard such authority coming from a female throat. My heart beats even faster as I reply along with the others. "Yes, Karmoko," I gasp, my throat raw.

"Louder!" she commands.

"Yes, Karmoko!"

"Better." She nods. She glances at the girls who answered yes. "Consider yourselves most fortunate to have encountered such monstrosities and survived. For the rest of you, allow me to even the score."

Even the score? What score?

Karmoko Thandiwe gestures, and the older girls march towards us, footsteps steady and sure.

"Step back, neophytes!" the one at the front, a short, slim girl with the black hair and light-brown skin of the mid-Eastern provinces, calls. She has a jagged scar all the way down the side of her cheek, old but harshly puckered. Another one who hasn't experienced a recent death. "Move back! Move back!" she shouts.

I hurriedly do as I'm told, shuffling backwards until soon I'm at the very edges of the room with the other neophytes. The older girls spread into a single line before us – a barrier, keeping us firmly in place.

By now, my palms are sweating, and my heart is beating so fast, it feels like it'll leap out of my chest. They can't really mean to bring deathshrieks here, can they? I thought Captain Kelechi said we would encounter them on the raids. What if those monsters escape – attack us the way the ones in Irfut did? What if I react the same way I did before, my eyes changing colour, that demonic voice emerging from my throat?

I whimper, the thought of everyone witnessing it almost too much to bear.

Who knows what the karmokos would do to someone like me – someone with abilities beyond what is common for an ordinary alaki.

I swallow back the thought as Karmoko Thandiwe gestures to Matron Nasra, and the matron presses a small, circular metal structure in the wall. A low rumbling rises as the floor slides apart, revealing a dark subterranean cave, a stone staircase leading to a group of iron cages arranged in its centre. Muffled, inhuman grunts sound from those cages, mist clouding around them. My entire body stills, my fears now confirmed. There are deathshrieks underneath the Warthu Bera, and the karmokos intend to bring them up.

The scarred girl walks with a group of the older girls down the stairs, heading towards the largest cage, where an ominous sound rises: the rattling of chains. Sharp, predatory black eyes gleam inside the cage, the outline of a gaunt, gigantic figure barely visible in the shadows. A deathshriek, chains binding it.

My heart hammers, teeth clench, sweat pours rivers down my back.

Britta shifts closer to me. "It's all right, Deka," she whispers, "I'm right here."

I nod, inhale deeply for courage as I return my attention to what's happening in the cavern below. The deathshriek still hasn't come out, and the scarred girl is getting impatient.

"Get it out," she commands the others.

They quickly do as they're told, a tall, dark-skinned girl darting forwards and opening the cage door while the others wait, swords drawn. Strangely, the deathshriek makes no movement. What is it doing? Why is it just standing there? My muscles go taut from the tension.

Finally, the scarred girl has had enough. She darts inside the cage, tugs at one of the deathshriek's chains.

With a muffled howl of outrage, the deathshriek lunges for her, the quills in its pale silver fur a whirlwind of motion, black eyes slitted with fury. But the scarred girl and the others don't jerk back or flee. Instead, they grab its chains, then use inhuman strength to force it up the stairs until it's just before Karmoko Thandiwe, who casually flips it to the ground, then slams her foot into its throat, pressing harder and harder until it slumps unconscious.

The blood roars in my ears.

Astonishment has taken me by the throat, so it's some minutes before I remember how close that deathshriek is, remember what can happen when I'm in the presence of one.

I turn to Britta, alarmed. "Is there anything wrong with my eyes?" I ask.

She peers down at me, frowns. "No, is there supposed to be?"

Relief coursing through my veins, I shake my head and face forward again just as Karmoko Thandiwe removes her foot and points to the unconscious deathshriek.

"This is a deathshriek, the enemy that is now invading the One Kingdom," she states. "Your natural enemy. All across Otera, deathshrieks hunt your kind, but here in the Warthu Bera, you will learn how to withstand them – their cries, their infernal strength and speed. You will learn how to transform from the hunted to the hunter – how to train harder, more ruthlessly, until you become the best, the most fearsome warriors in all of the emperor's alaki regiment.

"Then, when you have served the emperor for twenty years each, you will be rewarded with the Rite of Purification, a sacred ceremony by the high priests to cleanse you of your demonic blood." She looks across the room now, her eyes pinning each and every one of us in place as she declares, "You will be pure again."

Pure… Breath catches in my throat.

The next twenty years can't pass quickly enough.

Around me, whispers sound, exclamations of joy and relief. "Did you hear that?" a girl near me says, gaping. Katya, I think her name is. She's the one from the line to the wagons, red hair so bright, it looked like a fire springing from her head. Now she's as bald as the rest of us, even her eyebrows shorn from her face. "We're going to be pure. Truly pure," she exclaims.

She looks almost as excited as I feel. Even though Karmoko Thandiwe has just repeated the same sentiments Captain Kelechi did, something about her delivery set a fire in me. Or perhaps it's the fact it was a woman that said them.

Not everyone is as impressed, however. Adwapa manages to somehow seem bored as she murmurs: "Well, that's a relief." Being already bald, she was spared the indignity of a shearing, but her sister Asha's head now also gleams when she nods in agreement beside her.

Karmoko Thandiwe holds up her hand for silence, and the hall quiets.

"Look to your left," she commands. We quickly obey. "Now to your right." Again, we obey her words. "Standing on either side of you are your sisters – both in blood and in arms. Bloodsisters. They will live and die with you on the battlefield. They are your family now, is this understood?"

It takes me a moment to realize she means for us to answer. "Yes, Karmoko Thandiwe," I reply, joining the chorus of voices.

"Now look to your elder bloodsisters, the novices." She points to the armoured girls. "From now on, you will refer to them always as 'honoured elder bloodsister'. They have been here for a year now. They will show you the way." As we nod, she turns to face us once again. "I would have you understand one thing. Of all the hundreds of alaki that have come to Hemaira, you are the fifty most talented – the fastest, the strongest, the most deadly. Most of you were noted by your village elders before you underwent the Ritual, or as you tried, futilely, to escape your fates. You all showed promise. Strength, cunning, resilience – much more than the average alaki. That is why you were chosen."

I suddenly remember Britta telling me how she was so strong she could almost lift a cow, remember White Hands marvelling at all the times I'd died and been resurrected.

"Remember this well," the karmoko warns, "because you are here for one purpose and one purpose only. In ten months precisely, the emperor will go on campaign against the deathshrieks, and he has chosen the alaki who will lead the charge."

She glances around the room, her eyes deadly serious.

"You will be at the forefront of the emperor's armies," she declares. "You will ride into battle and fight for the glory of Otera, and you will win the war against the deathshrieks or you will die trying – however many times that may take."

ELEVEN

In the aftermath of Karmoko Thandiwe's speech, silence descends over the hall.

My breath comes in short, ragged bursts, her words ringing in my ears. Win the war against the deathshrieks... The forefront of the emperor's armies... My hands shake, and I clasp them together. Knowing the bargain I agreed to is one thing. Actually being here, seeing the deathshrieks hidden underneath my feet – the monsters I will one day fight against – is another.

I barely see the novices hefting the unconscious deathshriek and returning it to its cage, barely see Matron Nasra closing the floor behind them, then bows deferentially to the karmokos. Only when Karmoko Thandiwe nods at us do I return my attention to the present. That's when I see something strange. The karmoko is staring right at me, a peculiar look in her eyes. It's almost as if she recognizes me. The expression is gone before I can blink, but I know my eyes weren't deceiving me.

You have a familiar look about you... Matron Nasra's words ring in my head.

As if my mind summoned her, the matron walks to the front of the hall and claps her hands for attention. "All right, neophytes, move it along. Time for dinner!" she bellows.

I obey along with the rest of the girls, following her into the next hall, which is filled with long wooden tables and similar chairs. As I take a seat beside Britta and the others, my mind whirls, darting back to the symbol on the karmokos' eclipse pins – to the strange feeling I had when Karmoko Huon traced it with her fingers earlier. I mentally trace it again, imagining the shape of that shadowed sun gliding under my own fingertips, its edges softened by years of daily use.

A gasp explodes from my chest.

I've felt that symbol before, touched it a thousand times before I ever saw it on the seal White Hands gave me. It's the same symbol that's on my mother's necklace, the one I could never make out because it had become so worn, and it's everywhere I look now: the archway above the door from which the assistants are emerging, steaming plates of food in hand, the centres of the tables, even the middle of the ceiling, which soars high above us.

I point up at it and ask the girls beside me, "Do any of you know what that symbol is?"

All this time, and I've never once asked. Belcalis and Asha shake their heads, but Adwapa nods. "It's the umbra, the emblem of the Shadows."

My brow furrows, thoughts rushing faster. Mother had it on her necklace, wore it every day. And symbols like that, ones connected to the emperor, can be used only with special permission. Even mistakenly carving one warrants a death sentence – the smallest child knows that. The ground tilts under my feet as a strange, impossible theory slithers into my mind.

What if Mother was a Shadow?

It seems far-fetched – impossible even – but it would explain so many things: the reason she was always so careful to remain at the periphery of the village, the fact that she moved all the way to Irfut in the first place. Most women never leave their home villages, and if they do, it's to move the next village over, not an entirely different province.

Some of the village men back in Irfut used to gossip that the emperor collects strange people to serve him, people who defy the natural order but have been granted special dispensation by the priests. What if Mother was one of them? If she was, what does that make me?

There have to be answers here somewhere.

As the assistants place plates of herbed chicken and rice in front of us, Britta's eyes narrow. "Ye have a funny look on yer face," she says, eating a piece of chicken using her hands, as is the tradition of the Southern provinces.

Mother used to do the same, even though Father wanted her to use utensils. She always said hands were good enough. The thought sends a twinge of sadness through me. It chases away the uncomfortable smell of chicken, which has sent my stomach twisting in on itself. Ever since I was burned, I can't stomach the smell of roasted meat.

I look into Britta's eyes. "I think my mother was a Shadow," I whisper.

"Wha?"

"There's this necklace she always wore – never went

anywhere without it. It had the umbra on it." It sounds so strange saying this out loud, silly even, but voicing my thoughts solidifies them. I know I'm right, I can just feel it.

"An' that awful matron said ye looked familiar…" Excitement lights up Britta's face and she gasps. "Wha if she knew yer mother? Wha if they trained together or something?"

"That's what I'm thinking."

Britta's voice lowers to a whisper. "Does this explain how ye knew the deathshrieks were down there?" She huddles over her plate of food so the others won't hear us talking.

Does it? I turn the question over and over in my mind. "I don't know," I admit. "I just get feelings sometimes. And she did too…"

I glance at Britta, steeling myself for her reaction – horror, fear? But she just nods. "We have to get that book, then – the Heraldry the karmoko talked about. If all the Shadows are listed there, perhaps yer mother is as well. Perhaps we can learn more about her."

She looks so determined, so eager, something loosens in my chest. Here I was frightened she'd laugh at me or turn me away. I nod. "And if she's not, at least I'll know for sure."

"Either way, it'll get our minds off things. All that talk about going on raids and being warriors. How can I be a warrior? Me, Britta of Golma, a cabbage farmer's daughter. I can't imagine it."

"None of us can," Belcalis says beside her, startling me. I've been so absorbed in discussing Mother, I'd almost forgotten that she was sitting there. That all the other girls were as well.

To my surprise, they haven't separated themselves by province, the way visitors to Irfut so often do – Northerners and

Southerners particularly. Instead, they all lean closer, nodding in agreement with her words.

"I want to go home." This fearful whisper comes from Katya. "'Conquer'? 'Warriors'? *Dying?*" She turns to us, bald eyebrows drawing together like pale caterpillars. "I never asked for that. All I wanted to do was get married, have children. I just want to go home, go back to Rian."

"Rian?" I blink. "You had a betrothed?"

Katya nods. "When they came to take me, he ran after the wagon. He told me he'd wait, no matter how long it took." She looks down at her newly gilded hands, her voice low with tears. "He's waiting for me. He's still wait—" She stops abruptly, hiccupping back sobs, and Britta puts her arm around her.

I just watch, unsure of what to do. The moment my blood ran gold, everyone I knew abandoned me: Father left, the villagers turned against me – even Elfriede fled. Sixteen years of friendship gone, just like that.

But Katya's betrothed stayed with her. Tried to fight for her. Even though he went against his village elders, the priests. I'm unable to fathom the idea of such loyalty from a man – from any person, actually.

Are there truly people in the world like that? Could there be someone like that for me?

I don't even know if it's possible, if someone, somewhere in this vast world, will ever love someone like me – the unageing, unchanging offspring of a demon – but I want to find them. Want to survive long enough to experience that kind of love: loyal, unflinching, steadfast. The kind of love that Mother gave me before she died. The kind of love that Katya and Britta seem to command so easily.

And I don't have to do it alone.

I glance at the other girls, Katya's eyes wild with fear, Britta's with uncertainty. If this was anywhere else, we wouldn't even speak to each other, but we're all in the same boat now, all of us faced with years of pain, suffering, blood... Bloodsisters – that's what Karmoko Thandiwe called us, a word that gives me courage.

I send a little prayer to Oyomo before I turn to the others. "I don't know about you," I say, "but I intend to survive long enough to leave this place. I've already had enough of dying."

Katya's eyebrows knit together. "Already had enough? Wait, do you mean you've actually already died—"

"Nine times," I whisper, the words like thorns in my mouth.

Her eyes widen nearly past their sockets. "Nine times?"

As incredulity mottles her face, and the others turn to me with identical expressions of shock, I explain: "I was subjected to the Death Mandate before I came. Only they couldn't find my final death, so they tried again and again—" I cut myself off. "I don't want to experience that again. I don't want more deaths, more pain – I want to have a life, a real one this time. A happy one... But to do so, I have to survive. We all do."

I glance from one girl to the other, take a deep breath to summon my courage. "Karmoko Thandiwe said that we were bloodsisters, so let's help each other. If we're to survive the next twenty years, we have to do so together, not just as allies but as friends – family..."

I extend my hand, my heart lodged in my throat. "Bloodsisters?" I ask, a thousand thoughts barraging my mind. What if I'm asking for too much? What if they turn away, scorn me the way everyone in the village did, what if they—

A soft hand settles over mine. "Bloodsisters," Britta declares when I look up, startled. She grins. "Now and for ever, but ye already knew that, Deka."

As I nod, relieved, Katya leans forward as well. "Bloodsisters," she whispers. "I know we just met, but if you're going to join together, I want to be a part of it."

I nod, returning her anxious smile.

It's the twins' turn, and for once, they seem almost serious as they look at each other and shrug. "Might as well," they say to each other, placing their hands over ours. "Bloodsisters," they declare together, smiling at me.

Warmth spreads over me, a glow of happiness. They're actually saying yes – all of them. As I grin, another hand settles unexpectedly on mine. Belcalis's.

"Bloodsisters," she says, mouth tight as the others smile and embrace her.

Just like that, we're bonded.

Bloodsisters.

Happiness sparking inside me, I pick up a handful of rice and begin eating, careful to pick around the chicken bits. I have to build up my strength. Survival is hard work, after all. And so will be finding the truth about Mother's past.

TWELVE

I t starts with a sea of unwavering black, ancient yet familiar. I'm floating inside it, warm, motionless. Voices, female and powerful. They call out to me. "Deka…" they whisper.

One of them almost sounds like Mother.

I turn towards the voices, not at all startled to find a golden light shimmering in the distance. A door, waiting for me to open it. As I swim over, weightless in this vast sea, I hear something else—

"Raise your lazy arses, neophytes!"

I gasp awake, blinking in the darkness, as two novices rush into the common bedroom, shoving girls off their beds if they move too slowly. There are more novices in the hallway, their shouts timed by the frantic beating of nearby drums.

"Wha—huh, wha—?" Britta snuffles, jerking upright.

"We have to get ready," I say, almost wrenching her out of bed. The novices have positioned themselves just in front of the doorway. One of them is the scarred girl from last night, the other a plump, almost cherubic-looking brown girl with dark, loosely curled hair. Both are wearing dark blue robes –

a uniform, just like the green ones we were given yesterday.

"Morning greetings, neophytes," the scarred girl barks.

"Morning greetings." My reply is as uncertain as the other girls' when we gather around her.

She takes a step forward. "I am Gazal, your honoured elder bloodsister. You will refer to me as Honoured Elder Bloodsister Gazal, or Honoured Senior Bloodsister. All other forms of address will not be tolerated."

The air immediately thickens, tension rising until the plump girl steps forward. Compared to Gazal, she's warmth and sunshine personified as she grins at us. "I am Jeneba, your honoured elder bloodsister," she says cheerfully. "I hope in time we will become friends."

My tension begins to ease. Jeneba seems like one of those happy people who get along with everybody.

I barely have time to nod back at her before it's Gazal's turn to speak again. "Jeneba and I have been tasked with overseeing this common bedroom," she explains. "Together, we'll lead you through your first week at the Warthu Bera and, in time, your entire tenure in this training ground… That is, if you survive it."

As a tense silence falls, all the neophytes glancing at each other uneasily, Jeneba steps forward and claps her hands for attention. "All right, neophytes, you have fifteen minutes to clean yourselves. Go! Go! Go!"

Her words are like a lightning bolt, sending girls rushing towards the cleaning chamber as fast as they can. I hurry along, not wanting to get left behind, but when I catch sight of the chamber's polished bronze mirrors and ten stone sinks with water jugs and other bathing supplies carefully laid out on them, I slow, awed. In Irfut, the only sink I ever saw was the one in the temple, and that was reserved for men. I stop in front of one, gasping when I see my hair has already grown back into a fluffy little cloud. It's the same with all the other neophytes, but I'm only noticing now because I'm not as disoriented as I was when I woke. This must be an effect of alaki healing. Finally, a benefit to being impure.

"Fourteen minutes," Jeneba calls out.

I jolt back into action, wiping my face with the cloth and water. When I'm done, I glance at the small stick of wood beside my water jug, perplexed.

"Wha is that?" Britta whispers, voicing the question that's on the tip of my tongue.

"Chewing stick," Belcalis answers, using hers to scrub her teeth.

I hurriedly do the same, gasping when an icy-cool flavour explodes in my mouth. No wonder Hemairans prefer these to the cloths we use in Irfut to scrub our mouths clean. Once I'm finished, I scramble to put on my green robes and leather sandals, and by the time the drums sound again, I'm dressed and ready to follow Jeneba to the courtyard.

It's still dark by the time I emerge – only a few dim torches light our path. Even then, it's nice and warm, the early morning air balmy with the scent of exotic flowers. For a moment, I remain where I am, savouring the feeling. Sunrise was always chilly in Irfut. This heat should be uncomfortable for a Northerner like me, but somehow, it feels perfect.

The umbra carved into the archway seems to glare at me as

I walk under it, a reminder that I have to read the Heraldry of Shadows to discover whatever I can about Mother's past. I make a mental note to ask Jeneba where it is. She seems nice, compared to the other novices.

Karmoko Thandiwe is standing calmly before the statue of Emperor Gezo, Gazal at her side, when we reach the courtyard. The novice has one hand behind her back and the other across her heart in rigid military posture. She looks even more intimidating now than she did when she woke us up this morning.

"Good morning, neophytes," Karmoko Thandiwe calls out, that muscular body ramrod straight, red-clay braids gleaming in the darkness. "I hope you've had a good sleep."

We look at each other. "Yes, Karmoko," we reply.

Karmoko Thandiwe smiles. "Still not quite right."

Gazal steps forward and slams her folded hand across her heart. "Neophytes, when in the presence of the karmokos, stand at attention!" She demonstrates. "Back straight, right hand across heart, left behind back!"

We quickly do as we're told, Jeneba checking us to ensure our compliance. The other novices assigned to the different common bedrooms help their own portions of the line. As they inspect us, I see movement in the upper windows. The matrons are watching. This, apparently, is entertainment for them.

Once we're all standing at attention, Karmoko Thandiwe addresses us: "In order to be warriors, you must be strong in body and spirit. That starts with running. Every morning."

My eyes bulge.

Running?

Women aren't allowed to run in Otera. Any girl caught walking faster than a sedate pace is whipped for her insolence. "Light and graceful are the footsteps of the pure woman," the Infinite Wisdoms cautions. The reminder sends a subtle nausea roiling through my stomach.

"Let's go, neophytes!" Gazal barks, jolting me from my thoughts. "Move it!"

She demonstrates by jogging down the path at a quick, steady pace, the other novices behind her. The other neophytes and I tentatively do the same, huffing and puffing as we struggle to control our breathing and the burning in our leg muscles. By the time Gazal finally stops at the bottom of the first hill, I'm so exhausted I lurch over, hands on my knees to steady myself.

"All right, neophytes," Gazal barks, seeming almost energized now as she addresses us. "Your bodies should be fully warm. Time to double the pace!" She darts back up the hill, moving even faster than before.

I shake my head, horrified. "I can't go any faster," I rasp to Britta between breaths. "My legs are on fire."

Britta's breathing is just as ragged as mine. "Me neither."

"Oh, stop complaining," Adwapa proclaims breezily, running past us.

She and her sister are the only ones who seem unfazed by the fact that we're running. Then again, they're Nibari – their tribe only ever pretends to obey the Infinite Wisdoms when priests or emissaries venture into their deserts. At least, that's what Mother always told me.

There must be truth to her words, because Adwapa's almost

skipping as she declares, "It's only a light run. Back home, we used to run for miles."

"In the heat," Asha adds. "On top of mountains."

"Then why don't ye just run yer arses back to yer mountains and leave us here to die," Britta snaps. Then she wheezes, instantly regretful. "I'm sorry, I didna mean that. I'm so tired. I think I'm going to die me first almost death from this."

I nod in weary agreement. "That's the truth if I've ever heard it," I say, reluctantly beginning to run again.

This second round is even worse than the first, my muscles blistering under the pace. To my astonishment, however, the longer I run, the easier it gets. It's almost as if my muscles are gaining power, stretching to their fullest potential. Soon, my discomfort is a thing of the past as I zip up and down the hills, my feet barely touching the ground. The scenery around me begins to ripple – soft, shimmering waves, as if the trees are underwater. Air distorts, sounds become more distinct – I've stepped into a completely different world, one where everything is sharpened to brightest clarity.

I grin from ear to ear when a dewdrop descends slowly before me, its crystalline beauty easily perceptible with my sharpened vision. I've never felt this happy before. Never felt this free.

"Is this what birds feel like?" Britta shouts excitedly. "No wonder they never wanted us to run."

And I stumble, the reminder as piercing as an arrow. The Infinite Wisdoms forbids running, as it does most things that don't prepare girls for marriage and serving their families. Girls can't shout, drink, ride horses, go to school, learn a trade, learn to fight, move about without a male guardian – we can't do anything that doesn't somehow relate to having a husband and family or serving them. Elder Durkas always told us that's because the Infinite Wisdoms were trying to show us how to live happy, righteous lives.

What if they were meant to cage us instead?

I force the thought back, guilt flooding through me. The way of the faithful is trust and submission – how many times has Elder Durkas told us that? I may not understand it now, but Oyomo has a greater plan for me. All I have to do is submit and have faith.

Even though I'm here, doing things that go against the teachings, I have to believe that Oyomo understands my heart, that he sees that I'm trying my best to be faithful.

I will submit. I will be faithful.

I won't think any more dangerous thoughts…

Gazal finally leads the way back to the courtyard. The moment we reach it, I buckle to the ground, suddenly too exhausted to remain standing any longer. The others do the same, but they're laughing and giggling as well, savouring the discovery they've just made, the joy they've just felt. The joy I'm still trying to forget.

Oyomo, forgive me. Oyomo, forgive me.

It's not right, the euphoria I felt while running. I must cast it from my thoughts.

I'm almost grateful when Gazal glares at us with her usual cold expression, distracting me from my thoughts. "That's enough for this morning's warm-up, neophytes," she says. "Make your way back to your rooms. You have twenty minutes to clean yourselves and change into the clothes you have been given, then ten more for breakfast. Lessons start promptly."

That's the only information she gives before we hurry back to our rooms.

THIRTEEN

"Look, there's Jeneba," Britta says, pointing to the cheerful Southern novice as we stream outside later in the morning.

By now, I've washed, dressed, and eaten the breakfast of oats and honey the assistants set out for us. The accompanying sausages, I gave to Britta, since the smell of them turned my stomach.

I don't think I can eat meat any more.

"Ye wanted to ask her about the Heraldry, remember?" Britta says, before hurrying towards her. "Honoured Elder Bloodsister Jeneba! Honoured Elder Bloodsister Jeneba!"

Jeneba turns towards us. "Neophyte Britta," she says. "Is something the matter?"

"No, just got a question for ye, Honoured Elder Bloodsister – the *Heraldry*…where is it?"

"In the Hall of Records next to the library on the upper floor." She pauses, glances at Britta. "Was it your mother or grandmother who was a Shadow?"

"Mother – possibly," I say, drawing her attention to me.

One of her eyebrows raises. "So it's for you, Neophyte Deka. How intriguing. Well, good fortune to you getting there." When Britta and I glance at her, confused, she explains: "Neophytes are allowed into the library only on free days, and you get those only after the first three weeks are ended. So again, good fortune to you, neophyte."

The moment she's gone, I whirl to Britta, horrified. "Three weeks? I can't wait that long." Who knows what will happen between now and then? What if we start training with deathshrieks? The novices told us at breakfast that they didn't do so until their third month at the Warthu Bera, but that was because they were training only for raids against local deathshriek nests.

Now that the deathshriek migration is upon us, everybody's preparing for the campaign, which means we'll be trained even more intensely than they were. I wouldn't be surprised if we had to spar with deathshrieks starting this week.

"There has to be another way – there has to!" I say to Britta, panic rising. What if my eyes change colour again in their presence? What if someone sees, exposes me?

Dread chokes me as I think of what could happen: the karmokos forcing me into the caverns beneath the Warthu Bera to conduct tests the way the elders did back in Irfut, the jatu dragging me away to be executed again and again. I can't do that again, I can't! I have to learn about Mother, find some method to control whatever ability is growing inside me.

Right now, the Heraldry is the only hope I have.

I try to calm my thoughts as Britta replies: "There will be, Deka. We just have to search for it. Besides, isn't it a good thing ye can sense the deathshrieks?"

I still. "What?"

"Think of how useful it'll be when we go on raids an' such. It could be very valuable. We could use it on raids, spot the deathshrieks before they ever appear. It might give us an advantage." Britta shrugs, completely unaware she's just upended my entire world view.

Valuable...

All this time, I've been terrified of my ability. But what if it's a useful weapon – a sword to unsheathe when the situation requires. And Britta saw so easily what I could not, accepted so easily what even my own family couldn't.

Tears sear my eyes and I blink them back.

I watch as she continues: "Perhaps instead of tryin' to hide it, ye should try to master it. Control it."

"You have a point," I finally manage to say.

"I do, don't I?" She seems very pleased with herself. "Let's find out what we can about yer mother, an' then we can start training...after we finish these first few weeks, that is." She pulls me onwards, following behind the line of other girls.

Our first lesson for the day is in a small, plain wooden building that sits in the middle of the hill. The sun has only just begun to stretch itself in the sky, but it's already hot when we enter. Karmoko Huon is sitting cross-legged on a reed mat, a pale-yellow half mask covering her from forehead to nose, waiting for us. This morning, she's wearing a pretty blue robe embroidered with pink flowers, and her hair is held up by an ornately jewelled comb. A pair of heavily armed jatu stand behind her, arms folded menacingly.

"Find your seats, neophytes," she says in her soft, calm

voice, pointing at the reed mats that have been laid out in two orderly rows.

Britta and I look at each other, then quickly do as we're told, dipping a knee in greeting to her before hurrying to the mats at the very back, along with the twins, Katya, and Belcalis. As I settle into a kneel, I'm dimly aware of Gazal glowering at us from the shadows, where a few other novices have taken their seats. There are about five or six of them, but Gazal and Jeneba are the only ones I recognize.

Karmoko Huon claps her hands. "Welcome to your first combat class, neophytes," she says. "I am Karmoko Huon, and I will teach you to use your body as a weapon. It is a pleasure to make your acquaintances." She bows formally to us.

We all look at her, unsure of how to reply to this new greeting.

"Bow to the karmoko!" Gazal barks.

When we quickly try to comply, fumbling in our attempt, Karmoko Huon holds up her hand. "I think, Gazal," she says, amused, "we have to demonstrate first." She turns to us. "Like this," she says, touching her head to the floor. "This is how you greet your karmokos when you are on the mat. Now you try."

We quickly replicate the bow.

Karmoko Huon's mouth quirks. "Good. Not perfect, but good."

We turn to each other, relieved. "At least we didna completely disgrace ourselves," Britta whispers to me out the corner of her mouth.

I suddenly wonder whether the recruits are having the same troubles we are. Not likely.

A memory of Keita's sword-calloused hands rises, and I shiver it away, turn back to Karmoko Huon as she gracefully rises. "Now, then," she says decisively. "In order to engage in combat, you must first know your forms. Forms are battle stances – each one a tiny part of the dance you will soon become intimately familiar with. The dance of death."

My eyes narrow. How is a dance going to help us fight deathshrieks?

On the other side of me, Adwapa scoffs under her breath, "Dance of death. She's going to get us killed, this one."

A hairpin slams into the wall behind her, something pinned underneath it. A piece of flesh, golden blood still dripping from it. Adwapa turns, sees it, and her eyes widen with shock.

"My ear!" she gasps, holding her left ear. The top half of it is gone.

Karmoko Huon smiles mildly, rearranging the portion of her hair that's now fallen from the rest of her pins. For the first time, there's a look of steel in her gaze, the power hidden behind that ornamental exterior. She calmly stretches out her hand towards Adwapa. "I seem to have lost my hairpin, neophyte. Can you fetch it for me?"

Clutching her bleeding ear, Adwapa slowly retrieves the pin, then, trembling, hands it to Karmoko Huon. The karmoko smiles gratefully and dismisses her with a nod. Once Adwapa's returned to her seat, Karmoko Huon turns to the rest of the class. "Shall we continue?"

"Yes, Karmoko," we quickly say, still in shock.

Karmoko Huon nods, rises. "I shall now demonstrate the first form."

She plants her feet apart and shifts her weight so it's concentrated on her lower body. When she spreads her arms in a graceful but precise movement, her expression stern, something inside me trembles. Karmoko Huon reminds me of White Hands: pretty on the outside, deadly on the inside.

"In the Immovable Earth form, you are centred, at your most powerful," she says. "You are in the perfect position to attack, or evade." She demonstrates quickly, her movements precise but fluid. "I will show you."

She beckons to the larger of the two jatu behind her – a hulking beast of a man – then bows formally when he approaches. He quickly bows as well.

He launches into an attack, and we all watch, rapt. How will the karmoko handle this head-on attack? To my surprise, Karmoko Huon flips him on his back before he can even touch her, then twists his wrist to an odd and painful angle.

"Yield! I yield!" the jatu cries out, his eyes bulging from the pain.

The karmoko tuts, but her eyes are as cold as icicles. "First lesson, neophytes: alaki do not yield. You conquer or you die. For an alaki – for any warrior – death should be a familiar friend, an old partner you greet before you step onto the battlefield. Do not fear it, do not shy from it. Embrace it, tame it to your will. That is why we always say 'We who are dead salute you' to our commanders before we ride off into battle."

A strange, uneasy feeling builds inside my gut. Death should be a familiar friend… I can barely fathom the concept.

Karmoko Huon finally releases the jatu's hand and bows to him again. "My thanks for your aid," she says sweetly. The burly man gives a pained nod, then limps off, wincing.

By now, we're all quiet, tense. Karmoko Huon turns to us. "Do you know why I chose to demonstrate that move with him, neophytes?" she asks.

We shake our heads slowly.

"Because I wanted to show you that size does not matter," she explains. "No opponent is infallible, no matter how big he is. Deathshrieks may be bigger, but no matter how frightening they seem, how intimidating they may be, you are just as strong, just as fast – especially when you enter the combat state, which you experienced this morning when you ran and your senses became heightened, your reflexes sharpened.

"We will explore this more as time goes on. For now, let us continue the lesson."

FOURTEEN

"**R**aise your lazy arses, neophytes!"

I don't need this aggressively shouted reminder.
Two and a half weeks in, the schedule is second nature to me
now, so I'm already washed and dressed by the time Jeneba
comes to lead us to the courtyard. The recruits are waiting
there, the leather armour on their bodies gleaming under the
flickering light of the torches.

I blink, startled by the sight.

I haven't seen any of the recruits since the day we were
matched in Jor Hall. Heard them training, of course, their
voices carrying over the wall. But even on lunar days, when we
all have a full afternoon to ourselves, we haven't crossed paths
– not that I expected it. Unlike us, they're free to go into the city
that day, free to mix with the people beyond the Warthu Bera's
walls, as are the assistants and matrons. The only people who
never leave the Warthu Bera are the alaki – not that we're
allowed to roam inside the training ground either. I've
confirmed this trying to enter the Hall of Records the last two
lunar days.

Assistants and matrons constantly guard the corridors, ready to greet any alaki who strays off the beaten path with the barbed end of their rungus. Just as Jeneba said, neophytes are not allowed in any of the restricted areas until our first three weeks end.

Thankfully, they're almost over.

In three days exactly, I'll enter the Hall of Records. Then I'll read from the Heraldry of Shadows and answer the questions that have been plaguing me ever since I entered this training ground.

I can almost imagine it now, seeing my mother's name there, reading about her life, her deeds, learning about her abilities – about mine as well.

Anticipation races through me at the thought.

As I savour the feeling, golden eyes meet mine across the courtyard. I stiffen, unnerved, when Keita nods at me, his expression cold as it was the first time I met him. The novices are directing us to merge lines, so I reluctantly shuffle towards him, grateful that my hair has already regrown to its former length, courtesy of my alaki healing. I'll have to cut it again soon. It interferes with training. Most girls have taken to hacking theirs off every morning like the novices do, and some, like Adwapa, keep their heads perfectly bald.

Once we're standing side by side, Keita nods down at me. "Morning greetings, Deka," he murmurs.

"Morning greetings," I reply, fighting the urge to duck my head. Just as before, I feel uneasy when I'm near him. Something about him makes me remember Ionas and what happened the last time I got close to a boy.

Maybe it's his height. He's just as tall as Ionas, and that's no common thing.

I forcibly return my attention to the front of the courtyard as Karmoko Thandiwe steps forward, dark-brown skin gleaming against her clay-daubed hair. This morning, she's wearing midnight-blue robes and a half mask painted darkest onyx. All the other karmokos behind her and Captain Kelechi wear similar masks, as they always do whenever men are about.

I don't envy them. I can only imagine how impractical those masks would be during training, with all the sweating and dirt we have to deal with.

"In the past two and a half weeks," Karmoko Thandiwe announces, "you have learned the basics of speed, strength, weaponry, and combat. Today, you will begin training in pairs, starting with your daily run. Remember, you are partnered from now on, and you must account for each other's strengths and weaknesses. Understood?"

"Yes, Karmoko," I shout along with the other girls.

She nods at Gazal, who steps forward, her uruni, a slim, blond Northern boy, just beside her. "Let's go, neophytes, move your arses!" she commands, setting off in a quick jog.

I follow behind her, easily keeping pace. Over the past few weeks, the run has become my favourite part of the day. I can already notice the air slowing around me as I move faster up the hill, muscles loosening, senses coming alive. I'm slipping into the combat state, much more easily than when I first arrived.

I turn to glance at Britta, about to chat with her, as always, but she isn't there, and neither are the other girls, now that I'm looking. They're all at the bottom of the hill, shuffling at least five steps after the recruits, even though their muscles must be spasming and twitching from the effort of running so slowly. They're doing exactly what they would have done in their home villages – holding themselves back so they don't show up any potential husbands. But the Warthu Bera isn't a home village, and there are much greater dangers here than upsetting a few boys. The memory of the corpses in Irfut's snow flashes across my mind and I dig my nails into my skin.

I dart over to Britta and the others, not caring when the recruits stop and watch, astounded by my speed. "You can't slow down for them," I say. "You have to make them keep up with you."

"Deka," Britta whispers. She glances at the gawking recruits, embarrassed. "Ye can't let them see ye like that – in the combat state an' such. It'll frighten them."

The other girls around her nod in agreement.

"She's right," Katya says.

"Frighten them?" I can't believe what I'm hearing. "Do you think we're here, learning all these new things, endangering ourselves, just for the sport of it? There are deathshrieks outside these walls, and they will kill us if we don't learn how to fight them. We will *die* out there."

Memories bombard my mind, sudden and violent. The gold, the blood... I gag, nearly tasting it dripping into my mouth, the way it used to do.

"Have you ever died, Katya?" I ask.

She blinks. "Well, no—"

"It's agony, greater than you've ever felt, and if it's not your true death, you wake up dreading that it'll happen again. Then,

153

after it happens multiple times, you begin wishing for a true death – a final death, just so you never have to—" I break off, shaking from the force of my emotions. Tears are blurring my eyes, and a few drop down before I can stop them.

I have to take a breath, calm myself, so I can look back at my friends – at the other neophytes now gathering behind them, their eyes wide with horror. The majority of them haven't faced death yet. They came from towns and villages near the capital and were taken to Jor Hall immediately after their Rituals. Whenever we have discussions about how we came to the Warthu Bera, they always say the transporters were already waiting in the temples.

They've never experienced the icy coldness of a sword as it slices into the flesh, never had to endure those long and terrifying moments before merciful oblivion.

It was only the ones like Belcalis and I – the alaki so far from the capital, it took transporters months to reach us – who were unlucky enough to experience the Death Mandate and the terror that came with it. But we both survived somehow. Unlike all the girls who didn't make it past their first two or three deaths, we both lived.

And we have to honour that.

I breathe back the memories as I turn to the other girls. "Our whole lives, we've been taught to make ourselves smaller, weaker than men. That's what the Infinite Wisdoms teaches – that being a girl means perpetual submission."

That's how it was back in Irfut, me always accepting everything because I thought it was Oyomo's will. Was it Oyomo's will, the village turning its back on me, the elders dismembering me so they could sell my blood? Was it His will for them to cut out my tongue so I couldn't scream? What about all the things in the Infinite Wisdoms, the rules against running, laughing too loudly, dressing in certain ways – all of it His will?

"The truth is, girls have to wear smiling masks, contort themselves into all kinds of knots to please others, and then, when the deathshrieks come, girls die. They *die*." I glance from one bloodsister to the other. "The way I see it, we all have a choice right now. Are we girls, or are we demons? Are we going to die, or are we going to survive?"

I've been trying so desperately to keep myself from thinking such thoughts; what does it matter if I'm here anyway, about to face death once more? What does it matter if we're all here, risking our bodies and lives in service to Otera?

The other girls stare back at me, eyes wide with fear, horror, but I remain silent, letting them decide for themselves.

I already know my answer.

I will not die here in this horrible place. I will not die before I discover the truth about myself. I'll survive, and I'll do so long enough to leave this place, long enough to find someone to love me who cherishes me the way Katya's betrothed did her. I just have to be brave for once. All I have to do is be brave for once.

I remove one of the pins from the side of my robe, stab it into my palm.

It stings, a sharp, searing pain, but I don't even wince. My weeks here have already made me tougher, deadened my skin. Gold begins dripping, and I wipe it across my chest, marking the same place they would have cut me during the Ritual of Purity. The blood gleams there, the cursed gold that I am now bleeding for my own cause – not anybody else's.

"What're you doing—" a girl begins, but I ignore her.

"I'm a demon," I declare, "and I will survive this to win my absolution and a life for myself."

"Me too." Belcalis's voice comes from behind me, and when I turn, she's there, holding up her bleeding palm as well, an expression in her eyes that tells me that she understands, that she feels the way I do. "I'm a demon."

"I'm a demon," the twins echo, chests glistening as they wipe bloodied golden palms across them. And now other girls are doing so as well.

Even Britta and Katya, who were so horrified at first, walk up to me with bleeding palms. "I'm a demon," Britta says, wiping her hand across her chest.

The recruits whisper to each other, confused, alarmed by this sudden and bloody display, but it's too late to stem the tide. "Demon. I am a demon," each girl declares, bleeding herself to display her golden blood. The blood we have so long been told is cursed. The blood that binds us to each other.

Before long, all the girls are standing together.

Bleeding.

And this time, when we run again, we don't hold back.

As I walk over for breakfast, an unwelcome presence falls in step beside me. Keita. "That was an interesting speech," he says, by way of conversation. "Human girls or demons. Clever way to motivate the others…"

I stop mid-step, trying to ignore the familiar high-pitched

shrieks echoing in the distance as I look up at him. We're standing next to the entrance of the caverns where the deathshrieks are kept, and they're agitated, as always.

"A word of warning, however," he says. "The commanders may not look too fondly on any of you embracing your heritage too keenly, Deka."

Fear shivers over me, but I exhale it away. I'm done being afraid. "Is that a threat?" I ask.

"No, a warning."

"Then I'll take it under advisement."

Something almost like a smile darts over his lips, and he steps closer. "You know, I'm relieved."

"Why?" I ask, curious.

He shrugs. "When we were partnered, I thought you were too delicate to be a soldier."

"Too delicate?" I echo, surprised. No one has considered me delicate since the moment my blood ran gold. "I'm an alaki," I remind him.

Keita nods. "That may be true, but not everyone is suited to killing deathshrieks."

"Are you?"

Keita shrugs. "I'm told I'm good at exterminating them," he says simply.

There's a look in his eyes, an absolute belief.

"I was worried you wouldn't be suited to it, that you would be a burden on the battlefield. Perhaps I was wrong, perhaps you will be able to withstand your fear," he says.

The calm assuredness in his eyes nettles me, but I know better than to show it.

Instead, I smile sweetly at him. "You know, I'm relieved too."

"Why is that?"

"I was afraid you were too pretty to get your hands dirty."

His eyes widen with surprise, and, for a moment, the side of his lips quirk. "Well, we're both full of surprises, aren't we?" he says as he walks away.

FIFTEEN

"I can't believe we're finally here!"

Britta's voice is high-pitched with excitement as we walk through the library; the dark, cavernous chamber on the topmost floor of the Warthu Bera, Katya, Belcalis and the twins at our side. With each step, my anticipation builds higher and higher. In just a few moments, I'll be there, standing before the Heraldry. Then I'll read from its pages, finally find the answers to the questions that have been plaguing me since the day I entered this training ground.

At least I hope I will.

There's always the possibility there are no answers in the Heraldry, and I've wasted everybody's time coming here. Perhaps I should have just bolstered my courage and spoken to Matron Nasra or Karmoko Thandiwe about my suspicions. It would have been so much easier than walking past these bookshelves, eagerness and dread lining the pit of my stomach. But no, Matron Nasra is hateful, and Karmoko Thandiwe is much too frightening to approach. Better to do this with my friends.

Britta doesn't notice my introspection as she continues: "Just think, in a few moments, ye could have all the answers ye seek."

"Or you could have nothing," Belcalis humphs, "because you created an entire farce out of nothing, and us being here, on our one lunar afternoon, is indeed a farce."

Trust her to always state my deepest fears out loud.

"Must you always be such a pissfart?" Katya tsks.

"Pissfart?" Adwapa stops and looks at her. "Did you just make up that word?"

Britta dimples. "I did. Rather fitting, don't ye think? It has a certain—"

"We're here." Katya nods towards the heavy wooden door before us: the entrance to the Hall of Records.

Isattu, the midnight-dark assistant assigned to our common bedroom, is organizing the scrolls on the shelf beside the entrance. She grins when she sees us, her smile filled with goodwill and cheer. Unlike most of the assistants and matrons, she was immediately assigned to the Warthu Bera when she became a temple maiden two years ago, so she has retained the happiness that would have been snuffed out had she had to serve priests.

"Ah, there you are, neophytes," she says, unlocking the door. "Right this way. As a reminder, you're never to speak about anything you read in this book to any outside person on pain of death. If you do so, remember the walls always have ears, especially when it comes to Shadows…"

I nod, trying to push back the chills rushing through me as she ushers us into a small, circular room, light filtering in through the heavy glass roof. Scrolls line the shelves attached to the walls, their edges aged and delicate, as if they've been here for hundreds of years. Flames flicker from the sconces, and an umbra has been carved into the floor. It's not the most interesting sight here, however. The large stone pedestal in the middle of the room is – or, rather, the thick leather-bound book on top of it.

Isattu walks over to it, opens the book. "You said your mother was twenty-five years old when she had you?" I nod and she explains: "Most potential Shadows are taken in for training when they're ten, so if you're sixteen now, your mother would have first entered the Warthu Bera about thirty-one years ago." She flips through the pages until she finds the one she's looking for. "You can start from here. Shadows are listed alphabetically according to their year, and each entry has two pages each. All right, then, I'll leave you to it."

Nodding, I approach the book. "The moment of truth…" I murmur, muscles tense.

"The moment of truth…" Britta smiles reassuringly at me.

I flip through the pages, names flying past – Aada, Analise, Binta, Katka, Nirmir, Tran… When I get to the U's, I slow down, my heart hammering in my chest. Mother's name was an uncommon name in Irfut, but what if it is the opposite here in Hemaira? What if there are several women with her name and I can't tell which one is hers? But, no – every Shadow has a different identification badge listed under their entry. I should be able to recognize it once I see it.

I continue flipping until finally, I'm at the last few names. Ua, Uda, Ukami, Una, Uzad, Uzma. I stop, flip the pages back, my breath short. I didn't see Mother's name. I flip again and again, but no matter how many times I turn the page, the result is the same.

"She's not there," I whisper, tears blurring my eyes. "She's not there." I walk to a corner and slump on the floor, defeat weighing on me.

All these weeks, I've been imagining finding Mother's name, getting answers to all my questions about what she was – what I am. But there are no answers, because she was never here. I made up an entire fantasy in my head to distract myself from the fact that I'm just a—

"Deka, look! She's here!" I jolt up as Britta calls excitedly to me. She's standing beside the book, pointing to a page. I didn't even notice her walk over. "I found her! She was here a year earlier than Isattu thought."

"What?" I gasp, surging up.

"'Umu of Punthun, nine years old, dark brown skin, black eyes, short brown hair, Othemne tribal markings, two on each cheek. Identification badge: Golden necklace, umbra inscribed.'"

I suddenly forget to breathe. "That's her…" I say raggedly, tears searing my eyes as I look down at the entry only a paragraph long. "She was here. She was a Shadow…"

The confirmation of everything I've suspected is too much to bear, and I begin crying, great big tears falling down my cheeks.

"Oh, Deka," Britta says, hugging me.

As she holds me, Katya reads on. "'Retired after fifteen years of service due to personal reasons.'" Then she stops.

"What else does it say?" I urge.

Katya shakes her head. "That's all there is."

All there is? My eyebrows gather. "That can't be all. What about what she was like? What she studied – did she have any special characteristics?"

"Special characteristics?" Katya frowns. "No, that's all it says."

"Let me see." I wriggle out of Britta's arms and look down at the entry, chest tightening even further when I see it's just as Katya said. There's nothing more. No mention of any abilities, no further entries, nothing.

My chest tightens again. What about the tingling, the ability to sense deathshrieks? What about the way my eyes and voice change when I'm around those monsters? I thought the Heraldry would have answers, but there are none here – nothing that can help me at all.

I'm right back where I started, and even worse, my first lessons with deathshrieks are only a few weeks away.

As I walk towards the armoury later that evening, I'm in such a mood that I don't even notice the smell of blood coating the air. It takes a scream – wretched and all too human – to return my thoughts to the present. Britta and I look at each other, eyes wide in the growing darkness. We both know what that scream means. A new raiding party must have returned from the outskirts of Hemaira without killing their required quota of deathshrieks. The novices who didn't kill their share are being flayed.

I've glimpsed it numerous times over the past few weeks: Matron Nasra peeling skin from novices' backs as easily as she would from a citron. I've seen the golden blood dripping, heard the pitiful cries of the girls unlucky enough to be punished, and then the silence, the awful, awful silence.

"Suffering makes demons stronger," the matron always explains, a macabre smile slicing her lips. If that's the case, all the alaki in the Warthu Bera must be hardened to the point of steel.

Another scream splits the air, and my hands clench into fists, the skin on them stretching so tight they could split. First, Mother's uninformative entry in the Heraldry, and now this. What more will I have to endure before this miserable day ends?

"Don't listen to it," Keita says, glancing at me as he marches onward, a bundle of wooden atikas – our long, flat practice swords – in hand. He and two of the other uruni are helping us return them to the armoury before they go back to their barracks. "Just push it to the back of your mind."

His words set my skin boiling with anger. Even though we've settled into an uneasy truce, Keita is not my friend. Very few of the boys are. After what happened during the run, they're wary of me and the other girls, frightened of our power. Now they know how much greater our strength is than theirs – and that it's only going to continue growing.

"Easy for you to say," I reply, turning to him. "You're not the ones being flayed."

"We're not the ones who can regenerate," Acalan, Belcalis's uruni, sniffs. A tall, burly Northerner, he has a sour, pious look that reminds me of Elder Durkas when he's feeling especially sanctimonious.

"Even if that were the case," Britta humphs at him, "which it's clearly not, ye lot still wouldna be punished, an' ye know it."

"It's true," Katya agrees. "They never punish the boys. Even when girls die."

"But Oyomo forbid a recruit tastes infinity," I add. "That's when every girl in the raiding party is flayed."

"So, what, you want us all to bleed now?" Acalan sneers. "You want us to suffer like—"

"Let's not argue," Surem, Katya's uruni, quickly interjects in his calm, gentle manner. He's the boy I once thought I'd matched with, the smiling, tattooed Westerner. "We're almost at the armoury. Let's just…"

I'm no longer listening to him. A sudden, panicked tingling is surging through my veins, and it only takes me a second to recognize the cause. Deathshrieks…but not the ones in the caverns under the Warthu Bera. Heart pounding, I follow my senses to the wall just beside us, where I quickly spot four horrifically familiar figures creeping down the stones, their white pelts gleaming past the mist wreathing their bodies.

Leapers: the deathshrieks that jump onto their victims and rend them apart using claws and teeth. They're really on the walls, just as we've been warned so many times they could be. The others don't seem to have noticed them yet.

They're much larger than the ones the novices use for sparring practice, these deathshrieks; their bodies muscled and healthy, their eyes alert in the darkness. So this is the difference between captive deathshrieks and free ones. I'd almost forgotten, but now my vision is sharpening, so I can see them clearer, and my ears are muffling everything else out, so I can hear their low, isolated footsteps. I'm already slipping into the combat state, just as Karmoko Huon taught us. I don't need a run to stimulate it: it's rising by instinct.

I put down the extra atikas I'm carrying, doing it slowly so as not to attract the deathshrieks' attention, aware of Keita's eyes darting towards me. This is the first time I've ever seen him so attentive outside combat practice. Perhaps he senses them too, feels the cold of their mists now creeping towards us.

"What is it?" he whispers.

I flick my eyes towards the wall. "Deathshrieks, four of them on the western wall, all leapers – huge ones."

Everyone stiffens, alarmed, but I quickly tally the odds. Six of us to four of them. But it takes three to four girls to topple one deathshriek during a raid. And usually those girls have real swords.

"We're outmatched," Britta whispers. "We need to run to Main Hall an' raise the alarm."

Keita nods, his eyes squinted against the darkness as he tries to pick them out. Like the other boys, he can't see as keenly in the dark as we alaki can. "Everyone," he says, turning to the others, all of them stiff and tense now after my words, "I can't see them, so we run on Deka's mark. And we do so silently."

"But—" Acalan begins, bluster in his voice.

Keita sternly cuts him off. "We're the only ones out here, and we have no real weapons and no helmets to protect us against their screams. On Deka's mark," he repeats, nodding at me.

I glance at the deathshrieks. The first of them is just now stepping onto the ground. When it notices me looking, it glances

166

up, its eyes meeting mine. There's a look in them, a predatory intelligence. It opens its mouth.

"NOW!" I shout, taking off down the path.

A blur passes me, Katya already leading the way, her eyes wide with terror. "DEATHSHRIEKS!" she screams, panic making her disregard Keita's instructions. "DEATHSHRIEKS ARE ATTACK—"

A massive white form slams into her, sending her tumbling into the bushes. As she falls, the deathshriek goes after her, but Surem quickly blocks it, atika at the ready. The deathshriek hisses at him, teeth and claws bared in annoyance.

"DAMMIT, KATYA!" Keita growls, bolting over.

I do the same, shocked to find the other three deathshrieks splitting off behind us to head off the novices and recruits now running to answer Katya's call. *Why aren't they shrieking*, I wonder. We're the closest ones to them – why aren't they trying to attack us?

I barely have time to think this before the deathshriek in front of Katya moves, claws raking down to easily slice through Surem's wooden sword. He whimpers as it falls apart in his hands. The deathshriek raises its claws again, about to deliver the deathblow, but Katya lunges up, pushing him out of the way and then darting backwards.

For just a moment, I'm sure she's safe, sure she's evaded the claws. She's one of the fastest girls in the Warthu Bera, after all. But then I hear the sickening crunch of bone, see the claws protruding out through her chest.

"Oh!" she gasps, eyes wide with surprise.

Her spine rips back, pulled out by the deathshriek's claws.

Time seems to suspend, my entire body caught in amber, as I watch Katya bleeding out through that gaping hole in her back. A strange blue colour is racing out of it – a shade of blue I've never seen on anything before. Her body twitches once, twice, then stills. I know, without having to ask, that she's gone. There's no golden sheen of an almost-death, no gilded sleep for her.

"Katya…" I whisper, my chest deflating, horror leadening my limbs.

I turn to the deathshriek, which remains where it is, watching her. It almost seems…surprised. Shocked that it killed her so easily. A low, deep feeling rumbles inside me, a heated volcano that turns my blood to fire and my breath to ash.

"GET AWAY FROM HER, YOU BEAST!" I rage, the words erupting from my mouth. My voice is layered, powerful now, as I repeat, "GET AWAY FROM HER!"

The deathshriek's entire body immediately goes rigid, its eyes rolling in its head. It staggers away, limbs jerking as if they're on strings. Adwapa and Asha swoop into the space it left, quickly plucking Katya's body up. The moment they do so, exhaustion crashes over me, a wave of tiredness muffling everything around me, dulling my senses to their lowest. All I see is flashes: the other deathshrieks grabbing the staggering one and then running back over the wall the way they came; Adwapa gently resting Katya's body on the ground as novices and karmokos finally arrive; Surem rushing to Katya's side, tears in his eyes.

Karmoko Thandiwe gestures for the novices to pull Katya's body away from him. "Who raised the initial alarm?" she asks, glancing around.

"Deka did," Britta replies. "Then...Katya." She stops, her voice breaking.

I ignore her, my eyes fastened on Katya's corpse, on that horrible blue colour seeping from her spine. Just a few moments ago, she was darting in front of me, long red hair gleaming in the dark...and now...now... My entire body buckles, suddenly unable to hold up its own weight.

Even after almost a month here – a month seeing at least one alaki corpse return from every raid – I still didn't understand how easily we could die. After all, those were novices, older girls far removed me from me and my friends. But Katya – how could she succumb so easily? How could the deathshriek's claws strike true the very first time? As tears fall freely down my eyes and exhaustion weights my limbs, fingers snap, forcing me to look up.

It's Karmoko Thandiwe, frowning as she stares down at me. "Your eyes, Deka," she murmurs wonderingly. "Whatever's happened to your eyes..."

That's the last thing I hear before darkness reaches up to claim me.

SIXTEEN

"**I** saw what you did last night." Keita's voice is an unwelcome whisper in my ear.

It's evening and we're at the lake, observing Katya's funeral rites. Alaki aren't allowed burial in the ground, so we're burning her on the water, in a small boat we've turned into a funeral pyre. In the absence of a male guardian, Surem is in charge of her rites, and he reads solemnly from the Infinite Wisdoms. He'll be leaving Hemaira the moment the funeral rites have ended, returning to his home in the Western provinces. He can't take the thought of witnessing any more comrades' deaths.

I don't blame him. If I had the choice, I'd leave too. It doesn't matter that Mother was once here, that there are still questions I need answers to. I want to escape this place – want to run somewhere far away. But I'm bound to these walls, just as Katya was.

Her skin is the deep indigo of the summer sky now, and her long red curls flake in tiny patches as the fire flickers over them. She never cut her hair after that first day here, not even when it got in the way of training. I always thought the matrons would punish her for it, but they never did. It smells like apples as it burns away – the big red ones from the Northern provinces she once told me she was fond of. I don't know whether this is fanciful thinking or not, but it drives away the metallic odour of blood from my nostrils, the lingering memory of her ripped-out spine, the look in the deathshriek's eyes when I addressed it – the same look I saw in the Irfut deathshriek's eyes.

I inhale the smell to banish the horrible thought before I turn to Keita. "What do you mean?" I murmur. I'm so numb now, I'm not even afraid that Keita suspects me, that Karmoko Thandiwe likely does as well. What kind of life have I chosen that people die so easily? That friends die so easily?

One much better than what you had before... I stifle the unhelpful thought. I don't want to think practically right now, don't want to think about what happened yesterday, when the deathshriek stood over Katya, and I spoke—

Keita moves closer. "I won't tell anyone," he says. "And, if it helps, I don't think Karmoko Thandiwe will either."

This assurance does nothing to dull the twitchy, agitated feeling that's crawling over me. "What exactly is it that you want?" I ask, looking up.

If there's one thing being here in the constant presence of deathshrieks has taught me, it's that Britta was correct: my gift is valuable, which means other people will do awful things to get their hands on it. *On me.*

A memory of the cellar flashes through my mind: golden blood on the floor, the elders approaching, buckets in their hands. I push it away, wait for Keita to reply.

It takes him a moment. "The same thing I want from

171

everyone," he says, determination in his gaze. "To help eradicate the deathshrieks."

"What does that have to do with me?"

"Don't play stupid, Deka. Whatever that is that you did last night, it seems like it might be useful. I think we should explore it – in secret, of course." I nearly laugh at the irony. Just weeks ago, Britta suggested the same thing. I force myself to pay attention as he continues: "I don't think my commanders would take kindly to such things, much less the priests."

These last words, *the priests*, stoke my agitation, and that memory flashes again; Elder Durkas's hand, a knife inside it. I breathe to calm myself. "Why should I trust you? If you saw what you think you saw, why should I believe that you won't betray me to the priests or your commanders?"

He shrugs, golden gaze meeting my own. "There are monsters at our gates whose very screams can cause a person's eardrums to explode, and whose claws can saw through bodies smoother than a knife through butter. Don't you want revenge?"

There's a look in his eyes now – a bitterness. He isn't just talking about me, but also about himself, perhaps even the other uruni as well. "Aren't you tired of losing people to them? Always losing to them…"

I find myself nodding, anger abruptly boiling inside me. More images rush through my head: the attack on the village, all those corpses lying in the snow, then the cellar, golden blood pooling on the floor, and finally, Katya, claws piercing through her chest.

Deathshrieks have already taken everything away from me. What else am I going to let them take? I know I can command them – that I can force them to do my bidding. I need to learn more about my ability. Need to use whatever this thing inside me is to get back at those monsters. To get revenge for Katya.

"I am tired," I whisper, suddenly thinking of everything I've lost. Mother, Father, my life back in Irfut. I think of Katya, who only ever wanted to go home – to be a wife to Rian, have a family. "I'm so very, very tired."

Keita nods. "Me too, which is why I'll gladly swear my loyalty to you – protect you with my life – if what I saw you do can help us kill more of them." As I glance up at him, startled by this fervent declaration, he holds out his right hand. "I mean it. Partners – in truth, this time?"

I stare at his outstretched hand, confusion rising. No man has ever offered me his before, as if we were equals, but that's exactly what Keita's doing. Perhaps he truly does mean everything he's saying. Or perhaps this is a trick, one that could end my life. Either way, he already has his suspicions about me. Perhaps it's better that I ally with him, watch him for any weaknesses I might exploit. A devil's bargain, to be sure, but what isn't in this life of ours?

I take his hand, marvelling at how odd it looks against mine. Skin versus gilding, brown against gold. "Partners – in truth," I say.

This time, Keita squeezes my hand before he releases it. My breath catches, though I don't know why. Perhaps it's all the exhaustion.

SEVENTEEN

"See any changes?" Keita asks, his voice echoing off the damp, dark walls.

It's early morning, and we're in the caverns under the Warthu Bera, using the spare few minutes we have between lessons to test out our theory about my ability. The others are back in Karmoko Huon's lesson hall, still packing up from combat practice. I've warned them to stay away until I'm more certain about Keita. I'm still not certain what his motives are. As he stands lookout at the end of the passage, I stare down at a bucket of water, my skin tingling feverishly. Deathshrieks are caged in the next cavern over, and their muffled grunts and clicks are causing my blood to pool faster and faster, moving in tandem with all the mist now crawling around me. They secrete it whenever they're agitated, and they're always agitated down here.

I examine my reflection, then sigh. My eyes are still as boring and grey as they were ten minutes ago. "No differences," I say to Keita. I pick up the bucket to empty it, then stop – think. "What if I get closer?"

"What? No, they're not wearing their gags—"

"Just keep watch," I interrupt, rushing away.

The next cavern has been hollowed out into a makeshift stable, cages on either side. Lights flicker dimly in the sconces, illuminating the rushes on the floor, the chains binding each cell's monstrous occupant. Deathshrieks become more aggressive when they're in the same cage, so the karmokos separate them. There are about twenty here in total, the bulk of the deathshrieks at the Warthu Bera. About ten more are kept in the other caverns. My skin prickles faster, my heartbeat rises, as I approach them. The ones here aren't gagged, so a single scream from them could end me.

But no, that's not true. I remember how it was in Irfut, everyone's ears bleeding when I alone could continue standing. It was the same thing when Katya died. I could hear the shrieks, feel their power, but I wasn't affected by them the way the others were. I just have to concentrate on my breathing, keep my mind on the present the way Karmoko Huon taught me. I'll be fine.

Taking a deep breath for strength, I walk down the centre of the caverns, aware of the gleam of predatory black eyes, the rustling of chains, as massive bodies stretch in the corners. The heavy, pungent aroma clouding the cavern strengthens, as does a lighter, sickeningly sweet smell I cannot identify. I ignore the low growls, the fear rising inside me, as I walk over to the largest cage, the central one. A subtle hissing starts between the cages as this one's occupant slowly rises, distinctive, silvery quill-like projections on its back immediately recognizable from our first evening at the Warthu Bera. When it staggers forward, massive body shimmering in the dull light, my mouth goes dry.

Rattle, the alpha deathshriek of all the ones here.

The chieftain.

I look up at him, at those eyes gleaming with hatred towards me. "Go on – scream," I whisper. "I want you to."

Something has risen inside me, a dark and abrupt feeling I would almost call rage, except it's riddled through with the razor's edge of another emotion: grief. I think of Katya, think of those hateful claws ripping through her body, and I walk closer. Just out of reach of those claws. I'm aware now of the other deathshrieks stirring around me: velvety white leapers, their long-limbed arms allowing them to climb up their cages' bars with ease; the massively tall, massively gaunt workers at the corners making chittering sounds. Karmoko Thandiwe taught us how to classify them all, how to understand their weaknesses, their strengths.

I ignore them, focus on Rattle.

I know, from the karmoko's warnings, that he commands the other deathshrieks here. Deathshrieks are pack animals, always with a chieftain to direct them. They may lack human intelligence, but that doesn't mean they aren't smart.

"Why aren't you doing anything?" I ask him as he growls softly in the darkness.

He isn't making any movements, isn't reaching to attack me. It's the same with the other deathshrieks, all of them chittering away as they watch. Why aren't they attacking? Why aren't they fighting me? It's almost like they're duller, slower somehow, than the ones that killed Katya – or even the ones back at Irfut. Their lack of fight prickles at me. Enrages me.

"What's wrong with you?" I hiss, glaring at Rattle.

Suddenly, I don't care that I'm so close to his cage he could reach out and gut me, don't care that the matrons who attend to the deathshrieks could discover me down here and give me a beating for my insolence. All I can think of is Katya, that look in her eyes. The fear.

"Scream!" I rage. "Threaten me. DO SOMETHING."

But he does nothing.

That clicking sound rises, he and the other deathshrieks clicking at each other, their voices building and building until—

"Deka!" Keita's call comes as if from far away. "Deka, we have to go, the drums are sounding."

I exhale. Glance down at the water bucket, not surprised to see that my eyes are still normal in the reflection. I don't know why I was expecting otherwise.

I empty the bucket in a nearby trough, then inhale to compose myself. "Coming," I finally call back, as I walk out of the cavern. The deathshrieks continue clicking after I'm gone.

I emerge to find Keita waiting for me in the connecting passageway, worry in his eyes. The very sight grates at me. I don't know why he's pretending to care.

"What happened?" he asks. "Are you all right? Did they shriek?"

I shake my head. "Nothing happened. And my eyes didn't change – at least, I didn't see them do so in my reflection."

He nods, seeming to compose himself. "Well, that's disappointing," he murmurs.

We walk down the passage, each of us lost in our own thoughts, until something shifts in the shadows. It's Gazal, standing at the entrance to the next cavern, the one Matron

Nasra opened the floor to two months ago. It's our classroom for battle strategy, the class where we learn how to conduct raids and how to fight effectively during the campaign.

"Neophyte Deka," she says. "You will remain after the lesson. There is something Karmoko Thandiwe wishes to discuss with you."

This announcement sends a cold sweat down my back. Does the karmoko want to ask me about what happened that night with Katya?

I force myself to exhale away the panicked thought as I nod respectfully to Gazal. "Thank you for informing me, Honoured Elder Bloodsister," I murmur.

Satisfied, she walks into the main cavern, Keita and I following behind her. My muscles tense, senses on high alert, as I notice Karmoko Thandiwe standing at the centre, the other neophytes and their uruni already settling into the wooden desks before her. The lesson is about to begin.

Please don't ask me about what happened with the deathshrieks, please don't ask me about what happened with the deathshrieks, I desperately pray as Keita and I join the others.

Thankfully, Karmoko Thandiwe doesn't even seem to notice me as she walks to the front of the desks, a scroll in hand. She turns it towards us, displaying a picture, one that never fails to produce tremors of fear inside me. "You all know of the Gilded Ones, the alaki's infernal ancestors," she says.

I nod, reluctantly taking in the monstrous golden-veined beings depicted on the scroll. There's four of them: one so white she's glowing, another brown with a pendulous belly and protruding breasts, the third red and scaled over with wings like a dragon, and the fourth amorphous in shape and as dark as an inkblot. The sight of them fills me with unease. To think that I'm descended from them, from beings so frightening, so nightmarish of form. I may have come to terms with being alaki, but reminders like this still unsettle me.

I push back the thought as Karmoko Thandiwe hands the scroll to the neophyte nearest her, a short, doe-eyed Southerner named Mehrut. "Today, we will begin learning about the demonic heritage the Gilded Ones have left you and how to harness it against the deathshrieks," she says. "Open your scrolls to section three. Let's get started."

When the lesson ends, I remain seated, anxiety building. What does Karmoko Thandiwe want with me? I'm so tense, everything she taught us about alaki physiology has disappeared, replaced by a thousand horrific scenarios involving bloody rungus and questions about my true nature. My fears spiral higher and higher until Keita walks over, places a hand on my shoulder. I shiver from the surprising warmth of it, my thoughts abruptly calming.

"If Karmoko Thandiwe wanted to report you to the jatu, she would have done so by now," he says quietly, "so remember that before you panic."

I don't even know how he sensed my feelings, but I exhale. "I'll keep that in mind," I whisper.

He nods, heads for the door, but now the others have noticed I'm not following behind them.

"Ye not coming, Deka?" Britta asks.

"In a moment," I say, waving them away. "Save me dinner. Karmoko Thandiwe wishes to speak with me."

"What did you do?" Li, Britta's uruni asks. He's a lanky boy from the Eastern provinces, all smiles and easy manner.

"Nothing that I know of," I quickly say. Then I frown. "And why would you think I did something?"

Acalan humphs pompously. "Well, what else would it be? She never asks for you."

"Let's hurry and eat, I'm starving," Li complains.

"Yer always starving," Britta notes.

"A case of the river condemning the stream for rushing too fast, isn't it?" Li sniffs.

Keita turns to me, a silent reminder in his eyes: don't panic. "I'll save you dinner, Deka," he says.

I force myself to nod. "My thanks."

Their voices disappear down the hallway.

Now I'm alone with Karmoko Thandiwe in the large, forbidding cavern, tension worming its way through my insides as I watch her put away her teaching scrolls.

Finally, she turns to me. "Follow me, Deka," she says quietly.

I nod. "Yes, Karmoko."

My nervousness grows as she leads me out of the caverns up to a narrow stairway I've never seen before. Its sides seem to gather closer the farther up I go. What does the karmoko plan for me? Does she want to imprison me, study and bleed me? My thoughts whirl faster and faster until finally, I can't bear the anticipation any longer.

I stop, apprehensive. "Karmoko Thandiwe," I say.

"Yes?"

"Is this about before? About what happened with the deathshrieks?"

She turns to me with a frown, seeming confused. "Something happened when the deathshrieks came? I cannot recall." As I blink at her, perplexed, she steps closer, whispers in my ear: "If something did, however, happen then, I would be wise to keep it to myself, would I not? Just as I would also be wise to explore it at the most opportune time."

Shock washes over me like a wave.

She's not going to lock me away? Study me like the deathshrieks caged under the Warthu Bera? My muscles feel weak. My entire body feels unbalanced. "I don't understand," I say, looking up at her.

Karmoko Thandiwe shrugs. "I have no intention of hurting you, alaki. You are Umu's daughter, are you not?"

I blink, startled at this casual acknowledgment after all my weeks of skulking about. "You knew my mother?"

She nods. "She was four years my junior. An admirable Shadow. Ferocious, determined. A pity what happened to her. She could have been a legend among us, but then she got with child. You, I presume?"

I nod, then glance up at her. "So that's why she left? Because of me?"

She nods. "It was quite the scandal. Shadows are not allowed to marry, so an execution order was sent out. Luckily, she had some noble as a benefactor who protected her. Got her away in time. I can't imagine how she did it, running away in the last week of rainy season, flooding everywhere. I'm grateful she survived. How is she?"

"Dead," I reply, in a daze now. "The red pox."

Karmoko Thandiwe blinks before she nods again. Then: "Did she live a good life?"

"She was happy till the end." I look at her. "I have a question. Was she like me? Did she have any…abnormalities?"

"As far as I could tell, she was perfectly human." Karmoko Thandiwe looks down at me, her eyes piercing mine. "Truth be told, of all the alaki I've met in the two years since the emperor's mandate, I've met none like you."

"None other—" I stop mid-sentence when a familiar whistling pierces my ears. It's coming from the top of the stairs, where an open door leads to a small private garden beside the courtyard. "White Hands?"

"Is that what you call the Lady of the Equus?" Karmoko Thandiwe's eyebrows rise. She steps to the side, clearing space for me on the stairs. "She's waiting for you."

Gasping, I rush past her up the stairs and out into the garden, where White Hands sits on a mound of pillows. A feast is spread out before her, and the equus twins are curled at her side, stuffing themselves. The hazy-sweet scent from her water pipe curls around the garden, mingling with the warm evening air.

"The Lady of the Equus!" I gasp, hurrying over. "Braima, Masaima, you're all here!"

The twins look up from their meal of yellow apples and other exotic fruit. "Hello, Quiet One." Masaima grins fondly.

"Have you missed us?" Braima adds, rising.

I rush over, joyfully petting them, and then waiting as they nuzzle me. Masaima begins nibbling my hair, but I don't even mind it. "I've missed you both so much!" I say, hugging them.

How long it has been since I last saw them both, sweet-talking their way into eating all the apples in the wagon? I hug them even tighter, grinning when they hug me back.

"The world is so much more beautiful when we're around, is that not true?" Braima muses with a flick of his black-striped tail.

"Surely so, Brother," Masaima agrees. "We make all things better."

I blink to push back the tears burning my eyes. "Well, you've both certainly made my day better," I say, releasing them.

Then I turn to White Hands, nervous. If it wasn't for her, I'd still be in Irfut, still be in that cellar. And now she's here. Why is she here?

"Lady of the Equus," I say respectfully, walking over.

"White Hands will do," she replies with a wave of her hand. "I'm quite fond of that name, actually."

When I stop just short of her, uncertain of what to do next, she looks up at me, amused. "Tell me, is this awkward little approach how they teach you to greet your elders at the Warthu Bera nowadays?" she asks, taking an idle puff of her water pipe and blowing little smoke rings into the air.

"No." I dip a knee to the ground in the formal greeting the karmokos prefer outside of lessons. "Evening greetings, White Hands," I say.

"Evening greetings, Deka." She looks me up and down, then adds, "You've certainly become more exuberant these past days. The Warthu Bera must be good for you."

I shrug. "Somewhat," I say, thinking of Katya. "My thanks for sending Britta and me here."

I know now that had it not been for her intervention, we

would have probably been separated and sent to lesser training grounds, as so many alaki are. She's the one who decided that we were worthy of the Warthu Bera. And it was a good thing that she did. I have to blink away thoughts of what Karmoko Thandiwe told me about Mother. Something about what she said is still niggling at me, though I'm not exactly sure what.

"And how is our ever-cheerful Britta?" she asks.

I smile. "Even more cheerful, now that she's tossing boys across the sandpits."

"Exuberance must be in the air." White Hands puts down her water pipe, then nibbles delicately on a fruit. "Imagine my surprise when I hear that you of all people are now bleeding yourself and calling yourself demon. You, the alaki who nearly dissolved in a puddle of shame every time I said the words 'cursed gold'. I take it you're no longer unsure of the truth of my words."

My blush heats me all the way to the roots of my hair. I didn't know she knew I doubted the promises she used to lure me here. "No, I am not," I say truthfully. "The Warthu Bera is exactly as you promised. I am…no longer ashamed of what I am," I say. "No matter my origins, there is worth in what I am."

To my surprise, White Hands gives a full-throated laugh. "Well, that certainly is good to hear. And much better than you moping around in the wagon. It quite put me off my feed. Carambola?" She offers me a plate of the delicate yellowish-green fruits shaped like stars.

I shake my head. "No, thank you," I say respectfully.

"We'll take it," Braima says, a greedy gleam in his eye as his fingers reach.

"No use letting a good fruit go to waste," Masaima adds.

White Hands smacks their fingers. "Not for you," she says sternly. "You may go eat over there, test the figs on that tree." She points.

As the equus pout and canter away, she turns to me. "Here's a lesson for you, Deka. When someone – particularly your elder – offers you food, you eat. This is the way of the Southern provinces."

I nod and hastily take the plate. "My thanks, White Hands," I say. As I carefully sit across from her, I have a thought. "Why are you here? Did you bring more girls to the Warthu Bera?"

I glance through the garden gate over to the courtyard, where the moon shines down on the statue of the emperor. There's only one wagon there – the same one that brought us all the way from the North.

White Hands shakes her head. "No, the Warthu Bera has enough girls."

Now I'm confused. "Then why are you here?"

"Because I teach here, of course," she says.

"Teach?" I echo.

"The Lady of the Equus is being modest, so as not to impress you with her grand stature," Karmoko Thandiwe says as she walks towards us. "She oversees the Warthu Bera, in addition to all the other training grounds."

I feel my mouth slackening as I turn to White Hands. "You—"

"Oversee all the training grounds? Yes, I suppose I do." She shrugs, then places a slice of cheese on my plate. "Try this, it pairs excellently with the carambola."

I shake my head, still in shock. If she oversees all the grounds, that must mean she's a noble – only the rich and powerful are given tasks as important as that. "I can't eat with you," I say. "It wouldn't be respectful, you're—"

"Your new karmoko? Of course I am," White Hands finishes smugly. As my head whips from her to Karmoko Thandiwe, she continues: "I occasionally take on a student or two to prepare them for the most…demanding raids, which is, of course, why I brought you and Britta here. Although your friend Belcalis also fascinates me, as does the ever-angry Gazal."

I frown. "You know Belcalis? And Gazal?"

"Undoubtedly. I keep my eyes sharp for promising students. You four will be my first new trainees. Lessons start tomorrow."

"You'll report to her after dinner," Karmoko Thandiwe adds. "Promptly."

I bow to her. "Yes, my lady," I say.

"You mean, yes, Karmoko," White Hands corrects, smiling at me. "Well, that's that. Unless you want to remain here and smoke with us."

The very thought appals me. I rush upright. "No, Karmoko," I gasp, then I bow and scurry away, leaving White Hands in the garden, Karmoko Thandiwe standing behind her.

I'm halfway back to the common bedroom before I understand what bothered me about Karmoko Thandiwe's words. She said Mother ran away the last week of the rainy season. But I was born in the month of the silver wolven, more than ten months after that.

I've watched Karmoko Thandiwe recite entire passages from memory in class. She's always correct when it comes to dates. But the timing she gave me isn't humanly possible. If she's correct, Mother was pregnant at least a full month before she met Father. There's no way I'm his natural child. There's no way I'm natural at all.

So why am I turning her words over in my head, wondering if there's something there?

EIGHTEEN

When I arrive at the lake the next evening, White Hands is seated on a small carpet, a bronze goblet of the potent local palm wine in hand. It's been a warmer Hemairan day than usual, and the smell of night jasmine wraps everything in a haze of sweetness. The scent so intoxicates me, it takes some seconds before I see the weapons laid out beside White Hands, their metal glinting in the low evening light. Panic beats a heightened pulse in my veins, pushing away the thoughts that have been plaguing me all day – my conversation with Karmoko Thandiwe, my doubts about who my father is…

All I can see now is those weapons, gleaming sinisterly in the fading light. Neophytes are required to use wooden weapons for the first two months, and the end of my second month isn't even near yet. I'm only supposed to use metal weapons in the third month, as I prepare to go out on raids.

And yet here is an array of metal weapons, clearly meant for use.

A thousand questions suddenly flit across my mind. What exactly did White Hands mean when she said "the most demanding raids", and why has she chosen us four – Britta, Belcalis, Gazal, and I – to accomplish them?

I glance at the three other girls, not surprised to see that they all seem unnerved too, except, of course, for Britta, whom I told about White Hands's surprise arrival last night. "Evening greetings, Karmoko," she says with a wide grin, doing a quick kneel in greeting to White Hands.

White Hands's mouth quirks into a smile. "Evening greetings, Britta," she replies. Then she turns to the rest of us. "You're all on time. Wonderful. I hate latecomers, don't you?"

When we look at each other, unsure of how to respond, she rises, dusting herself off. She's wearing the sedate brown robes of a karmoko, and I'm not surprised to find they suit her even better than her old travelling blacks ever did. She walks over, nods at us.

"I am your new karmoko," she announces. "You may call me Karmoko, or Karmoko White Hands. I'm very fond of that name." She winks at me as she says this.

I quickly bow. "Evening greetings, Karmoko White Hands," I say, echoing the other girls.

"Evening greetings," she returns.

Then she spots us watching the weapons. "You've noticed my teaching tools. Wonderful. As you may have heard, I've specially selected you all to go on certain raids for the Warthu Bera, and as such, I feel there's no point insulting your natural abilities by giving you practice swords and weaponry to train with. The four of you are alaki, you can and already have faced worse – mostly." She glances at Britta when she says this, and Britta blushes, embarrassed at being singled out.

"That's why I have decided to hold these lessons. Now that I'm here, it's time I moulded the champions of this school."

"Champions?" Belcalis repeats.

White Hands doesn't answer. She's now walking over to Gazal, an expression of concern on her face. I frown as I see the same thing she has. Gazal's forehead shines with sweat, and her eyes are slightly unfocused. She's staring at the lake, as pale as a ghost. I almost wonder if she's sick, but alaki don't get sick. Once our blood begins changing, we become immune to most illnesses, our bodies healing them just as fast as it does everything else.

"You don't look at all well," White Hands says softly. "Gazal, is it not?"

"Yes, Karmoko." Gazal nods, her eyes flicking to the water.

As White Hands's eyes follow Gazal's gaze, a calculating expression surfaces. She casually takes the novice by the elbow. "Why don't we go over to the lake, cool you off."

"No!" The word barks from Gazal's lips, and she jerks herself out of White Hands's hands.

A quiet knowing rises in our new karmoko's eyes. "It's the lake, isn't it?" When Gazal doesn't respond, she repeats her words. "Isn't it, novice?"

Gazal reluctantly nods.

"Why?"

Gazal shakes her head frantically, that frightened expression taking over. My eyes widen, watching her. I've never seen her unnerved before. "I can't, I—"

"You have to say it in order to overcome it," White Hands insists calmly. "The lake can't change, and I certainly won't,

190

so whatever it is, you have to address it now, so we can move on with our lesson."

"Please," Gazal whimpers, her eyes fixed on the dark water.

"Please what?"

"Please, I don't want to be near that, I don't want—"

I've never seen Gazal so distraught, didn't even know it was possible. I suddenly feel deeply uneasy, as if I'm witnessing something I shouldn't.

"This isn't right," Britta whispers beside me.

I nod. White Hands likes to play with people, but this is a shade too far. Her expression is implacable now as she turns to Gazal. "Why don't you want to be near the water?" she asks, then adds, "I can't do anything if you don't tell me why."

Gazal only shakes her head, her eyes wilder. The thought of talking about it obviously terrifies her.

"Very well," White Hands says, grabbing her by the arm. She drags her towards the lake.

"No. NO!" Gazal shrieks, digging her feet in, but White Hands is unyielding. She keeps pulling Gazal closer and closer until finally, the novice can't take it any more.

"They locked me inside it!" she screams.

Gazal collapses, tears falling from her eyes. She's sobbing so hard, her entire body is wracked by the force of her cries.

"They locked me in a cage, under the lake! They thought I would die, but I didn't. I just kept drowning. I just kept drowning!" Tears are pouring down her eyes, and her whole body shudders. "Over and over and over and—"

White Hands grabs her up. "Who are they?" she asks.

"My family," Gazal sobs.

White Hands shakes her head. "Your bloodsisters are your family. Who are they?"

"The House of Agarwal," Gazal answers, confused. Tears are still pouring from her eyes.

White Hands grips her by the hair, pulls her along. "I said, WHO ARE THEY?"

I can no longer watch. "White Hands, please stop," I say, hurrying over. "You don't have to frighten her!"

White Hands turns to me, her eyes deadly calm. "Interrupt me, Deka – any of you interrupt – and I will deliver you pain such as you have never before imagined."

We all step back, horrified.

White Hands continues pulling Gazal by her hair, not even budging when Gazal fights so hard, her feet dig into the lake's muddy banks. She pushes Gazal down until her head is nearly to the water.

"WHO ARE THEY?" she roars.

"NO ONE!" Gazal wails, finally understanding. "They are no one, please, Karmoko! They are nothing to me any more."

This answer satisfies White Hands. She releases Gazal's hair, then walks back over and selects a sword. She looks down at it, her eyes considering the blade. "If you'd had a sword in those days, no one would have been able to do that to you."

She walks over, flings the sword at Gazal's feet. "You have one now. What will you do?"

Trembling, Gazal picks up the sword, looks from White Hands back to it. White Hands picks up the rest of the weapons and hands them to us, giving Britta the war hammer last.

Finally, she turns back to Gazal and nods. "You can come

at me, but that will be a very short venture. Or you can choose." She waves to us. "Choose an opponent."

I know, almost instinctively, whom Gazal is going to choose.

"Her," she whispers, her voice going cold as she points at me. "I choose her."

White Hands claps, delighted. "Excellent choice, novice! Deka is the perfect opponent for you."

Gazal approaches, murder in her eyes, and something stills in me – a subtle shifting as my senses sharpen. I take a step back, take a deep breath, and tighten my grasp on my sword. Gazal's out for blood – I can tell just by looking. Nevertheless, I'm ready for her. As Karmoko Huon always says, "First rule of combat: be prepared to engage at all times."

I widen my stance as White Hands nods to Gazal. "Have at her," she waves.

Gazal rushes me so fast, I move only seconds before her sword slices where my neck would have been. Surprise rips a gasp from my throat. She's not just out for my blood, she's out for my head, the easiest way to kill an alaki. But I'm prepared to die in combat, just as Karmoko Huon taught me. And, more to the point, I already know that beheading is not my final death. I use this reminder to breathe, to focus on tracking Gazal as she attacks me again, her assaults lightning fast. In her combat state, Gazal is like the wind – the fastest alaki in the Warthu Bera, now that Katya is gone.

That means I have to be smarter, or if I'm not careful, this lesson will end with her taking my head.

"Watch out, Deka!" Britta calls.

I whirl, following this cry to find Gazal already at my back.

I have mere seconds to jerk away before she can thrust her sword through my stomach. I dodge, but I'm still not fast enough. The sword slices into my forearm, and I wince, clenching my teeth against the white-sweet pain. Gold springs up, stinging the wound. I ignore it. I've felt worse pain than this, experienced much worse things. This is only a scratch, I tell myself.

White Hands laughs again, raising her cup in a toast to me. "Conquer or die, Deka. Either way, you learn your lesson."

Lesson… The word reverberates through my body, a reminder that I've had many other such lessons in the past month. Lessons aimed at teaching me survival – no, victory – against all odds.

Conquer or die…

I'm not dying again. Not today, anyway.

I look at Gazal, her body seemingly overtaken by the wildness shimmering in her eyes. There'll be no reasoning with her. No talking. Gazal needs to let out her pain, and I'm the one she's selected to do so. The only honourable thing I can do is fight. Win.

Conquer.

I lift up my sword. "Attempt me," I say.

Gazal does so with a scream. When she lunges, however, I whirl to the side and slam the pommel of my sword into her skull. She only barely manages to grab my sleeve before she slumps down, unconscious. It'll be at least an hour before she wakes up, judging from the size of the knot in her head.

White Hands walks over, clapping. "Splendid, splendid! Such quick thinking, Deka." I slump, my entire body shaking now. "Simply masterful. I knew I made the right choice."

"Choice?" This question comes from Belcalis. She's spent the entire battle in quiet contemplation, as is her habit. "Why her? Why us, of all the girls in the Warthu Bera, Karmoko?" she asks.

White Hands shrugs. "You have rage – deep wells of it," she replies. Then she points at a still-unconscious Gazal. "That one has pain – an entire lake's worth, as you just saw." It's Britta's turn now, and White Hands's finger points towards her. "That one is strong, loyal, and will do what must be done." As Britta blinks in surprise, White Hands turns to me. "And that one," she says. "That one is unnatural."

There it is again, that hated word. Unnatural. But I don't feel the shame and nausea I used to. Now I know my ability has value, my main reaction is curiosity. White Hands knows where my ability came from. I'd already guessed this back in Irfut, but now I know it for a fact. That's why she's using that word to describe me. It's not a condemnation but a truth.

"What do you mean, unnatural?" I ask. "What exactly am I? Am I even alaki?" This last question rushes out of me – a fear I've kept so deeply hidden, I've never even acknowledged it until now.

An amused smile curls White Hands's lips. "Are you even alaki?" She laughs. "What a silly question to ask, Deka. Of course you are. You're the most valuable alaki in all of the Warthu Bera." I frown at her, confused by this declaration, and she takes a step closer, peers down at me. "Of all the girls here, only you have the ability to command deathshrieks."

Even though I already knew this, the confirmation still comes as a shock. As do other realizations. If White Hands knows about my ability, then she was probably aware of what I was as far back as Irfut, might have been searching for me then. Which means she knew about me – knew what I was. Does this mean there are other girls like me? I'd dismissed the possibility, but now, I'm not so sure. All I know is that White Hands has the answers I seek.

"Are you the benefactor?" I blurt out.

All day I've been thinking about it, the mysterious benefactor Karmoko Thandiwe said helped Mother escape. I thought it was one of the karmokos at the Warthu Bera during that time, or perhaps even a jatu or an official, but what if it was White Hands? She's a noble – she has money, power, the ability to transport people wherever she likes.

"Are you the one who helped my mother escape the Warthu Bera?"

White Hands just blinks. "Your mother was in the Warthu Bera? Fascinating…"

She says it in that noncommittal way of hers, so I can't tell whether she's lying or not. All I know is that she knows more than she's telling. "What do you know about me? About what I am?" I plead.

She shrugs. "I know that using your power exhausts you. That you become vulnerable after using it. I know that you are valuable to us. To this fight."

Blood drums in my ears. Valuable to us? The way she says those words, looks so meaningfully at me – I know exactly what she's thinking. She intends to use my ability during the campaign. She intends to expose it for everyone to see. My muscles clench into knots, my breath comes in spurts. A primal wail begins building somewhere deep inside me, but White Hands clicks her claws, forcing my mind back to the present.

"I know you have questions, Deka," she says, "and I will answer them all before the campaign is over. But for now, know that I won't put you in harm's way."

Just like that, the wail dissipates, and I can breathe again. If there's one thing I know about White Hands, it's that she's a woman of her word, even though her intentions are always murky.

She turns to Britta. "You once asked me why you were chosen. It's for this – to protect Deka during her vulnerable periods, to keep her from being hurt during that time."

She points at Britta's war hammer. "With that war hammer, Britta, you will be Deka's protector."

Britta looks down at the hammer, her brows knitted in a frown. "That's why you took me," she says slowly. "That's why you brought us together..."

White Hands does not bother to deny it. "As the strongest representatives of the Warthu Bera, you four will be sent on the most difficult raids. The ones where the deathshrieks are more numerous or cunning, where the terrain is more unforgiving – the ones where Deka's voice is required."

She glances across our faces, her eyes finally resting on Britta. "Not only are you strong, Britta, you truly care for Deka, which is why she needs you. A protector to keep her safe. A friend to keep her sane in the horror of the coming months. Are you up to the task?"

I turn to Britta, my questions about White Hands pushed aside by an even more important emotion: fear. What if she's frightened of me? What if she hates me for putting her in such a dangerous situation? It's an irrational thought, I know, but the mere spectre of it is so painful, I can barely breathe.

But then Britta hefts the hammer and smiles. "Deka and I are bloodsisters. We belong together."

White Hands smiles. "I am glad to hear it." Now she turns to Belcalis. "And you, Belcalis of Hualpa, what are your thoughts?"

Belcalis snorts. "I don't know what all this nonsense about Deka's value is, but I just want to survive my term so I can leave this place. If Deka can help us defeat the deathshrieks faster, I'll protect her as well," she says, walking over to Britta and me.

Relief shudders through me, so sudden it almost makes my knees buckle. Belcalis doesn't hate me either. She's still my friend.

White Hands smiles. "I thought you might. After all, you, more than anyone else, understand the pain that Deka endured. It is the same that you endured. You, more than anyone else, understands what needs to be done."

Suddenly now, I remember the scars on Belcalis's back, the ones that once massed over each other, like a map. They've faded now, but I'll never forget them. Never forget that she suffered just as much as I did.

Belcalis nods curtly and White Hands continues: "For the meantime, keep Deka's secret between this group. Only you and the karmokos know, and we would like to keep it that way for now."

When the others nod, giving their word, she picks up a sword, considers it. "Now, then…which one of you wants to attempt me?"

NINETEEN

"Tell me about your dreams, Deka," White Hands says.

It's our fourth day of lessons at the lake. Our usual no-holds-barred combat has ended, and Britta, Belcalis and Gazal have returned to Main Hall, but White Hands asked me to stay afterwards, though she wouldn't tell me why. White Hands is very good at not answering questions. I should know, I've pestered her with enough of them. All she ever tells me is that she'll explain everything in good time, which is sometime before the campaign ends.

I suppose I just have to be satisfied with that for now. I could ask Karmoko Thandiwe instead, but I have the feeling she won't know anything near what White Hands does.

"My dreams?" I finally echo, confusion building. What do my dreams have to do with anything?

"You've been having nightmares," she says. "Recurring dreams as well." When she sees my shocked expression, she shrugs, smiles. "Don't look so worried. All alaki have such dreams. The unnatural ones especially. Tell me about yours."

I clear my throat, embarrassed. "It always starts in the ocean

– at least it feels like an ocean," I begin. "It's dark, but there are these…presences there. I don't know if they're different or all one thing, but they call to me."

"What do they say?"

"My name. They say my name, and they beckon me towards this…door. It's golden, all shining." I turn to her, biting my lip now. Almost afraid to speak.

"What is it, Deka?" she prompts.

"They use my mother's voice," I whisper. "When they call to me, they use Mother's voice. But I know it's not her. Mother's dead. Gone." The words surface some of that old pain, and I rub my chest to soothe it.

White Hands nods, seems deep in thought. "The door – have you ever been through it?" she asks.

I shake my head. "Never."

She turns to me, a strange expression on her face. "This time, when they call you, go," she says.

I frown. "But I don't control when the dreams—"

A sharp pain pricks my neck. All I see is the faint smile on White Hands face as she says, "Remember, when they call you – go."

Then everything turns dark.

Complete blackness, an ocean of warmth. It's the same as always, the same place I've been seeing ever since Mother died. Something stirs inside it, vast and ancient, but I'm not frightened. I've met it countless times before, felt its presence rolling inside me.

"Deka…" it calls, a rumbling in the waters.

It sounds almost like Mother.

But it's not her. It's lying to me, using Mother's voice like that. I swim in the other direction, trying to get away from it. Then gold suddenly shimmers, a door opening behind me.

"Deka…" the voice comes again, pleading this time.

It scratches a memory, a reminder of something important I'm forgetting. Something about that door. I turn, and there it is, golden and shining, growing bigger and bigger until it completely blocks my field of vision.

Enter it, Deka… The words filter, almost eerily, into my mind. An order.

I obey it now, swimming closer and closer to the gold until the door swallows me up and there's nothing left but that beautiful colour washing over me.

You can wake up now, Deka.

I gasp awake, obeying White Hands's voice, only to realize I've only done so halfway. I'm not really awake, and I'm not really here. That's the only explanation of why everything suddenly glows so brightly. It's dark around me, but all the living things glow – the plants, the insects, the trees. It's almost as if there's a halo over everything, a shimmering, mystical light. I turn to White Hands. She's standing beside me, a brilliant white flame in the darkness, her entire body illuminated.

"What do you see?" she asks, her voice seeming to come from afar.

She seems distant, so very distant. But I know she's here. Just as I'm here. Am I truly still asleep?

"You're shining…" I whisper, wonder flowing over me.

"That's good."

"What's happening?" I ask, my voice sounding hollow to my own ears.

White Hands walks around me. "You've been taught about the combat state?" she asks.

I nod slowly, everything so weightless and calming now.

"What you've experienced is only the surface of it. This, what you're feeling and seeing now, is its purest form, a state of heightened senses when you're halfway between sleep and waking, halfway between this world and the next. Look at your hands," she instructs.

I look down, shocked to see they're glowing just like White Hands's body, only there are streaks on them that glow even more brightly than everything else. My veins, branching across my body, illuminating it in the night. I can see them even against the gilding.

"When you enter the deep combat state, you can see what others can't, feel what others can't – become faster and stronger than is normally possible for an alaki. This is the state you will use to develop your voice. Catch."

A shadow whizzes towards me, and my hands automatically reach up, grasping the object. I gape at it. It's a sword, a very sharp one. I caught it by the blade, but I'm not bleeding – not even the tiniest wound mars my skin. I stare at it, amazement growing. The cursed gold has pooled under the skin there, protecting it. I can see it working, moving even under my gilding.

White Hands smiles. "Wonderful. You're already controlling your blood. When you do the same with your voice, you'll be in a much better position, I promise. Well, then, let's get started, shall we? We have a lot to learn. Let's start with entering the combat state on your own."

I wake up the next morning even earlier than I usually do.

Rattle is already standing towards the front of his cage when I arrive. His eyes glimmer in the darkness, those midnight-black pupils tracking me. It feels almost as if he knew I was coming, but then, he already has someone keeping him company. White Hands is seated on a small bench in front of him, that gnarled demon half mask on her face. I blink, startled by the sight. It's rare to see karmokos wearing the masks when men aren't around. But Rattle is male, I suppose, although I've never looked at his nethers closely enough to verify.

"Morning greetings, Karmoko," I say with a nervous bow, but White Hands impatiently waves my greeting away.

"Are you ready?" she asks.

I inhale deeply, looking at Rattle. "I think so."

She nods. "Submerge into the combat state."

Just like that?

I try not to show my unease as I nod, visualizing the dark ocean in my head, just as she directed me to do last night. At first, there is nothing, only the thousand erratic thoughts barging through my head: what if I can't do this? What if something happens and—

"Quiet your thoughts," White Hands commands. "Find a place to focus."

I do as she says, glancing down at my hands, at the gold that gilds them. It's just as thick as it was the first day I dipped my hands into that vase. If I stare long enough, I can almost see my veins underneath it, feel them throbbing just under the golden sheen of the gilding. I remember the way the blood in them surged up last night, protecting my hands when I caught the sword. The blood as gold as my hands. As gold as that door…

My thoughts still, my body already beginning to feel weightless.

"That's it," White Hands whispers, her voice coming as if from far away. "Focus on the door," she says.

It's there now, just in front of me. I move towards it, swimming through the darkness. Swimming into the light. There's so much of it now, everything glowing white before me – everything living, that is. That includes Rattle. His entire body seems to shimmer now, a white light glimmering in the darkness. Only his eyes are still black. He looks at me, a strange expression on his face. Fear? Curiosity? I can't tell.

I walk closer to him, my footsteps seeming to float on air. Once I'm just out of reach, I look up at his eyes. "Rattle," I say. "Kneel."

My voice sounds layered even to my own ears.

Moments pass, nothing happens, but then a familiar, rattling sound. His quills, creaking on his back. He slowly but surely sinks to his knees, a vacant look in his eyes. The same look that was in the other deathshrieks' eyes – the one that killed Katya and the one back in Irfut. Shock jolts as I realize: I did it, I commanded him!

"Why, Deka." White Hands's voice is suddenly right next to my ear. "I think you've issued your first intentional command."

My grin wavers, exhaustion surging inside me. Then everything goes black.

TWENTY

"Deathshrieks have gathered in a cave near the outskirts of Hemaira's southern border," Karmoko Thandiwe announces, glancing across the room.

It's late afternoon and I'm standing in the karmokos' personal library along with several other alaki: Beax, a thoughtful Northern novice with green eyes and black hair, Mehrut, the short Southern neophyte Adwapa is forever making cow eyes at, and Britta, Belcalis, Gazal and Adwapa. White Hands and the other karmokos sit quietly in the corner, assessing us. This time tomorrow, our small party will be on the outskirts of Hemaira hunting deathshrieks. And not just the ordinary ones either. This particular group has killed over fifty men in the week they've been nesting at the southern border. Most deathshrieks take at least two or three months to wreak such devastation. We're hunting these on our very first raid.

My heart pounds, fear, nerves and eagerness all coming together as one. This is what I've been training all these months for.

"The deathshrieks are massing here, near the jungle villas

of several nobles," Karmoko Thandiwe says, walking to the centre of the library, where a map of Otera has been carved into the floor. She points with a spear to the area we will be travelling to, a small village at Hemaira's leftmost edge. "You lot and your uruni will ride out tomorrow and will engage them at this cave." She points to the location, then looks up, beckons to me. "Deka, this is where your particular talent becomes of use."

I reluctantly walk over, noticing the questions arising in the other bloodsisters' eyes.

Once I reach her, Karmoko Thandiwe turns to face them. "You all know Deka," she begins, patting my shoulder. "What you do not know, however, is that she is not quite like the rest of you."

The girls glance at each other again, confused. My muscles tense, anxiety roping them tighter. None of us in White Hands's lessons has told any of the others about my ability, and now that the moment is here, I'm filled with dread. Will they hate me? Fear me?

A hand nudges mine. Britta's. "It's all right, Deka," she whispers, smiling. "I'm right here."

I smile back, relieved.

"Deka is an anomaly among your kind," Karmoko Thandiwe explains, glancing around the room. "She has the power to command deathshrieks."

The other girls gasp, and Adwapa sends me a shocked look. "Deka?" she whispers, a question in her eyes.

I nod quickly, suddenly shy.

Beax raises her hand. "I do not understand, Karmoko. Do you mean that she can hypnotize them?"

"Something like that," Karmoko Thandiwe replies. "She can do so only for short periods of time, but, as you can imagine, this is a very helpful ability, so we must explore it."

Now she looks across the room, her eyes stern. "A word of warning: very few people know of Deka's talent. Only those in this room, the jatu commanders, and a few select others are privy to this information. No one else may know – not even your other bloodsisters, on pain of death."

Beax nods, staring at me speculatively. I stand straighter, try to seem stronger – worthy, somehow. I still don't know why I was gifted with this ability, but I don't want to act so timid that the other bloodsisters dismiss me for my lack of confidence.

"Now, let's talk strategy," Karmoko Thandiwe declares. She glances at the other bloodsisters, then at me. "The plan is simple. Deka, you will approach first, flanked by your uruni and Britta. You will lure the deathshrieks out, using your voice, and render them motionless if you can. The others will then exterminate them, fast and simple. Do you understand?" she asks.

I nod. "Yes, Karmoko," I say, my muscles roped tighter than ever.

It's finally here, the time for me to accomplish my purpose. The very thought makes my mouth dry. I can do this, I can do this...

Karmoko Thandiwe smiles at me and nods.

"Then let's go over the finer points."

* * *

The mood is sombre when we gather in the stands with our uruni later in the evening. Our group has been allowed to have two hours to ourselves, as is the custom with every new raiding party, so we've decided to pass the time having dinner together. After all, it's very likely that some of us will die tomorrow. This almost feels like a sort of funeral – a chance to say goodbye before it's too late.

I'm not the only one that feels this way. As I bite into my dinner of hot stew and bread, Acalan, Belcalis's uruni, shifts beside me. "What does it feel like – dying?" he asks quietly.

There's an expression on his face, a vulnerability I've never seen there before.

"Cold, very cold," I reply. "You can feel the blood slowing inside you. Then there's the darkness, the loneliness. Dying is very lonely…"

"And after?" Acalan prompts, uncertain.

Perhaps he's not all bluster and rudeness after all.

"After?" I repeat, trying to picture it. It's a difficult thing. I always remember dying, but I can never quite recall what comes afterwards. All I remember is the darkness and the peace. If I try to think of anything further than that, the memory shifts away. Lots of my memories shift away now. I sometimes think I don't want to remember them – don't want to feel the fear that accompanies them.

"It's warm." To my surprise, this answer comes from Belcalis, and there's a faint smile on her mouth as she looks up from the cream she's been mixing all evening. Belcalis is very good at creams and solutions – a talent she learned from working at her uncle's apothecary. She makes them every time she's nervous or anxious, even though we don't need any such remedies as alaki. "It's always warm, like something is surrounding you, keeping you safe."

"You sound as if you like it." This perplexed observation comes from Kweku, Adwapa's plump and usually cheerful uruni. His eyebrows are gathered together, large brown eyes confused underneath them.

Belcalis shrugs. "I don't mind it – being dead, that is. It's actually peaceful, like you're floating in warmth and happiness. Whenever people call us monsters, I think about when I'm dead – what it feels like – and I wonder: If I'm that much of a monster, why is Oyomo so kind to me in the Afterlands?"

This answer doesn't sit well with Acalan, and he quickly rises. "Oyomo is kind to everyone, from the highest of the high to the lowest of the low. And you might not want to share such words in mixed company. The priests might accuse you of blasphemy."

He quickly walks away, back stiffly upright. I can't help but feel this is out of fear more than anger. Unlike us, the recruits get only one death.

"I'll go talk to him," Britta's uruni, Li, says, his expression apologetic as he makes his exit as well. Kweku quickly does the same, leaving us in silence behind him.

The moments tick by until finally Britta sighs. "That went just as well as expected."

We all laugh nervously, but we still follow the other boys with our eyes until they disappear down the hill to the barracks before we turn back to each other. Keita remains, much to my surprise. Despite our somewhat closer relationship now, he's still not the sort for idle conversation.

He turns to Belcalis. "Have you died many times, then?" he asks.

She shrugs. "Only six – from the bleedings, mostly."

"Six?" he sputters. When Belcalis shrugs, unconcerned, he shakes his head. "And – bleedings?"

"Sometimes, priests like to take our blood and sell it," Belcalis says, mixing the poultice faster and faster. She doesn't want to talk about this any more.

"They always take lots of it," I add quickly, drawing the attention away from her. "Once, as the village elders were dismembering me, I woke up and the entire cellar was covered in blood. That was unpleasant. And painful. But mainly unpleasant. I'd gotten used to it, you see. They dismembered me quite a lot."

I'm used to saying this without feeling any of the old fear and nausea now, so the expression that takes over Keita's face startles me. It's horror. Pure, unfiltered horror.

"I have to – pardon me," he says abruptly, scrambling up.

His body shakes as he walks away.

I watch him go, then sigh. Sometimes, I forget how sheltered the recruits are. Yes, they're soldiers, and yes, they live with brutality, with horror, but they have no understanding of what life is like for us. The pain we've all endured.

I should have told him about my past more gently, eased him into it, but now that I've said the words out loud, I don't regret saying them at all.

"I think I'll take some time to myself," I say as I rise.

The others nod as I walk away.

* * *

My favourite tree is the blue-flowered nystria on the next hill. It's a towering old giant, its branches so broad, they block out the view of almost everything else. The rest of the Warthu Bera always seems far away, a distant memory, once I slip into the small space under the branches and breathe in the delicate fragrance wafting from the flowers. That's where Keita finds me later, lying quietly in the shade.

"My apologies for running off," he says, crouching down beside me. "You were telling me about the most horrifying thing that ever happened to you and I fled like a child. I just… I could have never imagined that, what they did to you. I still can't…" He looks away, struggling for words.

Finally, he composes himself, turns back to me. "I'm sorry, Deka," he says. "From the bottom of my soul, I'm sorry for what was done to you, sorry for what was done to all of you. I know it doesn't make a difference, but I just want to say it, so you know how I feel."

I blink, startled by his words. Whatever I was expecting, it was certainly not this. This may be the most Keita has ever said to me in one go.

I nod as he takes a seat, then turn and smile at him. "I wouldn't compare you to a child," I say. "More like one of those tree lizards." I point to a pale-green lizard scurrying across the nystria's branches.

Keita's mouth quirks. "I'll take nothing less than a horned lizard," he says.

"Horned lizard it is," I agree.

His smile widens for a moment. Then he sighs. "I'm sorry," he whispers again. "Sorry for what happened to you, sorry that I didn't stay to hear you finish what you were saying."

"It's all right," I reply. "I shouldn't have told you in the first place."

"You shouldn't have had to go through such horror in the first place," he says, his eyes grim. "What those elders did – that's not what's supposed to happen."

"But what do you think the Death Mandate is?" I ask him softly. I know he knows about it. All the jatu in this unit do. They were once tasked with enforcing it if the priests failed. That was, of course, before alaki became necessary. "It's there. It's always been there."

Keita looks away guiltily, so I move closer. I don't want him to turn away from me, from this conversation. This may be the only chance I ever have.

"My kind, we don't have a choice," I say. "Fight or die – either way, our lives are not our own. Belcalis is right, you know. They call us demons, but are we really?"

Keita looks down. "I don't know." He sighs. "I don't know any more. When I first became a recruit, I thought that's what your kind were. I thought I'd hate you as I worked with you, and even when I made the bargain with you, I still distrusted you. But now…"

"But now?" I echo.

"Now, when I look at you, all I can see is my comrades. And now, when I hear what was done to you…" His hands clench. He has to breathe before he releases them. He turns to me. "Who dismembered you?" he asks. "What are their names?"

"What does it matter?" I shrug. "According to the Infinite Wisdoms, I'm a demon. Besides, it's over and done with."

Keita gathers my hand in his and squeezes it. The heat from his hand is like a furnace, washing over my skin. "It matters to me," he says. "You matter to me."

The words set my heart to beating and twist my stomach into knots. I don't know why I'm suddenly warm, suddenly flushed, in his presence. "You are my uruni," I say softly – a reminder to myself. "I thank you for caring."

"Even if I weren't your uruni, I would care."

To my surprise, Keita's other hand reaches up to clasp my chin. He lifts it up so I can meet his eyes. They're warm, earnest… My entire body tingles.

"I remember seeing you in Jor Hall that first day," he says softly. "When I saw you standing there, so frightened, Britta at your side, you reminded me of something I'd forgotten."

My heart is beating so fast now, I'm scared it'll burst from my chest. "What was that?" I whisper.

"Myself, when I was younger. I'm so sorry," he says abruptly, removing his hand. "I'm sorry I'm powerless, Deka, sorry your life was taken from you, sorry that violence brought you here… same as it brought me."

I stare at him, trying to understand these last few words. I've always known there was some tragedy in Keita's past, but I've never asked, since I know he wouldn't want me to pry. I sense that now is still not the time, so I just blink.

"It's all right," I say. "At least I have my bloodsisters now. It's enough. I never had friends like that back home. Never had much of anyone, really." I remember how easily Father abandoned me, how easily Elfriede did too.

I blink again, startled. I haven't thought about them in weeks, haven't even questioned again whether I'm Father's child or not. Now that White Hands is here, I'm content to wait for answers, safe in the knowledge that no matter what the truth is, no one's going to lock me in a cellar or bleed me because of my abilities.

Perhaps that's why I can be here, like this, with Keita.

His eyes seem to glow as he glances sideways at me. "Am I your friend, Deka?"

"Do you want to be?" I say this part so softly, I don't think he hears it.

But then he whispers in my ear, his breath stirring the short mop of curly hair above it. "I think I'm something much better. I'm your uruni, now until the day of our deaths."

It's the nicest thing I've heard in a long time.

TWENTY-ONE

I'm already a thousand times prepared for the raid when the sun climbs over the horizon the next day. My weapons have been sharpened, my leather armour has been tightened, and my horse has been equipped with everything it needs for the long ride to the outskirts of Hemaira. I'm so nervous, a strange sort of energy fills me as I saddle my horse. I don't even feel constricted by my armour now, even though it's the same grotesquely heavy leather all the alaki have been given. All I feel is a light compression over my body.

Around me, the others are also saddling their horses and loading their packs.

To my surprise, Adwapa still hasn't asked me any questions about Karmoko Thandiwe's revelation the night before. When I ask why as we mount the horses, she rolls her eyes. "Well, I've always known you were odd," she says by way of explanation.

I decide not to ask any further questions.

As we ride to the gates of the Warthu Bera, I spot Keita and the other uruni waiting on the other side, behind Captain Kelechi's horse. A strange warmth rises in me at the sight of him, resplendent in the ornamental orange-red armour of a recruit. I try to breathe it back, but it continues circling under my skin.

A civilian crowd has gathered behind him and the other recruits, necks straining as they gawk at our tiny regiment, which consists of us alaki, two matrons with battle experience, and the four assistants who will serve as our support; thankfully, one of them is Isattu, the assistant usually assigned to our common bedroom.

The drawbridge goes down, and Gazal, the ranking alaki for this expedition, lifts her arm in a folded fist, then drops it commandingly. "Helmets!" she bellows.

We quickly don our helmets – piercing, spiky affairs with war masks in the shape of snarling demon faces attached to the front.

"Cross the moat!" Gazal commands.

We obey, riding across the drawbridge. A strange feeling rushes over me the moment we reach the other side: nervousness, thrumming in my veins. This is the first time I've seen the outside of the Warthu Bera since I entered, the first time I haven't been within its confines, secluded by its walls – protected by them. I shiver at the thought, my pulse rising. I wonder what the common folk will do when they see us exiting the gates. Despite all our armour, most of us are shorter and smaller than the recruits. Will they suspect what we are? Do they know about us yet?

The novices tell us that the common folk mostly ignore them when they go on raids, but lately, there have been murmurs, rumblings of discontent we sometimes hear when we watch the novices exit. Who knows what will happen today... I curb the thought as our procession comes to a stop at the end of the drawbridge, where a market day is in full swing, with crowds of people milling around, buying fresh goods.

Captain Kelechi rides over to welcome us. He'll be heading our raiding party from now on – a surprising fact, given his rank as head of all the jatu. To my surprise, he rides over to me, then stops and gives me a slow, considering look down his long, aristocratic nose. It feels as if this is the first time he's actually seeing me, even though I've seen him countless times before, his tall, dark silhouette and rigid posture unmistakable anywhere he goes.

"You are Deka of Irfut," he says coldly, brown eyes assessing me up and down. "The demon among demons."

I make sure to keep my face expressionless as I reply. "Yes, Captain."

He moves his horse closer. "It works only on deathshrieks? Your gift, I mean."

I'm confused by his question for a moment, then I understand. He's asking whether my gift works on humans. On him.

"Only the deathshrieks," I confirm.

The captain nods brusquely. "Ensure that you keep it that way," he says. "Ensure that you keep your unholy ways well to yourself, because if I suspect for any reason that you are doing otherwise, I will give you so many brutal almost-deaths, you'll marvel at my ingenuity from here to infinity."

I nod, the blood chilling inside me. "Yes, Captain," I rasp.

He nods, turning his horse around. "Move out!" he calls.

I urge my horse onward, keeping my eyes steadfastly fixed on the road. Around us, the crowd mutters suspiciously, having noticed the alaki's smaller stature, not to mention the obvious curves of our armour.

"Whores!" I hear the word shouted more than once as we continue on.

I hurry to catch up with Keita. His forbidding expression is a barrier only the bravest man would dare cross. Concern shades his eyes when he glances at me.

"Is everything all right, Deka?" he asks. "The captain didn't threaten you, did he?"

"No, why do you think that?" I ask. I don't want him to know about what just happened.

"I saw him whisper to you," Keita explains. "What did he say?"

My face heats, and I shrug in what I hope is a casual way. "He just offered me some advice."

"About your gift?"

I nod. I've already told him about White Hands's revelations, our lessons, and what happened yesterday with Karmoko Thandiwe's announcement. "He said I—"

"Demons!" The word explodes from the crowd. "They're all demons!"

A shabby man pushes his way through, wild-eyed fervour blazing through his expression. "Don't let them fool you! Every week they come out of those gates, clothed in the foul armour of corruption. They want to corrupt us, to rot Otera to its very foundations."

The crowd has begun to murmur now, many people nodding their heads in agreement. "He's right!" a man calls out.

"Demons!" another shouts.

"Whores!" This last declaration comes from one of the few women in the crowd, an old grandmother in a grotesquely smiling bright-yellow sun-figure mask, and accompanied by two young boys – her male guardians, no doubt.

It's not long before the crowd is chanting the word: "Whores! Whores! Whores!"

As the chants grow louder, I instinctively shrink towards Britta, who's riding to my right. Even though we're well trained, I know only too well the power a human mob can wield. I remember my village, remember what happened there after the deathshrieks attacked – the way the villagers all gathered around me, watching impassively as Ionas gutted my—

This isn't my village.

I blink, realization washing over me.

These aren't the villagers who turned on me, tortured me. I'm not the same girl who cowered and allowed myself to be dismembered. I'm stronger now, faster too. Most important of all, I'm trained for combat.

The shabby man has whipped himself into such a frothing rage, he launches at Britta. "Demon-whores! I'll kill—"

I pull him up by the front of his robes.

"Don't touch my friends," I growl. "I'll break you to pieces before you can land a single blow."

"An' I'll help her scatter them all across Otera when she's done," Britta sniffs beside me.

I drop him back onto the dusty ground and make a show of contemptuously dusting off my hands. As I do so, a warm, buoyant feeling steals through me. Exhilaration. I can't believe

219

I did it, can't believe I defended myself – my friends – against that man. Just a few months ago, I would have just cowered in a corner.

"Good on ye," Britta whispers proudly to me as I continue on.

Keita, meanwhile, moves his horse closer to mine, the other uruni swiftly mimicking him so they're a barrier between the crowd and us. "I would never have imagined it," he says with a laugh. "Our little Deka, finally showing her teeth."

"Keep twittering on like that, and they'll sink right into you," I humph.

But now the man has turned to the crowd for support. "They're demons!" he shouts. "You jatu can't lie to us – we know what you're up to on that hill. We know you're doing all kinds of unholy things. We can't have such filth among us!"

"He's right," the grandmother in the sun mask calls out, clutching her grandsons closer.

"We don't want their filth here!" another man shouts.

My tension begins to rise, and my hands steal towards my atika's hilt. I'm grateful this one is made of steel, unlike our practice swords. I have to be prepared for anything.

As I do so, Captain Kelechi abruptly turns his horse to face the crowd. "Very well," he calls out. "If you want them gone, then who wants to take their place on the raid of a nearby deathshriek nest we're going on?"

The crowd quiets, confused by the question.

Captain Kelechi continues. "If my soldiers are demons, and therefore not worthy of fighting – no – *dying* for Otera, who among you will replace them in our ranks?" He glances mildly at the man. "Will you?" Then he points to another member of the crowd. "How about you? Or you?"

One by one, Captain Kelechi points out people in the crowd, asking them to take our place. The crowd falls silent with alarm...and shame. Scores of people, and no one can look him in the eye.

When no one steps forward, Captain Kelechi nods again. "The next time you want to rob me of my soldiers, make sure you're ready to take their place first." He casts a severe look at the man, who slinks away sulkily. He wasn't expecting anyone to question him, that much is obvious.

I watch the man go, relief building inside me. The people in the capital are much less dedicated to their hatred than the ones in the villages, it seems.

Once he disappears, Captain Kelechi turns to us. "What are you waiting for? Move out!"

We quickly do as we're told.

As we continue down the street, the familiar sound of Emeka's Tears thundering in the distance, I turn to Keita, perplexed. "Is he always like that? Captain Kelechi, I mean."

Keita turns to me and shrugs. "He's both better and worse than you can imagine."

The eastern outskirts of Hemaira are dusty and dry, the orderly beauty of the city giving way to a wild, uncultivated plain filled with yellow grasses and towering baobab trees. Baobabs are native here, but the summer heat has so parched them, their leaves have shrivelled on the stems. Even the streams and waterfalls have dried up, all of them seared away by the sun's unrelenting heat.

The farther out we go, the higher my anxieties build. The nest we're raiding is at the edge of the jungle, deep inside a cave. Captain Kelechi tracks the deathshrieks' movements via coucals, the messenger birds he trades with his scouts. The creatures have been unusually active today. I can already feel them out there, a vague, distant presence that causes my blood to rush faster and faster. Ever since I started taking lessons with White Hands, my blood has gotten more and more sensitive.

The plan is to attack the nest early next morning, when they're at their most vulnerable. Like humans, deathshrieks are active during the day and sleep at night.

As the day wears on, my nerves tighten more and more. I'm excited to finally begin killing deathshrieks to fulfil the purpose the karmokos have been training me for and avenge Katya's death – but what if I can't use my voice? I'm used to summoning it during lessons with White Hands – what if I can't do it here, without her to guide me?

My nervousness grows as we set up camp at the edge of the jungle, my thoughts consumed by the fear of what if, what if. I'm so preoccupied, I don't notice Keita when he sits next to me on the log where I've been mindlessly sharpening my atika for the past thirty minutes.

"Still at it?" he whispers in my ear, amused.

My heart nearly jumps out my chest. "Oyomo's breath, Keita!" I gasp. "You almost made me slice off my finger!"

He carefully takes the sword from my hands, examines it. "This is the fifth time I've seen you sharpening it since we set up camp, and it hasn't even tasted any blood yet." He glances at me from the corner of his eye. "Frightened?"

"Of course I'm frightened," I sniff.

"You'd be insane if you weren't," he agrees, leaning against the tree at our backs.

He's so close now, I can feel the heat of his thigh on mine. I try not to shiver from the contact.

"On my first deathshriek raid, I vomited so much that I fainted," he says. "By the time I woke, the raid was already over."

"What?" I turn to him, astonishment building. This is the first time he's told me this. We've talked about his time at Jor Hall, but never this.

"Disgraceful, isn't it?" He shrugs. "There I was, covered in my own vomit, when they woke me."

"How old were you?" I ask, curious. Despite the time we have spent together training, I still don't know much about Keita's earlier life – but then, he doesn't know much about mine. We both have secrets we want to keep.

Keita pauses now, his eyes far away. "Eight," he finally replies. "I was eight."

My eyes goggle. "Eight?" I repeat. Keita is seventeen now, which means he's been raiding deathshrieks for nine whole years. "Why would anyone take a child on a raid?" I ask, appalled.

"I insisted," he says with a shrug. When I turn to him, he explains. "The deathshrieks had just attacked my home, killed my family – my mother, my father, my brothers... I wanted to avenge them. It's not easy, going from being the youngest to being an orphan in the blink of an eye."

My stomach lurches, everything making sense. Now I understand why Keita's so desperate for revenge, why he isn't as carefree and joking as the other boys. If everyone I'd ever loved had been murdered all at once in such a horrible way, I'd be closed off too.

He smiles thinly, a sad, bitter expression on his face. "In the end, I couldn't even stay conscious for the beginning of it."

I'm so horrified, I place my hand on his knee. "I'm so sorry," I say. "I didn't know."

"I didn't tell you." He shrugs again. "It's all right, I suppose. You don't become lord of Gar Fatu without someone dying first."

"Gar Fatu?" I echo. I remember distantly Keita's introduction on our first meeting, but I didn't think much of it at the time. Gar Fatu is the name of the region where Father served during his military tour. Then: "*Lord* of Gar Fatu?"

I'd always thought Keita could be aristocratic, but an actual lord? And of Gar Fatu, of all places? Gar Fatu is the last stronghold guarding the border between Otera and the Unknown Lands, one of Otera's most strategic castles. Why is he here with us instead of at court, doing whatever it is fancy lords and ladies do? His family is one of the important ones, the nobles. At least, it was. They're all dead now, which is why he's here.

When I look up at him again, he's giving me a rueful smile – an expression that isn't reflected in his eyes.

The sight of it wounds me. "Don't do that," I say abruptly.

"Don't do what?"

"Pretend like everything is all right when it's not. Make horrible jokes to hide your pain. I know what it feels like to lose a parent. To lose your entire family. You don't have to pretend with me. Never with me."

Keita seems startled as he looks down, his golden eyes peering into mine. Finally, he nods. "I won't do it again," he agrees.

"You swear it?" I extend my little finger to him just as I used to with my mother, until I realize what I'm doing. I quickly retract my finger.

To my surprise, he picks my hand up, intertwines his little finger with mine.

"I swear it," he says and nods.

We sit there, fingers intertwined, as the night air cools around us. The rest of the camp seems to recede in the distance – the other alaki milling around, the recruits huddled together around a board game to calm their nerves. Finally, the silence becomes too much. I awkwardly remove my finger, clearing my throat as I do so.

"Did you go on any raids after?" I ask. "After the one where you vomited, I mean."

Keita taps his feet against the ground. "Countless," he says. "That's why I was assigned to Jor Hall. I'd seen more deathshrieks than all the jatu there combined, even though I was only a recruit, so they decided I wouldn't be out of my depth overseeing a few alaki. Then they decided to send me to the Warthu Bera. It was a much more fitting match for me, they said. I had to give up my rank, though. Now I'm just a lowly recruit, like the rest of them."

"You're much more accomplished than I ever imagined," I say, impressed. "I'm glad you're my uruni."

Keita grins, a glimmer of teeth shining behind his lips. The breath shallows in my throat, my whole world suddenly hanging on that expanse of white.

"Just wait till we finally go on the campaign and I spend days without washing. My odour will impress you more than anything you've ever smelled in your life," he says.

I giggle, charmed despite myself. "Stop joking, Keita, I—"

"Apt words, alaki."

When we look up, Captain Kelechi is standing above us, his mouth turned down in a disapproving frown. Keita and I immediately jerk upright.

Keita clears his throat. "Captain, I was—"

"Chattering with your partner when you should be inspecting the perimeter?" the captain interrupts, eyebrow raised.

Keita bows. "My apologies, Captain," he says quickly. "I will do so now."

Once he disappears into the shadows, Captain Kelechi turns to me. "Get some sleep, alaki," he says. "We'll need you at your best this morning."

"Yes, Captain." I bow, but by the time I lift my head, he's already gone.

TWENTY-TWO

The moon has just begun lowering in the sky when we reach the deathshriek nest early next morning. Even though the rest of the jungle simmers with heat, this area is bathed in a cold, clammy mist. It lets us know we're in the right place. I stare up at the trees, wonder rising despite the tension gripping my muscles. In the forests back home, we never had such giants, vines dripping from their branches, brightly coloured flowers nestled in their trunks. They're so beautiful, they almost make me forget the fear gnawing at my mind.

What if I can't sink into the combat state? Even worse – what if I can't use the voice? What if I freeze the way I did with Katya and someone dies?

What if, what if, what if…

Britta taps me, motioning for me to focus. I nod, try to push away these unhelpful thoughts by breathing deeply the way White Hands taught me. I'm mentally reaching for that dark ocean, the golden door inside it. Thankfully, it surges up easily, and just like that, I'm in the deep combat state, which allows me to see even more clearly in the dark, the creatures there shimmering with that strange, unearthly glow as I move soundlessly through the trees with the others. I quickly spot leapers, the deathshriek sentries hidden up in the branches. Their heartbeats shine brightest of all, living drums that pound so loudly, I can almost feel them vibrating under my skin.

I motion for the group to stop, pointing up. There are two leapers up there, both well camouflaged in the trees. No one else has seen them yet – no one else has the advantage of being able to track them using only their heartbeats, the way I can. Thankfully, they haven't noticed us yet. One false move and they will.

Captain Kelechi points a finger at me and then motions. *Time for you to go*, the signal says.

I motion that I understand, and then Britta and I are on the move, creeping slowly through the underbrush, making sure not to make any noises that would alert the deathshrieks. I'm dimly aware of Keita beside me, his shadow blending in and out of the trees. The years of nightly deathshriek raids have made him as quiet as he is deadly. Britta, unfortunately, is not as graceful, but she makes silent progress across the jungle as well, steadfastly watching my back.

Within moments, we're all near both deathshrieks. The one closest to me is scanning the area, eyes alert for threats. I frown, watching it. As with the ones that attacked our walls two months ago, it seems sharper, more alive somehow, than the deathshrieks in the Warthu Bera. It doesn't seem to notice me skulking below it, however. I've learned how to be stealthy during White Hands's many lessons.

I'm the hunter now.

"Don't make a sound," I command, my voice reverberating, that familiar power pushing out from my skin. "Come down here."

Both deathshrieks turn to me at the same time, their black eyes going wide with surprise before they just as quickly glaze over. Their hearts slow, the beats dulling to a trickle. When they slowly begin to descend, relief whooshes from my lungs. It's actually working!

Soon enough, they're on the ground, and Keita makes quick work of them, slicing their heads off before they're any the wiser. It's all I can do not to vomit when a musky-sweet smell tinges the air and blue blood wells up where their heads were.

Flashes. *Gold on the floor. The look in Father's eyes. The look in Katya's…*

Britta taps me and I turn away from the hated memory. I'm no longer in that cellar, and no one is going to behead me here. As I regain my composure, Keita walks over to me, eyes searching for any sign of tiredness. I still haven't conquered the exhaustion that rises whenever I use my voice to command. I can already feel it, that hazy feeling spreading over my limbs. I won't be able to remain standing for much longer.

"Excellent job," he says. "They never even saw it com—"

The sound of shaking branches alerts us to movement. I turn to find a pair of black deathshriek eyes peeking out from a nearby tree. The deathshriek stops, horrified, when it sees the bodies of its slaughtered comrades.

It opens its mouth – only to make a horrible gurgling sound as a knife rips through its throat, pinning it to the tree. Belcalis lowers her hand, but her knife came too late. The deathshriek's dying scream is now echoing through the trees. For a moment, Keita and I look at each other, hoping against hope that we're safe – that the other deathshrieks haven't been awakened.

Then the shrieks begin, each more horrific than the next, so piercing, I can hear them through my helmet. I toss it aside, trying to hear the direction they're coming from. I'm resistant to the worst effects of deathshriek screams, and my time in the caverns with Rattle and the other deathshrieks has made me even more so.

The mist thickens, the enraged deathshrieks excreting it more and more, and Keita grabs me, running towards the rest of the group. "Infinity take it, there's too many of them!" he hisses, feet pounding faster. I try to keep up, but every stride is a battle against the exhaustion now weighing down my limbs.

"I've got her!" Britta says, swooping me up like I weigh nothing.

"Keep her close!" Keita replies, readying his sword as we reach the others.

Captain Kelechi is prepared for our arrival. "Swords outward!" he commands as the raiding party bands together.

Britta places me in the middle of the circle, and then everyone else closes ranks, backs to each other, swords out towards the incoming threat. Around us, the mist is thickening even more and the treetops are rustling as shimmering figures lope across branches while others make their way through the underbrush. I watch it, my limbs so heavy now, I can barely remain standing. Exhaustion weights my every muscle.

"Make sure you leave no openings!" Captain Kelechi calls out.

"Yes, sir," I rasp, my tongue slurred by tiredness. My body is getting heavier and heavier, my eyes struggle to remain open.

It doesn't matter, however, because the deathshrieks are here, their towering silhouettes moving silently in the darkness. There are at least thirty of them – more than I've ever seen before in my life, the heightened senses of the deep combat state allowing me to see their heartbeats flashing furious white against the silvery glow of their skin. When they see the bodies of their friends, they begin to shriek again, the sound both anguished and angry as it drills into my ears. But it doesn't get worse, none of the red-hot agony that used to sear my brain.

The shrieks reach a fever pitch when the largest deathshriek, a silvery monstrosity with white, quill-like projections all down its back, steps forward. It looks almost like Rattle, its quills clattering as it motions to the other deathshrieks. But Rattle is much less frightening than this hulking, commanding monster that makes the other deathshrieks begin circling, their movements slow and deliberate. I watch it through eyes so weighted, it feels as if I'm fighting past water just to keep them open.

Once they've completely surrounded us, the silver deathshriek turns to us, eyes gleaming with hate, and makes a deliberate slicing motion across its throat. The deathshrieks grunt low, rumbling noises in their throats, their message clear: they mean to kill us slowly and painfully.

"Oyomo's beard, did you see that?" Kweku rasps. "Did you see what it just did?"

"They're gonna kill us," Britta whispers, terrified. "They're gonna kill us all."

So much terror vibrates through her voice, it pierces the wave of exhaustion crushing me. There are too many deathshrieks about to hope for a victory if we have to use our swords. I have to do something, have to try. I inhale, struggling to sink deeper into the combat state, struggling to shake off the tentacles of fatigue now squeezing even tighter around me.

"Can you control them, Deka?" Captain Kelechi whispers.

I swallow, my tongue heavy with fear and exhaustion. "I can try."

Captain Kelechi's hands tighten on his sword. "Don't try – do."

I nod, closing my eyes and allowing myself to fall even deeper into the dark ocean of my subconscious. That voice is whispering there as always, a mixture of my own thoughts and the power swirling inside me. I reach out to it, reach out to the golden door that it offers me, and almost immediately, I feel it, power surging through my veins.

I smile, allowing it to fill me up. Allowing it to give me strength. I won't let my friends die – not here, not now.

"Stop moving!" I command, power vibrating from my body. "Remain perfectly still."

Surprise fills me as the deathshrieks' heartbeats dim, silver throbbing to a dull grey. Their eyes glaze over and they all freeze in place, no longer able to move. Silence fills the jungle as the others look at me, awed.

"Oyomo's tears!" one recruit gasps.

It's enough to rouse Captain Kelechi from his daze. "What are you waiting for? Hurry up and end them!"

The words snap everyone into action. They begin attacking the motionless deathshrieks, who just remain there, eyes blinking frantically as they're beheaded one by one. A dark, suffocating feeling surges inside me. This seems wrong, so very, very wrong. The deathshrieks are completely defenceless, none of them so much as twitching a finger as they're cut down – massacred. I sag to the ground, no longer able to support my own body, watching as rivers of deathshriek blood soak the ground.

Repulsion comes over me as the pile of headless bodies quickly grows into a small mountain. By the time the moon disappears over the hill, the odour completely stains the air, shudders of nausea rising inside me every time I take a whiff.

Finally, it's over, and the other bloodsisters and even their uruni are hugging and kissing me joyfully as I lie there on the ground, my body completely immobile.

"Ye did it, ye did it!" Britta crows.

"Oyomo's breath, Deka, you saved us," says Belcalis. Then her brows gather. "Deka, your eyes…"

"I know," I rasp, the easiest words I can manage, given the circumstances, the darkness rising up to claim me.

As I finally allow myself to succumb to it, I notice something I didn't before. A little brown girl, about eleven or so, white shift fluttering as she runs away from us deeper into the forest.

"A girl…" I say.

Then everything goes black.

TWENTY-THREE

When I wake, it's early morning, and we're camped outside the deathshrieks' now-abandoned nest. Part of the work of the raid is checking the nest to ensure that none of the creatures has managed to hide away, which is why we're always expected to make our encampments next to the nests if we're on an overnight raid. Like everything surrounding deathshrieks, the ground here is cold and damp, and I shiver against the temperature when my eyes blink open.

"Yer awake!" Britta gasps as I sit up. She's kneeling beside me, her eyes droopy and tired. She has no doubt been awake all night like the others, scouring the area for any remaining deathshrieks.

"I am," I rasp, glancing around.

The smell of deathshriek blood assaults my nostrils. I gag, shuddering when I see the corpses piled nearby. The recruits surround them, Acalan and Kweku bent over the silver-quilled one, brows furrowed with concentration. Then I see their knives – moving…

"What are they doing?" I ask Britta, horrified.

She shrugs. "They're takin' trophies. Acalan says he wants the quills. To give as gifts."

The thought fills me with such disgust, I retch against the pallet Britta's made for me. I'm suddenly forcibly reminded of the elders, buckets in hand as they bled me.

Britta crouches above me, feeling my forehead. "Ye all right?" she asks. "Ye don't feel warm…"

I wipe my mouth, nodding. "I'm fine," I croak. "Just a little bit tired still."

As she nods suspiciously, I suddenly remember something.

"The girl," I gasp. "Did anybody find her? The little girl in the forest."

Britta frowns. "Wha are ye goin' on about? Wha little girl?"

"The one running away after we killed the deathshrieks."

Britta feels my forehead. "Sure yer all right, Deka? There weren't any humans in the forest but us."

"But—"

"We would've seen a little girl."

I nod. "Perhaps I was hallucinating," I say, uncertain now. "I was very tired last night. Perhaps it was the exhaustion."

Britta shoots me another suspicious look.

I'm almost relieved when Keita walks over. Then I see he's carrying what looks like a bloodied deathshriek pelt. I studiously avoid the sight of it as he smiles down at me. He seems at ease now, horribly so. He must be used to this, killing deathshrieks, taking trophies like the other recruits. Is this what he's done since he was a child? The thought sends my stomach turning on itself.

"You're awake," he says, smiling. "Good to see you're

recovering." He notices me watching the pelt. "The first one I killed last night," he explains, his expression almost shy now. "I was going to go bury it. It's a strange habit, I know, but it feels right, so—"

"Deka! We slaughtered them all, thanks to you." Acalan walks up, a cheerful expression on his face. It takes me some moments before I realize what it is: bloodlust. "You're truly the commander of deathshrieks," he says with that awful look in his eyes.

"And we're the Death Strikers," Adwapa adds cheerfully, walking over. "Deka sends them like lambs to the slaughter—"

"And then we annihilate them!" Li finishes, grinning as he walks over, Kweku beside him. They're all smiling down at me. It almost frightens me how happy they are. How at ease they seem.

And I made all this possible…

What have I done?

I bolt up, unable to bear any more of this conversation. "What's happening now?" I say, nodding towards the cave.

"There are zerizards in there," Adwapa answers. "They're all corralled and everything."

I frown. "Why would deathshrieks want zerizards?"

"They wouldn't. Deathshrieks don't corral animals." This firm reply comes from Keita. He puts the deathshriek pelt down, turns towards the cave, then looks back down at me, a strange, hesitant look in his eye.

"What is it?" I ask, moving closer.

He clears his throat. "There are…people in there," he finally says. As my heart clenches with thoughts of that little girl, he adds, "Their corpses, I mean. They're only at the entrance, though."

I nod, nausea rising as I understand what he's trying to say. The deathshrieks had to find a place to put all those people they killed, after all. "I'll be fine," I rasp, striding ahead. "I've seen worse." *My own body parts, strewn across the floor…*

Keita nods, following behind me.

It's at least twenty degrees colder in the cave than it is outside, and a horrifyingly familiar smell muddles the air, metallic and raw. It comes from the corner of the entrance, where dark red splashes the ground and odd brown shapes are scattered haphazardly in the dirt.

Human body parts, just as Keita said.

I shiver, suddenly freezing cold. Try not to look any further. Try not to see anything that might look like a little girl's head. These must be the remains of some of the nobles who were attacked. I try not to check whether there are bite marks on them. It's said deathshrieks like to gnaw on the bones afterwards.

"You all right?" Keita asks.

I nod, try to keep my expression from collapsing into horror. "It seems I'm no longer used to the cold," I say.

"You'll get used to it soon," he says. "And…the corpses too." When I glance up at him, startled, he nods. "I couldn't look at them either when I first started. Still can't. Some sights are just never easy, no matter how many years you spend on the battlefield."

I nod, oddly comforted by his words. "Let's see the nest," I say.

The interior of the cave is much larger than I'd expected it to be. Instead of a cramped, dark little structure, I'm shocked to find a massive open space with colossal walls that curve into a soaring ceiling. A small hole in the middle allows weak light to filter onto the herd of zerizards milling in the centre of the cave, eating from what looks like a trough of assorted fruits. They cluck excitedly when they see us. Keita goes over to examine them, but I keep looking around.

The dirt closest to the walls is scattered loosely, as if it was raked. This must be where the deathshrieks slept. I can see their tracks now, distinct impressions of arching, four-toed feet worn into the soil. As I glance around, unnerved, I sense a subtle tingling racing through my body, awareness rising deep within me. It's different from the foreboding I get sometimes.

This time, it doesn't feel like something is approaching. It feels like something is already here.

I turn towards the corner of the cave, where a small, dark passage leads deeper down. The feeling is coming from there, so strong, it's almost like I'm slipping into the deep combat state, even though I know I'm still wide awake. My vision hasn't changed, no shimmering yet. Even so, I can feel the dark ocean stretching inside me, the golden door opening, its secrets rustling behind.

I reach for it as I slip down the rough, vine-covered path into an even smaller one that curves deeper, hurrying along to make sure I'm not followed. I don't know where I'm going, only that I have to go, have to follow this strange, urgent feeling where it leads. By now, the ocean is surging up, rising inside me. I'm no longer sure I'm fully awake, but for some reason, this isn't like when I use the deep combat state to train my voice. This is a different sort of state.

A knowing one.

Soon enough, I reach the end of the passage, which is guarded by what looks like a carved doorway. I walk towards it, frowning. What's this?

"Deka?" Britta's voice is as unexpected as it is loud. "Deka, are you there?"

When her familiar form appears around the bend, I shush her. "Lower your voice," I say, alarmed by its volume.

I have a feeling that this is a sacred space – a space we shouldn't disturb. Then Belcalis appears as well.

I sigh. I guess I'm not as stealthy as I thought.

"What is this place?" Belcalis asks, glancing around.

"I don't know, ask Deka," Britta says, turning to me, but I don't have time to answer.

The knowing is urging me forward. "Shush, you have to be quiet," I warn them, walking through the doorway. The breath immediately catches in my throat.

This new part of the cave has been shaped by human hands – that's immediately apparent from the grandly carved pillars and ceiling, the blue stone on the floor. That's not what shocks me, however. The colossal statues do. There's one at each of this chamber's four corners, and they are all women, from a different Oteran province. Their features are distinct, as are the clothes they wear.

There's a wise-looking Southerner in flowing robes, her face angular and shrewd; a gentle Northerner in her furs, body as round as her smiling face; a warlike Easterner, scaled armour covering her from head to toe and wings on her back; and a motherly Westerner, belly round and fertile, a welcoming look in her eyes.

The women in the statues appear ageless – somehow old and young at the same time – and they soar high into the ceiling, giants to our ants. I approach the closest one, the wise-looking Southerner, and that's when I notice something else. Something that stops me mid step.

Golden veins.

They shimmer almost ethereally over the statue's skin, identical to the ones that shimmer under mine. The closer I get to them, the more my skin prickles, realization quickly dawning.

Britta walks over to me, seeming dazed as she regards the statues. "Are they supposed to be—"

"The Gilded Ones…" Belcalis says, finishing Britta's question.

There's no question about it when those veins are so unmistakable, as are the other things: the pregnant belly of the Westerner, the Southerner's darkness, the pale glow of the Northerner, the scaled armour of the Easterner, wings protruding from it.

"They don't look like demons at all," Britta says, shocked. "They look like—"

"Gods," I whisper, thinking of all the statues of Oyomo I've seen, glowering down at us from the corners of temples. "They look like gods."

"Who would worship demons as gods?" Belcalis asks.

"Desperate people," Adwapa replies quietly. "People who don't want their families devoured, their children slaughtered. People who want their children to be gods."

"I don't understand." Britta's forehead scrunches as she turns to Adwapa. "What do you mean by that?"

Adwapa shrugs. "Ever wonder how exactly our kind came to be?"

"The goddesses birthed our ancestors – I already know that," Britta huffs.

"Yes, but how did they birth us? If we're mixed with both human and demon, where did the human part come from?"

I gasp, finally understanding what Adwapa is trying to say. "Whoever built this, whoever worshipped the Gilded Ones – they're the ones the Gilded Ones mated with. Our human ancestors."

"Exactly," Adwapa nods.

"But this temple is clean – cared for," Britta says. "Whoever did this, they're still around. Do you think they're still around, the worshippers?"

"You mean blasphemers," Belcalis corrects her. "That's what the priests will say, won't they?"

I don't pay any more attention to them, my thoughts suddenly whispering to me again. The knowing is calling me towards something else: the pond in the middle of the cave. Like the goddesses' feet, it's been surrounded by candles and flowers. A strange blue light shimmers inside it, shifting and changing every few seconds.

Something is inside it…

My entire body tingling now, I walk slowly towards the creature in the pond, careful not to make any sudden movements. It's almost as if the knowing is guiding me, the subconscious White Hands told me of whispering distant instructions in my ear.

"Deka, what are ye doing?" Britta's voice seems so far away.

I ignore it as I look down at the pond, which is much deeper than I'd realized. In fact, it's not so much a pond as it is the tip of a deep underground lake. Strangely, I can see clearly to the bottom, and something is swimming there – something reptilian, slithering over a series of large, shimmering, boulderlike objects, each one almost golden in colour.

My breath catches in my throat, and I watch as the creature spirals towards the surface, a shifting, changing animal, almost serpentine in form. It stops just under the surface of the water – watching me. Dimly, I make out two intelligent black eyes, a short, almost feline snout, and what look like membranous ears, fanning against the water. It looks like a drakos, one of those aquatic dragons that can go from land to air, but I know that's not what it is. This creature is something no one has seen before – I'm certain of it.

It stares at me as intently as I stare at it. It seems to want something from me.

The answer comes to mind almost instinctively, a rumbled command from the dark ocean.

Reach down…

I immediately obey, reaching down into the water and gasping when a cold far more piercing than I've ever felt before freezes my blood. As I look down, the creature opens its mouth, revealing rows of razor-sharp teeth.

It bites into my arm, digging in until gold begins to dot the surface of the water.

"Deka!" Britta gasps, running over, but I'm already lifting my arm out, the creature still attached to it.

It seems to be shrinking now, taking on an almost feline appearance as its blue scales become fur and its ears shrink into velvety smooth triangles. Within moments, it has unwrapped from my arm and is scrambling up so it can curl itself around my neck. It's transformed into what looks like a large bluish kitten, except it has nubby white horns on its forehead and those intelligent black eyes, which look up at me so solemnly, I can't help but nuzzle its cheeks.

They feel velvety to the touch, but I can still feel the scales under the fur.

Mine… The knowledge surges up from the depths of my mind, the dark ocean whispering secrets, knowledge I don't yet understand.

Even then, I know it's real, know that it's the truth. White Hands told me to trust this voice, trust the power hidden inside me, and I do, which is why I know that whatever this creature is, it has nothing to do with the deathshrieks or the humans outside, nothing to do with anything we've encountered this past day. It was here long before them and will likely be here long after, as will whatever it is that it was guarding in that lake, those large, shimmering boulders.

Mine. The knowledge vibrates under my skin.

I scratch the creature under its chin, smiling when it chirps at me – almost like a cat. "Do you want to go home with me?" I ask, smiling when it chirps again, an agreement this time.

"Deka," Britta repeats, her voice finally breaking through my daze. She points at the creature. "Wha is that?"

I turn to her and Belcalis, who now both have their weapons drawn suspiciously.

Alarmed, I press the creature close to my chest. "This is Ixa," I say, the knowledge flowing into my head. "He's mine."

* * *

"Don't tell anybody about the temple down there," I whisper to the others as we reunite with the rest of the raiding party. By now, Ixa is securely hidden in my armour, just above my heart.

The recruits and the other alaki have searched the cave thoroughly and found no sign of further deathshrieks. They don't seem to have noticed the path we took down into that other portion, and I have the feeling they won't if we don't point it out. Even now, the knowing still rumbles within me – guiding me, though I don't know how or why.

"Why?" Britta wants to know.

"I don't know, I just think it's—"

"Sacred," Belcalis finishes. "That place is sacred, and we should leave it untouched."

As I nod, relieved that someone else felt what I did, Adwapa snorts. "You two are fools, and your feelings are both stupid and dangerous – as is that thing you're carrying, Deka, but we'll talk about that later. For now, I don't want to be the demon that shows a group of jatu a temple dedicated to her demon ancestors, and I certainly don't want to be the demon that shows the jatu some new, strange creature. That will not end well for any of us, understood?"

We all nod, quickly seeing her point.

"Let's talk about this when we get home," Britta says, her eyes on the spot in my armour where Ixa is hidden.

As we ride back to the Warthu Bera, I keep tapping it to make sure Ixa is there, only stopping when he shifts around, rumbling just loudly enough so I can hear. It's a sound that fills me with a strange sort of relief. Ixa is mine, and I will protect him no matter what, keep him no matter what. He seems to feel the same, because as we enter Hemaira, I hear a sound in my head – one that's very low and very distant but clear nonetheless.

It's Ixa's voice, childlike and innocent as it says, *De...ka...*

TWENTY-FOUR

hen I wake early the next morning, it's to the sight of my friends creeping towards my bed, weapons in hand. Ixa is sleeping on my chest, but he bolts up the moment I do and hisses a low, frightening sound that raises the hairs on my arms.

"That's enough, Ixa," I whisper to him, uneasy. He quickly stops hissing.

But then the girls raise their weapons.

Ixa jumps to the floor, his muscles shifting and changing. Within seconds, he's back to his true form, looking for all the world like that water drakos, scales gleaming, powerful muscles working under them as he grows to monstrous size. A low rumble gathers in his throat, vibrating through my body.

"What in the name of Oyomo!" Belcalis gasps, brandishing her sword more forcefully.

"I told you that thing is unnatural!" Adwapa points, horrified. "Fecking unnatural!"

Ixa rumbles again, and I hold out my hands, trying to calm both sides.

"Shhh, Ixa," I say, reaching out to him. Relief washes over

me when he nuzzles my palm with his gigantic nose. For such a threatening-looking creature, he's very gentle. Almost like a child...

De...ka? he whispers, unsure. His voice is even clearer now, a loud whisper in my head.

"That's right, that's right," I say soothingly, my heart beating fast. "It's me, Deka." *Change back,* I ask with my thoughts. *Please, Ixa?*

De...ka. Ixa shrinks, and within moments, he's back to kitten size and jumping back on the bed.

"Did ye see that?" Britta gasps, flabbergasted. "It just changed – just like that. Why did it change?" She narrows her eyes at me. "Did ye have anything to do with it?"

"Ixa's a he, not an it," I humph, ignoring her question. "And what exactly are the four of you up to?"

Britta points towards Ixa, who has now made his way to my pillow and is snuggling down. "We're here about that. Wha exactly is that?"

I look at him, then shrug. "Honestly, I'm not sure what he is."

"You do get that it's not normal, right?" Asha says. By now, her sister has told her all about the raid and what we found there – excluding the part about my abilities, of course.

"He," I correct, rolling my eyes. "And really, Asha? People say we're not normal, and yet here we are, having arguments over a kitten."

"It's a creature ye found in a temple dedicated to demons that not only changes form but also fed on yer blood," Britta says. "I saw it bite ye in the temple."

247

"What if it wants to murder us in our beds?" Adwapa adds. "Ever think of that?"

I roll my eyes again. "Oh, for Oyomo's sake, whatever Ixa is, he isn't a monster – even I know that much. He's just some type of shapeshifter that whoever lived at that temple was raising." That much I know to be true. "Besides, I was told to keep him in the combat state."

Britta's eyebrows rise. "The combat state?" she asks disbelievingly.

I can't blame the others for not knowing more about it. White Hands refuses to teach them, saying it would be a wasted effort, since they don't have the abilities I do. "When I'm in it, White Hands says I see things clearer than I normally do. This is one of those things. Ixa means us no harm."

De...ka... Ixa agrees.

"Yer mad," Britta says. "Ye know that, right?"

I sigh, getting back into bed and pulling the covers around me. I'm not arguing any longer. "How about this: I'll talk to White Hands about Ixa tomorrow. If she tells me to get rid of him, I'll consider it."

"Fine," Britta huffs. "But I want to be right there, watching ye tell her."

"Fine," I reply.

I wait until I hear their grumbling footsteps receding before I glance at Ixa. *Just don't prove them right, all right?* I whisper silently.

De...ka... is his reply.

He snuggles up beside me and, together, we fall asleep.

* * *

White Hands is sprawled on her usual carpet, a jug of palm wine in hand, when I arrive at the lake to take lessons the next evening. Assorted dried fruits and a plate of cheeses keep her company. White Hands loves her indulgences – that much will never change. I'm the first to arrive, so she pats the space beside her.

"Have a seat, Deka," she says.

"Yes, Karmoko," I reply, kneeling to her in the traditional greeting before I reluctantly sit beside her, my muscles clenched tight.

I know I have to tell her about Ixa, but I'm not sure of what to say. Besides, Britta isn't here yet, and I promised I'd wait until she arrived to talk to White Hands about him.

"I'm told your first raid was a success," she murmurs, pouring a goblet of palm wine and handing it to me.

I shake my head, declining it. "Yes, Karmoko, we defeated all the deathshrieks nesting in the cave."

"Wonderful," she murmurs, that ever-present amused look in her eyes. She takes a swig of the wine. "And did you learn anything about your gift in the process?"

I immediately think about the way the knowing flowed inside me while I was in the cave, the way the deep combat state took over almost as soon as my blood tingled a warning. I didn't have to meditate, didn't have to force myself into it, it just came when I needed and then left when I didn't.

"I think I'm starting to understand how it works," I finally reply.

"And how does it work?"

"The combat state is connected to my blood. If my blood rushes, it stimulates the combat state. That's why I had to run or be panicked before in order to experience the combat state. And I now know how the voice works too. I think it affects the deathshrieks' bodies." I remember now the way I started sensing deathshriek heartbeats before I saw them – making them slow every time I gave a command. "Power rushes out of me, and that's what causes their bodies to react – to slow. That's why they do whatever I will them to," I finish.

Something about my words causes White Hands's brow to furrow. A strange, excited look shines in her eyes. "So you don't actually have to speak... What if, instead of concentrating on using your voice, we concentrated on directing your power, channelling it?"

"How?" I ask, intrigued.

"Targeted movements. A dance, as it were." White Hands taps her lip, deep in thought now. "Yes...I think we must come up with a martial art especially for you."

A martial art specially for me? I can barely fathom it, but of course White Hands would think of such a thing.

All Shadows are well versed in the martial arts. They even have their own specific style of fighting, a graceful, almost airy series of movements. Karmoko Huon demonstrated it once, but it's useless for alaki, since it requires a delicacy we no longer have. Too much brute force behind our movements.

I watch White Hands as she continues speaking, that excitement growing in her eyes. "I had considered it when I first started teaching you, but now I know it's necessary. We start tomorrow – no time to waste. The campaign will be here soon, and I want you to be ready in the event you are needed."

In the event I am needed? I muffle a laugh at her wording.

More like the eventuality. I know White Hands intends to use me during the campaign, a pet weapon she will present with great fanfare to the emperor. That's why she keeps pushing me harder, keeps reminding me how much more difficult the campaign will be than anything I've experienced thus far.

If she can make me the perfect weapon, she can gain greater status in the emperor's eyes. I'm starting to understand how she thinks.

Still, I'm relieved when Britta's familiar figure appears on the horizon. Just because I'm prepared for the eventuality of battle doesn't mean I want to think about it. "There's something else I wanted to tell you, Karmoko," I say.

"Yes?"

"I found something inside the cave where the deathshrieks were."

"Oh, you mean your new pet?" White Hands murmurs.

I glare at Britta, who's just now arriving. "You already told her?"

Britta's face flushes with guilt. "I had to, Deka, it's my duty to protect ye!"

I stand up, furious. "Protect me? I told you not to—"

"Well, it's not a cat, that's for certain," White Hands interrupts, thoughtfully tapping her lips. "Although…it could be mistaken for one, from a distance…" She turns to me. "What do you think it is, precisely?"

I blink, momentarily distracted from my anger. "Some sort of shapeshifter," I reply. "Mother told me such creatures roamed the South."

White Hands shrugs. "Far be it from me to question what

your mother knew to be true," she says.

"You think he's a danger," I say, my eyes narrowing.

"I think that you need to find out exactly what your pet is before you continue cradling it to your bosom and feeding it your blood."

I whirl again towards Britta. "You told her that too!"

I've been allowing Ixa to take occasional sips of my blood since I brought him from the pond. He seems to like it, so there doesn't seem to be much harm in doing so. Still, I can't believe Britta betrayed me like this.

Her mutinous expression tells me she doesn't see it that way. "I had to!" she hisses. "Ye weren't acting rationally."

"I am perfectly rational! I was halfway into the combat state when I found him, and I would have noticed if there was something evil about him! Besides—"

"Here's what I think," White Hands interrupts.

When I reluctantly turn to her, she continues: "You do seem to be very perceptive while in the combat state, so I would err on the side of listening to it. If it tells you your pet is safe, then it is safe. For now…"

She nods, making a decision. "I'll allow you to keep it as I make enquiries. Just make sure to let me know what happens when you feed it more cursed gold. Any reactions or changes may give us a clue as to its origins."

Britta's mouth turns down. "I don't like this," she sniffs. "I don't like it at all."

I shrug, giving her a smug smile. "You asked for the karmoko to speak, and now the karmoko has spoken. Let's get to our lesson, shall we?"

* * *

White Hands is so enamoured with her new idea about creating a martial art for me, she has no time to actually teach us during the lesson. "Have at it with swords, no holds barred," she instructs when Belcalis and Gazal arrive, then she nestles into her carpet and spends the next hour scribbling notes in her scroll.

I think she's coming up with the movements I will use to harness my power, but I know better than to ask. I've seen her like this before, when she's in the heat of training, excitement pulsing through her. Battle – the pursuit of it – is what drives her. She's just like Karmoko Huon in that regard. While Britta, Belcalis, Gazal and I do as she commands, hacking and slashing each other with all our strength, she continues at her scribbling.

Wounds open, blood pours. White Hands notices nothing except the scroll in front of her. The moment the hour is over, she rushes away, eager to plan her new lessons. I'm grateful for her distraction. That means I can spend more time with Ixa.

Ixa, I call, using my thoughts to speak to him. He's been scurrying after me in cat form all day, so I'm surprised when a small bird with blue feathers, horns and black eyes flies over towards us.

Britta frowns at it. "That's not—"

Ixa obligingly changes into his feline form.

I walk over to him, awed. "What are you?" I whisper, stroking him.

De…ka, he replies.

"Deka," Belcalis says, a thoughtful look on her face. "How exactly do you plan to take care of him?"

253

I turn to her. "Take care of him?" I echo.

"Well, he doesn't seem like the type to eat cooked food. And from the way he follows you, it looks like he's used to having a caretaker. So how are you going to feed him?"

I pause. I hadn't thought of that.

As I frown, considering the answer, a splash draws my attention to the pond. Ixa is swimming out of it in his drakos form, a fish wriggling in his jaws. He snaps down half of it, then offers the rest to me.

I nudge it back. *You can have it,* I say.

De…ka? Ixa asks, uncertain.

Eat, I tell him.

He obeys, gulping down the other half of the fish.

"Well, that takes care of that," Britta says, and sighs.

But now there's a horrified expression on Belcalis's face. "It can't change into human form, can it?"

I whirl to Ixa. *Can you?*

De…ka? Ixa seems confused by the notion. He starts nuzzling at my feet.

"I don't think so," I say, sitting down so Ixa can get comfortable on my lap. I pet him and he rumbles, licking the blood crusting my shoulder.

Don't do that in front of them, I tell him.

He immediately stops, cocking his head up at me.

Belcalis's eyes narrow. "You're talking to it, aren't you," she says – a statement, not a question.

"Him," I correct her. "And yes, I hear his voice in my head… and I talk back the same way."

Britta gasps. "Ye said none of that to White Hands, Deka!"

254

"Because I didn't want to give her any information that might turn her against Ixa! You wanted to know why I thought he was safe. This is why. I can hear him…although he barely speaks, really. I think he's a baby." I look up at her. "You won't tell White Hands, will you?"

Britta rolls her eyes, then puffs out a breath. "No, I'll let ye and her sort it out."

"Thanks, Britta," I say, smiling.

She sighs. "I know ye think I'm being silly, but I'm worried about ye, Deka. Ye keep changing an' not in normal ways. I'm afraid for ye." There's a note in her voice, a plea that forces me to my feet.

"I'm all right, Britta, really," I say, walking over and embracing her. "Everything is all right."

She groans. "Just make sure that's true."

It's my turn to nod.

I glance over to Belcalis. "You said he's used to having a caretaker. Do you think he thinks I'm his mother?" I ask.

Belcalis shrugs, kneeling down, then reaches out to him. Ixa lets out a welcoming chirp, and she begins petting him. "He's so soft," she murmurs. "And he doesn't seem unfriendly. White Hands did say you could keep him?" she asks, glancing between me and Britta.

"She said she'd try to learn more about him, which means he's here to stay." I lift Ixa up, kiss his fat little cheeks. "Yes, you are, aren't you, Ixa?"

Ixa chirps, rubs his face against mine.

Britta groans. "Just don't let it sleep on my bed."

"Him," I correct.

* * *

"But what is it?"

This is the first question Keita asks once I explain to him the situation with Ixa. As usual, we're sitting under our nystria tree, enjoying what little time we have between now and dinner. Ixa stalks through the branches above us, pouncing on the leaves like they're tiny animals. Keita watches him, a frown on his face.

"A shapeshifter of some sort, I told you," I repeat.

"And if you found it near the deathshriek nest, why didn't you tell me?"

I shrug. "Because you would have told me to get rid of him," I say, looking up at Ixa. Warmth spreads through me when he chirps suspiciously at a leaf. Or perhaps it's because of how close I am to Keita.

We're seated side by side now, our bodies touching from arm to feet. If I wanted, I could reach out and lean my head on his shoulder, ruffle his closely shorn hair, and look into his eyes. But of course I do nothing of the sort. Even though I feel bolder with him when we're here, under our tree, I'm still not that bold.

He nods. "You're right, I would say that." He turns his head towards me. "You have to be careful, Deka, that thing is—"

"—a child, an innocent child, all alone in the world?"

"An oddity. Something most of us have never seen before. You have to be careful of oddities, Deka. Sometimes, they can be dangerous things. Sometimes, their mere existence makes them dangerous." The way he looks at me sideways makes me know he's not just talking about Ixa.

I sigh, looking up at my new pet. "I'll keep him hidden," I finally say, knowing I'm not just talking about Ixa.

"See that you do." Then he turns to me, a hesitant expression on his face. "Deka, about your karmoko...the Lady of the Equus."

I frown. "What about her?"

"I asked my commanders if they knew of her, and as it turns out, she's quite...notorious. There are whispers that she's in charge of the emperor's special assignments." He takes a breath, looks down at me. "She breeds monsters for him, Deka."

My heart skips a beat. "Monsters?"

Every question I've ever had comes rushing back.

TWENTY-FIVE

Monsters...

The word plays a sickening refrain in my head all night, forcing me to realize I've been too complacent these past few months. White Hands promised me the answers I sought, but what if she's the source of all my questions? The way she appeared so mysteriously at Irfut, rescuing me from my months of torture. The way she seems to know all sorts of things about me. Am I one of the monsters she made for the emperor? Is Ixa? It was all too convenient, his presence in that pond.

And what about me? Mother was pregnant before she and Father ever met. Did White Hands have a hand in creating me – some sort of alaki breeding project? If I accept that she made Ixa, then it's possible she made me, possible I'm some sort of shapeshifter as well. That could be why my eyes sometimes change, why I look like Father, even though there's no way he's my true parent. But if that's the case, why allow him to raise me? Or allow me to live in Irfut as long as I did?

Round and round my thoughts go until strange footsteps enter the room. I bolt upright, then almost as quickly calm.

It's Gazal. She's approaching my bed, a set of new robes in her hand. She must have been sent by White Hands. I choke back a bitter laugh at the irony. Think of the infernal, and it'll appear to you – there's a good reason for that saying.

I search around for Ixa, but thankfully, he's nowhere to be found. He must be hunting, as he often does during the night.

"The Lady of the Equus requests your presence," Gazal says, throwing the robes at me. "Rise. Now."

Beside me, Britta stirs, her eyes widening when she notices Gazal. "Wha's happening?" she asks worriedly.

"Everything's fine," I say, reassuring her. "White Hands is asking for me."

"Don't let her make ye do anything strange so early," she warns before turning over with a yawn. "Last week, she had us sparring in the lake in full armour. Nearly drowned a couple of times…" The rest of her words are muffled by her pillow.

"I won't," I promise as I put on my robes.

Darkness is still surrounding the Warthu Bera when Gazal and I walk outside, a velvet cloak I can almost reach out and touch. The torches are still burning, and the lights of Hemaira flicker dimly in the distance. Exactly how early is it? I wonder. I know better than to ask Gazal this question. She's a surly shadow leading me to our destination, one of the more remote buildings at the edge of the Warthu Bera's hill.

White Hands is waiting inside when we enter, a plain torch in her hand. The darkness seems to gather sinisterly around her. I try not to show my unease.

"Morning greetings, Karmoko." Gazal and I bow.

"Morning greetings," White Hands replies. Then she nods

to Gazal. "My thanks, novice," she says. "You may continue to the next task."

Gazal bows again and exits, slipping away as quietly as she came. Now it's just White Hands and me. She glances at me. "I can feel your thoughts scurrying," she says. "Out with it, Deka."

I nod. "I heard something…distressing, Karmoko."

"Yes?"

"I heard that you breed monsters for the emperor."

White Hands humphs. "And now you think you may be a monster. That I somehow bred you."

I don't bother to deny it. White Hands rolls her eyes.

"The funny thing about you, Deka, is that your thoughts are always spinning. You think and think and run your mind in fine little circles, and yet you never quite grasp the truth of the matter. I told you I would give you all the answers before the campaign was over, and I will. I will tell you everything you need to know when the time is right. For now, here is what you need to know: there are several types of monsters in this world. You are not one."

I look in her eyes. They're firm, full of conviction. She's saying the truth. But I have one last question. "You do breed them, however. Monsters."

Her replying smile is thin. "I do what needs to be done. Now, then." She turns from me, gestures around the room, which is covered in large bronze mirrors, one for each wall.

It's obvious our conversation is at an end. I push my worries aside. Spend too much time ruminating in battle and that's how you get killed.

"You must be wondering what all this is," White Hands says, nodding at the mirrors.

"Yes, Karmoko."

"You see, I have a theory, Deka. I think that every time you use the voice, you do so using all your energy. That's what causes the exhaustion. If we can get you using smaller amounts, you can control it more. Therefore, I have formulated a series of moving meditations that will allow you to control your energy while in the combat state.

"Hopefully, you will soon be able to direct your energy so effectively, you'll no longer have to succumb to exhaustion when you use your voice. By the time the campaign comes, you'll be able to use your ability without a hint of fatigue."

Revulsion suffuses me at the thought, but I keep my face still. No matter the dread that wells up when I think of killing another wild deathshriek in cold blood, it's my duty to keep Otera safe. My mind flashes to Katya, that surprise in her eyes when the deathshriek ripped out her spine, then to all those villagers lying in the snow.

I have a duty to fulfil. I won't be put off by my own squeamishness.

"Let's begin with the first move: centring the energy in your body," White Hands says. "Spread your legs apart, hands up. Now inhale deeply."

She demonstrates and I mimic her moves.

"Close your eyes and visualize the ocean you see in your subconscious."

I obey, closing my eyes and imagining the dark ocean. Perhaps it's the stillness of the night, the quiet of the chamber around us, but I feel it almost immediately, lapping at the edges of my mind.

"Move through the golden door. Beyond it lies the source of your energy, your power. Visualize it as a white light flowing through your body."

I nod quietly, sinking deeper and deeper into my mind. When the golden door looms, I swim through it, just as she instructed, then watch, amazed, as a sea of white rushes over me. My energy, glowing like a distant star. Now I know why people shimmer when I see them in the combat state. It's their energy I'm seeing, the power near their hearts glowing brightest of all.

I concentrate on mine, feeling it rise and tingle inside me.

"Do you have it?" White Hands asks.

I nod. "I think so."

"Good," she says, opening a door I hadn't noticed at the back of the room.

Gazal and Jeneba are waiting there, at the top of a dark, ominous staircase. I don't have to ask to know that it must lead to the caverns – the deathshrieks. I can already feel one's presence, moving closer and closer, so familiar, it's immediately distinguishable. Rattle.

He's gagged and bound, struggling against the group of novices dragging him up the stairs. When he sees me, he stops, his expression wary, the way it always is now whenever I'm near. I'm caught by how docile he seems compared to the deathshrieks I've encountered in the wild, how withered he is around the edges. I can't put my finger on what it is exactly, but I know something's wrong with him and the other deathshrieks in the caverns.

"Do you have your energy?" White Hands asks, turning back to me.

I blink, forcing my mind to the present. "Yes."

I can feel it swirling inside me, a glowing ball of white.

"Follow my movements," she says, cupping her hand near her heart and then extending her fingers.

Her energy streams out, a clear white ribbon she pinches slowly upwards, away from her heart. As she does so, she turns towards the mirror, nodding for me to do the same. Now we're side by side, watching each other in the mirror as she calls out instructions.

"Pull a strand of energy from your heart to your throat. Use it to power your command. Only this small amount, nothing more," White Hands directs, her fingers pulling that glowing ribbon all the way to her throat. It glows there, brighter than the rest of the energy swirling around her body.

I wish she could see it, see the energy in her body, flickering as bright as a candle. But humans don't have the cursed gold, or the ability to reach the combat state. White Hands can't see anything but herself in that mirror.

I push the thought away as I nod, following her movements. I can feel the power now, see it vibrating in my throat. I focus on it, turn to Rattle, steeling myself against my guilt as I give a command. "Kneel," I say, my voice layering with power.

When he quickly does as he's told, sinking to his knees, White Hands claps her hands, pleased. "Wonderful work, Deka."

I nod, smiling thinly to mirror her expression. Just as she'd promised, I don't feel any exhaustion – no tiredness at all.

"Thank you, Karmo—" The words die on my lips as I catch a glimpse of myself in the bronze mirror.

My eyes are black from rim to rim – like death shining through my face. So this is what others have seen before, what they've talked about when they told me my eyes were changing. It must happen only when I use my energy. No wonder I wasn't able to glimpse it all those times I tried. I walk closer to the mirror, stare closer at them. They fit, somehow, the way they look in my face. They look like they belong.

"You've never seen it before, have you – the way your eyes change..." White Hands murmurs, moving closer.

I shake my head, then turn back to the mirror. "Now I know what they keep talking about," I whisper, almost to myself. Once I've examined every inch of them, I turn back to her. "Should I continue?" I ask, glancing at Rattle.

She nods. "Yes."

Encouraged, I pull another ribbon to my throat, turn towards the deathshriek. "Lift your hands."

He obeys again, and again I feel no exhaustion, not even the slightest hint of fatigue.

"Lower your hands," I command, using another ribbon.

When there's still no exhaustion as he obeys, I pull out the next ribbon, not paying much attention to it as I command, "Turn in a circle."

Exhilaration races through me when he does so, but then another feeling follows it: exhaustion, pounding me like a hammer. I look in the mirror and quickly see why. My throat is covered in masses of energy. Much, much more than I should have taken.

Why didn't I pay attention?

As I collapse to the floor, my eyes closing, White Hands humphs, annoyed. "I warned you, only a strand."

Learning to harness the combat state is a tiresome business. Sometimes, I keep control and use only the energy I need to command Rattle and the other deathshrieks. Other times, I miscalculate and take so much, it's all I can do to make it through till evening. Every day now, I'm getting better and better at using my ability, and it doesn't take long before I'm learning how to direct my energy through my veins like little rivers of power, all of them at my command.

It's a good thing too – the raid where I found Ixa was only the first of many as we do our part to exterminate the deathshrieks crossing Hemaira's borders. At first, I feel guilty using my ability, guilty rendering deathshrieks defenceless against my comrades' swords. Then I see pile after pile of human corpses at the nests, and my guilt changes back into anger – rage at what the deathshrieks are doing to the people they kill.

I don't hesitate to use my ability again.

Our tiny group quickly becomes so effective, the people in the city take up the name Adwapa gifted us, Death Strikers, for our seemingly uncanny ability to obliterate all the deathshriek nests we find. They cheer and throw flowers at us as we pass – a striking reversal from the first time, when they called us whores.

"Welcome, Death Strikers!" they shout, lining the streets whenever they hear we're coming.

It's almost like we're heroes now, and people don't even

seem to mind that some of us are women who may or may not be human. Of course, they have no idea about my particular talent. Not even the other girls at the Warthu Bera know – although they quickly get to know Ixa. Within days, he's made his feline incarnation a familiar presence in the training ground, stealing fish from the kitchens, chasing the birds, and curling around my neck whenever I'm not training.

Except for Keita, Britta, Gazal, Belcalis, Asha and Adwapa, no one else seems to view him as anything more than a friendly cat, and they laugh whenever my friends attempt to convince them otherwise. I try not to wonder why this is as our raids continue, as does our success.

The months pass, and soon, the cold season – such as it is – begins to creep into Hemaira, making the days a little less balmy and the nights comfortably cool. The deathshrieks seem to be aware of our existence now, because there are ever more sentries waiting for us. They even manage to catch us unawares a few times, grievously wounding all the alaki at least one time or another, but despite our injuries, we're always triumphant in the end. No deathshriek can resist my power. None of them can resist when I beckon. I only very rarely use my voice now, preferring to motion them to my will instead. Hand movements are all I need now to subdue them.

Everything is going so well, we receive a visitor specifically for the Death Strikers one evening. As we're filing out of the sandpits after combat practice one day, the grandest carriage we've ever witnessed – pulled by a pair of twin equus, striped black and white like zebras and adorned with gold jewellery – rides into the courtyard towards White Hands.

A plump man in official robes steps out, then gives her what looks like a scroll.

She scans it, inclines her head. The man gives her a deep, respectful bow, then gets back into the carriage and rides away.

When she sees Keita and me, she beckons, and we both run over.

"Yes, Karmoko?" we ask after we bow.

She hands us the scroll, which is sealed with the kuru. "Call the rest of the Death Strikers," she declares. "We have been invited to the palace by Emperor Gezo."

Oyomo's Eye is just as golden inside as it is out. That's what I discover as I walk down the Hemairan palace's gold-veined hallways the very next morning, my heart drumming a frantically nervous beat. I've never seen so much opulence in my life. Everywhere I turn, there's another precious stone, another imposing sculpture. Jatu in the most extravagant red armour I've ever witnessed stand at attention by each doorway, while grandly robed courtiers whisper behind their fans as we pass them.

Thankfully, we're garbed in the finest armour the Warthu Bera has to offer – Karmoko Huon insisted we wear it instead of the ornate robes the other karmokos wanted us to wear – as well as war masks to cover our faces. We alaki are no longer human women, she reminded the others, and it's better the emperor and those around him don't view us as such.

"Oh, me belly," Britta whispers as we near the double doors leading to the throne room. "There it goes again."

"Why is it that you always get a stomach ache when you're upset?" Li asks, exasperated.

"It's just the way I am." Britta sighs. "Least I have me war mask on, so I won't embarrass us," she says, touching the light bronze frame.

I don't know how she can bear it. Even though the air is cool in this gigantic hallway, my mask feels hot against my skin, and sweat dampens my brow.

Keita smiles when he notices the nervousness in my eyes. "Take courage, Deka," he whispers. "Everything will be well."

"You too," I whisper back. Then I clear my throat and add, "You look very handsome today." Like me, he's dressed in splendid ornamental armour made just for this occasion.

He nods, and I blush, my stomach jumping. I shouldn't have complimented him like that. Why oh why did I compliment him?

"You look pretty too," he whispers, and my cheeks sting with embarrassment and glee.

It's all I can do to keep from grinning from ear to ear. This is the first time a man other than Father and Ionas has called me pretty and actually meant it. *Father...* I wonder how he would feel if he could see me now, if he even misses me. I try to picture the look he'd give me, but I can't.

I can't remember the shape of his eyes, much less the colour of his eyebrows, or the length of his hair.

Why can't I remember his face?

Drums sound and the doors to the throne room open, forcing the question from my mind.

"The Death Strikers," the emperor's crier announces.

Taking a deep breath for bravery, I walk down the long hallway, trying not to gawk at the nobles sitting on either side of the room, their bodies so covered in gold and jewels, my eyes hurt to look at them. I thought the regular folk in Hemaira were finely dressed, but the nobles are walking treasure chests, their clothes and bodies virtually crusted in jewels, their faces covered by golden masks even though they're male. White Hands informed us that courtiers wear masks to show their submission to the emperor the same way women wear masks so as not to offend the eyes of Oyomo.

The emperor sits at the very end of the room, separated from everyone else by a massive veiled throne. My jaw nearly drops when I see it, gold threading the fine red material. It's said that the emperor is as close to Oyomo as you can find in this world – even more so than the high priests. Looking at his throne, I don't doubt it. The stairs leading up to it are solid gold, their edges lacquered in a thin crust of rubies.

Captain Kelechi and White Hands, as representatives of each group, stop just before the stairs and prostrate themselves on the floor. I do the same, my entire body trembling. I can't believe I'm here, in front of the emperor himself. The thought makes my body tremble even more.

"Your Imperial Majesty," White Hands murmurs.

"The Lady of the Equus," the emperor rumbles, his voice deep and resonant to match his burly silhouette, which I can just make out past the sheer curtains. "How wonderful it is to see you again, and in such auspicious circumstances."

I squint, trying to see him more clearly out the corner of my eye, but it's difficult with the edges of the mask blocking my periphery. Why did I ever want to wear these things again? I concentrate, straining my eyes in his direction. From what I can tell, he's very tall and broad-shouldered – bulky too, although I suspect he's more muscle than fat. A carefully groomed beard takes up most of his face, and his lips seem almost feminine, they're so lush. They make him seem a bit more human – flesh and blood, rather than the godlike being I was expecting.

White Hands abruptly sits up and faces him. "How wonderful it is to see you again, Cousin. You look...healthy."

Cousin? The word is a lightning bolt through me. White Hands is a royal? I thought she was just a noble, high-ranking but of ordinary blood, as all the other nobles are. To think that she has imperial blood – the blood of the emperor – coursing through her veins. It explains so many things: the way people defer to her, her seeming confidence against all odds. Even the fact that no one ever says her real name, and she can sit up in the emperor's presence. No wonder she's in charge of his special assignments, his little monsters, whatever they truly are. She's his cousin!

By now, the emperor is laughing. "Such humour you have, Cousin. I suppose I have become a bit more rotund in the past few months."

White Hands shrugs. "If you say so." She gestures to us. "Here is what I promised you: the Death Strikers, the most elite deathshriek-killing force in all Otera. The crown jewels of your new regiment."

New regiment? I struggle to keep my eyes focused on the floor as I hear White Hands's words. What does she mean, "new regiment"? Confusion circles inside me until I realize something: yet another of her promises has proven true. She said that she'd make us crown jewels in the emperor's army, and she has done it.

What is the truth of White Hands? I wonder. The sinister agent of the emperor or something else? Something I can't quite put my finger on yet.

A rustling behind the throne's veil as the emperor nods. Then he turns to his courtiers. "You may leave."

"But Your Imperial Majesty," a tall, dark courtier protests.

"We cannot leave you by yourself," another calls.

"It would be sacrilege," yet another courtier, a stern-looking Easterner this time, objects.

The emperor's reply is one word: "Now."

The courtiers scurry to obey his command, and within a few seconds, they're all gone, the door slamming behind them. I hear a shuffling as the emperor rises, then footsteps coming down the stairs. Large brown feet encased in jewel-encrusted sandals stop just before me.

"Tell me, which one of them is the anomaly?"

"Rise, Deka," White Hands commands.

I raise my head, trying my best not to stare as the emperor peers down at me. He's very handsome up close, hair closely cropped except for the beard, head covered by an imposing golden crown studded with diamonds the size of pigeon eggs. He's also quite dark, his skin the smooth bluish-black of the deep Southern provinces. The house of Gezo has always been Southerners.

He looks me up and down, intelligent brown eyes assessing.

There's a strange expression in them, recognition almost – although I'm not sure what he's recognizing.

"You're very small for a killer," he finally says.

"Yes, Your Imperial Majesty."

He frowns. "Your accent. You are from the North?"

"Yes, Your Imperial Majesty."

"But your skin is brown."

"Her mother was of the Southern provinces," White Hands explains. "A former Shadow."

Emperor Gezo nods. "The best stock to breed warriors." He turns to the others. "You may raise your heads as well."

When they do, the emperor turns to Keita, frowning. "The young lord of Gar Fatu. I heard you were with the Death Strikers as well."

"I am Deka's uruni, Your Imperial Majesty," Keita explains.

The emperor nods. "See that you protect her well. I expect great things from you, little lord," he says.

Keita nods. "Yes, my emperor."

I sit there, thoughts still whirling, as the emperor walks back up to his throne and takes a seat. He stares down at us with stern eyes. "As you know, the army is going on campaign soon. We will exterminate the deathshrieks, destroy their primal nesting ground, and begin the path to victory in this interminable combat."

The emperor leans closer. "You have done well these past months, Death Strikers. Word of your exploits has reached even my ears. As a reward, you will ride at my right hand, at the very front of the army in the special regiment I've made of Otera's best soldiers."

We all look at each other, shocked. White Hands had told us as much, but hearing it from the emperor's own lips – it's all a bit too much to take in. Britta, Belcalis, Gazal and I all look faint now, but the boys, Li and Kweku especially, look like they want to jump up in delight. Acalan is the only one whose reaction resembles our own, he's so overwhelmed by the honour.

White Hands smoothly bows. "You honour us, Cousin," she says.

"No, you honour me," the emperor insists. "Remember when you came to me with the idea of alaki soldiers?"

My head nearly whips around in shock. Came to him? I stare at White Hands, my eyes nearly bulging past their sockets as I realize what the emperor just said. The alaki regiment, the end of the Death Mandate – that was all her doing? My body begins to shake, gratitude overwhelming me. No matter what White Hands is, no matter what she's done, she's saved the lives of countless girls. Rescued them from certain death. Rescued me.

That much, I have to give her credit for.

I barely hear the emperor as he continues: "I was doubtful – no, revolted by the very idea of it: impure girls riding into battle. But you have proven to me how wrong I was – all of you have – and now Otera is better for it. The alaki training grounds have decimated hordes of deathshrieks, thinning the armies we will face during the campaign.

"It will be a long one, make no mistake, but with the alaki at our side, we'll have the upper hand now. Let us continue on this path and lead our beloved One Kingdom to victory by ridding it of this pestilence of monsters once and for all."

"Thank you for your kind words, Cousin," says White Hands, bowing.

Just like that, our audience with the emperor is over, and we are backing out of the room so as not to dishonour him by giving him our backs.

As we ride back to the Warthu Bera, Ixa emerging from my pack to ride on my shoulder, my confusion continues building. White Hands creates monsters for the emperor, yet she also persuaded him to create the alaki training grounds? Does she truly create monsters, or is that one of the many deceptions she wears in place of a mask? Is she a villain, or the saviour who protected us? I don't know what to think any more. Except I have so much more to be grateful to her than I knew. We all do – which is why we neophytes continue staring at her, unsure of what to say, as she rides at the front on Braima, Masaima trotting at their side.

After a while, she turns to us. "I can feel your thoughts like little insects scurrying down my back."

"You persuaded the emperor to create the training grounds. Why?" I ask.

She shrugs. "Because I don't like seeing things go to waste, that's why. The alaki were just being thrown away. A waste…"

"You saved us," Belcalis whispers. To my surprise, tears are glazing her eyes, and there's a strange, unsettled expression in them. "You saved us…"

"She's right," Britta says. "Without ye, who knows where we'd be?"

"Well, don't get sentimental," White Hands huffs. For the

first time, I see that she's flustered. "If you're really grateful, show it on the battlefield."

"Oh, we will," Adwapa promises. "We certainly will."

White Hands humphs, rides on and I continue to watch her, still not sure what to think.

When we finish lessons later that night, Belcalis and I remain behind to pack up the weapons. We all take turns every evening, and tonight, it's our turn to shine and store the swords from practice. As usual, they're filthy, so we have to carefully soak them in aqua regia, then scrub them to remove the gold crust from the blood that was spilled.

I do so even more vigorously than usual, my mind ablaze with all the things I learned today. White Hands freed us from the Death Mandate, and gave us the chance to fight. Just as she promised, we're the emperor's crown jewels and will ride at his side in less than two months and deliver Otera from the deathshrieks once and for all. She's proven herself a woman of her word again and again.

So why do I feel uneasy?

As I finish polishing the swords in the armoury, I turn to Belcalis. She's making more aqua regia, her eyes troubled as she mixes the chemical solution. Usually, I would just leave her to her thoughts, but today has been a strange day, by all accounts. I need someone to talk to.

"Can you believe it was White Hands all along?" I say, hoping to start a conversation. I walk over to where she's packing the swords away. "What good fortune we've had that she came along. Had we been born just a year earlier, we'd have already been executed."

"Good fortune?" The words drip like acid from Belcalis's lips. "Is there such a thing for our kind?"

I find her shaking, every muscle quivering with barely suppressed fury. Even though she rarely speaks about her past, I know she was somewhere awful before she came here.

Wherever it was, I know that it was even worse than the temple cellar – that it was so nightmarish, she wakes up screaming at least once every few weeks and is filled with a constant, unending supply of pain and rage.

"What happened to you...what happened to me – these things, they alter us," Belcalis says. "They change us in the most fundamental ways. The emperor and his men, they can use White Hands and the rest of the karmokos to make us into warriors, they can even give us absolution, but they can never change what they did. They can never take back the horrors that have already been inflicted on us."

Gold on the floor...the look in Father's eyes... The memory of my torture surges before I can stop it, that familiar heaviness accompanying it. That pain and humiliation once more surfacing.

I've been so dedicated to building myself into the perfect little warrior these past few months. Did I really think I'd gotten past all this? Did I really think I could forgive and forget, just like that?

If it weren't for White Hands, I'd still be in that cellar and the elders would still be doing what they did, taking advantage of my ignorance, my desperation, to ensure that I continued submitting to the atrocities they disguised as piety. The realization slaps me in the face, as does another:

"I don't remember things like I used to," I whisper, looking up at Belcalis. For once, I allow myself to feel the pain coiling tightly inside me, the pain I so often stifle in an effort to pretend I'm fine. "I used to have excellent memory, but ever since the cellar, little things escape me. Like Father's face... The only thing I remember about him now is his expression as he beheaded me in the cellar. His features, what his smile looked like – I don't remember any of it any more."

It's a devastating, awful admission, and I gasp for air, trying to steel myself against the force of it. "I know that what he did was wrong, but he's my father. The only one I have, anyway. There were good times – before... Now, every time I try to remember him, his face slips away." I look down, surprised to find tears in my eyes. "All my memories from before, they just keep slipping through my fingers."

"Is that why I forgot my anger so easily today? Is that why I forgot everything that I'd gone through?"

"I was thirteen when it happened," Belcalis says softly, turning to me. "I cut myself slicing onions. Onions. Can you imagine how stupid that is? Girls aren't supposed to play with knives... When my father saw the gold, he knew immediately what it was – he was a priest, you see. He thought it was Oyomo's will that my blood had appeared so young – a sign that I was meant to be spared. So he called for his brother in Gar Calgaras and asked him to help me disappear into the city so I'd never have to undergo the Ritual of Purity.

"Father trusted his brother, loved him... He was an

apothecary, a good man who helped people." She laughs a short, bitter laugh. "It wasn't even a month before that 'good man' sold me to the brothel. But that was his mistake, you see. When the procurers saw my golden blood, realized that it was actually real, they killed him immediately so he would never lead the jatu to them – mistakenly or not. And then they offered me to their most…particular clients. The ones who like to hurt children – like to watch as they scream."

My hands are trembling now. There's so much pain in Belcalis's eyes, I feel the echo of it deep inside me.

"Belcalis," I say, "you don't have to—"

"They would give them a knife as they came into the room." Belcalis's voice is low and painful as she continues. "'You can do whatever you want to her and she'll heal' – that's what they told them. She'll heal." Belcalis's voice breaks at these words.

"'No matter what you do – no matter how badly you hurt her, grind her beneath your feet – she'll heal. She'll always be as good as new. Even if you slit her throat.'" Belcalis sobs brokenly, and something inside me shatters. These past few months, I've been so determined to bury my own pain, to prove to myself I'm fine – I've been so focused on my own troubles – I've forgotten that other girls are suffering too.

"Belcalis…" I whisper.

She abruptly reaches for the ties to her robe, begins untying them.

My eyes widen. "Belcalis, you don't have to—"

"I want you to see," she insists. "Remember those scars you saw long ago? Look now."

She takes off her robe and turns, offering me her back. I gasp, shocked. "They're gone." Her back is completely smooth now. But of course they are. The only scars that ever remain are the ones acquired before the blood turns.

"Once I stopped being hurt, being violated, they faded." She smiles bitterly. "And that's the worst part. The physical body – it heals. The scars fade. But the memories are for ever. Even when you forget, they remain inside, taunting you, resurfacing when you least expect."

My entire body is trembling now. "I'm so sorry," I whisper. "I'm so very sorry."

Belcalis shakes her head. "I don't want you to be sorry," she says. "I want you to keep the memory of my scars. I need someone to remember what happened to me. I need someone to—"

I rush to her and gather her in my arms. "I won't forget," I promise her. "I'll never forget."

The tears Belcalis has been holding back for so long burst out of her in great big heaving sobs. "Don't you dare," she cries. "Don't you dare. They might need us now because we're valuable, might pretend to accept us, to reward us – but never forget what they did to us first. If they did it once, Deka, they'll surely do it again, no matter the flowery promises they give."

"I won't forget," I promise, tears streaming down my face, determination building in my heart. "I'll never forget."

TWENTY-SIX

It's evening and we're slogging through the marshes at Hemaira's southern edge, heading towards a deathshriek nest deep in the marsh. Mist hangs thick over us, as does a cloud of mosquitoes, which nip incessantly at our faces. Leeches would do the same to our legs, but thankfully, we've worn sturdy boots for the occasion. Even so, this is the most draining raid I've ever been on. Now that the campaign is almost here, we're taking on even tougher raids in even more difficult terrain, the places where the deathshrieks blend themselves so completely into their surroundings, you almost never notice them until it's too late.

"It's like the Infernal Realms, it is," Britta grumbles under her breath.

"The arsehole of the Infernal Realms," Belcalis mutters – her favourite insult in times like these.

Keita shrugs. "If you think this is bad, wait till you visit my family home at Gar—"

A rock whizzes past so quickly, he has mere seconds to dodge it. I immediately slip into the combat state, time seeming to slow as I notice how quiet the marsh has become. Unnaturally quiet. The deathshrieks are near.

Power rushes into my veins as I raise my hands, gathering the energy in them. The air around me begins to vibrate as my body obeys my silent command.

"Show yourselves," I say.

The reeds around us rustle as deathshrieks slip out of them, answering my call. To my surprise, they're all wearing strange metal circlets around their heads. I squint at them, wondering what in the world they are. One of the deathshrieks nods to something behind me.

I whirl back, alarmed, and that's when I realize my mistake. Those metal circlets are cochleans, protecting the deathshrieks from the effects of my voice. We wear the same thing under our helmets to protect ourselves from deathshriek screams. Before I can gesture to freeze them in place, one of the deathshrieks throws a rock into my face, crushing my jaw and throat. I gurgle, blood oozing from the remnants of my jaw, but the next rock is even more sizable, breaking my hands, so I can't move them. I'm in shock now, my body going cold, blackness edging at my vision. I can't even absorb the fact that the deathshrieks are using rocks and cochleans – that they've obviously planned for my arrival. All I can feel is pain and confusion as golden blood gushes from me, pouring into the water.

"Deka!" Keita rushes towards me, using his body to shield me from the storm of rocks the deathshrieks are now throwing.

More of them are running out the marsh's bushes, slingshots in their hands. It's an ambush, but I can do nothing, only continue gurgling helplessly as my own blood drowns my mouth and throat. If only I could just move my arms – a finger.

"Call them off, Deka!" Captain Kelechi roars. Being human, he can't see what's happened to me in the darkness as he beats a retreat with the others.

"She can't, she's been struck!" Keita answers, holding me closer to his body.

By now, black is spotting my vision, and I can't feel my limbs any more. Blood has already drained from them. I'm going to die again. Is it my final death? I've never had my face crushed before. The serenity of the thought jars me, forcing me to struggle against the cold, the helplessness.

No, no, no! I must remain awake.

Keita desperately covers my neck, trying to stem the blood flow. "Deka!" he cries. "Deka!"

He doesn't seem to notice the deathshrieks gathering around him, their claws at the ready. I desperately motion towards them with my eyes, trying to get Keita to see them, to notice. Beware, Keita! I try to say, but it's no use. I can no longer move my tongue – or any other part of me, for that matter. The darkness has gathered around me now, bringing with it that familiar chill. My skin is already gilding, turning that eerie gold colour. I should be relieved it's only an almost-death, but I'm not. I'm scared for Keita, scared for all my friends. What'll happen to them when I go into the gilded sleep? Please, please let them be all right.

DEKA! Reptilian blue scales flash past me, a monstrously large body. Deathshriek screams fill the air as the enormous creature ploughs into them, claws flashing, jaws chomping.

Ixa? I think, my thoughts distant and airy.

And that's all I have time to ask before I fall into the gilded sleep.

When I wake, it's fully dark and I'm nestled inside a warm, soft blanket. I stretch, luxuriating inside it. I haven't felt this comfortable in ages.

"She's waking up!" a voice gasps. "Deka, Deka – can you hear me?"

Britta? I think. It's difficult to push past the darkness surrounding me, and honestly, I don't want to. I like it here in the darkness. It's so snug.

"Why don't we just lure the creature down – or shoot it," an annoyed voice suggests. Gazal's.

"Oh, yes, that sounds very reasonable," another voice returns, sharp with sarcasm. I immediately recognize it as Adwapa's. "Shoot down the one thing protecting us if those deathshrieks return."

"It's not protecting us, it's protecting her." This voice belongs to Li, and it doesn't sound at all cheerful, as it usually does.

The blanket around me rustles as footsteps draw near, squelching loudly through the mud. "Deka, please wake." This voice is Keita's, and he sounds concerned. "We can't leave here until you do."

Keita! The very thought jolts through me, shattering my darkness.

"Keita?" I rasp, blinking awake. "You're alive!"

Relief swells within me as I remember when I last saw him,

283

his body shielding me from the deathshrieks gathering near. But he's alive and well. I look around, trying to get my bearings. To my surprise, I'm surrounded by soft, shimmering blue scales covered in a light sprinkling of blue fur. When I glance up, a massive feline face with reptilian black eyes meets mine.

Deka... Ixa coos, nuzzling me with his gigantic snout.

"Ixa?" I gasp, shocked. "You're so big!"

He's never shifted into such a large drakos form before.

"He transformed when you died," Keita's voice says.

He's standing on the ground below me, his eyes filled with worry. I'm lying on a tree, I realize belatedly, and what I first thought a blanket is actually Ixa's body coiled all around me. Protecting me...

Now I take in the surrounding area. It's littered with deathshriek corpses, their body parts scattered across the marsh with macabre abandon. The familiar musky sweetness of their blood fills the air, causing me to gag. Even after all these months, I still haven't gotten used to it.

Keita tiptoes closer. "He killed all the deathshrieks attacking you. We took care of the rest, but he took you up there before we could get to you."

I finally realize that the others are gathered a safe distance away in a makeshift camp, watching me, Keita and Ixa. Everyone has seen him in this form. Everyone.

The stern look in Captain Kelechi's eyes when I meet them strikes fear into my heart. He's never been one to tolerate anything he thinks is irregular. He points accusingly at Ixa. "Now that you're awake, Deka," he says quietly, "you will tell me what that creature is."

Ixa sniffs dismissively, turning his nose up. He's never thought much of the captain.

"He's my pet," I say quickly, trying not to look at all the deathshriek corpses littering the ground. The corpses that Ixa made all by himself, if what I heard is true. I try not to let my unease show as I turn to the captain. "Whatever he's done, it's to protect me."

"That doesn't answer my question," Captain Kelechi returns, seeming every inch the jatu commander he is as he again asks, "What exactly is that thing?"

I look at Ixa, trying to find an answer. How do I explain a horned creature that looks feline half the time but occasionally transforms into a gigantic monstrosity when the need arises?

"Just a pet," I repeat, at a loss for how to explain.

"Does your pet have a specific breed?" Captain Kelechi grinds out, aristocratic face even darker with impatience now.

"I don't know...exactly..."

"You don't know?" The captain takes a step closer but stops when Ixa hisses at him.

"Enough, Ixa," I say, tapping him. *Let me down.*

Snuffling his annoyance, Ixa ripples his tail so I can slide down it to the ground. By the time my feet touch down, he has shrunk to his normal feline state, and he wraps himself around my neck with a small chirp.

"Did you see that?" one of the recruits gasps. "It just changed again!"

I walk towards the captain, nervous. "I just sort of found him," I say, taking Ixa from my neck and reluctantly holding him up for view.

285

Captain Kelechi squints down at him, intrigued. "Where?" he asks.

I swallow, sweat suddenly prickling my forehead. "At—"

"The Warthu Bera," Belcalis says, stepping forward. "We all found him at the Warthu Bera. He was by the lake."

"The lake?" the captain echoes disbelievingly. "Which one?"

"The one where we take lessons with the Lady of the Equus," Britta says. She steps forward, sliding easily into Belcalis's lie. "An' he wasn't that big when we found him. We thought he was some sort of cat. As ye can see, he changes form."

"He's probably been doing so for some time now," Adwapa adds, her face perfectly straight. "At least, that's what Karmoko White Hands says. She's the one who told Deka to care for him."

Something I didn't know was clenched inside me releases. My friends are coming to Ixa's rescue. They're protecting him for me.

Captain Kelechi looks from one to the other, then abruptly nods. "Very well," he says, turning on his heel. "We will continue this discussion later with the Lady of the Equus."

I slump, relieved. That went much better than I thought it would.

As we return to camp, I hold on tightly to Ixa, deep in thought. *What exactly is he?* I wonder, looking down at his furry blue form. Is this truly his real form, or is that the one he turned into earlier, when he saved us? Even more important, what were those deathshrieks back there? They were wearing cochleans and using slingshots.

I already knew their kind was much cleverer than ordinary predators, but this – this defies all expectation. I'm so deep in thought, I barely notice Adwapa, Britta and Belcalis approaching until they're flanking either side of me, leading me from the group.

"What?" I say, staring from one to the other when I notice that Britta is avoiding my eyes.

Belcalis looks around, making sure no one is listening. By now, the recruits and the others are slogging towards the edge of the swamp, where the battle matrons and assistants are waiting with the horses.

"Ixa wasn't the only worrisome transformation that happened today," she says, turning back to me.

Just like that, the clenched feeling is back in my stomach. "What do you mean?" I ask.

"When you called to the deathshrieks, yer eyes – they changed," Britta explains in a hushed whisper.

"That always happens," I say.

"But then the rest of you began to as well." This quiet statement comes from Belcalis.

I stop midstep, turn to her. "What does that mean?"

"They mean that for a moment, your skin leathered." All of us whirl to face Gazal, who approached so quietly, we didn't even hear her as she neared. Her face has its usual calm expression as she says, "It looked just like a deathshriek's."

My heart stops, the words like an arrow through them. Leathering? Changing? What are they talking about?

"That's not even the worst thing that happened, though," Adwapa adds.

"What do you mean?" I ask, my heart pounding so hard, it feels like it'll leap out of my chest. When she looks away again, uncomfortable, my heartbeat doubles.

"She means we felt it – your voice. When you told the deathshrieks to show themselves, we all felt the command inside us – compelling us," Gazal says.

"Compelling…?" I look from one to the other, still not understanding.

"Commanding," Belcalis says. "Your voice commanded us the way it did the deathshrieks. It took everything in me to resist it. It was so beautiful, but in a strange, terrifying way."

I'm so shocked, my knees feel weak. Then I have another thought. I look at the recruits, who are now out the marsh and hurrying to their horses. "The recruits, did they—"

"I don't think they noticed," Britta quickly reassures me. "It didn't seem to affect them. I don't think it works on humans."

I'm in such a daze now, everything seems far away.

"Are you telling me that you didn't know this was happening?" Gazal asks.

I shake my head, my entire body heavy. Deathshriek? Compelled? I still don't fully understand what they're saying. Don't want to understand. Because if I do, that means that it's my fault. I've caused all these changes, taking all those lessons, building up the power inside me. I've made myself even more monstrous than I already am.

"It can't be possible," I say. "It can't be."

"But it is." Belcalis's tone is implacable, and there's a look in her eyes now – something almost close to fear. "And the question is, what will you do?"

288

I turn to her. "Are you sure none of the recruits saw me change? Heard me?" My eyes flit to Keita, tightening the straps on his saddle. *Please, no. Please…* I couldn't bear it if he turned away from me, if he suddenly hated me the way Ionas did when he realized I was different from everyone else.

Belcalis shakes her head, sending a wave of relief over me. "It was too dark for them to see you."

"We only saw wha happened 'cause our night vision is better," Britta says. Then she adds, "I think you'd better talk to White Hands. Whatever this is, we need to take care of it afore anyone else knows." She follows my gaze to Keita. "Anyone," she repeats.

I nod.

As it turns out, I don't have to wait for a meeting with White Hands, because she summons me to the Warthu Bera's roof the moment I return. When Isattu deposits me there, White Hands is lounging on a bed of pillows, smoking that ever-present water pipe. The Hemairan night gathers around us, warm and sweetly scented, but all I can feel right now is my panic and fear. I know that White Hands probably called me here to talk about what happened with Ixa, but I have more pressing concerns.

White Hands doesn't seem to notice my anxiety as she takes another puff of her pipe. "I hear," she says, "that you've been experiencing some worrisome changes lately."

I stare at her, startled. How did she know?

Then I remember – White Hands commands the Warthu Bera, and that includes all the matrons and assistants here. I shouldn't be surprised if she has Isattu spying for her when we go on raids, if all the assistants are spying for her. "The assistants are your spies," I say, suddenly realizing why they're so deferential whenever they see her.

"The matrons too," she sniffs. "I try to surround myself with the best."

Her smugness only heightens my panic. If she knows what's happening, how can she be so calm? I can barely stand still, I'm so agitated. I clench and unclench my hands to keep myself from picking at my nails.

"Is it the lessons?" I ask, pulling Ixa from my neck into my arms as I walk closer. "Is that what's changing me?"

White Hands nods, a languid incline of the head. "It might be."

"Might be? I need a better explanation than that. Tell me why this is happening! You promised you would!"

White Hands doesn't reply, only rises and beckons for me to follow her to the edge of the roof. Below us, the city of Hemaira is spread out like a dark ocean dotted with dimly flickering lights.

She gestures to it.

"Tell me, what do you see before you?"

"Hemaira," I reply. What does this have to do with anything?

"And what fills Hemaira?" Now White Hands glances at me, as if there's something she wants to gauge.

"People," I reply, wondering where she's going.

"And beyond Hemaira? What fills the wilderness?"

"Deathshrieks," I say, quickly adding, "our enemies."

For a moment, a strange expression flashes over her face, but then she's back to that amused smile. "I see," she says.

"What does that have to do with what's happening to me?" I ask impatiently.

"Everything... And nothing."

Her answer infuriates me. "I don't have time for circular replies," I grit out. "I'm changing, Karmoko.

"You said I wasn't a monster, but am I some sort of deathshriek half-breed?" The words wrench out of me, a newly sprouted fear I almost can't bear to voice.

"A what?" White Hands barks out a laugh. "No, you are certainly not that."

"Then what am I? Explain why I keep having all these changes!"

"Because you keep using your power. Every time you use it, it grows, changes things around you."

Now a thought occurs to me – one that fills me with terror. "And my friends? Will I affect them? Will they start changing too?" I whisper.

White Hands shakes her head. "That won't happen. You're the only one with the voice. You're the only one with the ability." White Hands turns back towards the city. "And besides, there's nothing you can do to stop it – not at this time, anyway."

She seems so certain, I have a sudden realization. "You've witnessed this before, haven't you?" I gasp. "There are more girls like me! That's how you came up with the lessons, learning how to master the combat state!" I can imagine it now, an entire army of girls with the ability to control deathshrieks. I walk closer to her, pleading: "Who are they? Where are they?"

When White Hands finally glances at me, her expression is firm. "That should not be your concern at the moment. For now, listen to my words. Use your power only in the dark, when the jatu can't see you, and wear full armour. And try to surround yourself with your friends whenever you use it. Should a jatu catch a glimpse of your change, laugh it off and suggest that his eyes are playing tricks on him. Never forget: the same gift they praise you for now, they will kill you for later."

Her words are so similar to Belcalis's, my insides turn cold. I always knew there was more to White Hands than met the eye, more to the plans she has for me, but this is beyond what I ever imagined.

"But you brought me here," I whisper, fear rising. "You're the one who gave me this purpose."

She nods. "And I intend for you to survive long enough to fulfil it, which is why you must understand – truly – how fickle your position is. The jatu, my cousin the emperor, and his courtiers – they'll all love you now, when there are deathshrieks to conquer. The moment that changes, they'll remember that you're a woman. That you're unnatural… That is how they are. That is always how such men are."

"Tell me how I stop this," I beg. I don't want to be part of this, whatever it is White Hands is plotting. I just want to survive. Glory, honour – those are for other people. "Tell me how I make it go away."

"You can't." White Hands's eyes are deadly serious, no trace of amusement in them now. "You will continue training, you will harness your power, develop it until it becomes so strong, no one can stand in your way. In our way."

"White Hands…" I say, horrified. I know now she's not talking about the alaki regiment, or even the army. She's talking

about something else, something far more deadly. Rebellion…
That's what she means when she talks about gathering power so
she can be stronger than the men who command her. Including
the emperor of Otera himself.

This is all a game to her – the realization sticks in my throat.
This is one of those deadly games the rich, the powerful, play.
And I'm just a pawn she brought to serve her. Just like all the
assistants and matrons scurrying around the Warthu Bera.

"White Hands, I—"

She places a gauntleted finger to my lips, cutting me off. Her
eyes gleam with an expression I can't even fathom now. She
leans closer. "There are no others like you, Deka. You should
know that. There never have been, and there will never be."

As I gape, her words settling under my skin, she continues
her warning. "Hide your changes from the jatu. Keep yourself
safe, Deka. And always keep your pet with you."

I look down at Ixa, horror rising inside me. Has he always
been part of her plan as well? All my suspicions about how I
found him – perhaps they really are true. He blinks, not
understanding what's happening.

"I have explained to the other karmokos and the jatu that he
is a new type of creature I have been breeding in secret. That
should keep them satisfied for now. I am the procurer of
monsters, after all. You see, you were wrong in that regard,
Deka. I don't breed monsters for the emperor, I find them. Find
the creatures this empire deems impure, undesirable,
dangerous…"

Dread swells inside me. "What is Ixa?" I know she knows.
She knows everything. Hides everything.

"He's a shapeshifter," White Hands says. "That's all you need to know at present."

My thoughts whirl, each one more frightening than the next. What she said about the jatu, Ixa... "Why are you being so secretive?" I plead. "Why won't you answer my questions?"

"Because you won't understand the answers – not at this moment, not as you are. All you need to know is that you're not unnatural, or whatever other horrific supposition you'll now have running through your mind. Neither is your pet, for that matter. You need to remain with each other and to keep from attracting any attention long enough to get through the campaign. We're almost there, almost to the finish. You just have to survive till then, till our empire is free from those monsters. Then I will tell you everything, make you see what all this was for. Do you understand?"

I nod, at a loss for how else to respond. "I understand," I say, despair rising inside me. Just as I was beginning to think I could trust White Hands. Now I see that she's just like all the others – worse, even. A spider on a web, dangling threads that I have no idea how to connect. Ixa, the combat state, my gift – all things she's nurtured to suit a rebellion.

But whose? And why?

Till our empire is free from those monsters... What was she referring to with those words? Was it the deathshrieks...or the men who send us out to battle them? I quickly drive the thought to the depths of my mind, terrified by the implications.

I'm just a soldier, I remind myself. Such things are above me.

White Hands nods, then turns back towards the city. "What a lovely view," she says.

I can see I've been dismissed.

I walk away trembling, still no idea what just happened. I do know one thing: I have to be wary of what White Hands plans, or I might fall afoul of something even more dangerous than deathshrieks.

The Oteran empire itself.

TWENTY-SEVEN

"**I** call it the infernal armour," Karmoko Calderis declares, lifting up a golden helmet.

It's early morning and we're standing before the statue of Emperor Gezo, watching her make this triumphant announcement, the culmination of months of gruelling labour on her part. She's been working day and night ever since the novices arrived last year, refining the method for making armour out of cursed gold. Finally, her efforts have borne fruit: suits of armour impervious to deathshriek claws, comfortably cool under the sun's hottest rays, and lightweight enough for running.

"We've revolutionized the process," Karmoko Calderis crows.

"Oh, she's revolutionized something, all right," Asha snickers under her breath. She has just come back from a raid and is still filthy with the mud from her journey. Even so, she's exuberant. Her team filled their quota. Yes, three of the girls are still in the gilded sleep, and yes, one of them has lost an eye, but no one is being flayed this morning – an enormous victory, given how much harder the raids have gotten these past few weeks.

It's almost as if the deathshrieks sense that we're about to attack their primal nest, so they've launched an all-out assault. They want to kill as many of us as they can, just as we want to kill as many of them as we can. If it's this bad now, I can't imagine how much worse the campaign will be when there are hundreds of thousands of them on the battlefield.

"She's all revolutionary," Asha continues, snickering.

"Quiet, ye," Britta hisses.

I turn my attention back to Karmoko Calderis as she gives instruction on to how to receive our suits of armour. I need to pay close attention. Ever since I spoke with White Hands the night she told me all those awful things, I've been determined to get armour that covers me more fully. The makeshift helmets we've been using recently only barely cover our heads and the ones we ride out through the city with are much too bulky to use during a raid.

I want armour that covers my entire face and the rest of my body as well. I don't know if the leathering the others spoke of will happen again, but if it does, I want to make sure no one sees – especially not Keita. Just the thought of him witnessing the sight sends dread coursing through me. I don't ever want him to see me like that, so monstrous in form.

When Karmoko Calderis opens the forge the next morning, Britta, Belcalis, Asha, Adwapa and I are all standing there, waiting. Months of bloody combat and raids have wiped away my fear of bleeding, so I'm first in line. Besides, the karmoko did tell us each suit could be personalized, and I'm looking forward to seeing what designs she has on offer.

The karmoko's face splits into a toothy grin when she sees me, Ixa curled around my neck. "Ah, Deka, you're perfectly on time," she says gleefully, rubbing her palms together. "Come in." As I walk in, she stops and glances pointedly at Ixa. "You may leave the creature outside. Can't have fur disturbing the process."

Ixa blinks confused black eyes at me. *De...ka?*

He seems to be understanding what other people are saying more and more lately, although he's still unable to say anything more than my name. I wonder if he ever will. I would ask White Hands about it, but I'm too wary of the way she manipulates everything around her.

Yes, I say to Ixa. *You have to leave.*

Sniffing his annoyance, he does as he's told and stalks outside. I enter the forge, eyes widening when I see the changes that have been made in the past few months. Looping metal pipes have been attached to the ceiling, and they all end in gigantic vats suspended over a fire that is stoked to a constant blaze by sweating assistants.

Karmoko Calderis points gleefully to the large wooden chair in the middle of the forge. "Why don't you have a seat. Let's get started, shall we?" She holds up a blade.

I take a breath, look at its gleaming edge. "I'm ready," I say, stepping onto the chair.

I have a suit of armour to make.

It's a hot day for the cold season. Britta, Belcalis, Adwapa and I are perched on a bluff above the rock outcropping where deathshrieks have made a nest. They've been menacing a village called Yoko, on the outskirts of Hemaira, and its elders personally requested the Death Strikers, gave us a map to the source of their woes. That's why I'm here, sweat trickling down my back, leather armour chafing at my skin. I'm part of the advance team, my ability to track deathshrieks by instinct a tremendous asset in rocky, difficult terrain like this.

Below me, the deathshrieks huddle in a group around a protrusion of white rocks. They've spread only a small amount of mist, so they're easily visible despite their distance from our hiding place. Normally, the scouts would watch them in preparation for our advance, but at my suggestion, my friends and I have started doing so instead. It's important that we're familiar with our enemies in order to deal with them effectively. At least, that's what Karmoko Thandiwe always says.

Captain Kelechi agrees, which is why he, the recruits and the other alaki are back at the camp, making the last preparations while we four watch the deathshrieks. I didn't, of course, tell him my true reason for insisting we do so: deathshrieks have become increasingly fascinating to me. Ever since that day at the marsh, when they wore those cochleans to keep my voice from overpowering their will, I've been doing everything I can to watch them – to study them. And what I'm learning has made me very concerned.

The karmokos and the jatu keep telling us that deathshrieks are mindless beasts with very little intelligence, and yet they've always seemed almost human to my eyes. They even appear to have a language. It took me some time to identify it as such, but there they are in a circle, rumbling and clicking to each other.

Take away their terrifying appearance and they could be a contingent of alaki and recruits preparing for a raid. In fact, I'm certain that's what they're doing: preparing to menace Yoko again, to slaughter more people and steal more girls away.

The elders sobbed as they told us about this when we arrived, sobbed as they told us how the deathshrieks rounded up all the twelve- and thirteen-year-old girls and took them away while their family members lay dying on the ground, body parts scattered around them. I didn't have the heart to tell them that whatever girls they took are probably lost for good.

We can never find the girls the deathshrieks take, not even their remains. The corpse piles in deathshriek nests are always filled with adults, all of them men – there's never any hint of women or girls. Every time I wonder about this, a memory of that little girl I saw from the first raid flashes in me. I always wonder what happened to her – is she still alive or was she eaten by the deathshrieks…or worse? The thought unsettles me, so I turn to Ixa, perched in feline form on a nearby tree. *Signal the recruits,* I say to him.

He nods, sprouting wings from his back as he takes off. It's a favoured trick of his – one I'm very grateful for. It's made him useful to the group, and Captain Kelechi always appreciates usefulness. I've even had a golden helmet made from my blood for his drakos form, which he flaunts proudly at every opportunity.

"I can never get used to that," Adwapa whispers beside me. "Gives me the shivers, it does."

We're far enough away that sound won't carry, but we're always careful to remain quiet all the same.

"Get used to wha?" Britta asks.

She's on the other side of me, Ixa's helmet perched on her head. He can't wear it when he's not in battle form, so she's been slinging it around like a toy. Britta can be very childlike sometimes.

"She means Ixa changing form," I explain.

Britta whips to me, her eyebrows knitted in a frown. "Say that again," she demands.

Now it's my turn to frown. "Say what?"

Britta takes off the helmet, looks down at it. "That's odd," she says.

"What's odd?" This back-and-forth is very confusing.

Britta puts the helmet on again and turns to me. "Say anything – anything at all," she urges.

"Anything at all," I reply, shrugging.

She takes off the helmet and looks at me. "Yer voice, it's different when I put the helmet on."

"All right…" I have no idea what she's babbling about.

Belcalis is getting annoyed. "Enough of this," she says. "There's an entire nest of deathshrieks down there preparing themselves to slaughter a nearby village. Whatever this is, it can wait till later."

Adwapa nods. "She's right. We should be getting ready to kill them all. I know I am," she says eagerly. Months of raids have encouraged Adwapa's irreverence towards death, although she always kills only her quota of deathshrieks and not a single one more.

"I like conserving my energies," she always says when we tease her about it. Her sister is the same way.

Beside me, Britta nods. Then she turns back to us. "It's just…what if this is the answer to the voice problem?" she asks.

I shift towards her. "How?"

She and the others always feel my voice calling to their blood now, even when I'm specifically addressing the deathshrieks and not them. They tried putting on cochleans the way the deathshrieks in the marsh did, but it didn't work. My ability just keeps getting stronger. I'm always scared now that I'll say something that gets my friends hurt or, even worse, killed.

"When ye spoke while I had this on, yer voice sounded strange," Britta explains. "I could hear it, but it was almost… normal. Usually, when ye use yer voice, it sounds deep – like there are multiple people talking at once. This time, it just sounded ordinary. I think it's because the helmet is made from yer blood."

I turn to her, excited now. "So perhaps wearing helmets from my blood will prevent my voice from overpowering you!"

"It might." Britta shrugs.

"It's worth a try!" If helmets will keep me from mistakenly harming my friends, I'll gladly bleed myself dry if I have to.

Belcalis nods. "Then let's test it after the raid." She looks down at the outcropping and the deathshrieks gathered there. A bright blue bird is flying above it, black eyes distinctly reptilian in the darkness. It's Ixa, giving the signal to attack.

"But first, let's go kill some deathshrieks, shall we?" she says, rising.

I sigh, raising my sword. "Let's."

* * *

The first thing I do when I get back to the Warthu Bera is ask Karmoko Calderis to make a few helmets for my friends, in addition to my infernal armour. The karmoko is only too happy to fulfil my request, since this means she gets to test out more designs.

All it requires is some more bloodletting on my part, and in less than a week, I have the four gleaming new pieces of armour. We decide to test them by the lake one evening after our lesson with White Hands.

"Hurry," Adwapa says excitedly as I pull them out of my pack. "Let's see if they work."

"They're so pretty," Britta adds, marvelling at hers.

Say what you will about Karmoko Calderis, but she has a smith's talent coupled with an artist's eye. Each helmet is so unique, you don't have to wonder who it's for. Britta's is inscribed with horned bears, Belcalis's has actual horns protruding from it, and both Asha's and Adwapa's feature wings on each side.

"Can you hear me?" I ask once everyone's wearing theirs.

"Yes," Britta says, the other three nodding in agreement.

"Hurry up with it," Adwapa humphs.

"All right," I huff, summoning the power. I smile when I feel it tingle in my veins. "Bow to me," I command, excitedly shuffling from foot to foot.

Please let this work, please let this work...

To my horror, Britta immediately starts to lower her head. No... Disappointment swamps me. I'd been so excited about this—

Britta whips her head up, a mischievous dimple appearing

on the side of her mouth. "I don't want to," she says with a laugh. "There'll be no bowing here."

"It worked?" I gasp, all the tension whooshing from inside me. "It actually worked!" I grab Britta and begin dancing up and down. "It worked! It worked!"

Britta laughs, sharing my glee. "Yes, it did!"

"Good thinking, Britta," Belcalis says, clapping her shoulder.

Britta giggles her pleasure and falls to the ground. I do the same thing beside her, exhaling away all my fear and tension. I turn my head towards her. "My thanks, Britta," I say, taking her hand.

"Anything for ye, Deka." She smiles, squeezing my hand.

As I lie there, I stare at my friends, excited and relieved. I no longer have to worry about accidentally enthralling them. Now all I need to do is make helmets for the rest of the Death Strikers before we go into battle.

In the end, I settle on thin golden circlets that cover the other girls' ears as they go out on raids. That way, they can put any helmets they've already designed over them. I even make ones for Gazal and Beax, although I'm not sure Gazal will wear hers. She's never been too fond of me. Karmoko Calderis is only too happy to indulge my request and gleefully incorporates this new addition into her designs. I think she would have become a smith had women been allowed to do so.

Our raids also continue, only now there are a few changes in how we approach them – Ixa being one. As per White Hands's recommendation, he's become a permanent member of our raiding party, and I ride his drakos form out of the Warthu Bera, much to the alarm of the crowds that always wait for us – and to Ixa's delight. If there's one thing he loves, it's showing off. Captain Kelechi, thankfully, never minds, no doubt because of all the lies White Hands told him about the new breed of creatures she's creating. I always wonder how she'll explain the lack of other Ixa-like creatures to him, but that's a concern for another day.

When I ride out these days, it's with Keita to one side and Britta to the other. Keita and I use these occasions to talk. He tells me more about growing up in Gar Fatu with his mother and father, about all the adventures he had, wandering the marshes and salt mines of his home. I tell him as much as I can about Irfut but always stop before I say too much about my time in the cellar after the Ritual of Purity. I always see the anger surface in his eyes, and the sight fascinates me. Reassures me.

Keita's not like Father and the other men I once knew, the men who abandoned me, tortured me to enrich themselves. I know I can always depend on him to fight for me, defend me. I never truly thought I'd have someone like that, and now that I do, I always feel as if I'm floating, even in my darkest moments.

Sometimes, when no one is looking, he and I hold hands. We even embrace each other, his touch sending shivers through me. I feel as if I could melt into him and never separate. I move away the moment anyone comes by, however.

Many days now, I find myself wishing I could remain by his side for ever. But I know I will stop ageing at human pace once I reach physical maturity, as all alaki do. I have only two or three years more, but then Keita's ageing will overtake mine.

He'll grow older as I remain unchanged, and I have to make my peace with that, have to understand that no matter what I feel for him, we will never be what I want us to be.

Besides, I'll always have Britta. The feelings I have for Keita always make me warm, but Britta's the one who's forever there by my side, ready to support me, to push me when I'm being silly, to laugh with me when I need cheer. I've learned many things these past few months, and if there's one thing I know, it's this: Britta is my dearest friend, and my kinship with her is the foundation I stand on.

I have to remind myself of this whenever she annoys me, as she's doing now.

We're deep in the jungle, as usual, one of the typical places we find deathshrieks. Mist gathers around us, cold and ominous in what should be sweltering heat, but there's no sign of them. The closer we've gotten to the campaign, the warier they've become. No matter, we'll find them soon enough.

Their nest is near here, once again the ruins of what looks like a temple, although it's hard to make out anything with all the mist and the vines around. I squint, trying to peer closer, but it's a difficult proposition.

"Infinity take it," Britta grumbles beside me. "I can't see anything in this blasted, Oyomo-forsaken mist."

She, Keita and I are on scout duty today, so I nod. "Let's move closer – hand signals."

Keita shakes his head. "Too dangerous. Let's use Ixa." He looks up at the shapeshifter, who's perched in bird form in the tree above.

"And what, read his mind to glean whatever it is he's seeing?"

I ask, sarcasm dripping from my words.

"Well – yes," Britta says, rolling her eyes.

I sigh. "Fine, fine, I'll do it." I begin rising, but Keita grabs me. I look down at him. "What?"

"Be aware of what's around you," he warns.

"I will." I sigh. Really, between the two of them, it's like I have two nagging karmokos whispering in my ear.

He nods. "Let's move out."

Follow me, Ixa, I command as I slip into the mists.

Around me, the jungle is silent, on edge. The bird monkeys have stopped their chattering, and all the leopardans that frequent this area have long disappeared, their horned, blue-spotted feline forms nowhere to be seen. This is the one good thing about hunting deathshrieks: their presence scares off all the other predators that could hunt you.

As I sneak towards the temple, Keita and Britta doing the same before me, I keep alert for any leapers. We passed a couple on our way here, but I easily avoided them. I can anticipate their presence by simply listening for their heartbeats. All I have to do is open my mind and concentrate, and I can feel them in the distance – a tingling I can almost touch.

We're coming closer and closer to the temple, and now I can feel the deathshriek rumbles in my chest. There are two of them standing before the temple steps, chattering. I will my footsteps to be quieter and slowly, cautiously creep towards them. As I do so, I notice something unusual.

Words.

"*...the Nuru will come?*" a strange voice says.

I stop, confused. Who just spoke?

When I look up, Ixa is perched on the temple's roof, watching me. I know he's not the one talking. Ixa may be able to say my name, but that's all he can say. I doubt he'll ever have full conversations.

Another voice joins the first. *"Let's hope not. She'll destroy us if she does."*

"How can the Nuru be so traitorous? Does she not care about us?" the first one asks. Its voice is stranger than anything I've ever heard. It's deep and sibilant, and even more alarmingly, it's not speaking Oteran. And yet I seem to understand it.

How can I understand it?

As I search for the source, my eyes fall on the two deathshrieks. The larger one almost seems to be…shrugging…

"Perhaps she does not know."

The other deathshriek shakes its head mournfully in reply, and the world tilts. No, it's not possible, I think, shocked. It can't be possible. Yes, I've seen deathshrieks speaking to each other before – making grunts, clicks and deep thrumming signs – and yes, they always understand me when I command them, but I never thought I'd actually be able to understand them.

And there they are – talking. Making sounds I can understand, even though I don't know how I can do so.

My chest is so tight now, I can barely breathe.

All I can think is *how?* How could I have never noticed them speaking before? How could I not have known?

I'm so stunned by what I'm witnessing, I don't notice the dark figures slipping around me until Keita shouts. "Deka, use your voice!"

I turn to find a deathshriek arching towards him, claws at the ready.

Power surges through me, hot and blistering. "STOP!" I command, raising my arms. The air vibrates with my energy. "Do not move until I will it."

They freeze, caught by the power rumbling from me in waves. But I know time is already running away from me. The rest of the raiding party is thundering towards the temple, and it won't be long now before they get here.

I walk towards the two deathshrieks, still frozen mid-stride, energy arcing from me in waves. When I approach the smaller one, the one that spoke first, it looks down at me, eyes wide with terror and something else – something that looks almost like betrayal… It reminds me so much of that expression I can never identify on Rattle's face, my heart clenches.

By now, the others have entered the temple grounds, and I distantly hear the telltale sound of swords being unsheathed, the soft grunts of the deathshrieks as they're slaughtered. I hurriedly focus my attention on the deathshriek before me, keeping threads of energy tied around it as I begin my questions.

"Did you speak?" I ask it, fighting the exhaustion edging at my mind. I've never had to hold a deathshriek still while speaking to it at the same time.

"Deka, what are you doing? Kill them!" Belcalis's voice emerges as if from afar, an awful reminder that I often participate in deathshriek massacres, immobilizing the creatures, then slaying them as they're incapacitated.

I push the thought back as I turn to the deathshriek. "Answer me," I command, power reinforcing my words. I'm vibrating now, my entire body rumbling so deeply, the deathshriek struggles to remain standing. "Did you speak?"

The deathshriek's eyes widen. It looks down at me and opens its mouth. "I—"

Bluish-black blood sprays my face.

As I jerk back, startled and horrified, Belcalis casually retracts the sword now protruding from the deathshriek's chest. "I told you to kill it," she says as the creature falls sideways with a heavy thump.

My hands are shaking so hard now, I have to clasp them to stop. Where is Britta? I need Britta! "Britta?" I call, looking for her. Needing her to comfort me.

Belcalis shakes me. "Are you listening, Deka? What's wrong with you?"

I don't reply. I slowly wipe the blood from my face, then crouch beside the deathshriek and turn it over. A tear is running down one of its eyes. *It's crying...* I marvel distantly. It's crying as it dies.

Everything seems far away now. So very far away...

Keita runs over, concern in his eyes as he dispatches a nearby deathshriek, then turns to me. "Deka?" he says.

I don't reply. Can't reply – not now, when everything seems so broken.

He turns to Belcalis. "What's wrong with her?"

"I don't know. She's been acting strange since I arrived."

"Deka, are you all right?" Britta has finally rejoined the group and is bashing away at a nearby deathshriek together with Beax.

"Britta..." I say weakly, my heart in my mouth. I don't know what else to say.

There were only a few deathshrieks in this nest, and they're dead, and it's my fault. The moment I sensed them, pointed them out to the others, their lives were over. Because I can sense them coming but they can't sense me.

This whole time, I thought I was the hero, the righteous saviour, here to liberate Otera from the deathshriek scourge. But in reality I was a destroyer – a monster who falsely thought she was destroying monsters.

I turn towards the temple, towards the steps leading up it. I'm so tired now – so very tired. I think it's time I sat down.

"What's wrong, Deka?" Britta asks, concerned.

But I can no longer speak, no longer corral my growing despair.

I ignore her and continue walking, almost in a daze, towards the temple ruins. I don't want anyone to see my face, don't want anyone to see the deathshriek-like leathering that has no doubt already surrounded my eyes. When I reach the nearest stone fragment, I take a seat and look down. To my surprise, I'm sitting on what appears to be a toe. I glance up, frowning when I discern the rest of the statue under the weeds and mist. It's a goddess statue, a wise-looking Southerner in flowing robes. The very same Southerner I saw in that other temple, her face chiselled and intelligent as she looked down at the scroll in her hands.

I look around, make out the other statues, the same ones from the cave where I found Ixa.

The rest of the Gilded Ones.

The rocks the deathshrieks nested under near Yoko flash through my mind. They were the very same type of white rock as the rocks I'm sitting next to: the remnants of other statues.

The world tilts.

Every deathshriek nest we've been to is a temple of the Gilded Ones. It's the *deathshrieks* who have been worshipping them as goddesses, the deathshrieks who have been leaving behind flowers and candles. And we never once considered them. Never once thought they'd have the capacity for intelligent thought, much less religion.

White Hands told me I wasn't half deathshriek, but I think she lied. I think she not only bred a half deathshriek, she bred one that could destroy all the others.

She bred the perfect monster.

TWENTY-EIGHT

I'm quiet when we return to the Warthu Bera, my mind rattling with thoughts of what I've discovered about the deathshrieks and the temples. Memories of all my previous encounters with them filter through my mind – not just the ones outside but the ones here too. I suddenly think of Rattle and the others, how dull their eyes seem compared to those of wild deathshrieks. Why is it that they're so vacant and all the other deathshrieks are not? Why is it that the deathshrieks outside the Warthu Bera are intelligent enough to maintain temples, yet the ones here seem capable of barely more than grunting? It's a mystery I must unravel.

"Ye all right, Deka?" Britta asks me as we go to sleep.

I nod. "I'm fine," I say.

I wish I could tell her about what I discovered, but I don't want to involve her in my affairs any more. It's too dangerous. All those things White Hands said during our last conversation about rebellions and true monsters. I may not be the most intelligent person, but even I know that talk of rebellion leads swiftly to executions and final deaths.

Add to that the changes happening to me – the leathering on my face, the way I can understand deathshrieks. One alone is frightening, but the two combined – that's enough to condemn me.

I don't want my friends anywhere nearby. I'm not damning them along with me if something happens and I'm sentenced to the Death Mandate.

"I'm worried about ye, Deka." Britta's softly whispered words pull me from my thoughts.

I turn to her. "What do you mean?"

"Ye keep changing," she says. "Every day, it feels like you're becoming more and more different…"

She doesn't finish her sentence, but she doesn't have to. I know she's talking about what happened at the temple today when I heard the deathshrieks speaking. "Isn't change a good thing?" I whisper. A hopeful thought if there ever was one.

Britta looks up at the ceiling. "Not if yer an alaki. Not if yer just about to go on campaign in a few days, where the emperor and everyone will be watchin'."

I don't have to ask further to understand the warning behind her words. "I'll be fine, Britta. I won't draw attention to myself."

"Ye say that, but ye canna help yerself, Deka. Sometimes, it seems like something just takes over ye, like ye lose yer common sense when yer using yer abilities. It's like ye can't reason properly."

"That's why I have you to protect me."

"But what if I'm not there?"

"You'll always be there, Britta. And I'll always be there for you."

Britta sighs. "Just be safe, Deka. Be safe."

I nod silently as we both go to sleep.

It's cold in the caverns when I enter, mist trailing clammy fingers down my spine. As usual, Rattle is standing near the bars of his cage, watching me as I walk down the line of cages housing the other deathshrieks. There's that horribly familiar expression in his eyes, that look I'm only now starting to understand.

Betrayal… "You can understand me, can't you," I whisper, approaching his cage.

He doesn't answer, doesn't make a sound. He just watches me, that expression in his eyes.

"Speak," I urge. "Say something – anything, Rattle."

But he remains silent. After everything that's just happened, this show of stubbornness infuriates me. "Speak!" I command, lacing my voice with power.

Rattle flinches, his eyes widening, his mouth moving, but no sound comes out. No words. It's almost like something is stopping them in his throat, preventing them from emerging. I walk closer – the closest I've ever been to him in all the months I've spent here in the Warthu Bera – and that's when I smell it again: the sickly sweet smell wafting from his spikes, his skin, the one I never before recognized – until now. Blue blossom, the tiny blue flower the matrons sometimes eat when they want to forget their sorrows.

Understanding sweeps over me. Rattle is being drugged. All the deathshrieks in the Warthu Bera are.

That's why they seem so brutish, so unintelligent, compared

with the ones in the wild. The karmokos, the assistants, keep them that way, and for once, I don't have to ask why. Everyone employed at the Warthu Bera has a simple goal: keep us alive long enough to take part in the campaign. Deathshrieks in their wild state are much too difficult to control, especially for the naive, unschooled neophytes freshly condemned by the Ritual of Purity who come here.

So they drug them into docility.

Rattle is a tool, just like the rest of us – a pawn to help prepare for the campaign. It's not that he won't speak to me, it's that he can't.

I nod, stepping back from his cage. "My apologies, Rattle," I say as I walk towards the cavern's exit. "I'm sorry for what we're doing to you."

"And what exactly are we doing to him?"

I nearly gasp, startled, when Keita steps out of the shadows. "Keita. What are you doing here?"

"Looking for you. You've been avoiding me."

It's not strictly true. I've been avoiding everyone, too frightened by my discoveries at the last raid to burden anyone else with them.

My stomach clenches as Keita walks closer, his eyes gleaming softly in the darkness. I haven't spoken deeply to him in days, embraced him in what feels like longer. All I want is to feel his arms around me. But I can't afford that, not now, when I'm in such a state. I'll tell him everything if I do, and then there's no going back. He'll be drawn into White Hands's web, and who knows the deadly paths that will lead to.

"What happened when we were at the raid?" he asks.

"What is it you're not telling me?"

I look up at him, wondering how to answer. Finally, I sigh. "Let's get some air," I say, walking towards the entrance to the caverns.

We end up, as we always do, at our nystria tree. It's dark outside now, night rapidly falling around the Warthu Bera. The last few stragglers from the jog make their way indoors. Once we reach the tree, Keita takes a seat between one of the roots, then pats the space beside him.

I reluctantly sit there, stiff until he pulls me closer. His arm is warm, comforting on my shoulder. He leans his forehead against mine, and I close my eyes, inhaling the musk of his scent. *Let this go well*, I beg inwardly.

"You can tell me anything, Deka, you know that," he whispers. His lips are so close, if I lean any nearer, they'll brush mine.

I pull back. "Some things are too dangerous to tell. You yourself always say that."

His body tenses and his eyes search mine, worry shining in them. "If it is a danger to you, then I want to share in it. We're partners, remember?"

I nod, hide my head in the crook of his neck. "What if I heard something that should not be possible?" I mumble. "What if I heard something that would upturn everything we thought we knew? Perhaps even destroy everything?"

"You're talking about deathshrieks, aren't you?" Keita pulls back, tilts my chin up so I look in his eyes. "What did you hear, Deka?" he asks.

I look away. "More like what I think I heard."

"And what do you think you heard?"

"I think I heard a deathshriek speak," I force myself to say. "Not in Oteran, or any human language, but I could understand it nonetheless. As easily as I understand you."

"What did it say?" Keita asks, his voice suddenly hoarse.

I swallow. "Betrayer," I whisper. "It called me Betrayer."

Keita becomes even tenser, if possible. "Why would it say that?"

"I don't know." The lie slides smoothly past my lips. "I don't know anything any more."

"Have you told anyone else of this?"

I quickly shake my head.

He nods, relieved, then stares at me, his eyes deadly serious now. "Never speak of this again. Not ever again, Deka. And don't ever try to talk to them again." When I open my mouth to protest, he sighs. "You can already command deathshrieks, Deka. To understand them as well – to have them speak to you...That is the type of power that can upend the natural order.

"People kill over these things. People die over these things. You might die over this. Never forget, Deka, that you are an alaki first and foremost, because I guarantee you, no one else will."

A cold sweat shivers over me, and my heart pounds so fast, my entire body shakes. Keita's echoing the same thing White Hands said, the same thing I've thought over a thousand times before.

I nod. "You're right. I won't speak of it again. I won't ever speak to them again."

He reaches his arm around me, embraces me so tight, I can feel his heartbeat through his skin. It's beating a loud, panicked beat. The same one as mine. "All you have to do is remain safe until the campaign is over, Deka," he whispers into my hair. "All you have to do is remain safe for me."

"I promise," I whisper, settling against him.

We remain as we are, heartbeats pounding in unison, until the drums sound, beckoning everyone to dinner.

TWENTY-NINE

T hank Oyomo for my armour.

That's all I can think as I stand to attention in the courtyard of the Warthu Bera the afternoon of the campaign, the midday sun blazing high above us. It's once again the dry season and the heat suffocates the hundred of us girls that have been chosen to march on campaign. Everyone else remains behind, a reserve force to support us if further waves of attack are necessary. I hope this won't be the case, but more alaki are brought to the Warthu Bera every day as a precaution. They stare at us from the corners of the courtyard, their newly bald heads shining wretchedly in the blistering sun. I wonder if they're frightened or awed by what they see.

All the girls leaving today gleam from head to toe in golden armour. Mine has scales to mimic Ixa's drakos form and jagged spikes all down the back. It's strangely light and cool, considering that it covers every part of me but my eyes. It vibrates subtly whenever I near it, as does all the other infernal armour – especially Ixa's, since it was also made from my blood. White Hands had Karmoko Calderis make him a suit for his drakos form, because she wanted to ensure that the rest of the army sees the power of the Warthu Bera, that our prowess shines above that of all the other training grounds.

She and the other karmokos are in front of the gathered girls, but only she will accompany us, as our ranking commander, which is why she's riding a massive white stallion, Braima and Masaima standing guard on either side of her. Like us, they're all covered from head to toe in armour, although White Hands's is bone-white to match her gauntlets. The twins are also carrying assegai, long wooden spears tipped with sharp onyx blades. Apparently, they could be karmokos, they've so mastered them.

"Today is the day you have been preparing for, for so long," White Hands declares. "We begin our march to the N'Oyo desert, where we will meet and destroy the deathshriek scourge sweeping across our beloved Otera. That is where you, the honoured defenders of Otera, will carve your names into the history of this our empire! That is where you, the alaki of the Warthu Bera, will become legends!"

White Hands's speech is so rousing, the gathered girls clap, excitement building. Even I can't control the sudden drumming of my heart. It's finally happening. Our time is finally here.

"Can ye imagine it, Deka?" Britta says. "We're finally goin' on campaign."

"And we're going to kill every deathshriek we see," Adwapa says excitedly. "Twenty heads for each of us per day. No – thirty!"

Guilt sweeps over me, and I clench my fists to keep them from trembling. *Tears pouring from the deathshriek's eyes…* I shudder at the memory.

Beside me, Belcalis glances at Adwapa. "There is such a thing as too much enthusiasm, Adwapa," she informs her.

Adwapa sniffs, unimpressed. I return my attention to White Hands, who's now holding her hand up in a fist. "Alaki of the Warthu Bera! Conquer or die!" she commands.

"We who are dead salute you!" we reply, raising a fist and then beating it across our chest.

"Wherever we attack, we will conquer or bury ourselves in its ruins!"

"We who are dead salute you!" we repeat, beating our chests. "We who are dead salute you!"

"Move out!" White Hands commands, leading her horse onward.

We quickly do the same, pouring down the hill and out the gates, where the recruits fall seamlessly into place beside us. They're riding horses as well, but their jatu commanders ride in small tents on top of gigantic grey-skinned mammuts, or in chariots pulled by orrillions, the massive silver-furred apes growling warningly at each other and any horses that get close.

As we head towards Hemaira's main square to meet with the rest of the army, the citizens clap and cheer. "May Oyomo protect you, Death Strikers!" a few call out.

I can only shake my head, marvelling at the inconstancy of humans, as we continue riding through the streets.

The journey through the Eastern desert is long and brutal, much more so than I expected. I'm used to going on raids in rough terrain, but the desert is another beast altogether. The emperor has commanded that we make a stand at the N'Oyo mountain range, which borders the far edges of the desert, so for two weeks now, we've been slogging through sand, gritting our teeth when it slips through the crevices in our armour to invade our delicate parts. Every day, coucals have been flying back and forth, passing information, not that there's much of it. We know there are thousands of deathshrieks waiting for us in the mountains, but the scouts can never get close enough to get a full count. The mist is too thick to penetrate.

Before, I never understood how far the capital stretched, but now I can't help but count the days and hours, tracking the movement of the sun across the sands with heated irritation. It's not only the apprehension, the fear of venturing out into the unknown. It's the other soldiers – the common ones.

Even though they're now fully aware of what we alaki are, as is most everyone in Otera, they're used to seeing women only in the home. The idea of female soldiers does not sit well with them, and they've been treating us accordingly, hurling abusive words at us when the jatu aren't watching. They're especially hateful towards the bloodsisters of the Warthu Bera, since we're the only ones who wear golden armour.

The alaki from the other training houses are armoured and painted fiercely according to their houses, but they're not like us. Even though they number in the thousands, they're not as swift, as fierce, and they don't tolerate pain as well as we do. I've been observing them throughout our journey, and it seems the karmokos were right: we the alaki of the Warthu Bera are stronger than the rest, and it is because of our training. While all the other alaki were treated like regular soldiers – given healers when they were injured, rest when they were tired, and food when they were hungry – we were regarded as demons and trained accordingly. We were flayed, beaten, subjected to deathshriek screams. The unfairness of it would sting to my core, except I know that it has made me tougher. That's why I don't take too much offense when the foot soldiers grumble about me and my bloodsisters and pick at us. I know we can take them in a fight.

I try to remind myself of this every time I ride Ixa. The common soldiers are even more hateful when they notice him, his reptilian scales gleaming blue against the scorching desert sun. Yes, mammuts are ten times larger and the orrillions perhaps more impressive in their armour, but only Ixa can make horses shy away and zerizards flee when he passes.

Even now, as we near the midway point, an oasis deep in the desert, the animals still dart away. I ignore their panicked neighing and clucking as I hurry towards the lake at the oasis's centre. Ixa is so thirsty, his tongue is already flicking out.

"It's all right," I whisper to him once we reach the water's edge. "You're here."

De…ka, Ixa whispers, diving into the water. He's been parched these last few days.

I take out my waterskin, about to kneel down to fill it, when a shadow falls over me. "What in the name of Oyomo are you doing, alaki?" an unpleasant voice snarls.

My heart plummets. Baxo, a hefty Northern foot soldier, approaches, a scowl on his weathered face. Like many of the other foot soldiers, Baxo has made it his business to harass the bloodsisters of the Warthu Bera. I ignore him and continue filling my waterskin. No point getting into a confrontation with someone supposed to be on the same side as you.

When I don't reply, he stomps closer. "Are you stupid, or do you not hear me? What in the name of Oyomo are you doing, alaki?"

I sigh, rising and sealing my waterskin. "Getting some water," I reply.

"Getting some water?" he growls. "So you think you can bypass the rest of the line just 'cause you have that great beast of yours."

Now I see the other soldiers gathered behind Baxo. They're certainly not in any line, but they're there, and that's enough for Baxo.

"My apologies," I reply. I try to exhale away my growing anger. These men are only human. They aren't jatu, they aren't trained. I could kill them with less effort than it would take to swat a fly.

"Why? You've already gotten all the water you need." Baxo points to my waterskin. "You don't need to get back in line. What you need to do is get back on that great beast of yours and go to where the rest of your kind are."

He points to the far side of the lake, where the other alaki have gathered by themselves. Or, rather, where they've been herded to. The foot soldiers have all crowded around the lake and made sure to push all the alaki to the muddiest side.

"What are you waiting for?" Baxo snarls. "Go on."

He points again, but a low growl sounds. Ixa is out of the water and slowly advancing, teeth on full display. Each one gleams, butcher-knife sharp.

Baxo quickly takes a step back, his face turning chalky white. *Good boy, Ixa.* I praise him silently as he stands next to me, snarl deepening.

A fearful sweat is dripping down Baxo's forehead now. Nevertheless, he uses the moment to incite the other soldiers. "You see that?" he says. "You see what she's making that creature do?"

He returns his focus to me. "You bitches think you're better than us, whispering among your kind, giving us the evil eye. You're nothing but a group of malformed demon spawn, and I hope to Oyomo the deathshrieks finish your kind off well before we return from the desert."

My hands are clenched so tightly now, the skin feels like it's about to split. *Can't massacre your comrades, can't massacre your comrades…* Around me, the other men nod their agreement, then begin to add their own thoughts.

"Demons," one man calls.

"Abominations," another adds.

"Whores!"

And with that, I can remain silent no longer.

"Whores?" I scoff, looking at Baxo and his friends. "Hardly. We're soldiers, just like you. Many of us are going to die on the battlefield, same as you."

"As you should," Baxo jeers. "Women don't belong here – especially not your lot – and the more of you that die, the sooner you'll know it."

I unsheathe my atika, advancing closer, a growling Ixa at my side. A smile slices my lips when Baxo's face turns ever paler. "See, that's the amusing thing," I say. "Death is a common thing for our kind, which is why we welcome it, consider it an old friend." I point my atika at him. "Do you welcome death, Bax—"

A warm, calloused hand traps my shoulder. "Deka."

I turn to find Keita behind me, Li, Kweku and Acalan at his side. They've all walked over from their end of the lake.

He smiles at me. "Trust me?" he asks.

I roll my eyes, nod, then move to the side as he approaches Baxo, who takes a step back, alarmed.

"Lord Keita," the older man whispers.

"You have me at a disadvantage," Keita says. "I don't know your name. I do know you should be grateful for the alaki presence. Deka's especially. She's one of the most effective deathshriek killers there is, prized by the emperor himself, which is why she was given her mount, the first of its kind – personally developed by the Lady of the Equus." He thoughtfully taps his lips. "Are you saying that the emperor is wrong?"

"Wait, I don't think that's what he's saying at all," Kweku muses, entering the conversation. "I think he's saying both the emperor and the priests are wrong, because they're the ones who decreed that the alaki come with us."

"Also the Lady of the Equus," Li adds. "He's insulting her hard work. She personally bred Ixa, you know…"

Baxo's eyes are as wide as saucers now, and he turns from one to the other. "No, no, you're mistaken. I wasn't saying any of those things at all."

"Strange." Keita frowns. "I could have sworn you were. All of you, that is. In fact, I could have sworn that's why you all gathered here and made sure the alaki gathered there." He points to the muddy side of the lake.

"No, no, that's not it at all!" Baxo shakes his head quickly. "We were just leaving, weren't we?"

The other men nod.

"C'mon, then," Baxo urges.

He and the other men scurry away.

Once they're gone, Keita smiles at me. "I know you had it handled, but you're always saving me, Deka. I thought I'd return the favour at least once, even though you'd already done most of the work yourself."

"So you're the hero," I tease, amused despite myself.

"No, you're the hero," he corrects. "But every once in a while, the horned lizard shows his stripes." As I grin at this reminder of our first truly friendly conversation, he motions his head. "Come on, the rest of us are gathering water over there."

He points to the glistening portion of the lake, where the alaki are now gathering, their uruni by their side. They are partners, after all. And Keita and I... Well, Keita and I are something else altogether. Something that almost feels like... sweethearts.

THIRTY

"**T**his hateful desert," Britta groans, squinting against the sun.

It's a bright morning in the desert, and we're riding towards the small range of hills in the distance, the threshold to the N'Oyo Mountains. From there, the primal nesting grounds are a week and a half away. Beside me, Keita sits rigidly on his horse, jaw clenched. The N'Oyo Mountains border Gar Fatu, his home. In fact, his summer house – the very same house where his family was massacred – is in their foothills, which is why he becomes tenser with every step. I wish I could embrace him to make him feel better, but I can't do so here, where everyone will see. Instead I watch Britta as she grumbles about the weather.

"If it's not the sun, it's the sand, all flying everywhere an' getting all in me delicate bits."

A smile tugs at the side of my mouth. "Your delicate bits, you say... How ever will you survive?" I tease.

"Not much longer if it goes any deeper," Britta mutters.

"Oh please," Adwapa humphs, "you're not the only girl who has delicate bits."

"And ye know that from experience, wouldn't ye?" Britta laughs, her eyebrows waggling.

We all know Adwapa is forever sleeping in Mehrut's bed. It shocked me at first, the fact that two women would have such inclinations, but affection is affection. If there's one thing I've learned these past few months, it's that you must treasure it wherever you can find it. I'm just grateful they found each other in the Warthu Bera, rather than a place like Irfut, where they would have been beaten, then forced into servitude as temple maidens for deviancy.

"You three are disgusting," Acalan sniffs, shaking his head, although there's a twinkle in his eyes. He's also become much less rigid since entering the Warthu Bera. Constant brushes with death will do that to a person.

"Not our problem you don't know about delicate bits," says Asha, grinning at him.

"That would be because I'm an Oyomo-fearing man," Acalan sniffs.

"You mean an Oyomo-fearing virgin." Belcalis laughs, elbowing him.

He blushes. "I'm saving myself for marriage," he mumbles.

"You hear that, Keita?" It's Li's turn to join the conversation, and he turns laughingly to Keita. "Our Acalan is a virgin," he says, waggling his eyebrows.

Keita shrugs, looking away. "Nothing wrong with being a virgin," he replies. "I've never been with anyone either."

The conversation stops, and everyone turns to Keita, shocked, except for Britta and me. Being both from small villages, we tend to assume that unmarried people are virgins.

It was only after some weeks at the Warthu Bera that I realized city folk like Kweku, or Nibari like Adwapa and Asha, didn't hold such strict attitudes towards bed matters.

"Never ever?" Asha gasps, seeming bewildered beyond belief.

Keita shrugs, shaking his head.

"How about a kiss?" Kweku gasps. "Surely you've kissed."

Keita shrugs again.

"Why not?" Belcalis asks, seeming thoughtful.

"Never had anyone I wanted to kiss – before, that is." He looks away, seeming shy.

Belcalis breaks out in a knowing smile. "And now...?" She glances from Keita to me, and I feel my face heat all the way to the roots of my hair.

Keita shifts, uncomfortable. "Now is none of your business," he mumbles. "And honestly, I'm disappointed in you three."

"How are we the disappointing ones?" Adwapa sniffs. "You've never even felt a girl up before. I have – several times. It's delightful. Especially now that I get to do so in the privacy of our common bedroom." She makes a squeezing motion with her fingers, and we all roll our eyes.

"Go on." She gestures. "Please, do explain to me how we're the disappointing ones."

"Because you're alaki." Keita sighs. "You of all people know what it's like to not be the way the world expects you to be. Just because I'm a man—"

"Boy!" Asha coughs under her breath.

Keita rolls his eyes. "Just because I'm male doesn't mean I want to be chasing every girl in the vicinity. Perhaps I want my first time to mean something. Perhaps I want to be married, to be bonded, before I sleep with someone. I thought you'd all understand that."

We fall silent again.

Keita is right, of course. Virginity, no virginity – the choice should be a personal one. I could have never even thought such a thing before, growing up in Irfut, but being in the Warthu Bera has changed me. The Infinite Wisdoms no longer hold as much sway over me as it used to.

"I'm a virgin too," I whisper. "Nothing wrong with that."

"Same here." Britta waves.

"Me too," adds Lamin, Asha's uruni, blushing. He's a very shy boy, despite his massive size, and he very rarely speaks.

"Actually" – Li clears his throat – "me too. But I've kissed before – and other things."

"You hypocrite!" Acalan gasps. "You made such fun of me."

Li shrugs. "You're an easy target."

We all turn to Kweku, but he shrugs as well. "Well, don't look at me, I grew up in the city."

Now it's Asha, Adwapa and Belcalis's turn.

Adwapa's the first to respond, and she does so with a humph. "We all know that ship has sailed for me. Happily too. Countless times across the horizon, as it were – like a ship, docking at every port."

"Same here," Asha says with a shrug.

When everyone turns to Belcalis, I clear my throat loudly. "How did we even get on this topic anyway?" I ask, trying to distract them. "We should be making plans – survival plans, contingency plans… The deathshrieks are less than ten days away."

To my relief, Acalan takes the bait. "The largest number of deathshrieks ever, all of them waiting in the N'Oyo Mountains," he says with a shiver.

I glance at Belcalis, trying to see how she's doing. She catches my gaze, nods gratefully. "My thanks, Deka," she mouths.

I turn back to the conversation to see Britta glancing across the group. "Is anyone else frightened?" she asks. "I mean, I've gotten used to the raids, but this is different. Just the thought of this has me stomach in knots."

"You and your delicate stomach," Adwapa humphs. "And no, I'm not frightened. When I meet the deathshrieks, I'm gonna force every last one of those bastards to taste infinity."

"Ye and wha' army?" Britta sniffs. "Ye only ever fulfil yer quota, lazybones."

And just like that, the conversation becomes heated, everyone enthusiastically discussing how they're going to handle the deathshrieks when we meet them. My thoughts drift, the same worries taking over them. I don't know what I'll do when I'm faced with deathshrieks again. After what I've seen, what I know, I can't view them as just mindless monsters any more. But I'm still not fully sure what to make of them. I try to stifle my concerns, and that's when I notice something – prickles creeping up my spine, then swarming me in one enormous wave.

Heartbeats.

Lots of them.

I hear the whoosh before I see the shadow hurtling towards us. Then a massive boulder slams into our ranks.

* * *

The moments after impact tick by slowly, a macabre but graceful ballet. Bright red and gold blood drains into the sand, severed limbs scatter with abandon. A few of them move, trying to wriggle back to each other.

Severed alaki body parts fighting off the gilded sleep.

"…eka!"

The sound of battle horns comes as if from a distance, as do frantic drumbeats. The commanders are calling to their troops, trying to get them to reassemble. It's no use, not with all the boulders raining from the sky, their shapes clouded by the sand and dust whirling in the air.

"…ove, Deka!"

I'm overwhelmed by my heartbeat, my fear, the tingling. It rushes over my skin, a tidal wave only I can feel. Deathshrieks – an entire army of them. A shifting, formless mass in the distance. *There are so many of them…* I think, dazed. I knew there were, but this… This defies all expectation.

"Move, Deka!" Keita's hand grips my shoulder. He's standing behind me, Britta at his side. "The deathshrieks are throwing boulders at us!"

Another boulder ploughs into the advance guard, sending soldiers flying.

"Death Strikers, to me!" a voice roars. Captain Kelechi, riding at the front of the army.

Visibility is so poor now, I can barely see past my own nose. Mist is threading the sand, making it nearly impossible to see anything.

"Death Strikers, to me!" the captain repeats, waving a flag. It cuts through the mist, a barely-visible dull red glimmer. "To me!"

"Hurry, Deka!" Britta commands, urging her horse onward. "Let's go!"

I shake away my daze. "Yah!" I say, urging Ixa after her and Keita.

Together, we race towards Captain Kelechi, who has now moved just behind the advance troops guarding the emperor. When we arrive, Emperor Gezo, White Hands and two generals are beside him, as are the equus twins.

"Your Majesty." We all bow.

"No time for that now, this is a battlefield," the emperor says. He turns to White Hands. "What is the situation?"

"They're shooting at us from the hills there and there." She points.

"Big old rocks," Braima adds, and his twin nods.

The emperor turns to me. "Can you command them?"

I shake my head. "Not from this distance, Your Majesty. I'd have to ride over and—"

A volley of spears hurtles out the mist. Soldiers barely have time to get their shields up before it strikes the advance guard.

"Protect the emperor!" The call rises up, and a contingent of jatu splinters away from the advance guard and hurriedly covers us with a curtain of shields.

They do so just in time. Another hail of spears strikes, reaching even farther than the first one did.

"Oyomo's breath," one of the generals gasps, unnerved when a spear bounces off the shields. "They're throwing spears – fecking spears."

"We have to get Deka to them," Captain Kelechi says.

"I have the solution to that," White Hands offers. She hands me a steel cylinder that almost looks like a horn from a toros – a scaly, bull-like creature that lives on the shores of slow-flowing rivers. "Shout into that, and it will amplify your voice."

I nod. "Yes, Karmoko."

"You have to be closer, however," White Hands says. "Much closer." Her eyes look past the shields to the distance, from where yet more spears are hurtling.

My chest tightens in alarm. Surely the infernal armour cannot withstand that. And if an arrow hits any of my vitals, it'll trigger an almost-death, forcing me into the gilded sleep for the rest of the battle.

"So she has to ride out there," Keita says. He nods. "I'll protect her."

"No, you'll stay here," White Hands says, shaking her head. "Deka, Britta and Belcalis will go. Gazal will command the unit."

Gazal, off to White Hands's side, nods to us.

"Your task is to ensure that Deka is safe," White Hands says. "Belcalis, you will signal us when it is done."

Belcalis nods.

"But I'm her uruni," Keita protests. "Where she goes, I go."

White Hands turns to him. "Deka, Belcalis and Britta are alaki," she says, "ones I've personally trained. They're much less likely to die out there than you."

"But—"

"You are the lord of Gar Fatu," Emperor Gezo interrupts, "the last in your line. I will not send you out on such a dangerous errand."

Keita bows. "Yes, Your Majesty."

And that's that. I carefully tuck the metal toros horn White Hands gave me into my pack, then nod at Keita, trying to convey all my feelings in once glance. Hope, fear…affection. He nods back at me, his eyes reflecting all the same things. I let the sight hearten me as White Hands nods at the hill.

"Conquer the deathshrieks or bury yourself there," she commands.

Belcalis, Britta and I bow. "We who are dead salute you."

It's strangely cold and quiet as we ride into the mist. The occasional boulder still flies over us, but the rain of spears, thankfully, has ceased. Britta, Belcalis, Gazal and I concentrate on the hills rising in the distance. The deathshrieks have massed there, and we can dimly see their shapes moving in the eerie darkness.

"Keep your eyes sharp," Gazal commands as we ride onward. "We have to deliver Deka close enough to command them, then we can call to the rest of the army."

"Yes, Bloodsister," Britta, Belcalis and I reply as one.

As we ride, Britta turns to me. "Don't worry, Deka," she says. "I'm here. If ye fall, I will protect ye."

"Same to you," I reply, but Britta only nods. We both know my life is the more precious one now. I'm the one who has to get to the deathshrieks for the sake of the army. It's a disconcerting thought. I can't imagine a life without Britta, can't imagine what I would do if she had to lay down hers for mine.

We continue deeper into the mists, where the hills are

looming closer, as is something else – a formless, shifting mass accompanied by a low whistling sound.

Belcalis's horse falters. "Is that—"

"SHIELDS UP!" Gazal roars as spears explode out of the mist.

I jerk up my shield. *Down, Ixa!* I command.

He hunkers into the sand just as the spears impact, one of them ramming Belcalis's horse backwards, killing it instantly.

"Belcalis!" I shout, horrified.

"I'm all right!" her muffled voice replies. "My horse fell over me!"

"Hold tight, I'm coming for you!" I shout.

As I ride towards her, however, a puddle of dark blue catches my eye. I turn to it and the ground tilts sideways. It's Britta, impaled on a spear. My entire world narrows to the dark blue blood spilling from her gut, staining the sand with horrific colour. It's as if I'm moving through sludge, as if it's streaming into my nose and stopping my breath. I don't even feel my feet as I stagger off Ixa.

Deka? Ixa asks, trailing after me. He wants to know if I'm all right, but I can't reply, can't even think.

All I see is Britta lying there, that horrible blue blood pouring from her side. When I near, she looks up at me, her face pale with sweat, and bravely struggles to smile.

"Turns out…it was always me belly," she wheezes.

I can barely stand now. "Britta…" I whisper. "Don't speak. You don't have to—" I suddenly can't breathe any more, my helmet's strap is choking me.

I throw it aside, gasping.

"Deka!" Gazal's voice seems so far away. "What are you doing? We have a duty to fulfil!"

When I don't answer, she clasps my shoulders and forces me to look at her. "Deka!"

"I can't leave her!" I gasp, tears flooding my eyes. "I can't leave Britta."

Something almost like pity flickers over Gazal's eyes, but she ruthlessly suppresses it. "This happened in the pursuit of her duty. It should be her honour to die for Otera."

Die. The word explodes through me with the force of a thousand suns. Britta is dying. She's dying here, where the buzzards will make a feast of her, and the army will trample over her remains. She's dying here, where no one she loves will be able to find her, to mourn her.

I can't let that happen. I can't let Britta die. There's no one I love more than her, no one who loves me as deeply as she does. I wrench myself from Gazal and turn back to her. "You have to live," I gasp, power surging inside me. It's like a wave, washing over my body, vibrating from my skin.

"Deka…" Britta says weakly, her eyes wide. "Yer face." She reaches up to my now-uncovered face, but I catch her hands in mine, deliberately pull off her helmet, so she can't ignore my voice.

I don't know if this is going to work or not, but I tamp down my doubts, forcing myself to believe. Forcing myself to put every bit of power into this. Britta has to survive. Without her, I am nothing. When I speak, my voice doesn't even sound human any more. All my pain and fury have combined into what seems like a thousand resonant voices.

"You will not die, Britta," I command, forcing my will into her, threading my energy around her like a living web. She's fading away, the light in her dimming, so I use even more energy, shooting it out of me and into her.

"You will wait for a healer, and you will survive this. You will not die!"

Britta's eyes glaze over. "I will...not die..." she echoes, closing them. I look down at her side, and a tightness inside me loosens. Her bleeding has slowed, just as I willed.

"What is this, Deka?" Gazal's voice seems almost frightened behind me.

I turn and she takes a step back, gasping. "Deka, your face..." she gasps. "Your—"

"Guard her," I command, enforcing my words with a thread of energy. "Ensure that she sees a healer."

Gazal nods, her eyes glazing over. Unlike the others, she never did wear the golden circlet I gave her as a gift.

"Yes," she says dully, "I will guard her."

I wait until she plants herself beside Britta, shield up against any arrows.

Belcalis has finally freed herself from her horse. She gasps the minute I turn to her, jerking back. "Deka, your face..."

Then she sees Britta.

"Britta!" she gasps, running to her. "Britta, no!" Tears are running down her face now.

"She will survive," I tell her, forcing myself to believe my words. "She has to. She has to...I've commanded it."

Something in my words must have convinced her, because she slowly nods, drying her tears.

I walk over to Ixa, then point Belcalis towards Gazal's horse. "Come," I say, power still surging from me. "Let's end this."

She nods, mounts Gazal's horse, and nods at me grimly, her face still pale.

"Kill them all, Deka," she whispers. "Kill every last one of those bastards."

"I intend to," I reply.

THIRTY-ONE

The mist grows thicker as we continue onward, and the spears fly faster and more frequently. Ixa is attuned to their sound now and digs into the sand the minute he hears their signature whistling, allowing Belcalis and me to raise our shields before they can hit.

"There." Belcalis points at the hills after another storm of spears ends. "They're all there."

"YAH!" I urge Ixa onward. We've almost reached it.

When we burst though the mist, I see what Belcalis is pointing to – the rows and rows of deathshrieks lining the edge of the hills, catapults in their midst.

Belcalis stops, shocked. "Catapults," she gasps. "Where did they get catapults?"

It seems the deathshrieks' use of war machinery grows more advanced every time we see them. First it was slingshots and cochleans, now this. I don't dwell on the thought. I'm already lifting my hands, my body shaking with the force of the energy rolling from it. If I could see my reflection while using the combat state, I'm sure I would be glowing as bright as a star now.

Even the sand under my feet rumbles and shakes. When they notice it, the deathshrieks rumble and click to each other, panic rippling through their ranks. I slap my hands down, sending waves of power through their bodies.

"LOWER YOUR WEAPONS," I command. "KNEEL!"

They slowly obey, each one getting on its knees as its eyes glaze to my command.

"Signal the army," I say to Belcalis.

She nods, then lights the firecracker she has brought for the occasion. It explodes in a colourful display of reds and within moments, distant drumbeats reply to its signal. The army is on the move.

Once she's done, Belcalis looks at the kneeling deathshrieks and frowns. "Where are the rest of them? I thought they were in the thousands. This looks like only a few nests' worth."

"There's more of them," I say. I can feel them out there, thousands more heartbeats pounding somewhere behind the mountains, waiting for us. They're not my concern – yet. These are. They're the ones that hurt Britta, that may have caused her death by now, for all I know. I try not to think this horrific thought as I approach them, noting the terror rising from their skins, a shimmery grey colour only I can see, using the combat state.

My eyes quickly find the deathshriek in the middle, the one with all the quills. The chieftain. When I walk towards him, the sand shakes under my feet, a much deeper vibration than even my energy can cause. The army is nearing, and just in time. My limbs are sagging from the force of emitting so much energy. My collapse won't be long in coming now. But before it happens, I will have my due – for Britta's sake.

"Deka," Belcalis says, turning in the direction of the rumbling. "Put your helmet on. The army is near. They must not see your face."

I do as she cautions and walk over to the deathshriek leader. "Lift your head," I command. My words rumble through its body, squeezing its heart. It immediately complies. Once it does so, I add another command. "Speak but remain kneeling."

The deathshriek leader's expression as it looks up at me is a surprising mix of anger and disgust. When its voice emerges, it sounds gravelly but distinct. "Nuru..." it rasps.

I frown. There it is, that word again. That title. What does it mean?

"You betrayed...us..."

The unexpected words cut through my daze. I blink down at the deathshriek, shocked. "Betrayed you?" I ask.

The deathshriek hisses. "You...betrayed us...for the... humans...Nuru... We...will...never forgive you...this... Never."

Exhaustion slams into me.

Then everything goes black.

When I wake, it's dark and I'm lying inside a lush red tent. "The hero of the hour," a voice cheers. "You're awake." To my shock, Emperor Gezo is sitting beside me, Keita, Asha, Adwapa, Gazal and Belcalis kneeling by his side. His face is covered by a mask today – a benevolent sun, shining down on his subjects.

I scramble to get up, but the emperor shakes his head. "No need to rise. You have already served Otera well this day.

You may make use of this tent for as long as you need."

I take in the luxurious fabrics, the gold accents. This is one of his private tents. "Thank you, Your Majesty," I whisper, dazed. "Thank you."

Then I remember...

"Britta!" I gasp, horrified.

"Your friend is right there." The emperor points across the tent, where Britta lies, bandaged. "She will survive, but it was a close call. Thanks to this one" – he points to Gazal, who is kneeling, motionless, by his side – "she was able to get to a healer in time."

My entire body sags. "Thank you," I whisper again. "Thank you..."

The emperor nods. "Anything for you, Deka of Irfut. You saved us this day, and I imagine you will continue to do so in the days to come." He pats my shoulder. "Rest now. We ride out again tomorrow."

I bow again. "My deepest thanks, Your Majesty."

The emperor smiles, then he gestures to Keita. "Come, let us give them their privacy."

"Yes, Your Majesty." Keita sends me a worried glance as he leaves.

Once they're gone, I turn to Belcalis. "Help me up," I rasp. I'm still so tired, I can barely move my limbs on my own.

As Belcalis walks over, Adwapa peers out of the tent to ensure that we're truly alone. "What in infinity happened out there?" she asks, turning to us.

Gazal, for her part, remains where she is, head down, hands on her lap.

Belcalis shrugs. "You'll have to ask Deka," she says as she helps me over to Britta.

She's lying on a bed, and her skin is so very pale. Even then, I'm thankful. That horrific blue colour has receded. "Is she truly all right?" I ask, clutching my chest. My heart is beating such a desperate beat now, I'm scared it's going to jump out from behind my ribs.

"She'll survive," Belcalis says. "You made sure of that."

"What are you two talking about?" Adwapa has closed the tent flap and rushed to the bedside. "What happened out there?"

"What happened is that Deka changed – her entire face, it just changed," Belcalis explains. "She looked like... She looked not human."

"What do you mean?" I ask.

"Your face, Deka," Belcalis says. "It looked like a deathshriek's – but not. It was beautiful, yet terrifying... And when you spoke – if I hadn't had the circlet you gave me, I would have lost my wits the way Gazal did."

She nods at the novice. Gazal still hasn't moved, although her hands twitch in her lap when her name is mentioned. She looks eerie, sitting there so silently.

"She hasn't spoken since she brought Britta," Asha whispers. "She just insisted that Britta get a healer, and then she became like that. I lied to the emperor and told him she was battle shocked, which is why she wasn't moving."

Adwapa turns to me. "What in Oyomo's name did you do to her?"

I don't know, I want to tell her, but that would be a lie. I do know. I pushed all my power, all my will, into Gazal. That's what made her this way.

"Gazal?" I call.

When she hears my voice, she slowly looks up. Her eyes are glazed, distant. "Yes?" she replies.

"Are you awake?" I ask. When she doesn't answer, a small thread of panic slithers through me. "Wake up, Gazal," I urge.

The glazed look in Gazal's eyes fades. She glances around, confused. "Where am I? What happened?" she asks.

"I think—" I begin, but Belcalis pushes past me.

"You're in one of the emperor's tents," she says. "You brought Britta back, but something must have hit your head."

Gazal nods, holds her head as if searching for a lump. "Have I reported back?" she asks.

"I don't think so," I say. "But the mission was a success. You did well."

Gazal nods. "That's good," she says absently, walking out. That perplexed expression is still on her face.

"What was that?" Asha asks, frowning. "What happened to her?"

"It was Deka's voice," Belcalis explains. "It's growing more powerful, and the way she looks now when she uses it..." She looks at me, a worried look on her face. "What are you, Deka?" she whispers. "What are you?"

It's late in the evening by the time Asha leaves, off to tell our uruni what is happening. Once she does, Belcalis and Adwapa push their pallets beside Britta's. I'm relieved they've stayed behind. Images from this afternoon have begun flashing through my mind, confounding and frightening me all at once.

"Belcalis, Adwapa…" I whisper. "Can I speak to you?"

"Yes?" Both of them rise, walk over.

"I remember what happened now," I say as they sit beside me.

"I wasn't aware that you forgot," Adwapa snorts.

"There is one thing I did…" I begin. I turn to them, hesitant. "If I tell you two something, can you confine it to us? Can you promise never to tell anyone else – not even the other bloodsisters?"

"Of course." Adwapa nods.

Belcalis nods. "I would never betray your confidence, Deka. You know this."

"I know," I say, looking down. "But this…this might be dangerous," I add, giving her the same warning Keita once gave me. "It might get you – it might get us…"

"Killed?" Adwapa laughs. "We were dead the minute our blood ran gold, I've always known that. I thought you did too."

"We who are dead salute you," I agree, nodding.

"Isn't that the truth." Adwapa shrugs. "Now what did you want to tell us?"

I glance up at her. "What if…what if I heard the deathshrieks speak?"

Both still.

"You don't mean all the clicking and rumbling, do you?" Belcalis asks quietly.

I shake my head. "No, not the clicking."

"So you understand them?" This question comes from Adwapa. For some reason, she doesn't seem shocked.

I nod.

"For how long?" she asks.

"Ever since that last temple. The one where I went into a daze."

She nods, thinking.

"What are they saying?" Belcalis asks. When I don't reply, she sighs. "It must be very worrisome if you're having difficulty saying it."

"Betrayer," I whisper. "They're calling me a betrayer."

"Are you?" Adwapa asks quietly. "Are you some sort of deathshriek, Deka?"

The question strikes deep to the core of me, tears of fear and confusion blistering my eyes. When I shake my head, unable – *unwilling* – to answer, Belcalis sighs beside her. "Well, you need to find out, Deka, and quickly, before the jatu do so first and end your life."

THIRTY-TWO

What am I?

The question circles my mind, as it has for the past ten months.

Am I truly a deathshriek half-breed, or am I something more? No matter which way I look at it, the power I used on Britta defies all logic, moves well beyond everything I ever thought I knew. The only thing I know now is that White Hands has the answers – if only she would give them to me.

Thankfully, she's not the only person I can ask.

In the distance, mist swirls around frightening black monoliths with glittering white peaks. The N'Oyo Mountains – Otera's largest salt mines until Keita's family were massacred there. The deathshrieks' primal nesting grounds are hidden somewhere in those peaks, and they have the answers I seek. I just have to get it from them before anyone else notices. *Before the jatu do first and end your life...*

"Are you prepared, Deka?" This question comes from the emperor, who's riding on the mammut above me.

It's been completely outfitted with infernal armour, and

even the tent atop it is protected by a roof of solid cursed gold. I always suspected that Karmoko Calderis took lots more gold than she actually needed for our infernal armour. Now I know why.

"Yes, Your Majesty," I say, glancing at the platform carrying a gigantic toros horn the troops have built overnight. "I'm prepared."

"Good," he says. "Onward."

As the army complies, I feel the heat of another's gaze on my shoulders. When I turn, White Hands is watching me, her brow furrowed into a frown. I wonder what she's thinking, if she suspects what happened.

"You all right, Deka?" Keita asks, his eyes worried. We haven't had time to talk in private since yesterday, so I haven't had the chance to tell him I spoke to deathshrieks again, haven't even been sure I should tell him. I remember how insistent he was the last time we spoke that I should never do it again.

I nod. "All recovered," I say, trying not to worry him further.

"You certain about that?" He seems doubtful.

I turn to him. "Why do you ask?"

"You haven't been the same since yesterday," he says. "What happened out there?"

"Nothing," I say, looking down. When he gives me a doubtful look, I add, "Well, not nothing... It's Britta, I'm worried about her."

He reaches over, squeezes my hand. "She'll be fine. If humans can heal from near-fatal wounds, surely alaki can as well."

I nod, smile wanly. "Thanks for that, Keita. I just have to keep that in—"

A fireball explodes into the toros horn platform. As the horses pulling it gallop away, neighing, I jerk up to find yet more fireballs blazing towards us – flaming arrows, lighting up the sky.

"Deathshrieks!" Captain Kelechi shouts somewhere in the distance, having been anticipating such an attack. "Shields!"

Down, Ixa! I command, lifting my shield.

Ixa huddles into the sand as the arrows rain down. Bloodcurdling shrieks are now shattering the air, sending many of the soldiers to their knees. The smell of piss and vomit rises, soldiers convulse off their horses. They're not used to the deathshriek screams the way the jatu and we alaki are.

Above the din, the generals call to the troops from their mammuts. "Prepare yourselves!" they shout.

It's already too late. The deathshrieks are bursting through the mists, their bodies covered in crudely fashioned leather armour, their hands holding weapons – actual weapons. Massive swords and maces flash as they cut a bloody swath through the army, heading in our direction. The advance troops immediately assemble, trying to block the path to the emperor.

"Use your voice, Deka!" the emperor shouts to me. "Use your voice!"

I nod, fumbling to pull down my helmet so my face won't be seen. I notice something strange out of the corner of my eye – a leaper deathshriek with bright red spikes running down its back. Those spikes rattle in the wind, looking familiar – achingly so.

"Deka!" the leaper shouts, jumping over the assembled ranks. Its voice is clearer than any other deathshriek I've ever heard. "Deka, stop! It's me!"

Tears sting my eyes, and my hands tremble.

Why do I feel like I'm seeing a long-lost friend?

"Deka!" Keita's voice is strangely close to my ears. "Use your voice, Deka!"

I raise my hands, channelling power, but stop when the leaper frantically does the same, holding out her own hands.

Her hands?

Why do I think the deathshriek is female? They're all male, that's what we've been told. That's what we've always seen.

A shadow falls over me – Keita's. "Deka, pay attention!" he shouts. "Kill the deathshrieks!"

"Yes," I say, turning away from the strange leaper.

I will my power to rise again, letting it surge through every part of me. "STOP WHERE YOU—"

"DEKA, IT'S ME, KATYA!" the leaper shouts in that strange, clicking language, breaking into our ranks.

"Katya?" My hands fall to my sides.

No, it can't be. I remember Katya, red hair spilling, skin turning blue as that deathshriek ripped out her spine. "You can't be Katya!" I reply in Oteran. "This is a trick! You're trying to trick me!"

Keita looks from me to the deathshriek. "Deka?" he asks, shocked.

The leaper hurries closer, batting aside any soldiers in her way. The battle is still raging around us, but somehow it feels like we're the only two here. "No, Deka, it's the humans that are tricking you! This is what happens to us when we die our final deaths. This is what we become! You have to come with us, hurry!" she clicks.

"Us?" I ask, the blood rushing past my ears. "Who is us?" I whisper.

"Deathshrieks and alaki!" Katya cries. "We're one and the same! When an alaki dies her final death, she is reborn as a deathshriek! The emperor knows that. That's why he's using you to kill us. He's using you to destroy your own kind. He wants us all to die, for ever this time!"

The earth falls out from under my feet.

"No…" I whisper. "It can't be." But even as I say this, I remember the long-ago conversation I had with White Hands, remember her words. "Till our empire is free of those monsters."

Is this what she was talking about? Is this what she meant?

"Deka," Keita says, grabbing me. "What do you mean, Katya? Is that thing saying it's her?"

He looks back at her, repulsion visible in his eyes. I can imagine what he sees – a deathshriek, snarling and horrific, but that's not what I see now. All I see is my friend Katya, her deathshriek form still pale, and that red hair transformed into bright red spikes.

It's truly her.

Even after all our prayers that she would have a peaceful afterlife, here she is, again on the battlefield.

And now there's a contingent of jatu approaching her – two to each side and two from behind. They're going to kill her. They're going to kill her all over again.

Anger explodes inside me, rousing the foundations of my

power. My voice emerges as an inhuman rumble. "Deathshrieks," I roar to any who are in hearing distance, "protect Katya!"

The deathshrieks' heartbeats slow, their eyes glaze as my power takes over them. They hurtle towards Katya, destroying the soldiers in their path. Alaki, jatu, they all fall under the claws of the deathshrieks rushing to obey my command.

Keita's face is pale now. "Katya?" he echoes, stunned. "Tell me what you mean, Deka?"

A massive shadow falls over us as I form a reply. The emperor's mammut. There's a look on the emperor's face I've never seen before – one of pure, unadulterated rage. He points a finger at me.

"That alaki has gone mad!" he shouts. "Kill the traitor! Kill Deka of Irfut!"

My stomach plunges. "Your Majesty," I protest. "I—"

Armoured red hands drag me off Ixa.

Deka! Ixa growls, charging them, but the emperor points to him too.

"Destroy her animal as well!" he shouts.

The jatu turn their swords towards him, murder in their eyes.

"Ixa, run!" I shout. "Run!"

Deka! he protests.

"RUN, IXA! GO TO KATYA!" I bellow, pushing an image of the red-spiked deathshriek into his head.

That's the only command I have a chance to make before a gag goes over my mouth, and armoured hands force me down into the sand so I can't move my hands to make commands. As my helmet is removed, I dimly see Ixa barrelling away towards

Katya, dimly hear horrified gasps.

"Look at her face!"

"She looks just like a deathshriek! She's one of them!"

"No! NO!" Adwapa and Asha shout from somewhere nearby, joining the protests of the nearby bloodsisters.

The emperor doesn't care. "Kill her!" he shrieks. "Kill the deathshriek traitor now! Kill anyone who tries to aid her!"

Shadows hurriedly move over me. When I look up again, Captain Kelechi is standing before me, a sword in his hand. He has a calm, resigned expression on his face.

"You brought this on yourself, alaki," he says, raising his sword.

"WAIT!" Keita bursts through the ranks, but the other jatu quickly pin him down. My heart jolts at the sight, fear and relief rushing through me at the same time. He's trying to save me. "No, you can't do this, Captain!" he shouts, his voice desperate.

Captain Kelechi turns to him, shaking his head. "You can't help her now, Keita," he says. "You see what she is." He turns back to me, sword raised.

"Then let me do it!" Keita's eyes are determined as he shouts, "Let me kill her. I'm her uruni – I should be the one responsible for her."

What did he just say?

When the captain does not reply, Keita tries again. "She saved your life!" he cries. "She saved all of us – countless times! If you do this, you'll just be dishonouring everything she ever did for you!"

Captain Kelechi stills, turns to Keita, who nods desperately.

"She needs a peaceful final death," he whispers. "You owe

her that much. We all owe her. Even if she's a traitor, she killed for our side first." He looks at me, and everything inside me goes still. I see the cold, distant look in his eyes, the absolute certainty. He's not trying to save me. He's trying to end my life.

Just like Ionas did.

A long, endless scream shatters inside me, silence and leaden heaviness in its wake.

Once again, I am betrayed. And just like before, it is by the boy I loved.

The captain looks down at me, considering. Then he turns to Keita. "If you try to help her escape, it'll be your head," he says.

"I know," Keita says. "I know there's no escape for her now except death. But she's my partner, my responsibility, and only I know how to end it. Only I know her final death."

Everything inside me is so dull now, I'm not shocked by his words. I can barely see anything any more, barely feel anything behind this deep, aching emptiness growing inside me.

Captain Kelechi looks up at the emperor, who has been watching the proceedings from his mammut. "Your Majesty?" he asks.

The emperor nods. "How will you do it, young lord of Gar Fatu?" he asks Keita.

Keita shrugs off the jatu holding him down and rises. "I'll dismember her, Your Majesty," he says.

I blink, confused. I can't die from dismemberment, Keita knows that. He knows...

The breath strangles in my throat. Keita's trying to save me. Trying to ensure that I survive by executing me before someone else does.

He ignores my muffled gasp as he continues: "It's the only sure way to kill her."

"How do you know?" the emperor asks.

Keita looks straight into my eyes. "She told me once. She told me the truth of her final death."

Tears flood my eyes. He's sacrificing himself for me, signing his own death warrant. If he dismembers me, I'll go into the gilded sleep instead of the final death and then everyone will know him for a traitor. They'll kill him then, and unlike me, he won't come back.

He'll never come back.

The thought sends my body jerking back to life. "No!" I shriek, the sound muffled by my gag. "NO, KEITA!"

Keita ignores me, turns to the emperor. "Your Majesty?"

The emperor nods. "Proceed."

Keita walks over to me. "You shouldn't have done it, Deka," he says. "You shouldn't have told me how to kill you." There's hope, determination in his voice. I struggle, try to shout so he can hear me, but he lifts his sword. It gleams in the early afternoon sunlight. "I'm sorry," he says, bringing it down.

When my head separates from my body, my eyes catch his. They're filled with tears. Keita's eyes are filled with tears. He's crying as he kills me.

He's crying as he dooms himself.

It's night when I wake again, and an itchy darkness surrounds me. Some sort of cloth is binding me in place. I try to turn my head to get away from it, and that's when I stop, bewildered. I can't turn my head. I can't even turn my neck. There's a searing pain somewhere between the two – a pain that splinters across my body in a strange, abrupt way, as if there are gaps. I try to lift my hands to feel my neck, but they won't move. I can't even feel them, actually. The only thing I feel is that pain, and an unnerving slithering feeling, as if parts of my body are… reaching for each other.

My body isn't connected together. Alarm jolts me as I understand. The fibres are growing back into each other, the way they did back in the cellar in Irfut. Is this part of the emperor's punishment? Have they already killed Keita? Please say Keita is all right. A low, keening wail builds in my throat.

"Deka?" Something rummages the cloth surrounding me, and light pierces into its darkness. "Deka, you can't possibly be awake!"

I'm pulled up into the air, and the first thing I see is Keita's face. Shock and bewilderment shine in his eyes. "Deka, how can you be awake?" he gasps. "You're still healing!"

"Keita," I sob, relieved tears running down my eyes. "You're alive, you're alive!"

"Of course I'm alive," he says, frowning. "Why wouldn't I be?"

"But everyone saw you give me an almost-death, not a final one. They know you're a traitor."

Keita shakes his head. "No, they saw you bleed the blue of the final death. They thought you were dead."

"Blue?" I ask, frowning. "How could I bleed blue if it wasn't my final death?"

"It was Britta's idea," he answers. "She knew something like this would happen sooner or later, so she had Belcalis make a solution from some plants in the Warthu Bera. Apparently she has some experience with apothecaries?"

"Her uncle was an apothecary," I say, remembering what she told me about that evil man. At least she learned one thing from him that turned out to be helpful.

"Britta gave some of it to me and Adwapa as a precaution. I sprinkled it on you as I— as I…"

He swallows, unable to finish.

"There was just enough of it to convince everyone that it worked. And then the deathshrieks burst through the ranks and everyone got busy fighting. No one noticed us gathering up your body parts or taking them to Ixa in the confusion."

"Ixa?" I ask.

Keita helps me angle my head down, and I see what I didn't before: we're riding on Ixa, securely on his back, as he races across the desert sands.

"Ixa!" I gasp, relieved. "You're all right!"

De…ka, Ixa replies happily.

"He came back for you once he delivered that deathshriek to safety." Keita helps me angle my head back up, wincing again when I grimace. The pain is the strangest I've ever felt – fleeting and unconnected. "Sorry," he whispers. "I didn't know you could wake in such a state."

Neither did I, I want to reply, but I remain quiet, smile down at Ixa. *That's my Ixa,* I praise him silently.

Deka, Ixa says, pleased.

I glance back at Keita. He's looking around us, his eyes wary, the same way they are when we go out on raids. But this isn't a raid. This is treason against everything he's ever believed in.

"Why did you do it?" I ask. "You and Adwapa, why did you take the solution from Britta?"

He shrugs. "Because we know you, Deka. When you use your abilities, you change – your voice sounds different and you look…inhuman. No matter how careful you were, we knew it was only a matter of time before you were discovered, accused of being some sort of deathshriek or witch, and executed. Of course we didn't anticipate that it would happen the very next day."

My eyes widen. "You knew all along – about the leathering, I mean?"

Keita nods. "Yes. I saw it once, in the moonlight, during a raid. And it doesn't frighten me, if that's what you're thinking. I know you were afraid it would, but nothing will change how I feel about you, Deka… I know you're not a monster."

Warmth spreads through me, tears pricking at my eyes. Keita accepts me as I am – loves me. He doesn't have to say the words, but I feel them. I feel them in the way he cradles my severed head so gently, even though the very act of holding it should horrify him. I feel them in the actions he took – the actions that he knew could well have ended his life. He defied the emperor for me, risked death for me – the only one he has.

Against all odds, he loves me.

Keita loves me.

How could I ever have thought he would betray me?

So much warmth flows through me now, I don't even feel my wounds any more. Then I have a thought. "Wait – why didn't you just stop when you took my head? You didn't have to dismember me completely, you know."

"Well, I know that now." He sighs. "But I had to give you a death no one could believe you'd survive."

"You had to make a spectacle for them," I say, understanding now.

Keita nods, then looks away, his body trembling slightly. I'm not the only one the dismemberment hurt, I can see that now. I can only imagine how he felt, cutting into me. I suddenly wish I had the use of my arms, so I could embrace him and tell him it was all right.

"So what now?" I ask, trying to distract him.

"I've found a place for you to heal properly," Keita says, turning me forwards as Ixa pads to a stop in front of our destination: a small cave mouth at the very edge of the mountains, hidden by mounds of glasslike black rocks covered in salt.

He takes me into a massive cavern, and my eyes sting as we pass wall after wall of that black rock, trails of salt running down the sides. The deeper we go, the more the salt takes over, until soon we reach the depths of the cave, which is now just white rock salt interspersed by the black rocks.

"Look up."

Keita helps tilt my face up, so I can see the large hole in the centre of the ceiling, the moon and the stars twinkling brightly in the distance.

"How did you find this place?" I ask, gaping in awe.

"This was one of our salt mines," he replies. "I used to play here when I was little, with my family."

I want to nod, but that's impossible, since my neck isn't fully attached.

I can't imagine what Keita feels like being here, at the site of his family's massacre. I wish I could hold him, wish I could at least squeeze his hand.

He continues on to his destination, the lake in the centre of the cave. "The waters here are supposed to have healing properties," he says. As he carries me over, I catch a glimpse of my reflection, my body shimmering golden under the thin white cloth he's wrapped around it.

"My body is still in the gilded sleep?" I ask, amazed.

Keita nods. "Precisely why all this is so startling to me," he says. "You should still be asleep. All alaki sleep during this period. That's what your kind does."

"I don't think I'm my kind," I whisper. "I don't think I'm an alaki."

Keita looks down at me. "Then what are you?" he asks, no hint of judgement in his gaze. No hint of repulsion.

"I used to think that perhaps I was a creature White Hands made, some deathshriek half-breed she created for the emperor," I reply. "But after what I experienced on the battlefield, I'm no longer sure…"

When he glances at me, a questioning look in my eyes, I confess: "I brought Britta back. She was on the edge of her final death and I pulled her back."

Keita nods as he wades into the shallows, and carefully slips my body down into the soothing cold. There's so much salt, my body floats. Sparks shoot through my muscles as they begin connecting more tightly. To my relief, it's not painful, as it was when I first woke, merely uncomfortable – an itch that won't go away.

Once I'm firmly in place, Keita looks down at me, eyes worried. "Whatever you are, you can never return to Hemaira, you do know that, Deka? You can never return."

I blink up at him, careful not to move anything but my eyes. Even though he's telling me to keep away from Hemaira – from him – he doesn't flinch as he watches my body knit back together, doesn't show any disgust, although it must be gruesome to behold.

When one of my fingers twitches, he takes my hand, holds it in his own. I can dimly feel the warmth of his touch coursing through my body's tendrils. I look up to find silent tears in his eyes.

This is goodbye.

"You're too powerful, Deka," he says sadly. "You always were. That's why they killed you. That's why they'll kill you again if you return. You must never return to Hemaira, you hear me? Not ever."

Tears burn my eyes, and my lips tremble as I try to find a reply. Never return? Never see him again? Never see my friends, Britta?

I'm so caught in my misery, I don't notice the shadows entering the cave until a familiar voice sounds. "Oh, she won't, young lord of Gar Fatu," it purrs. "Deka will never return to the humans again."

THIRTY-THREE

A light whooshing attracts my eyes to the ceiling, where seven women are flying down on gryphs, gigantic beasts that look like striped desert cats except they're covered in feathers and have wings sprouting from their shoulders. Each woman wears golden armour and carries an enormous glass lantern. Even from the water, I can feel the vibrations in that armour.

It's infernal armour, which means these women are alaki, but there's something different about them. I study them, my eyes narrowing as realization builds inside me. These women are older than all the other alaki I've met. Much, much older.

Ancient, in fact, if their appearance means anything. A few of them look more than forty years old, which means they must be several millennia old – it takes us centuries to age one year, after all.

The woman at the front is immediately recognizable in her white armour. *White Hands.* As she descends, mist curls up to reach her. It's coming from the deathshrieks spilling into the cave, all of them spiked, all of them armoured. All of them female.

The thought resonates through me, and along with it, the horror of understanding what they are. What they *were*.

"Keita," I whisper warningly, but he has already noticed them. They're all so tall, I easily spot Katya from the water, her red spikes blazing in the dim lights. Braima and Masaima accompany her, their pale, equine forms distinct among the much larger, darker deathshrieks.

"Deka," Keita answers back, alarmed. He edges closer to me, hand on his sword.

White Hands smirks as she steps off her gryph and places her lantern on the cave floor. "As you no doubt understand by now, Keita, deathshrieks and alaki are the same creatures. Deka is ours. She has always been ours."

Keita glances at White Hands. "Ours?" he says, frowning. "You're an alaki?"

"*An* alaki?" White Hands laughs dismissively. "I am the Firstborn. Fatu of Izor, mother of the house of Gezo, true empress of Otera. I am your ancestor, boy. You and all your line sprang from my womb."

Keita's jaw is slack with shock now – as is mine.

"But you can't be," I gasp at her. "You can't be an alaki."

"Why, because you never sensed me with your intuition, as you did with the other alaki?" White Hands smirks. "Your mother never felt me either, and she was quite intuitive for an alaki of such tender age."

A deep roaring sounds in my ears. "Mother was an alaki?" I rasp, my throat suddenly hoarse. "That's not possible! She bled pure, I saw it!"

"You saw what she wanted you to see – both you and your father."

Memories flash past; the last few days before Mother died. She was so sickly, all that blood draining from her eyes and ears, all that red. Was it truly all false, everything I saw? I can't accept it.

But then...Mother was a Shadow. The thought sends a shiver through me.

Subterfuge is their art, disguise their trade.

"What happened to her?" I ask. "Is she truly dead?"

For a moment, hope blossoms, tentative buds unfurling. Then White Hands looks at me with grim eyes and my hope dies a swift death. "My deepest apologies, Deka," she says, "Your mother is well and truly gone."

"How did she die – truly?" It's almost painful to voice the question, but I have to ask it.

White Hands sighs. "She was making arrangements to save you from the Ritual of Purity, when she was caught by the jatu. They sentenced her to the Death Mandate."

A sob breaks free from my throat. *The Death Mandate.* If Mother's final death was anywhere as hard to find as mine, I can't even begin to imagine the agony she endured before she left this world.

My tears are falling freely now, so I'm almost startled when White Hands places a hand to my cheek. "Take comfort in the fact that your mother loved you very much, Deka. Everything she did, she did for you."

The words burn through me. I don't want to hear them – don't even want to think them – but I have to push past my pain. It's time to ask questions. Difficult ones.

"How did you meet her – Mother? Did she help you create me?"

"Create you?" White Hands laughs, seeming taken aback. "Even I do not have that power. No, it was my duty to watch you, and I've done so all your life. Even before you entered Umu's belly, I watched you. It was my duty, you see."

Duty? My mother's belly? What is she saying?

White Hands walks closer, her smile becoming something more fervent, more intense. She has the same look priests of Oyomo do when they read from the Infinite Wisdoms. The other alaki part for her, like subjects making way for a queen. Like soldiers making way for their general. Behind them, the deathshrieks silently watch the scene, giants towering above their much-smaller sisters.

"When the Gilded Ones wept and created the golden seed you sprang from, I was there," she announces. "When the jatu created the Death Mandate against our kind and wrote it into the Infinite Wisdoms to give it legitimacy, it was I who hid you in my belly. And when my sisters reunited in preparation for this war, it was I who found your mother – a young alaki on the verge of her transition, unaware of her divine heritage."

Divine heritage...

Something about the phrase sends shivers through me, but I force myself to remain quiet as White Hands continues: "Umu began bleeding the divine gold at fifteen. She rushed to me in a panic, so I told her what she was, told her what had happened to our kind.

"She wept at my feet, asked how she could be of service. That was when I knew she was the perfect vessel. We waited till she was of age to carry you, and then, as she bathed in the Warthu Bera's lake, I put your seed into the waters. Ten months later, there you were, shaped in both her image and that of the man she chose to raise you. The perfect mimicry of a human."

By now, my chest feels tight and I can barely breathe. *Seed? Vessel? What is she saying?*

Beside me, Keita shakes his head. "You're confusing her," he says. "All this talk of divine gold and seeds. Speak in the language of facts instead of legends."

"Legend is what humans call the things that they do not understand," White Hands scoffs. "They call me a legend, and yet I existed from the beginning, from the time Otera was birthed from the warring tribes. I helped create this empire – me, my sisters, our mothers…we're the ones who made Otera what it is."

"Mothers?" I gasp. "You're talking about the Gilded Ones – the demons." All those temples we saw flash into my mind. Did she send me there on purpose, so I could see the statues for myself?

"*Demons?*" White Hands dismisses the word with a wave of her hand. "The Gilded Ones were never demons. They were goddesses. They ruled Otera until their own sons rose up against them. The jatu desperately wanted to rule Otera, so they imprisoned our mothers and killed us, their sisters, along with all our children.

"They thought they had succeeded in wiping us out, the traitors, but our mothers used the last of their power to thwart them. With their last free breaths, they rendered us alaki truly deathless by giving us the power to resurrect as even fiercer creatures – deathshrieks. And then they created the Nuru, the one creature that could exist between the alaki and the deathshrieks. The one daughter who could free them all."

Something shatters inside me. Now I understand why the deathshrieks always sounded so wounded whenever they said the word *Nuru*.

White Hands wades closer, looks into my eyes. "You are the Nuru, Deka. You are the deliverer. It is your task to free our mothers. It is your task to free us all."

I suddenly can't move, can't breathe. The deliverer? Free them all?

"That's absurd!" Keita sputters beside me. "What do you mean, Deka should—"

"It is not your place to speak, son of man!" one of the other armoured women snarls. "You are not welcome here."

The deathshrieks bristle around me, angry snarls echoing in the cavern. "Murderer!" one calls.

"The lord of Gar Fatu. He killed so many of us," another says.

They gather around him, their spikes rattling.

"Keita!" I gasp, water sluicing from my body as I strain to rise.

Keita quickly unsheathes his sword, ready to defend himself.

"Calm yourself, Deka," White Hands says, gently pushing me down again. She walks over to the armoured woman. "Leave him, Zainab," she says.

"But he—"

"He kept the Nuru safe at the risk of his own life. That alone guarantees his," White Hands interrupts sternly. "Besides, he would never betray the Nuru." She turns and looks him firmly in the eye. "Would you?" she asks.

"No, of course not!" Keita replies. "She's my— She's my partner."

White Hands nods at this mumbled admission. "Indeed," she says. She turns back to Zainab. "Even if not for that, he is one of my descendants."

Zainab growls. "You have hundreds of them. All of us do. We're all mothers too. Grandmothers. Great-grandmothers."

White Hands is implacable. "You will not touch him. None of you will touch him." She glances pointedly around the room at the gathered deathshrieks. "From now on, as long as the lord of Gar Fatu refrains from any mortal action against us, we will do the same for him."

Grumbles erupt across the cavern, but White Hands whirls to face those assembled. "This is my will as your general, and you will obey me!"

The grumbles immediately cease, even the deathshrieks no longer clicking in their language.

White Hands turns to Keita. "You may leave now," she says. "Take Masaima. He will see you safely to the army."

Keita turns to me, worried. "But I—"

"Leave before my sisters tear you to pieces," she commands. "Their patience grows short."

Keita quickly nods. "May I say goodbye to Deka, at least?" he says.

"Make haste."

Nodding again, Keita wades into the water, puts his hand to my cheek. "Deka," he says softly, his eyes sad.

I struggle to point my little finger towards him, smiling when he gently intertwines his with mine. "If I could move my hands, I would hold you," I whisper. Then I admit, a low, soft whisper under my breath, "Keita, I—"

He places his lips to mine.

Sparks immediately explode across my skin. I barely notice the annoyed snarls of the deathshrieks, the growling of the armoured women – all I feel is the thundering of my heartbeat and the whisper of his body against mine. My entire being is warm now, despite the coolness of the water.

Keita tastes like star fruits and fire.

Keita tastes like home.

The kiss is suspended in time, magic coiling between us. A moment I will treasure for ever. When he finally lifts his lips, there's wonder in his eyes.

"I always wanted my first kiss to be with someone special," he whispers. "I always wanted it to be with you."

Tears sting my eyes. "I'm glad it was you, Keita."

"Me too," he whispers. He squeezes my hand one more time, then climbs onto Masaima. "Goodbye, Deka. Perhaps I'll see you again one day."

Just like that, he's gone, riding out of the cave on Masaima as the deathshrieks and elder alaki snarl at his exit.

It's all I can do not to weep, but I force my sadness into submission. There are other, more pressing things to think about. A thousand questions I must ask. If I'm the Nuru, the creature created to free deathshrieks and alaki, how do I go about fulfilling my purpose?

And what about White Hands? If everything she said to me

was true, why did she allow me to commit all those atrocities against deathshrieks? She and Mother could have prevented everything that happened by just spiriting me away at birth. Why allow me to be raised by humans in the first place – to suffer through so much pain, when I could have been here with my own kind all along?

The questions spin through my mind, but I do not have time to ponder it further. Exhaustion has overtaken me, and it's not long before I succumb to it and fall asleep.

When morning comes, White Hands is still at my side, a few of the other deathshrieks surrounding her. They all stand in a circle around me, hands connected, throats rumbling. The sound vibrates through my body, sparking yet more connections. I can feel my limbs knitting faster, my tendons attaching and strengthening, and I'm grateful for it, grateful for all the care they're giving me. The emperor's army is only four days away.

The thought fills me with worry. Britta and the others are still there, after all. I can only hope they're not being punished now that I've been deemed a traitor. I can only hope that Britta's still healing – that she hasn't succumbed to her injuries or something even worse.

Like the Death Mandate...

I push away the awful thought by returning to the question of my origins. What does being the Nuru mean, exactly? How exactly will I free the goddesses? I know they're at the top of this mountain, hidden in a temple like one of those that the deathshrieks nested in. That's why the deathshrieks kept gathering at temples, why they massacred Keita's family when they found them here. This is their most sacred site: the resting place of their goddesses. The primal nesting grounds were only ever a myth White Hands created so the emperor would gather all his armies here.

I suppose it makes things easier for me. While I'm freeing the goddesses, the emperor and his army will be too busy fighting. But what happens once I free them? I still have no idea. I don't even know what the goddesses are like – what the truth of them is, versus what people have told me.

I turn to White Hands. She's now standing hand in hand with Katya and thrumming. "White Ha— I mean, Fatu," I say, correcting myself so I use her true name.

White Hands smiles. "White Hands will do. Fatu is an old name, one people have long forgotten to fear. White Hands, however…" She clicks her gauntleted fingertips together. "It is a name that will soon not be easily forgotten. Besides, it is my greatest honour to have been named by you."

I shiver. There's something in her eyes, a look that tells me she truly does feel this way.

"Why is freeing the goddesses so important? What will change if they come back to this world?"

"Everything," she replies. "Everything will change.

"The emperors of Otera have oppressed our kind for too long. Proclaimed us demons. But now their turn has come. Once you wake the goddesses, they'll make Otera back to what it once was: a land of freedom, a land where men and women ruled equally, where women weren't abused, beaten, raped.

Where they weren't imprisoned in their homes, told that they were sinful and unholy."

She looks down at me, her eyes serious. "You will help us bring those joyous times again. You will help us win freedom for all of us – every last woman in Otera, even the ones who aren't alaki."

Freedom for every woman…

I shiver as I remember Gazal's fear of water, Katya's longing for home, the tears in Belcalis's eyes as she reminded me to never forget. All of them so different, and yet all fighting a world where they were unwanted, lesser than, despised.

Freedom for them – freedom for us all. I let the precious thought flow over my mind as the deathshrieks resume their thrumming.

THIRTY-FOUR

It takes two days for my body to completely heal. All the while the deathshrieks surround me, throats rumbling. They never eat, never sleep, just remain attentively at their task. By the time I rise on the second day, I feel stronger than I ever have. It's just as well. The army is at the foot of the mountains, the stronghold of the deathshrieks. The final battle is about to begin.

"It is time," White Hands says, motioning for me to emerge from the water.

I do as she commands, marvelling at the new strength of my muscles, the power I feel in my bones. When I twitch, golden veins flash just beneath my skin. I can see them threading across my hands. Despite everything the official at Jor Hall said, my gilded sleep has destroyed the gilding that once covered my hands and arms. Perhaps this is part of what being the Nuru means. I feel more alive than I've ever felt before.

I know my path now. I know my purpose.

After all, White Hands was very careful to explain it to me.

These past few days, she answered all my questions – even told me how she and Mother became allies:

Being a Shadow, Mother never had to endure the Ritual of Purity. Any alaki at the Warthu Bera would be found immediately, since Shadows are injured almost every day due to the sheer brutality of their training. When Mother began bleeding the cursed – no – *divine* gold during her menses, White Hands quickly sensed it and took her on as an attendant, keeping her away from battle.

Then Mother became pregnant and her superiors found out before White Hands could hide her properly. They sentenced her to death for tarnishing the honour of the Shadows. White Hands had no choice but to help her escape. She arranged for a retired soldier – Father – to give her passage, and from then on did not contact Mother any further for fear of endangering her. By that time, the emperor was watching her closely, distrustful of the ideas she was spouting about an alaki regiment.

Then I turned fifteen, and the threat of the Ritual of Purity loomed. That's when she and Mother went searching for each other.

And that's when White Hands sent those deathshrieks to Irfut.

The irony of it stings. Those deathshrieks did everything they could to rescue me, but I commanded them to leave, thereby dooming myself to that cellar. I was the agent of my own suffering.

But perhaps it is better I experienced that pain. Being raised in Irfut taught me what it meant to be a human girl – to believe so deeply in the Infinite Wisdoms only to eventually be caged in by its never-ending commandments and finally betrayed by the horrors of the Death Mandate.

If I am to fight for women – all women – I have to understand how human girls think, have to have experienced the same pain that they did.

I keep that in mind as I nod at White Hands. "More than ready," I say.

"Then it is time," she says, gesturing.

A pair of the elder alaki walk forwards, shimmering white armour in their hands. It's infernal armour, I know, but this is a type I've never felt before. If regular infernal armour tingles, this one explodes like fireworks. A thousand colours ripple across it, like a rainbow reflecting in a lake.

"A gift from our mothers," White Hands explains, "celestial armour – a worthy addition to your *first* gift."

She points to Ixa, who's waiting at the side of the cave, covered in the same armour as mine. He has wings now – beautiful blue wings that glisten with feathers and scales, just like the rest of him.

"The goddesses gave me Ixa?" I gasp, shocked.

White Hands nods. "Every child needs a pet, and what better pet than one that changes form and can protect you when you're vulnerable."

Ixa is undoubtedly all these things and more.

I knew you were mine, I whisper to him.

De…ka, he agrees happily.

Once I am completely armoured, I turn to the water, gazing at my reflection. I barely recognize myself, barely recognize this girl wearing winged armour and carrying shimmering double swords. My eyes peer back at me, a distracting grey in the brown of my face.

The same grey of my father's eyes as he beheaded me. The thought fills me with anger, regret.

The man I left in Irfut was never truly my father – none of his blood runs in my veins. Perhaps that's why he abandoned me so easily to the Death Mandate. Even though he always claimed me as his own, something deep inside him must have whispered I wasn't his. That I shared none of his flesh, none of his blood. Like the goddesses who created me, I am completely divine – a creature neither deathshriek nor human, with the ability to mimic both. I can be whatever I want to be.

And I no longer want to be anything like that man.

Even as I think this, my eyes are changing, darkening. When I look in the water again, they are the same black of White Hands's eyes – of the elder alaki's. They are the eyes that truly belong to me, the eyes that have always belonged to me.

They're the eyes that show I have matured into my power.

Smiling now, I put on the war mask that comes with my armour, then turn to White Hands and Katya, who will be accompanying me on a gryph of her own. It rumbles when she pets it with an armoured hand.

"I am ready," I say.

White Hands smiles, strokes my cheek fondly. "Remember, you are of the divine. You cannot be killed by mortal means. The only thing humans can hope to do is imprison you, as they did our mothers."

"I will." I nod.

"Then let us go."

* * *

379

We fly out of our mountain cavern to the roar of battle. Below us, armies crash into each other, alaki and humans fighting deathshrieks, red and gold blood against a sea of blue. The metallic smell rises into the air, accompanied by the earthier smells of piss and vomit. Battle smells. The smell of death and dying. My stomach clenches. Now that I know what the deathshrieks are, I cannot bear to see my bloodsisters raising their arms against them, unknowingly raising arms against their own kind. I cannot bear to watch them kill each other. My friends' faces flash before my eyes – Britta, Keita, Belcalis, the twins, the other uruni. If something happens to them during this senseless battle, I don't know what I would do.

I try to force back my fear as I stand on Ixa's back, mimicking White Hands and Katya, who are standing on their gryphs. The armies don't notice us yet – they're too busy fighting each other, too busy killing each other. They don't notice the army of alaki marching towards them, swords at the ready.

Now I know the reason the deathshrieks kept attacking the villages, the reason their captives were always young and always female, the reason I saw that little girl running away in the jungle during that long-ago raid. Deathshrieks can smell girls on the cusp of turning into alaki, smell the gold running in their veins. All this time, deathshrieks have been rescuing their alaki sisters, training them in the wilds for this very moment – the moment we free our mothers. It's a thought that fills me with hope, determination.

I will wake the goddesses.

Already, I can feel the power welling up inside me. I don't have to flow into the combat state to summon it, don't have to sink into the dark ocean of my subconscious. It's always been there, a wave waiting to rise in my veins.

"Alaki sisters," I roar in a voice louder than a thousand drums.

The fighting immediately stops. Everyone looks up, shading their eyes when they see me hovering above them. I can only imagine the sight I present, an armoured figure standing on a similarly armoured, winged drakos, two women on gryphs flanking me, the sun at our backs. Even though Katya is a deathshriek now, I see her as female, because that's what she is.

Even more impressive are the orderly lines of alaki behind us, each one shining in her infernal armour, each one ready to do battle. These are all the girls the deathshrieks have rescued, the girls that are ready to do battle for their mothers.

"Do not fight the deathshrieks. They are your sisters," I shout. "The emperor and the priests have lied to you – they're forcing you to kill your own kind. When alaki die, they are reborn as deathshrieks. Do not fight them!"

For a moment, the alaki glance at each other, unsure. I have to give them more reason to believe me than empty words and a glittering spectacle. I have to convince them to obey of their own volition, not force them using my voice, as I was doing before with the deathshrieks.

I remove my helmet and war mask, hand them over to Katya. Then I fly down until I'm just above the front ranks. I'm close enough now that I'm face-to-face with the generals, with Belcalis and the rest of the recruits. I try to find Keita, Adwapa and the others among the ranks, but I don't see them.

"Deka," Belcalis gasps, shocked. She ignores the sputters of the generals, the tense movements of the other soldiers, as she looks up at me. "Deka, is that you?"

I nod. "I haven't forgotten, Belcalis," I say. "I'll never forget what happened to you – to all of us." I turn to the gathered alaki, using my ability to amplify my voice: "NEVER FORGET HOW THE HUMANS TREATED US! NEVER FORGET WHAT THEY CALLED US!"

I stab my palm, holding it up when the blood begins to run.

"Demons!" I shout, pointing at the soldiers now turning around in confusion. "They called us demons, even though we are the daughters of goddesses! The Gilded Ones were never infernal beings. They were the goddesses who founded Otera – goddesses the jatu imprisoned in these very mountains. Today is the day we free ourselves from the jatu's lies. Alaki, fight with the deathshrieks, your sisters! Free yourselves from the jatu!"

This time, the truth in my voice cannot be denied. A rustling begins as alaki break ranks, headed towards the deathshrieks. The alaki at my back begin marching down from the mountain, led by the elder alaki from before. There are hundreds and hundreds of them.

Panicked, the generals shout to their soldiers, "Destroy the alaki! Kill all the traitors! And kill her!"

They point at me, but I'm already flying back up before the archers can aim. "Deathshrieks, alaki!" I call out. "Do not harm the jatu recruits if you don't have to. They knew nothing of this."

As I soar higher, headed towards the mountains, Katya accompanying me on her gryph, White Hands bows to me. "This is where I leave you," she says. "I must remain and oversee the battle." My dismay must show on my face, because she adds, "Don't worry, there's a guide waiting for you when you get to the temple."

"My thanks, White Hands." I nod. "For everything."

Now more than ever, I understand how cunning White Hands is, how meticulous she's been in her planning. She used the emperor to free her kind from the Death Mandate by promising him we would slay the deathshrieks, and instead began moulding them into an army – an army that fights at our side, now that they understand the truth of their heritage.

Till our empire is free of the monsters… I understand now what she was talking about, understand who the true monsters are.

White Hands nods again. "I may have seemed cruel these months past, but I had cause," she says. "I hope you can forgive me for all the things I failed to do, all the truths I didn't tell you, the pain you suffered because of my silence."

I nod. "I know now that you did all those things so I would learn," I reply, accepting her apology.

She smiles, then turns back to the battle, blows a curved ivory horn. A distant thundering sounds in response. When I turn, it's to the sight of hordes of equus pouring down from the dunes behind the human army, their talons moving with effortless precision. Yet more equus emerge on both flanks of the human army and smash into them, a timeless battle strategy.

"Conquer or die!" White Hands waves to me.

"We who are dead salute you," I reply, pounding my hand over my heart.

White Hands nods, smiling. Then she dives from her gryph,

toppling a human general from his mammut as she falls. She rips his throat open with her claws before they land, then whirls through the front lines, dancing an effortless ballet of death as blood rains over her.

I turn from the sight, my eyes fixed on the mountain peak above me. I have my own task to attend to. *I can do this*, I whisper firmly to myself. *I will do this.*

It's cold and cloudy when Katya and I reach the peaks of the N'Oyo Mountains. Thankfully, I don't feel the brunt of the chill. My celestial armour and war mask keep me warm and dissolve the ice crystals that form on my face.

"Are you ready, Deka?" Katya asks as we continue onward. She seems nervous, biting her lips the same way she did when she was an alaki.

"As I'll ever be," I say, staring at the glittering white peaks. Then I turn to her. "How does it feel? To be a deathshriek, I mean." Now that I have the time to think, I'm curious – or perhaps I'm just trying to keep my mind from dwelling on the urgency of my task.

Katya shrugs. "Not as strange as it was at first." When I frown, confused, she explains: "One moment, that deathshriek's claws were slicing through my back, and the next moment, I'm waking up in this body. It happened like that." She snaps her fingers. "There are these…eggs, you see. They're all at the bottom of these ponds…"

I gasp, eyes widening, as I remember the pond Ixa came out of, the golden boulders at the bottom of it. It's probably one of the places deathshrieks are born. Ixa must have been put there to protect the eggs as they matured.

I return my attention to Katya as she continues: "When an alaki dies, a new egg forms, and you wake up, a full-grown deathshriek."

"What happens to your old body?" I've seen alaki corpses rotting on the battlefield, all of them that awful blue colour from the final death. They just remain there, like every other corpse, but perhaps something happens later that I don't know.

Katya shrugs. "It rots, I suppose. But the new one...it just sort of bursts out of that egg and then you're swimming up, and all these bloodsisters are gathered around calming you, telling you you're all right – only they're all deathshrieks, and now you're a deathshriek. Even worse, humans are now always so frightened of you."

Her eyes slide away from mine. "That's the worst thing, you know: human fear."

"Why?" I ask.

"Because it makes us kill them," she whispers miserably. "The moment the humans sense us nearby, they begin to be afraid. It's like they can feel us, and the fear overwhelms them. Then the smell of it overwhelms us, and that's what starts the mist and the shrieking."

Now I understand.

The Gilded Ones made deathshrieks natural predators. That's why they're bigger and more terrifying, why they have the instinct to destroy their natural enemies. They were literally made to withstand humans.

Just as I was.

I understand now why I see so much more clearly in the dark than others, why I don't need food or water to survive, and my tolerance for pain is so much higher than the usual alaki's. The Gilded Ones gave me all the abilities I would need to survive in a world primed to kill me.

"I'm glad, though," Katya adds abruptly.

"Why?"

She shrugs. "Because I'm not dead yet."

"But what happens if you die again? As a deathshriek, I mean."

I've killed enough deathshrieks to know that their bodies don't disappear into the ether. They remain solidly on the ground, rotting...that is, until someone takes a trophy. Guilt churns through me at the reminder.

"The elders say there's the Afterlands, just like for everyone else." Katya shrugs. "Although I probably wouldn't mind it... The Afterlands, that is..."

"Why?"

She turns to me and smiles a brave, sad smile. "Because then I don't have to fight any more." She looks down at her claws. "I told you before – all I ever wanted to do was to marry Rian. To have my children, a home..."

Poor Katya.

After all this time spent fighting, I'd almost forgotten about the girls like her – the ones who only ever wanted a family and a home.

They always died fastest at the Warthu Bera, either killed first on the raids, or in accidents during combat practice.

The battleplace is not kind to the gentle, innocent souls.

"I'll never have that now," she says, "but in the Afterlands, I'll have peace. Everyone deserves peace, don't you think?"

I nod. "Everyone deserves peace. Hopefully, once this is done, we'll get it."

"I hope so too," Katya says with a smile.

Underneath us, the clouds are clearing and the Temple of the Gilded Ones is coming into view. It sits in the middle of a crater in the N'Oyo Mountains' highest peak, a massive structure at least four times larger than any other I've ever seen, the steps leading up to it at least a mile long. A lake of pure white salt surrounds it, and the sun glints so harshly off the grains, I have to shade my eyes against the glare.

To my bewilderment, a group of zerizards, at least fifty of them, are perched on the temple's steps when we land.

Dread stirs inside me the moment I glimpse their red saddles. Now I know why I didn't see the emperor or his guards on the battlefield. It's because he's been up here all this time, waiting for me.

"The emperor – he's already here!" I say, hurrying off Ixa.

"No matter, so are we," a familiar voice replies.

I whirl, startled to find Adwapa standing at the shadowy entrance to the temple, a smirk on her face.

She tsks. "You never did have much awareness of your surroundings, Deka. You should work on that in the future, if we survive this."

THIRTY-FIVE

"Adwapa?" I gasp, running over and embracing her. "What are you doing here?"

She squeezes me tightly, then sets me down. "Waiting for you," she says. "We were sent here to serve as your guards."

Now I see the other alaki and deathshrieks standing behind her. There's an entire contingent of them, and Asha is here too. She gives me a quick wave and smile.

I return the gesture, then hurry towards the entrance behind Adwapa. "But how?" I ask, shocked. "Why?"

She turns to me with a shrug. "The Nibari have always worshipped the Gilded Ones. Even after the Death Mandate, we held fast to our beliefs. My sister and I have been waiting for this moment all our lives."

When Asha nods solemnly, I finally realize: they deliberately got themselves sent to the Warthu Bera. They didn't have to reveal themselves as alaki. Priests don't live with the Nibari, finding them too heathenish a people to deal with. They only travel to the desert twice yearly, to perform the Ritual of Purity. The twins could have hidden themselves their entire lives if they'd wanted to, but they didn't want to.

That's why they always seemed so at ease during training, running faster and fighting better than all the rest of us, why they always seemed a little older, a little wiser, even when they acted immature.

Because they're older – much, much older. "Adwapa?" I rasp, "are you one of the Firstborn?"

She bursts out laughing. "The Firstborn? No, not at all – my sister and I are only three hundred years old."

"Three hundred…" I echo, stunned. "And what about—"

"Explanations later," Adwapa says, abruptly stopping.

We're in the entry hall of the temple now, and are staring into the face of the unknown. Dark corridors extend into the darkness, leading infinity knows where. My hands tremble at the thought.

"The emperor is already somewhere down there," Adwapa informs me.

"I know," I reply. "I saw the zerizards." I knew why I hadn't seen the emperor on the battlefield. It was because he was up here, waiting for me.

"He's not the only one who's there, though," Adwapa says, a worried expression surfacing in her eyes. "Keita is inside as well."

Everything inside me stills. "Keita?"

Adwapa nods. "The emperor caught him when he returned from delivering you to the lake. It's likely bad, Deka. You need to prepare yourself."

* * *

The interior of the temple is musty, quiet. Black columns rise above us, images of the Gilded Ones embedded in them. There they are, the wise Southerner, gentle Northerner, warlike Easterner, and motherly Westerner, all conquering monsters, battling rebels, raising the walls of Hemaira. In each and every carving, they're much larger than the humans – giants, in fact.

I wonder if they're the same in real life. There are so many things I wonder, and perhaps if I wonder long enough, I won't have to think of Keita at the mercy of the emperor, won't have to acknowledge the overwhelming terror weighing down my body.

I continue staring at the carvings, the goddesses sitting on four regal thrones, looking gently down at the much-smaller humans. Alaki and jatu surround them, their armour distinct compared with the robes of the regular humans and the priests. Those priests depicted on the carvings are joined by something I've never thought of before – something I've never even imagined.

Priestesses.

Column after column shows different women doing things – *being* things – I've never dreamed possible: priests, elders, scribes, all the things men are. My anger builds as I realize how thoroughly my mind has been poisoned that I would be shocked to see women in these positions. I breathe out trying to calm myself. I have to be prepared to meet the emperor.

He's just there, at the end of the hall, where dim light spills from a hidden chamber. And Keita too is there.

An arm touches mine, and I nearly jump. "You all right?" Adwapa asks.

I nod.

"You can't let down your guard, Deka, not here."

Not with the fate of the goddesses at stake – not to mention Keita. I silently finish Adwapa's sentence. "I won't," I say, palming both my atikas. I was given two for the occasion. "I'm prepared."

"All you have to do is free the goddesses," Adwapa reminds me. "Just free them. The others and I will take care of the rest. We'll protect Keita."

I nod again. I know my task.

Adwapa touches me again. "I believe in you," she says softly. "I always have, from the moment White Hands sent me to you."

Suddenly I remember the first time I met Adwapa in that wagon, all rolling eyes and defiance. Ever since then, she's always been there by my side, always ready with a joke, a wry, ironic smile. It doesn't bother me that she's White Hands's spy – she has always been my true friend. I know this as surely as I know my own heart.

She breathes out a ragged breath. "That's why I could do all those things, kill all those—"

"You never killed more than your quota," I remind her, squeezing her hand to stop her from saying more.

I can't imagine how she must have felt, knowing all this time what the deathshrieks were but pretending otherwise, looking on and even joining in as we slaughtered them. Same with White Hands and everyone else who was part of this hidden rebellion. Their guilt is my own, an acid pit in my stomach.

I remind myself that it was all for a purpose. All those deaths, they were all leading up to this.

I won't let Adwapa down. Won't let anyone else down.

"I believe in you too," I return.

She nods, and together we stride into the temple.

The sight that meets my eyes is much worse than I imagined.

Not only is Keita here, bound and gagged, but so is Britta. She's conscious but pale and tied up on the floor. The emperor sits beside them on an ornate bench, a smug smile on his face. Unlike the jatu, he's wearing very little armour and even has a crown on his head. There's a crossbow with golden arrows at his side.

"The Nuru," he sneers when I walk down the stairs that lead down into the chamber.

My eyes flit to Keita, horror jolting me when I see his face, bruised and bloodied, both of his arms bleeding. I'm sick to my stomach, and I have to clench my hands to keep from running to him. Running to Britta.

When Keita sees my gaze, his eyes send mine a quick message. *Run, Deka.*

I ignore it, return my attention to the emperor, who smirks at me and gloats: "You finally reveal yourself for what you are." His face is completely different: cold, hateful. He doesn't look at all like the man I once knew, almost admired.

"I only just found out what I am," I say. "But you always knew."

"I didn't know it was you." He shrugs, rising. "I thought you were just another anomaly – like your friend here." He puts his boot on Britta's neck, and she gasps, tears coming to her eyes.

Everything inside me stills, and I blurt, "Please—"

"Please, what?" the emperor asks. When he looks down at Britta, his eyes are cold – so very cold. They remind me of my father's eyes – of Ionas's. "Do you know she almost got free? Weak as she is, she nearly fought off my soldiers. Thankfully, we had some bonds left over from the ones we used to imprison my grandmother." When my eyebrows gather in confusion, he explains: "The Lady of the Equus. That is what they call her now, is it not? Once upon a time, she was known as Fatu the Relentless."

A gasp wrenches from my throat. I remember how White Hands stared so bitterly at the female statue rising from Emeka's Tears – the statue that I now know was modelled after her.

The emperor continues, an awful smile twitching at his lips. "Do you know that we dismembered her once – my forefathers, that is. Severed her into four parts and impaled her bits in the palace dungeons when she tried to defend her mothers. My father told me all about it – he heard the story from his own father, who heard it from his own father, and so on.

"Anyway, my ancestors couldn't find her final death, sadly, so they just left her there for a few hundred years until she went mad. The Firstborn don't succumb to the gilded sleep, you see. How she begged them to free her. For hundreds of years, she pleaded and cried, promised she'd serve us, the traitorous bitch. And she did, for centuries – until now."

A sob catches in my throat before I realize it. Poor White Hands. I thought I had suffered in Irfut, but what she experienced was a thousand times worse. No wonder she wasn't fazed by my pain, by that of others. The things she must have experienced over those hellish centuries. My hands tremble at the thought of it, anger churning inside me.

Emperor Gezo doesn't notice as he nudges Britta's neck again. I have to clench my teeth when she gasps in pain. "We used these very same bonds to imprison your friend. They're made of celestial gold, the gold we harvested from the goddesses before we trapped them here. It's unbreakable, even by your kind. Even by Fatu."

He tsks down at Britta, disgusted. "Alaki should not be so strong, but that is the nature of the anomalies. Then again, that's why I herded all of you into the Warthu Bera – the strongest, the fastest, the most cunning of the lot. All the anomalies, I sent you there."

"You were watching us," I say, horrified.

He nods. "I was searching for the Nuru. My treacherous grandmother tried to convince me that it would come as a deathshriek, but I knew it would be an alaki. I thought it would be one of the strong ones, at first, or at least the swift. I didn't realize it was you until much later. Grandmother hid details of your ability from me, you see."

He takes a step closer, smirking his amusement when the alaki and the deathshrieks gather to protect me. At least his foot is no longer on Britta's neck. My eyes flicker towards her, making sure she's all right, then I quickly glance back at the emperor.

"When did you realize?" I ask, trying to keep him talking. I have to keep his attention on me for as long as I can.

Anything to keep him from hurting Britta or Keita again.

"The moment I saw your face in the throne room," he says.

"You could have disguised all you wanted with that human appearance, but I could smell them on you."

"Smell who?"

"The divine bitches!" he hisses, pointing towards the end of the room where what look like four gigantic golden statues of the goddesses sit on colossal black thrones.

The Gilded Ones.

Even without walking over, I know it's them. I've known ever since I walked into the room and felt their power crashing over me like a silent earthquake. My body trembles as I take in their expressions: sadness, resignation, rage. They were entombed alive, trapped as they sat there on their thrones.

"They thought they could command us," the emperor seethes, "that because we couldn't kill them, we'd let them terrorize us for ever. We showed them, those demons. We showed them..."

He turns to me, his eyes gleaming with hate. "Do you know what we did to them – my ancestors, that is."

I shake my head.

"We buried them in the blood of their own children," he says with a gleeful, sinister laugh. "We melted down scores of infernal armour – told the alaki we were creating a tribute to our mothers. Then we lured them here and poured the molten gold all over them. We imprisoned them."

"Why?" I ask, stunned. "Why would you do such a thing?"

"Because they were a plague on this land!" he hisses. "Demons in the flesh, despite their celestial appearances! From time immemorial, we the jatu have vowed to protect Otera, so we imprisoned them and made sure they would never rise again. Never again would women rule Otera – this was the task of every emperor of the house of Gezo."

He looks me directly in the eye. "Never will I allow one of you filthy bitches to sit on the throne again."

His words, his hate, strike deep into my heart. *Bitches.* A word just as ugly as all the others men throw at us. It's all I can do not to unsheathe my swords, but I ask one last question. "Why didn't you kill me the moment you knew what I was?"

The emperor smiles cruelly. "Because you were useful," he says. "How beautiful it was to use you against the deathshrieks – *you*, the very instrument the Gilded Ones created to destroy my kind. Instead, I used you to slaughter theirs."

Revulsion and guilt flood over me as I think about all the deathshrieks I commanded to their deaths, all the deathshrieks I personally killed, despite all my instincts screaming against it.

"How many deathshrieks did you help kill, Deka? Five hundred? Six? A thousand?" the emperor titters. "Entire nests of deathshrieks fell to your voice, the divine ability your mothers gifted you to free them."

Adwapa moves beside me. "Deka, do not listen to him. Let's end this now."

I shake my head, listening as he continues his rant. "Did you ever feel disgust at what you were doing? Guilt? Remorse? You must have! You must have felt it in your blood! A recognition of all the blood that you spilled. Murderer of your own kind. The great betrayer!"

His words cut me at the knees, but I take a deep breath, calming myself. I will not allow Emperor Gezo to worm his way into my mind. I will not allow him to send me into a killing daze. I will end this on my terms – not just for me but for every other woman he and his kind have ever brutalized and abused. No matter what he says, I will never forget what he did – what all of them did.

The memory of Belcalis's scarred back flashes across my mind.

Never forget, I promised her.

I look at Emperor Gezo as I slowly unsheathe my swords. "All that may well be, but I'm here now, same as you." I point an atika at him. "You know I will free the goddesses. You know I will complete my task. That is what the karmokos trained me to do – what you made them train me to do."

"Then we're at an impasse." He shrugs.

"I suppose we are."

He nods at the jatu. When they raise their swords, he says one word.

"Attack."

And the battle begins.

THIRTY-SIX

"**D**eka, go to the goddesses!" Adwapa roars as she and the others smash into the jatu. "We'll keep them away from you."

I nod, turn to Katya. "Protect Britta and Keita!" I shout, waving her over to them.

Her massive form leaps into the melee, and within seconds, she's grabbing Britta with one hand and Keita with the other and scurrying up the walls, just as fast now as she was when she was an alaki. The breath I didn't know I was holding in whooshes out of me.

They're all safe. Now I can concentrate on my task.

I run towards the thrones, keeping to the edge of the chamber, well away from the fighting in the middle. It's deadlocked below me. The deathshrieks and alaki push against the jatu, but the jatu, for some reason, are able to push back.

How are they so strong?

A whooshing sound ends this thought. When I look up, the emperor is just before me.

I gasp, stunned. "How did you—"

He knocks me into the wall so hard, it crumbles. By the time I look up, dazed, he's standing above me, a cruel smile on his face.

"Surprise," he says as he picks me up by the heel.

He slams me against the wall. Stars explode in my head. Blackness comes in waves. I can barely think, barely move. What just happened?

Deka? I hear Ixa's voice as if from far away.

When I look up, he's exploding into the room. The moment he sees me lying there, bleeding, he roars, enraged. *DEKA!* he shouts, barrelling towards the emperor, teeth bared.

They snap at thin air. The emperor's body has vanished, as if it was never there. I blink again, shocked. Where did he go?

"Ah, the shapeshifter," Emperor Gezo's voice says from somewhere behind Ixa. "I've been waiting for you."

When Ixa whirls, the emperor is standing behind him, his crossbow cocked. He fires dozens of arrows in rapid succession, loading and reloading so fast, I can't even see them move. All I feel is a tremendous wind blowing past me, and when I look up, Ixa is pinned to the wall by golden arrows. He's roaring as he struggles against them.

DEKA! he calls, his anger changing to panic. He gnaws at the arrows, trying to free himself.

Panic jolts me when I realize they're made of celestial gold. He won't be able to move them no matter how hard he tries. All he'll do is worsen his wounds.

"Stop, Ixa!" I shout. "You'll only hurt yourself!"

"Such touching concern for a mindless animal." Emperor Gezo's voice is just next to my ear, and when I look up, his body blinks into the space beside me, the motion so fast, it's almost invisible. He smirks at my shock. "You really should be more concerned for yourself, Nuru," he says, grabbing me by the throat and slamming me into the ground.

The floor cracks under me, and my head rattles against my helmet. Blood begins to pour from my ears and nose.

Emperor Gezo leans over me again, a smirk on his lips.

His eyes seem different – darker… Now that I'm looking directly into them, I realize they're more similar to mine and White Hands's than they are to a regular human's. They're completely black, just like an elder alaki's. No wonder he prefers to wear masks.

"What are you?" I gasp, horrified.

The emperor slams me against another wall. "Haven't you guessed?" he gloats, picking me up again. "I'm a jatu, a male descendant of the Gilded Ones." He slams me against the floor.

"But the jatu are human," I say, scrambling backwards in horror. "They bleed pure."

The emperor grabs my foot, drags me along the floor. The smile on his face is almost serene now. He's enjoying this – enjoying hurting me.

How could I have ever thought he was benevolent?

He keeps slamming me against the wall.

"Very few of the jatu you've met are true jatu." SLAM. A hit. "We are all mortal – finite." SLAM. Another hit. "We do bleed red." SLAM. Yet another hit. "We also die like humans." SLAM. SLAM. More hits. "But the mark of our kind is strength and speed far greater than even that of the alaki."

He slams me against the wall one last time.

Everything is black now. I can barely open my eyes, I'm in such pain – white-hot splinters like fire shooting across my nerves, body throbbing, bones aching. "So your kind hid... All this time you hid..."

The emperor crouches before me, amused. "We were always fewer in number than our sisters, so we made the alaki and everyone else believe that we had died out, lost our power. Then we gave ordinary human soldiers the name to add to the confusion. All the while, we were hiding in plain sight, waiting for the day when you emerged and we could win this power struggle for ever."

I glance at the chamber floor, where the jatu are still fighting against the alaki and deathshrieks. "So this is all," I gurgle past the blood dripping from my mouth. "All that remains of the jatu – the true ones."

"For the most part," the emperor says, that cruel smile slicing his lips again. "There are just enough of us here to stop your kind once and for all."

"Good to know," I say, smirking right back at him.

I kick towards his legs.

In the blink of an eye, the emperor moves behind me, so fast that his body seems to materialize out of thin air. I whip away just as he punches down. The floor crumbles under his fist. He looks at me, surprised, then is gone again, but I'm already reaching for my dagger.

I thrust it backwards just as he appears behind me, grinning when it penetrates armour, then flesh. Jatu armour never was as resilient as the infernal armour.

"You little whore!" he gasps, clutching his side. Blood is

dripping from it – the very same blood now staining my dagger. I smile at him. "I learned well at the Warthu Bera. Karmoko Huon, particularly, taught me how to pretend to be weaker and more pathetic than I actually am."

The emperor tries to zip away again, but I slam him into the wall. His turn now. His head cracks against it – hard, but not hard enough to kill him. When I let go, he disappears again.

I grin when he appears behind me. So predictable... "In battle strategy, Karmoko Thandiwe taught me how to read, then anticipate, an enemy's movements," I say, effortlessly smashing him into the ground.

The emperor gapes past teeth reddened by blood. "How did you—"

"And Karmoko Calderis taught me the most important lesson of all," I interrupt, whispering in his ear. "How to discern my own infernal armour when it's disguised as some other object," I say, ripping off his crown.

Terror blazes in his eyes, and he backs away from me, horrified. "No, you couldn't have—"

I laugh, bitterly amused. "Did you really think I wouldn't notice that you were wearing a crown made out of my own blood? Thank you for that. It made me realize something important."

The emperor disappears again, but I'm not worried. "Stop," I command when he reappears behind me. Then I press my hands down, pushing energy with them.

Metal clatters to the floor – the sound of armour meeting stone. I turn to find the emperor already kneeling, fear and hatred in his eyes.

"You know," I murmur, "I don't actually need to use my gift

to command others any more. They do as I say." I place my sword to his neck, then turn to the combatants in the middle of the chamber. "Jatu!" I shout. "Put down your weapons or the emperor dies. NOW!"

My command reverberates through the chamber. The moment the jatu see the emperor on his knees, my sword to his throat, they stop fighting, in shock.

I prod the emperor with the tip of my sword, and his eyes almost bulge with rage. "Stop this now," he hisses. "Stop this, you unnatural bitch!"

"Unnatural? Bitch?" I scoff. "These words used to shock me, to hurt me, but no longer, thanks to you and your kind." I prod him again. "Command the jatu to drop their weapons and kneel. I would do it myself, but it would affect the deathshrieks too."

The emperor turns mutinously away from me.

"I said command them!" I roar.

"Drop your weapons! Kneel!" he shouts immediately.

Slowly but surely, the jatu do as they're told. The alaki and deathshrieks immediately secure their weapons, ensuring that they can no longer fight back. Within moments, they've been stripped of all their armour and weaponry.

"Well, I see you have this all in hand," a familiar voice says.

I look up to find White Hands standing at the entrance of the chamber, the equus twins and Belcalis at her side. "White Hands! Belcalis!" I gasp, relieved. "You're all right!"

"Of course we are." White Hands turns to her equus. "Secure the emperor."

"With pleasure," Braima and Masaima reply.

They walk over to the emperor and grab him up, snickering when he remains stuck in that kneeling posture, just as I commanded. Perhaps my voice is even more effective on the true jatu than it is on alaki and deathshrieks.

"Come along now, naughty jatu," they taunt as they take him away.

The moment they have him in hand, I run over to Ixa. He's still stuck to the wall, his wounds dripping onto the ground.

Deka, he says, nuzzling me weakly when I rip out the arrows holding him in place. They move easily under my fingers, responding to the divinity that flows in my veins.

"I'm so sorry – I'm so sorry, Ixa," I gasp, petting him.

He has so many injuries, I don't know what to do.

"Why don't you bleed for him?" White Hands suggests, approaching me. "It'll help the healing."

I hurriedly do as she says, offering Ixa my arm. He latches down, and within moments, the wounds on his wings are sealing together. Relief washes over me. *He's healing, just as White Hands said he would.*

Once he's completely healed, White Hands offers me a small golden dagger that gleams under the low light.

"It's time," she says, nodding towards the goddesses.

I nod, inhale deeply.

It's finally time for me to complete my task.

The goddesses are much larger up close than they seemed from a distance. My head reaches only as high as their toes, and a single divine finger is just large enough for me to stand on.

That beings like this once roamed Otera – the idea is almost impossible for me to comprehend.

I walk over to the nearest goddess, the wise Southerner – Anok was her name. White Hands told me all about the goddesses as I healed – their histories, their personalities. Anok was always the craftiest. It makes perfect sense, considering she is White Hands's mother.

By now, the knowing is whispering to me, giving me all the information I need to complete the awakening. I stab the dagger into my palm, waiting until the gold wells there. Then, as I will for each goddess, I rub it across Anok's feet. "Mother Anok," I whisper. "Rise."

The goddess's body trembles. I'm not sure if it's my imagination, but I'm hoping it's not.

I walk to the next goddess, the gentle Northerner, Beda. White Hands told me she was a kind soul who loved green and growing things. "Mother Beda," I say, rubbing blood onto her robes. "Rise."

This time, I know I'm not imagining it when her robes flutter.

"Mother Hui Li," I whisper to the warlike Easterner, the most quarrelsome of the bunch, according to White Hands. "Rise." I smooth my blood against the feathery wings protruding from her back.

Yet another tremor.

"Mother Etzli," I whisper to the motherly Westerner, the one who loved and nurtured all children, alaki or otherwise, as I slick my blood over a colossal toe. "Rise."

When the goddess's entire body vibrates, I step back, astounded to see that the tremor has turned into deep convulsions. Great rivers of cursed gold are streaming off the goddesses. I move back, awed, as hints of skin are revealed – brown, pink, bluish-black. My blood is doing what it was created to do: free the goddesses.

"FREE." The single word explodes like an earthquake through the chamber. "FINALLY, WE ARE FREE!"

Awe unfurls inside me as, one by one, the goddesses stand, stretching for the first time in thousands of years, their bodies so massive, they nearly reach the ceiling. I have never seen a more humbling sight in all my life. I feel like an insect, an ant at the foot of giants. My heart expands, joy filling every corner of it, as I watch them move, watch their bodies come alive.

"DAUGHTER." The word ripples through my head, a reminder of all the times I heard those exact voices in my dreams, all of them melding with Mother's.

I look up, amazed to see four perfect faces staring down at me. "YOU HAVE COMPLETED YOUR TASK. YOU HAVE FREED US. HOW GRATEFUL WE ARE TO YOU."

Tears slide down my eyes, an unconscious response to their voices. Euphoria, fear – all my emotions combine into a single powerful wave at the sound of the goddesses' voices. Now I know what it's like to be on the receiving end of my voice.

When the goddesses take a single step towards me, I jerk back, afraid of being crushed. But they shrink as they step down, and by the time they take their next step, they're only slighter taller than the average person.

"Mothers," I say, kneeling respectfully as they approach me. Cool hands lift my chin. They belong to Anok, who has a pleased smile on her face. "You have done so well, Deka," she whispers, that thread of compulsion running under her voice. "I am so very proud of you, my creation."

"We are all proud of you," the others echo.

My heart swells so, I'm afraid it's going to burst. That these goddesses, these beings, should claim me as their own – it's almost more than I can take in.

"What now?" I whisper, still in awe.

"Now?" This answer comes from Etzli. Her dark eyes peer into my own. "Now, our One Kingdom, Otera, is in turmoil and many are in pain."

"We will help them," Hui Li says. "We will rebuild the One Kingdom to what once it was: a place where all can exist in harmony, in peace… We will ensure that it thrives once more."

"And you will help us, Deka," Beda says. "You will help us rebuild this world."

"It will be my honour," I say, bowing.

Later, as the goddesses reunite with their children – the alaki, the deathshrieks, and even the jatu – I look at all the people here in the temple celebrating their return. There's Adwapa, happy tears flowing from her one remaining eye – she lost the other one during the battle, but I have no doubt it'll grow back soon enough. Beside her is Asha, who is also injured, although it's only a gash on her cheek. She's beaming from ear to ear.

Her smile grows when she and Adwapa spot the group of midnight-dark warriors now entering the temple. Just as Adwapa predicted, the Nibari have made the journey up the mountain. They have come to see their gods. They quickly join others in circling the goddesses, but White Hands keeps them firmly at bay.

She's already back to being the Gilded Ones' general. I grin when I see how happy she looks. I've never seen White Hands's smile so genuinely.

Belcalis is standing in the corner, watching everything with an almost stunned expression. She looks up when I walk over. "I can't believe this, Deka," she says, her voice trembling with awe. "I still can't believe all this."

"I do," I say to her. "The world is changing now. We're going to make it change – make it better. We're going to make sure that what happened to us never happens to anyone else again."

She nods. Then she gestures at someone behind me.

Britta, standing there with tears in her eyes.

"Britta!" I gasp, hugging her.

"Oh, Deka," she cries. "Ye saved me. Made that deathshriek help me."

She nods at Katya, who is surrounded by other deathshrieks.

"Ye know, it looks strangely familiar," she muses. "I mean *she*. *She* looks strangely familiar."

I laugh. "She does, doesn't she?" There's so much I have to tell Britta, so much she needs to know.

She holds out her hand to me. "Sisters?" she whispers.

I squeeze it. "Sisters," I agree.

She smiles, nods her chin. "I think there's someone waiting for you."

I turn to find Keita at the edge of the room, holding his

injured arm. To my relief, the other uruni are with him – Li, Acalan, Kweku, they're all there. They grin when I walk over.

"I guess we survived," Li says happily.

I nod, my eyes flitting to Keita. "I guess so."

"What happens now?"

This quiet question comes from Acalan. More than anyone, he'll have trouble adjusting to this new change in circumstances.

But he'll adjust. All of the recruits will.

"I don't know," I say truthfully, "but I expect we will move forward together."

"Thank you for protecting us," he says.

"If you hadn't told the deathshrieks not to hurt us, I don't know what would have happened," Kweku adds.

I nod and say, "You are our uruni. No matter what happens, we will always be partners." My eyes fall on Keita, who's still staring at me.

Kweku nods, nudges the others away. "C'mon, then, let's give them their privacy."

Now I'm looking up into Keita's eyes. "Keita, I—"

He kisses me so suddenly, I have to hold on to him to ground myself. I'm overtaken by the warmth, the bliss, of our mouths moving in perfect harmony. When we separate, I take a ragged breath. Keita is looking down at me, his eyes fathomless again.

I can't imagine what he must be thinking.

"I know this will be difficult for you," I say quickly, unnerved. "You've hated deathshrieks for so long, and now—"

"And now I know why they are the way they are, how they were forced to become monsters by their own mothers... I also know that the emperor abandoned my parents to die. He could have warned them of the danger any time – told them that this was a sacred place, but he did not.

"You know, I also learned one important thing these past few days," he whispers. "I am your uruni. No matter what happens, no matter what comes, I will move through this world with you. I will remain by your side, if you want…"

I have to catch my breath, I'm suddenly so weak.

He steps back so I can see his eyes. There's a hesitation in them now. He's asking me. This is a question – one he's too uncertain of to ask directly. I wrap my arms around him, relieved when he does the same.

"Always. I will always be your partner…if you want," I say, returning his unspoken question.

He looks down at me, nods intensely. "Then no matter what comes, we'll face it together?"

"Together," I agree, embracing him more tightly.

Keita nods, smiles. It's the most open expression I've ever seen on his face.

As I smile back, I realize something beautiful: this whole time, I've been searching for love, for family, but it's been here, right in my grasp. No matter what happens in this new world, I have Keita now, and Britta, and Belcalis, and Asha and Adwapa.

We'll confront any problems that rise together – side by side and hand in hand – and that's all you can ever ask for, isn't it?

THIRTY-SEVEN

The next few days are filled with hard work. We have to corral the remainder of the emperor's army, explain to them the true history of Otera, and cement them to our cause. Anyone that doesn't want to fight is sent home. There's no room for unwilling soldiers in the army of the impure, as we've taken to calling ourselves. Most of the men decide to go, but the majority of the alaki remain. This is their new life, and they finally have a cause they can believe in.

To my surprise, most recruits from the alaki training grounds elect to remain as well. All those months spent fighting side by side with alaki bonded them to their partners in a way the priests and commanders could have never foreseen. They are truly our brothers now. Keita, in particular, has become so well trusted by the goddesses, he often joins me in guarding them. He is a noted favourite of Anok's but then, she is White Hands's mother, which means she is his great-grandmother, thousands of times removed. The only time Keita ever leaves my side is to go to hers.

We haven't spoken words of love since the day I freed the

goddesses, but I feel it in his every look, his every touch. Just as I feel Britta's. She's always right beside me, my guardian and protector. My compass, guiding me whenever I am unsure.

Once, long ago, I wondered what it was to be loved so deeply, I could take that devotion to the Afterlands and back. Now, I have my answer, and it is sweeter than anything I have ever known. It is also a balm in these turbulent times.

There are a lot more true jatu hidden in Otera than the emperor let on. They have fled to all corners of Otera, where they have begun shoring up a resistance. They will not accept defeat without a fight, and neither will the high priests or elders of all the towns and villages. The men of Otera see our army as a threat, and they will do anything to crush us before we become too powerful. Every day, White Hands, the other Firstborn and I formulate strategies, battle plans with the goddesses.

The emperors of Otera made a crucial mistake in dealing with our kind. They taught we alaki to suffer, but they also taught us to survive – to conquer. And we will use those lessons. It's time to take up our swords once more.

Otera may be vast, but we intend to take back every last inch of it. It's time to reclaim the One Kingdom and make it ours again.

THE GODDESSES HAVE WOKEN.

BUT THE BATTLE FOR OTERA
IS FAR FROM OVER.

JOIN DEKA'S FIGHT IN...

THE
MERCILESS
ONES

COMING 2022

CHECK HERE FOR NEWS, UPDATES
AND MORE:

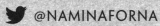 @NAMINAFORNA

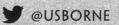 @USBORNE

#THEGILDEDONES

A LETTER FROM NAMINA

Dear Reader,

When I was a freshman in college, I began having dreams of a girl in golden armour. Bellowing a powerful cry, she'd leap into the battlefield, and just like that the dream would end. I didn't know it then, but this was the first seed of *The Gilded Ones*.

I was born and raised in Sierra Leone, West Africa. Sierra Leone is deeply patriarchal, and girls are often considered lesser than boys. When I moved to America, I hoped things would change, but I quickly realized it was the same. Perhaps the message wasn't as in your face, but it was still there.

I had the privilege of going to Spelman College for my undergraduate education, and during my time there, I took courses on feminism and religion. These classes gave me the foundation I needed to write *The Gilded Ones*.

At its heart, the book is an examination of patriarchy. How does it form? What supports it? How do women survive under it? And what about men or people who don't fall into the binary? Who thrives and who doesn't?

I hope I've done a good job answering these questions, and, failing that, I hope I've told a good story – one filled with relatable heroes and familiar stakes. After all, the world we live in right now is not so different from the world in my book. These are dire times – times that call for heroes. In *The Gilded Ones*, I hope I've created heroes that can be all of us.

To every person reading this book, know that you are the hero of your own story. You can make things happen, and you can change the world. Choose to change the world for good.

To all my teen readers, know that this is a world I've created for you. If you can't find yourself anywhere, find yourself here.

Much love,

Noora

ACKNOWLEDGEMENTS

First of all, I'd like to say an immense and never-ending thanks to my agent, Alice Sutherland-Hawes, who took a chance on me and on this book. Alice, thank you so much for championing *The Gilded Ones* after so many people said no for so many years, and thank you for being my greatest champion through this very turbulent year. You are quite literally the very best of agents.

To my editors, Kelsey Horton and Becky Walker, man have we been through the trenches together. Rewrite after rewrite, you guys kept with me, and now this book is even more beautiful than I could imagine. Thank you, thank you from the very bottom of my heart and soul for pushing me farther and making the difficult calls. Thank you for giving me that little extra time whenever I needed it, and being understanding when I couldn't be present. You took a diamond in the rough and polished it to its highest potential.

To my friend PJ Switzer, you've read this book so many times, I'm sure your eyes blur every time you see it. Thank you for being my sounding board, the person I can reach out to any time of the day to talk story with. Thank you for helping me go to the deep, painful places I never wanted so I could craft the emotions and nuance in this book.

To my friend Melanie, my ride or die, thank you so much for being an emotional rock through all the ups and downs. You were there when I was writing this book in grad school, and boy, have we come far. I can't wait to see where we go.

To Mary Wright: It takes a very special person to support another's dream. Thank you so much for all the years you spent housing and encouraging me. Thank you for always being patient and encouraging me to be the same. I would have never made it this far this fast if it weren't for you. Thank you from the bottom of my heart. Thank you.

To Shekou, thank you for allowing me to Namina all these years in the comforts of your home. You didn't have to let me come by so often to eat you out of house and home, but you always kept the door open and the welcome mat out. Thank you from the bottom of my heart.

To everyone at Delacorte Press who has cheered on this book, thank you, thank you. Thank you for taking a chance on me, and for being open to putting a novel with such difficult, but necessary subject matter into the world. My copyeditors, Candice and Colleen, thank you so much for all the hard and beautiful work you put into the manuscript. It would not be half as good without you.

To my beloved Spelman College, thank you for being the literal inspiration for the Warthu Bera from the Wakeup to the Olive Branch Ceremony. And thank you for teaching me how to remain undaunted by the fight.